A LUCKY SIXPENCE

A LUCKY SIXPENCE

Anne Baker

A LUCKY SIXPENCE

HEADLINE

First published in 2018
by HEADLINE PUBLISHING GROUP

1

Cataloguing in Publication Data is available from the British Library

ISBN 978 1 4722 5156 5

Typeset in Baskerville by Avon DataSet Ltd, Bidford-on-Avon, Warwickshire

Printed and bound in Great Britain by CPI Group (UK) Ltd, Croydon, CR0 4YY

Headline's policy is to use papers that are natural, renewable and recyclable
products and made from wood grown in well-managed forests and other controlled
sources. The logging and manufacturing processes are expected to conform to the
environmental regulations of the country of origin.

HEADLINE PUBLISHING GROUP
An Hachette UK Company
Carmelite House
50 Victoria Embankment
London EC4Y 0DZ

www.headline.co.uk
www.hachette.co.uk

CHAPTER ONE

Wednesday 12 May 1937

I T WAS A FINE spring morning and a public holiday. For months civic dignitaries all over the country had been planning celebrations for the coronation of George VI, and for Milly Travis the excitement had built until it was sky high. It was also her thirteenth birthday.

The Travis family were eating their breakfast. 'I love the fountain pen, Dadda, thank you,' she sang out. He'd also given her thirteen shillings, one for every year she'd lived. He did the same every year, but he said it was to be put in her post office savings account to buy something important. She must learn to look after her money; it must not be frittered away on fun. She carried on tearing open the cards from her school friends.

Elizabeth, her nineteen-year-old sister, believed in spending her wages and having all the fun she could – 'A public holiday,' she said to Milly. 'Blissful, I don't have to go to work,' though she loved her job in the best dress shop in New Brighton's shopping centre.

New Brighton was a holiday resort at the mouth of the Mersey; a place given over to fun. It had both the largest open-air swimming pool and the longest promenade in England.

Milly, or Emilia as she'd been christened, had gone to her shop and Lizzie had bought her a new dress for her birthday. She was wearing it now and said it was easily her favourite present. Both Father and Mum disapproved of it, though Mum had bought her a new hat and new shoes to wear with it. 'They think you're too young to have a bit of style,' Lizzie told her. 'They don't understand that every girl needs a change from gingham dresses and Peter Pan collars.' At the shop, Lizzie's boss thought it exactly right for Milly.

During the last week Milly had taken part in a display of keep-fit exercises at the swimming pool, enjoyed a tea party at the Embassy Rooms and been given a shiny penny showing the new King's head, and at school she'd been given a commemorative mug and tickets for four free rides at the local funfair. She rated the free rides very highly.

Dadda had frowned and said, 'You know I don't approve of the amusement arcade, it's not a suitable place for young girls. Don't go down there today. The pubs will be open late and the young lads will take celebrating too far.'

Dadda was Major Esmond Travis and on the council. He liked to arrange things, but he hadn't got his own way on the matter of the licensing hours.

Lizzie whispered, 'I'll take you, Milly. Today should be given over to enjoyment; we'll count it part of the Coronation festivities.' Despite their father's disapproval, Milly had been before with her friends from school, and she knew Lizzie went quite often.

The girls were looking forward to a great day. Their parents took them to the town hall in the morning for a civic ceremony. Dadda had lost one arm in the war and wore his imitation limb which ended in a leather glove, so nobody would know. He was up on a dais with his colleagues on the council, and because he was an important person they had been given seats on the front row.

Their mother looked smart in a new hat with pink flowers on the brim and she and Lizzie sat one each side of her. 'You're proud of Dadda, aren't you?' Milly whispered.

'Yes, he does a lot of work for others, and I'm proud of my two girls too,' Mum said, squeezing her hand.

Afterwards they watched the mayor's procession of floats, decorated with flowers and flags going through the streets, and were swept up on a wave of pleasure and excitement. Brass bands were playing rousing tunes, and they'd heard some of the ceremony broadcast from Westminster Abbey being relayed through the streets.

Everybody was out this morning and they met lots of people they knew. Dadda had friends he played chess with, and he knew some of the fathers of Lizzie's boyfriends, of which there were many.

They normally ate lunch at one o'clock. Dadda was a stickler for having meals on time, but today their meal of beef casserole and rice pudding with rhubarb was delayed until nearly four, and afterwards Dadda went out to another civic ceremony.

Lizzie had it all planned: the girls washed up hurriedly and made a cup of tea for Mum. Lizzie took it to her and said, 'You won't mind if I take Milly to the fair for an hour or so to have her free rides?'

'All right, love, but don't be late home. It's back to school and work tomorrow.'

They lived on the edge of town and were going down the lane to catch a bus to the promenade, when Lizzie grabbed her hand and started to run. 'Come on, I can see one coming. We don't want to miss it.'

Once in the crowd in the arcade Milly felt bewitched by the screams of people on the high dipper, the roar of engines and the yells of glee from the bumper cars. She took the tickets for her free rides from her pocket. Lizzie asked, 'What do you want to try first?'

'Let's go into the arcade.' There was an indoor amusement arcade as well as an outdoor fair. A ragtime band was blasting out from the swingboats and a caterpillar ride had clashing music that almost drowned it out. There was every sort of ride and sideshow imaginable: dodgems, a big wheel and huge merry-go-rounds of every sort.

Milly watched the one in front of her; it had rearing horses to ride, galloping giraffes and even motorbikes. Anticipation soared. 'This one.'

She pulled her sister towards a huge motorbike on the outside row. It took an effort to get astride and the handlebars stretched her arms wide apart. Two young men were collecting fares and one was coming towards them. 'Oh my goodness,' Lizzie said as she climbed on behind her, 'this fellow tries to chat me up every time I come here.'

Milly offered her free ticket but he ignored it and smiled at Lizzie. 'Why hello. I've seen you here before. You must be the most beautiful girl in the country.' He had a cheeky grin and curly hair. 'I'd like to know you better. My name is Ben McCluskey.'

'Ben for Benjamin?' Milly asked.

'No, it's short for Benedict,' he said, 'and I don't care much for it. What's yours?'

Lizzie was silent. 'It's Elizabeth,' Milly told him. 'Elizabeth Hardman, she's my sister.' Everybody loved and admired Lizzie. She was the golden girl of the family with long blonde curls that reached halfway down her back, but tonight they were pinned back so she no longer looked like a child. Milly knew her own hair, straight and a plain brown colour, was not considered nearly so attractive. Lizzie was full of spirit and accepted as the family beauty; she was also daring and full of fun. Milly was very close to her.

'Elizabeth is a bit of a mouthful,' Ben said. 'Are you known as Betty?'

She laughed. 'No, it's Lizzie,' she said.

He looked doubtfully from one to the other and said, 'You're not much alike.'

He seemed to be looking over her head. Milly straightened up and said, 'Half-sister, we have the same mother but different fathers.'

'Why is that?'

Lizzie offered him her four pennies and said icily, 'Our mother was widowed and married again. We are a very respectable family.'

'I'm sorry,' he said. 'I didn't mean to suggest you weren't.'

'Hadn't you better take our fares?' Lizzie went on. 'Your boss won't be pleased if you neglect your duties.'

'I'm the boss.' He smiled. 'I own this roundabout. If you'll talk to me you can have free rides. So can your half-sister.'

'Thank you,' Milly said. The roundabout was filling up. He moved away to start the ride. 'Isn't he kind?'

'He's trying to pick me up,' Lizzie said. 'Father would be horrified.'

'But he's nice and he's good-looking and he likes you.' The ride started slowly but soon the motorbike was spinning round faster and faster, rising and falling at the same time. Foot-tapping hurdy-gurdy music was blaring out and Milly's head began to spin. It was a delicious feeling, but far too soon it was slowing. She was reluctant to get off.

The man was heading towards them again. 'Don't go,' he pleaded. 'I'd never do anything to harm you. Stay and talk to me. Are you on holiday or do you live here?'

'We live here,' Lizzie said.

'Good, in New Brighton? So do I. My home town too. Whereabouts do you live?'

'Out Oakdene way,' Milly said.

'That's the posh end of town.'

'Perhaps it was once, but there's nothing posh about it now. Our house is so old the rain comes in on the top landing.'

'You didn't have to tell him that,' Lizzie muttered into her neck.

Milly felt she had to explain. 'Years and years ago our house was a dairy farm and Dad's family sold milk from a horse-drawn cart, but then the big dairies took over and sold milk more cheaply and took all the trade.'

'It ruined his business?'

'Our grandparents' business, yes.' Sometimes Dadda talked of the pain of having to sell off his farmland to support the family. Building work had taken place all round them and terraces of houses were creeping closer.

By the time Milly had had four free rides and not used one

of her free tickets, Ben was wearing Lizzie's wariness down.
She seemed to like him better. When he returned, Milly asked,
'Whereabouts do you live?'

'I'm in lodgings down here; just behind the ham and chips
parade.'

She'd heard her father speak of that area in derogatory
tones. 'Do you like living there?'

'Yes, it's great. Just behind the prom, in the middle of town
and handy for working here. So your dad's a farmer?'

'No,' Lizzie said, 'he lost an arm and had other terrible
injuries in the last war so he hasn't been able to work since.'

'I'm sorry . . .'

'No need to be, he's not my dad. He's Milly's.'

'How about letting your sister go home, then I could take
you for a drink? One of the posh hotels if you like.'

Milly was relieved to hear Lizzie's outraged tone. 'No! It's
her birthday and I've brought her here as a treat.'

'I'm thirteen,' she gulped, sliding off the motorbike. 'Thank
you for the rides but I'd like to try something else now.'

'Come and see my shooting range,' Ben said.

'We don't want to shoot. We know nothing about guns.'

'I could teach you.'

'No,' Lizzie said, 'we don't want to know anything about
war and guns.'

'They aren't real guns, of course, come and see them. The
rifle range belonged to my dad, but I've been running it since I
was sixteen.'

'Aren't you living with your family?' Milly asked.

'No, my grandpa brought me up but he was getting old
and wanted to go home to Ireland, so he fixed me up in

Mrs Philpin's lodging house and she's looked after me since.'

'From sixteen?' Lizzie asked. 'And does she look after you?'

'Yes, she's great.'

'How old are you now?' Milly knew all adults considered this vital information.

'Twenty-two.'

'But what about your mother and father?'

'My mother died having another baby and my dad got homesick. Eventually he went back to Ireland to go into business with my uncle.'

'You've been very unlucky that way,' Milly told him. She studied his face; he was very young to be running his own business and making his own way in the world. And he was very interested in Lizzie.

'I've got by. Do come and see my rifle range. I've got lots of prizes there,' he said. 'You could choose one as a birthday present.'

A crowd clustered round the rifle range, assessing the performance of those shooting and waiting to have a go themselves. Milly's eye was taken by the prizes they could win displayed on the shelves. 'You mean I can choose one of those?' She took in the choice he was offering her. 'Those teddy bears are lovely,' she gulped.

'Don't be silly,' Lizzie said. 'You're thirteen and far too old for teddy bears.'

'A nice ornament for a girl's bedroom,' Ben said. 'Not too old for that. Or perhaps you'd prefer one of the soft toys?'

Milly's eyes lingered over the woolly lamb but her mind was made up when she saw the kangaroo with a baby in its pouch. It was made of purple plush and was absolutely gorgeous.

'Father would say you shouldn't accept it,' Lizzie said. 'Anyway, it'll be a bother carrying it round for the rest of the time we're here.'

'I'll take it back to my roundabout,' Ben said, his eyes smiling at Milly. 'I'll look after it for you until you're ready to go home. You will come back to collect it and have a last ride with me?'

'Of course,' she agreed. 'Thank you very much.'

'See you later then.' But he was grinning at Lizzie now.

'Isn't he lovely?' Milly asked when he'd turned away. 'Kind and very generous too.'

'He's only being generous to you because he thinks it'll make me like him more.'

'But you do like him, don't you?'

Lizzie smiled. 'What is there to dislike about him?'

'That means you do,' Milly said happily. 'Let's have a go on the swingboats.'

The time sped past as Milly used up her free tickets and Lizzie treated her to a turn on the dodgems, the big wheel, and a pennyworth of chips.

They watched the activity at McCluskey's rifle range for a while. Milly saw some of her friends from school and Lizzie saw her boss. Everybody was at the fair tonight.

9

CHAPTER TWO

FINALLY, LIZZIE LED THE way back to Ben's merry-go-round saying, 'Mum said we mustn't be late home. We should go.'

Ben greeted them like long-lost friends. 'Not without having a last ride.' He ushered Milly towards a rearing horse and half lifted her onto its back. He was talking to Lizzie as he turned up the volume of the music. Milly felt marvellous as she was bobbed up and down and whirled round to 'Camptown Races'. The magic was definitely here. She was sorry to feel it slowing to a halt. Ben was coming towards them with the kangaroo he'd given her.

'I'll walk you to your bus,' he told Lizzie. The crowd in the fairground had thinned; he linked arms with them both.

Milly said, 'This has been the most perfect birthday ever.' She didn't want it to end. She saw the roll-a-penny stall. 'I haven't spent my new penny yet,' she said. 'You roll it for me, Lizzie; see if you can win more money, then I can come again.'

'Your chances of winning are not great.' Ben had an infectious chuckle. 'Old Bill has to make a living from this.'

'I call her Lucky Lizzie,' Milly said. 'She's always very lucky.'

'She'll need to be.'

'She never fails to win a raffle prize when Dad takes us to one of his charity parties.'

The roll-a-penny stall was circular, with the owner standing in the middle trying to entice everyone to play. His counter was marked out in squares, each one showing a prize between two pence and a shilling. As the prize went higher the squares got smaller and to win, the player had to roll a penny down a small chute and have it settle on a square without touching any of the dividing lines.

Milly expected Lizzie to drag her home, but tonight Ben said, 'Sure, try your luck. Why not?' He was prepared to indulge her to the hilt.

'It's getting late, we ought to go.' Lizzie hesitated but she accepted Milly's new penny and kept it poised at the top of the chute for a second.

'Do you mutter "abracadabra" or something over it?' Ben laughed.

'No, nothing at all,' she let it roll down the chute, 'it just happens.'

The penny wobbled and finally settled exactly in the middle of a square marked 6d.

'You've won a sixpence!' Milly shrieked. 'I knew you would.'

The owner tossed a small silver coin to Lizzie. 'Gosh,' she said, 'I've not seen one like this before. It's brand new. I shall keep it for luck.'

'Lot of new coins about right now,' the owner said. 'It's the Coronation.'

'A lucky sixpence,' Milly cried, 'but you've lost my penny. You've got to have another go.'

'Try and stop me.' Lizzie was feeling in her pocket for coins. 'I'm feeling lucky.'

'Surely you won't go on winning?' Ben said.

Lizzie let another new penny roll down the chute and this time it landed on a square marked 3d. The owner pursed his lips and threw two dark pennies to join it and pushed all three towards Lizzie.'

'Have another go,' Milly breathed.

Once again, the bright penny rolled across the counter and this time Lizzie won five pence. She pushed her winnings into Milly's hand and used the new penny to have another turn. She won another three pence. Milly felt ecstatic. 'I told you she was lucky.'

'I wouldn't have believed it,' Ben breathed.

'I want to have a go.' Milly chose one of the new pennies and let it roll in exactly the way Lizzie had. It came to settle over several lines.

'Rotten luck,' Ben sympathised.

Milly was getting anxious now. 'Come on, let's go, we don't want Dadda to get home before us. He'll be cross.'

Lizzie reluctantly agreed and they left. Out on the promenade there were miles of fairy lights and Milly could see a ferry boat on the river all decorated and lit up. Beyond that, the lights of Liverpool twinkled; it was like fairyland. A large crowd was waiting at the bus stop, but a bus was just about to pull in. 'I hope we get on.' Lizzie was worried now, but it was full long before their turn came. There were calls of, 'Is there another bus coming?'

'Yes, the next bus will be the last tonight and it'll be going to the bus sheds.'

'That's no good to us,' Lizzie wailed. 'It's not going our way.'

'Oh gosh,' Milly had a sinking feeling, 'we're going to be very late home. We'll have to walk.'

'Is it far?' Ben asked.

'Yes,' Lizzie groaned, 'we'll be in trouble.'

'Not that far,' Milly said.

A rowdy group passed them, noisily slurring the few words they could remember of 'Land of Hope and Glory'.

'Listen to them,' Lizzie said. 'Father was against letting the pubs stay open longer today.'

'Don't worry,' Ben said. 'I'll see you safely home.'

'But then you'll have to walk all the way back,' Milly pointed out, 'and what about your merry-go-round? Don't you need to look after that?'

'I have Duggie Bennett to do that,' Ben grinned at her, 'and he won't be busy at this time of night. Which is the shortest way for you? Come on, step out and you'll soon be home.' He took one of each of their arms and started to whistle a brisk march.

Milly was relieved when they reached their lane. They were silent and tired now, but she could see the hall light shining out to guide them to the front door. Her heart seemed to miss a beat when she noticed the light showing between the curtains of their parents' bedroom; they must be waiting up for them. Suddenly, she realised a car was turning into the lane behind them; its headlights lighting everything up.

'Oh, heaven help us,' Lizzie exclaimed. 'This is Father coming home in a taxi. We'll be in for it now.'

It drew up beside them and Major Esmond Travis, wearing

his formal dinner jacket and his row of military medals, leapt out and said angrily, 'What are you two doing out at this time of night?' Milly was shocked into silence and it seemed Lizzie was too. 'And who is this with you?'

'My name is Ben McCluskey,' he said politely.

'But what are you doing here? I don't know you.'

'I'm seeing your daughters get home safely, sir. They missed the last bus and had to walk.'

'Elizabeth! You've been into town and taken Emilia with you? I expressly told you not to go tonight.'

'Sorry, Father.'

Ben had taken Milly's kangaroo when she got tired and had carried it most of the way; now he handed it back to her. 'I'd better go, Lizzie,' he said. 'You know where to find me. Perhaps you'll come tomorrow?'

'Yes,' she said.

'No,' Dadda thundered. 'I forbid it. Go into the house, both of you. Emilia, what is that monstrosity?'

'A kangaroo, Dadda.' He stood glaring at it, breathing heavily.

'It was given to Emilia as a birthday present,' Lizzie said frostily. 'You surely wouldn't ask her to hand a birthday present back?'

His lips were straight and his expression stern. Milly knew they'd be in for a row once the taxi driver had been paid off.

Elsie Travis had had a bath an hour ago and had been working herself up ever since. She was waiting for her daughters to come home, willing them to get here before Esmond. She didn't want to tell him they were still out. She'd told Lizzie not to be late and thought she'd understood she was to come home earlier than usual, because she had Milly with her. She shouldn't have allowed Milly to go to the fair.

They'd had a good day of celebration, a day of happiness and hope for the future, but it had left her more anxious than ever. She was never at ease at church parades and civic ceremonies with Esmond's colleagues. She couldn't join in the small talk and she had to remember what Esmond kept telling her, that their wives did not intend to exclude or intimidate her.

Everything had gone so well for Esmond today: all the speeches, the pomp and ceremony and rejoicing. They'd all enjoyed the martial music, the floats and the flowers and the lovely day out – until now. Like everybody else, Elsie had completely forgotten that the threat of war was on the horizon. For the last few years all of England had watched what the Nazis were doing in Europe and shuddered. It was less than twenty years since they'd had the last terrible war, the war that was meant to end all wars.

Elsie had been a teenager at the time, and she remembered it well. Her father had been killed at Passchendaele. Her mother had carried on running the family corner shop, a small grocery business, and that had sheltered them from the acute shortages that had brought hunger to the rest of the population.

None had more reason to remember the war than Esmond. He had served in the trenches from the very beginning and survived until he lost his arm at Verdun in 1916. He was living in absolute dread of another war.

Could she hear a car coming? Elsie shot out of bed to open the curtains again. No, all was dark and silent in the lane outside. It was past eleven; where were the girls? Esmond said she gave Lizzie far too much freedom, and she should never have allowed her to take Milly to the fairground tonight.

Elsie felt fraught. She must stop coming to the window; it was impossible to see anything but the glow in the sky above the fairground, the lights of the town and the ships heading into the Mersey estuary. Where were the girls?

Suddenly there was the noise of the taxi at the door and of several voices. Disaster! They'd all come home together. Esmond would know exactly how late the girls were and she knew how he'd feel about that. She leapt out of bed, reached for her dressing gown and ran downstairs to join them.

Esmond was white with fury. 'I told Elizabeth not to go into town tonight and not to take Milly to the fairground,' he was shouting. 'She blatantly disobeyed me, and not only that, she's picked up some lout from the fairground.'

Elsie leaned against the banister to get her breath. She ought to tell him she'd given them permission but her nerve failed her.

'Those girls have far too much freedom. We should not allow them out in the evenings like this. It's not safe for them after dark.'

She had to bring this to an end. She sounded desperate to her own ears. 'Esmond, it's getting late and high time they were both in bed, it's school and work tomorrow. Come along, you two.'

She kissed them and gave each a brief hug, then sent them upstairs. 'Goodnight, no hanging about, get into your beds as quickly as you can.'

'I suppose,' he cried, 'you told them they could go? You should have had more sense.'

'I'll pour your nightcap for you,' she said, heading towards his study where he kept his whisky.

Her hand was shaking as she reached for the bottle – how many times had Lizzie told her not to say that? 'He may have only one arm, Mum, but he's more than capable of opening bottles and pouring himself a drink.' They all knew that if a cork didn't come out easily, he'd sit down and hold the bottle between his knees, and he'd developed more than average strength in his one wrist.

'Let him do what he can,' Lizzie had urged. 'There's no need to wait on him hand and foot.' But Elsie couldn't forget that once it had been her job to do exactly that. How could she when she'd been his housekeeper for six years before she became his wife? It was a habit she was finding hard to break. She gave him his drink and went back to bed alone.

He'd calmed down by the time he came up to bed, but she knew he was still angry with Lizzie. All the same, he was asleep long before she was. She listened to his regular breathing and thought about him – her second husband.

She'd known him since Lizzie was eight months old and she'd had to find a job. Elsie had replied to an advert in the local paper and become Esmond Travis's housekeeper. She'd walked the mile or so to his house and worked from nine to five with a half day on Saturday. During the first year he'd hardly spoken to her apart from pointing out the jobs he wanted her to do. He kept himself apart and she thought him introverted, but he did have friends who came to the house. He was interested in chess and the editor of the local paper came regularly for a game.

He was considerate and kind to her, but by nature he was habit-bound and changed nothing in his routine. Life at Oakdene Farm was always stable and predictable.

Jasper Hardman, Lizzie's father and her first husband, was as different to Esmond as chalk and cheese. While her working life had been stable, her life at home with him had been a nightmare. There they rocked from one problem to another.

In time, Esmond began to talk to her more; he unbent, asked after Lizzie and became more sympathetic. She was still wary of him, and occasionally conscious of the need to placate him. Things had stayed like that for years.

By then she had no one else to confide in, and as she always found Esmond kind and helpful she'd begun to talk about her problems. From time to time he even spoke of his own difficulties. He'd told her that he'd been fighting in the trenches when he'd lost his arm, but he didn't want to talk about it much.

His left arm had been amputated above the elbow, and at the beginning just to think of that had given her collywobbles. She'd never seen his arm bare and didn't want to, but before they were married he'd felt he must show it to her. 'You have to know what you're letting yourself in for,' he'd said.

She'd had to try hard not to flinch but now she was used to it. That was not his only injury; apart from the bullet that had to be removed from his arm, he'd had to have pieces of shrapnel removed from his chest and that had left him with scars all down his left side.

She knew by the way his face twisted that he was sometimes in pain, but he never complained. He seemed to radiate sincerity and honesty and they were the qualities she missed most in Jasper.

He spoke with regret of the collapse of his family farm, of his inability to follow a worthwhile career, and his enforced idleness. 'But you were a war hero and badly injured,' she said. 'You couldn't work.'

'I should have tried harder. I might have felt more fulfilled if I had. A man needs to work, Elsie. Everybody needs something to fill their day.'

Elsie marvelled that anybody would want more to do. For her there weren't enough hours in the day to get through her work. 'But you have your career working for the council,' she said.

'That isn't a career; it is unpaid voluntary work to fill my time. I'm just a lonely old man, tossed aside in the modern world. I don't fit in.'

CHAPTER THREE

THE NEXT DAY AT school Milly couldn't stop yawning, but Lizzie came home from work brimming with energy. 'I went to see Ben in my lunch hour,' she whispered. 'He's taking me to the Albion Hotel tonight for a drink.' Milly could see her sister was excited. 'Don't say anything to Father. I don't want him to know.'

But Major Travis was not over the anger he'd felt last night, and over their evening meal of steak and onions, he said, 'Elizabeth, you showed a lack of responsibility towards your younger sister by taking her into town last night.'

'I'm sorry, Father.'

'You keep saying you're sorry but you go on doing things you know are wrong. You never stop to think.'

'I was able to have my free rides, Dadda.' Milly smiled at him. 'I really enjoyed them.'

Dadda snorted with disgust. 'I've been thinking about that fellow who brought you home, Lizzie. I don't think he's a suitable person for you to know.'

'Why not?' she demanded.

Milly saw Mum close her eyes in resignation.

'You know why not. You let him pick you up in the fairground. I don't think you should see him again.'

Lizzie was bristling with indignation. 'Father, I am nineteen years old and capable of making my own friends. I do not need your help.'

'I'm thinking of your safety,' he said coldly.

'You don't need to. For your information, Ben is taking me to the Albion Hotel tonight for a drink.'

Milly knew she couldn't have said anything worse. Dadda was outraged. 'He's a fairground lout and I've told you before that I don't like you going to public bars.' Dadda liked his whisky and he bought sherry for Mum, but he was dead against Lizzie letting a drop of alcohol pass her lips. 'I forbid you to go.'

'Ben isn't a lout,' Lizzie said, 'and I'm going. You can't stop me. You were rude to him last night but he behaved with dignity.'

Milly felt she had to support her. 'He was very polite to you, Dadda, and he was kind and generous to us, very gentlemanly, I'd say. He walked all the way out here and back, just to see us safely home.'

She knew she'd said the wrong thing when Dadda said, 'This has nothing to do with you, Emilia.'

Mum put in desperately, 'Lizzie, Father is seeking to protect you. It isn't easy to judge character. Not without experience. None of us want you to get into trouble.'

'I won't. I can take care of myself.' She pushed her plate away and stood up. 'I'll go now so you can finish your dinner in peace.'

'Don't be late home,' Mum pleaded.

'You can expect me when you see me,' Lizzie retorted and was gone.

'Don't be hard on her, Esmond,' Mum said. Milly could see she was almost in tears. She felt the tension tightening across the table and ten minutes later heard the front door bang behind her sister. Dadda and Mum were silent and tight-lipped as they ate apple pie and custard. They didn't want her to know how hurt they'd been by Lizzie's outburst. But it was too late: over the years she'd heard more than enough to know exactly how things stood.

Mum remained silent as Milly helped her clear away and wash up while Dadda went to brood in his study. Her family was not normal. It had always seemed divided into two camps. She and Dadda clung together; he was old and couldn't help being habit-bound and formal. He was also gentle and kind to her; affectionate, always ready to stop and talk, and he encouraged her to come to his study and talk to him. He told her all sorts of interesting things. But he was not Lizzie's father and was stiff and strict with her, as though he couldn't love her in the same way. Lizzie resented him and let it show. An open row could flare up about nothing at the drop of a hat.

Lizzie and Mum were the opposing camp. Milly didn't doubt that Mum loved her too, but she showed extra affection for Lizzie. As though she was making allowances for her, trying to protect her from Dadda's strict discipline. Sometimes, Mum seemed to appeal to her to make allowances for Lizzie too. She thought that odd as Lizzie was nearly seven years older and more than confident about fighting to get her own way.

Mum left out a slice of apple pie and the remains of the custard for Lizzie to have when she came home. 'She didn't eat all her dinner,' she said. 'I don't like you girls cutting out meals.'

Milly loved them all and wanted them to be a normal happy family, but how could they be?

Lizzie knew Father had not had the last word in that argument, and that he'd carry on where he'd left off the next time he saw her. It happened at dinner the following night. 'You used to have some very nice friends, Elizabeth. Harry Barr used to come here to collect you to take you out. He could converse on anything, a very polite and able young man. Why don't you see him any more?'

That was enough to make Lizzie bristle once again. 'He was no fun, all work and duty, and he couldn't make up his mind whether to join the police force or the merchant navy. He finally settled on a life at sea, so he's not around any more.' Anyway they'd had a tiff. She couldn't remember what about now.

'I remember Harry Barr,' Milly put in. 'He was as handsome as a film star.'

'No doubt, Father, you found him acceptable because his father is a friend of yours, and also a senior policeman.'

Father was trying to smile at her. 'A very senior policeman, he is in charge of the Wallasey force now.'

'You liked his cousin too, didn't you, Charlie something?' Milly said. Lizzie kicked her ankle under the table to shut her up.

But it was too late; Mum started. 'Then there was that other very nice lad whose father was the editor of the Wallasey *Gazette*.'

Lizzie said caustically, 'Father plays chess with him.'

'Eric Thornley, I think,' Milly put in. 'He was good-looking too.' Lizzie's boyfriends had to be to interest her.

'Yes,' Lizzie said. 'Actually, Eric Thornley was a pain in the neck.' She had thought herself in love with him once, but he had an ego almost as big as Father's. The truth was he'd thrown her over or she might still be seeing him, but that wasn't something she would admit to her family. It was none of their business.

'I won't stay for pudding, Mum,' Lizzie added hastily. She knew exactly what was coming. Father would remind her that he'd paid for her to go to St Monica's, a private school where he thought all the girls were suitable friends for her, though she'd hated it and insisted on leaving at sixteen. 'Will you excuse me please?' she said and stood up. Father didn't answer so she went anyway. He always thought he knew best. He only let her leave school on the promise that she'd go to a secretarial college in Liverpool, though she'd told him a thousand times she was interested in fashion and wanted to work in a dress shop.

Anyway, she'd walked out of that after three months. She'd been rubbish at shorthand and what was the point anyway?

Milly was crossing the hall heading for the stairs when the front doorbell rang. 'I'll get it, Mum,' she called. It was Laurie Coyne.

The Coyne family lived a hundred yards further up the lane and were their nearest neighbours. Laurie was at the University of Liverpool training to be a vet like his father. She liked him; he had been taking Lizzie out for the past year or so. Everybody accepted Laurie as Lizzie's boyfriend and both their families seemed to approve of the match. 'Come in,' she invited.

'Better not,' he said. 'I've got my new dog with me and his paws are wet.'

Milly went out on the step to stroke him. 'Oh, he's lovely.'
He had a narrow head and a lean body on long legs. 'Is this the
greyhound you told me about?'

'Yes, he's just retired from racing at Belle Vue and he
needed a new home.' Laurie had already told her about the
popular new sport of greyhound racing and the new stadium
near Manchester. The dog had short brown fur; his friendly
and alert brown eyes stared up at her, his tongue came out to
lick her hand and he seemed full of energy.

'He's not old. What's his name?'

'Well, he raced under the name of Prince Igor, but he
answers to the name of Mutt.'

Milly laughed. 'Mutt, that's a bit of a come-down, isn't it?
Did he win?'

'Often, he was quite a star, but they're all retired between
three and four years of age. They don't win as often when they
get older. Is Lizzie in?'

'No, she's gone out.'

'Oh!' He was surprised. 'We were going to the pictures
either tonight or tomorrow. I came to see which it was to be.
Looks like it'll be tomorrow now.'

'She's got a new boyfriend,' Milly said. 'I don't think she'll
want to go out with you any more.'

'What?' He seemed shocked. 'Who is he?'

'His name's Ben McCluskey. We met him at the fair last
night. He's very handsome, got lovely brown curls, and he
looks at her as though he wants to marry her.'

Laurie's smile seemed to crumble. 'Oh my goodness! But,
Milly, that doesn't mean . . .'

'Oh it does, she thinks he's exciting, lots of fun. She says

25

Dadda is prejudiced against him because he works in the fair. He forbade her to go out with him tonight but he couldn't stop her. She said she was old enough to choose her own friends and she went.'

'He works in the fair, you say?'

'Well, he owns the rifle range and the best merry-go-round there. I like him too. He gave us free rides.'

His smile was sardonic. 'In that case you would like him.'

'It's not just that.' Milly felt a touch of sympathy. She knew what it was to long for Lizzie to come home, only to find she meant to go out with someone else as soon as she'd eaten. 'I'm afraid everybody wants to take Lizzie out and most want to marry her. She's very pretty – has she said she'd marry you?'

'Milly! Mind your own business.'

'Dadda approves of you though.'

He sighed. 'Fat lot of good that does me.'

'Personally,' she said, 'I think if Dadda's approves of her friends it puts her off them.'

He was biting his lip, the picture of disappointment.

'I'll come to the pictures with you,' Milly offered. 'Nobody ever asks me.'

'You?'

'Yes. I know you haven't much money because you're still at school learning to be a vet like your dad.'

'University,' he said haughtily.

'Yes, but I can pay for myself. Well, I've got eightpence. Which seats would you want to sit in? I know the cheapest are ninepence at night but I'll give you the other penny on Saturday when Dadda gives me my pocket money. Will you take me instead of Lizzie?'

'No,' he said.

'Why not? I know I'm not as pretty as she is, but at least I don't think you're staid, old-fashioned and pedantic.'

'Did she say I was that?'

She had, but Milly didn't want to confirm it. 'I think you're very handsome and I'd have you as my boyfriend. Why don't we go to the pictures tonight?'

'No, I've said, Milly.' He was edging away from the door.

'Lizzie takes me to the pictures sometimes; she took me to the first film I ever saw. It was *Modern Times*. Did you see that?'

'No, not my sort of thing.'

'She's taken me to others since, though Dadda thinks they are quite unsuitable for me. I would like to go again if you'd take me.' She could see he was about to say no again. 'Why not?'

'Lizzie will come with me tomorrow, I know. We have an understanding.'

'I doubt it. Is there something the matter with me?' she demanded.

'Nothing that a decade won't cure. Grow up, Milly, you're just a kid.' He was backing down the steps.

'Are you taking the dog for a walk? I'd like to come with you if you are. Lizzie's gone out and Mum and Dadda are just sitting by the fire, I'm bored on my own.'

Laurie turned and with an air of resignation said, 'All right, but you'd better get a coat.'

A moment later, Milly shot out to join him, struggling into an old coat. 'I wish I could have a dog, then I'd be able to take him for a walk every day.'

'Wouldn't you get fed up with that?' he asked and without

waiting for an answer began to tell her about a seagull he'd found in the lane with a broken wing. 'I've tried to reset it,' he went on. 'It wasn't easy, I hope I've done it right.'

'Your father will know, won't he? What does he say?'

'That it's probably going to die anyway, but it might just be able to fly again when it recovers from the shock. I'll need to take care of it for a week or so. Would you like to come up and see it?' he asked. 'I shall need to check it again tonight.'

The days were getting longer and it was still light. 'Yes please.'

The seagull looked pretty sick with its splinted wing hanging uselessly down on one side. 'I wouldn't give much for its chances,' Milly said. 'It looks pretty miserable.'

It was confined in a cage placed in a sheltered spot outside the shed in his back garden. 'I've splinted it with cocktail sticks – they were the lightest thing I could think of.' He took two bowls from its cage, refilled one with water and the other with bird seed, and put them back.

'It's spilt most of the first lot of bird seed on the floor of the cage,' Milly said. 'Will it ever be able to fly and look after itself in the wild?'

'There's a chance it might, but the only humane alternative would be to kill it now. The wildlife would do it if I did not. Probably eat it too.'

'Ugh,' but Milly could see the sense of that.

'I'm looking after some rats too.' He took her inside the shed and in another cage were two rats. 'I'm looking after these for a friend, who has gone away on holiday.'

'You showed these to Lizzie, she told me.'

'She didn't like them.'

28

'No, she couldn't believe anybody could, and they aren't even white.'

He opened the cage and took one out. 'They're very friendly,' he said, putting it against his lapel and stroking it. 'This one is called Bobby and the other is Billy.'

'I don't care for them either.' Milly tried not to pull a face as she pushed the scabby apple and wilting cabbage leaf he'd brought for them into their cage.

He laughed. 'My friend keeps them in his bedroom, but my mother said I wasn't to bring them in the house.'

Milly put out a tentative hand and tried to stroke it. 'Lizzie says you care more about animals than you do about humans. I think she finds that off-putting.'

Laurie's laugh had a hollow ring. 'Thanks for your advice.'

His mother came to the back door. 'Laurie, I'm making cocoa. Oh, hello, Milly, I didn't know you were here. Would you like to come in for a cup of cocoa too?'

Milly found there was sponge cake and it was partaken round the table in their very up-to-date kitchen with his parents. They talked about all sorts of interesting things and an hour flew past. She'd have stayed longer if his father had not said, 'Won't your mother be getting anxious about you, Milly?'

So, knowing it was time she went, she stood up. 'It's dark outside now, and it's overcast, so no starlight,' Mrs Coyne said. 'Laurie had better see you home.'

Milly could see reluctance on his face and knew he'd put his slippers on when they'd first come in, so she said, 'No need, Laurie, I'm not a child any more, I can get home alone.'

'Are you sure, Milly?' his mother asked.

'Yes, I can't possibly get lost, can I?'

Laurie saw her to their front gate. The kitchen light was on in Oakdene Farm, beckoning her on, and there were twinkling lights everywhere as well as the orange glow in the sky over the seafront. She walked home wondering how she could convince the Coynes that they didn't need to treat her like a babe in arms. She didn't feel like a child, though there was nothing in her life but school and homework. Everybody thought she was too young for any sort of fun.

She sighed with frustration; Lizzie could have anything she wanted straight away. Any boyfriend she might choose. How could she grow up more quickly?

CHAPTER FOUR

LIZZIE HAD NEVER BEEN inside the Albion Hotel before and found it very grand. Ben escorted her to a plush sofa in a corner, well away from the crush round the bar, before getting the drinks. She couldn't keep her eyes away from him. He was wearing a new Fair Isle pullover and had tight curls all over his head. His dark eyes kept meeting hers and neither of them could bring themselves to look away.

She'd asked for a glass of sherry because that was what Mum drank at home; actually she'd have preferred lemonade but was afraid Ben might think that childish. His fingers touched her hand as he slid the drink on the table in front of her, and it sent little shivers up her spine. She had never met anyone who had such an effect on her as this. Ben was lovely. He never stopped talking – either he was telling her about his life or asking about hers – and he made his glass of beer last for ages so it didn't matter that she didn't like the sherry.

He walked her home, of course. 'Has your father gone out tonight?' he asked. 'Just think how he'd harangue me if he caught me kissing you.'

She laughed. 'No, he stayed in, but there are other houses off this lane. Only recently four big new ones have been built, so there's no guarantee that our neighbours won't catch us.'

All the same, once the darkness enfolded them behind the high hedges he pulled her close and kissed her. Lizzie tingled from his touch and raised her lips for more. Ben was definitely not a lout and she liked him very much; in fact, she was more than a little in love with him already.

Over the following weeks Lizzie never seemed to be at home in the evenings, and at breakfast she was sleepy and dreamy-eyed. She had never looked more beautiful; her eyes sparkled, her hair shone. Milly heard her parents talking about her, their tension growing. They were afraid she was 'getting involved with that lad from the fair'. At meal times, sparks were flying more often between Lizzie and Dadda.

Milly followed her to her bedroom one evening when she was getting ready to go out. 'Do me a favour,' Lizzie said. 'Would you press this dress for me? Otherwise I'll have to do it when I come in tonight.'

'Ben is taking up all your time,' Milly said. She was missing Lizzie's company. 'You must like him more than Laurie.'

Lizzie laughed. 'Yes, he believes in having a good time, enjoying himself.'

'More than Laurie?'

'Laurie hasn't much time for fun. He's more interested in animals and his exams.'

'Well, he's got to pass those, hasn't he?'

One Saturday afternoon Lizzie took her to the fair again and Ben was even more generous with free rides on his merry-go-round. 'Stay on as long as you like,' he told them, but Lizzie wanted to consult the fortune-teller.

'That's a waste of money,' Milly said. 'Dadda says fortune-tellers will tell you what you want to hear. They're just guessing, it's their way of earning a living.'

'She could be right.' Ben grinned at her, and Milly stayed on for ride after ride until Lizzie came back.

It seemed to take a long time. 'What did you ask her?' she wanted to know. Lizzie wouldn't say.

'Was it when will Ben propose?'

'Shut up,' she said, getting into the racing car to have a free ride.

Milly had thought it impossible to spend too much time having free rides on Ben's merry-go round but now she wanted to try something else. 'I only have tuppence, Lizzie,' she said. 'Come to the roll-a-penny stall, and see if you can win enough for me to go on the ghost ride.'

Lizzie needed no persuading. Milly watched the first penny roll down, wobble and finally settle into a square that won her threepence. Lizzie was all smiles; her eyes were shining. 'I'll try and win a shilling for you,' she whispered. 'I'll try giving it a bit of a push.'

Sometimes she did lose her penny stake, but she kept going and was consistently winning small amounts until her winnings finally reached a shilling. Even Milly felt her fascination; it was intoxicating.

They were there long enough for Ben to come looking for them. 'Come on,' he said, 'Old Bill is looking fed up. If you carry on winning like this he'll ban you from playing at all.'

'Surely not,' Lizzie laughed, reluctant to move on.

'Come on,' Ben urged. 'Take Milly for a last go on the bumper cars, I'll ask Jack if we can all have a free turn.'

Milly loved the bumper cars, and Lizzie was sparkling with happiness. 'What an easy way to get money,' she laughed, patting Milly's pocket. 'More fun than working for it.'

They put Milly on the bus to go home alone, but she'd had a lovely time and now had one shilling and tuppence in her pocket.

Milly thought there was no better place to live in the whole wide world than New Brighton. They had a big map at school showing it at the mouth of the Mersey estuary, on the north corner of the Wirral peninsula. It had a marvellous beach with views across the Irish Sea and up the river to Liverpool. In the summer it had donkey rides.

Dadda was equally proud of his home town and could tell Milly stories about its history, if she could get him in the right mood. He'd told her about the lighthouse that had been showing a light for sailors since 1683, and Fort Perch Rock, completed in 1829, with guns to protect the port of Liverpool. That was now a museum.

At that time, a Liverpool gentleman named James Atherton bought much of the land along the seafront, aiming to build on it a high-class residential and holiday resort for the gentry, like Brighton – hence the name. A few grand houses and a couple of splendid civic buildings were built up the bank overlooking the river. He didn't live to see it finished but others carried on.

They had a pier to provide both entertainment and frequent ferries to Birkenhead and Liverpool.

New Brighton Tower was a copy of the Eiffel Tower and when first built was the tallest building in the country, taller than Blackpool Tower. It was built in sumptuous gardens with a ballroom and a huge theatre at its base, and also a cycle track, a roller-skating rink, a restaurant and shops. The tower had to be dismantled after the Great War because it was rusting due to lack of maintenance, but the Tower Ballroom and theatre were still here.

Also in the gardens was the enormous Palace Amusement Centre with a covered arcade which stayed open throughout the year where Ben had his merry-go round and rifle range. There was also a huge outside fairground with a big wheel, go-carts and boats on a lake. Milly considered the fairground to be the best part. 'I think,' she said to Dadda one day, 'that New Brighton is a wonderful holiday resort, don't you?'

'Well, it is our home too, but it has a problem. It is too close to a huge urban conurbation, and it has plenty of ferries, buses and trains to bring people here cheaply. Most people would describe it as a day-trippers' paradise, rather than a resort.'

'Oh dear!'

'When the sun comes out, they flock here in droves and swamp us locals. I blame the funfair for that.'

Milly knew New Brighton was part of the town of Wallasey, and Dadda called that a dormitory town because Liverpool workers lived there and used the ferry to get to work. She preferred to think of the old days when it had had a reputation for smuggling and wrecking and secret underground tunnels and cellars which were said to still exist.

Milly went to school in Wallasey and thought it rather a dull place; New Brighton was definitely the best part.

CHAPTER FIVE

ILLY COULD SEE THAT Lizzie was really enamoured of Ben McCluskey. She could understand that; she'd taken to him too. Lizzie was always telling her about the exciting places Ben took her. She'd had drinks and dinners in the Grand Hotel and also in the Albion. He'd taken her dancing in the Tower Ballroom and to the theatre and restaurant in the gardens nearby. 'He's marvellously generous, loads of fun, and wants us both to have a great time.'

She was rushing home from work every night to eat her dinner and leaving as soon as she possibly could to meet him. Mum protested that she was overdoing it and would tire herself out. Dadda was cross about it.

Tonight Lizzie was trying to rush the washing up. Father had said she must not go out until the kitchen had been cleared up after the evening meal. 'It's not fair to leave everything to Mum and Emilia.'

'I'm going to be late,' she fretted to Milly when they were alone in the kitchen.

'Don't worry, I'll finish off here,' she said. 'There's not much more to do, you go.'

'Thanks, I'll make it up to you later.' Lizzie flung the tea towel on the kitchen table and shot upstairs to get ready. Five minutes later she swept back wearing a new camel coat. 'Milly, love, I've just come across this in my pocket.' She put a green and gold button on the table. 'It came off my cardigan on the way home the other night. Would you be a real sport and sew it back on for me?'

Milly sighed. 'I do have homework to do, but all right, just this once. Where is it? Your cardie?'

'Er . . . I put it away. In my wardrobe, I think, or is it in the top drawer of my tallboy? Gosh, Milly, will you look? Thanks a million. You're the tops.'

Once Milly had finished mopping round the kitchen, she examined Lizzie's button and slipped it in her pocket. That cardigan was a real eye-catcher; she'd told Lizzie she'd love to have it when she grew tired of it. The buttons were lovely too. She'd see to that next.

She went upstairs to Lizzie's bedroom. Where did she say it would be? Yes, beneath her hanging clothes in her wardrobe. There were several cardigans there flung on top of shoes, but not that green one. She tried the top drawer in her chest of drawers, and there it was, the lovely green cardie she'd worn to work.

Lizzie loved clothes and was always buying them from the shop where she worked. Milly felt she could do with more. She dug lower to see more of a blue pullover and as she lifted it out an old newspaper cutting was caught up with it. It fluttered down to the bedside rug. Milly picked it up and idly smoothed it out.

SUICIDE OF WAR VETERAN

A child of six came home from school alone on Tuesday to find her father dead. Jasper Anthony Hardman, aged 29, of 15 Park Street, Wallasey, killed himself by . . .

Milly let the paper flutter from her nerveless fingers. She could feel her heart pounding, and the strength was ebbing from her knees. Jasper Hardman had been Mum's first husband and Lizzie's father! This was about them. Why had nobody told her that Lizzie's father had killed himself?

She'd not heard so much as a whisper about this, not even from Lizzie. His death was never talked about in the family; never mentioned. Milly wanted to kick herself: why had she never asked how or why he'd died?

With shaking fingers she picked the paper up to read some more. Oh goodness! He'd cut his wrists with a razor blade. This was horrible. It was making her feel sick. She ran downstairs and flung open the sitting room door. Mum was sitting on one side of the fireplace knitting and Dadda was on the other. Milly brandished the newspaper cutting at them, and slowly Dadda put his coffee cup down.

'Why didn't you tell me about Lizzie's father?' Milly demanded. 'Why has it been brushed under the carpet and forgotten? Surely I have a right to know what happens in the family?'

They both stared at her in stunned silence. Her father removed his spectacles. 'It hasn't been brushed under the carpet, Milly. That hasn't proved possible.'

'But nobody told me he'd killed himself. Why did he do that?'

'Well – war can have a terrible effect on the minds of men who fight in it.'

Milly nodded. 'You'd know, Dadda; you were in it too. Was he injured?'

'No, but he was caught up in the thick of the fighting in the trenches, and saw many of his friends killed. Afterwards, the Spanish flu epidemic swept across the country, and he was very ill then. It was a hard time for everyone. Elsie, you'd better tell her what she wants to know.'

'And I want to know about Lizzie. It says in the newspaper that she was only six.'

'Yes.' Her mother pulled herself up in her chair. 'Poor Lizzie, it really did upset her – she came home from school alone and found her father . . .'

'Found him dead, it says.'

'Yes, sitting in his armchair. After that she used to wake up screaming in the middle of the night, it gave her nightmares. Perhaps it still does.'

'No,' Dadda said. 'No, Elizabeth sleeps soundly, she never wakes us now. I think she's been over it for some years, Elsie.'

'Lizzie was very young; you can understand her being frightened?' There was a tremor in Mum's voice; Milly could see it upset her to talk about it even now.

'Of course. I would have been too.'

'Jasper would not have wanted his young daughter to come home and find him in that state.' Dadda sounded impatient. 'He didn't think it through. If he had, he'd have known the effect it would have on his wife and child.'

'But where were you, Mum?' Milly felt icy cold, but she could understand now why Mum was more protective of Lizzie than she was of her.

'At work,' she said. 'Her father used to look after Lizzie when she wasn't at school, they were very close.'

'You went out to work?' She'd heard Mum say from time to time that she ought to get a job, but Dadda said married ladies did not go out to work, and that Mum had more than enough to do looking after the family and the household, with only

Gladys coming in the mornings to help her with the rough.

'Yes, I went to work in those days. I had to. The shipyards were idle; the country was in a deep depression. We had no money, nobody had much. Jasper had worked for Cammell Laird's before the war but there were fewer ships being built there then. He'd tried everywhere but could get only temporary jobs.'

Milly asked, 'Did you work in a shop or an office? What did you do?'

Dadda said, 'Your mother was working for me as my housekeeper.'

'What?' Milly had heard of that before but still found it hard to believe. 'Oh, but of course, you didn't live here then – when it happened.'

'No,' Dadda said, 'that was at fifteen Park Street in Wallasey.'

'I don't know where that is,' Milly said, though she knew some parts of Wallasey well.

'Look at the time! I have to go,' Dadda said. 'The taxi I've ordered will be here in five minutes. Your mother will explain everything to you, Milly.'

She sat in Dadda's empty chair. They heard him shout his goodbyes from the hall and the front door close behind him. Her mother remained silent and looked troubled.

'Please tell me,' Milly pleaded.

'You know about it already.' She looked up, her pale eyes worried. 'There's not much more to tell.'

'But, Mum, there is. You were Dadda's housekeeper before you were his wife. Isn't that a bit . . . odd? Unusual?'

She sighed. 'Not really.'

A LUCKY SIXPENCE

* * *

Lizzie knew Ben had been watching for her; she saw his face light up as she approached his merry-go-round. As soon as it stopped she claimed a racing car for the next ride, and he came leaping across to join her. 'I was afraid something had stopped you coming.'

'Nothing would stop me, but I am a few minutes late. I started to press a dress for tomorrow, but persuaded Milly to take over. I have to look decent for work.'

He dropped a quick kiss on her cheek. 'You're always very smartly dressed, beautiful too. Have a ride or two while I tell Duggie to take over.'

'The fair's busy tonight.'

'It will be from now on, it's June, after all.'

After one ride Ben was back. She loved his tightly curling hair and impish smile. 'Where are we going tonight?'

With the light nights and increasing number of holiday-makers, it wasn't easy to find anywhere private, and it was privacy they sought. Lizzie longed to feel his arms round her. The beach was the best bet at night but there was no shortage of other couples seeking privacy too. Down on the beach under the pier in the shadow cast by the promenade, the night was a little darker. His arms pulled her close, and Lizzie was settling into the bliss of his kisses when they almost tripped over a couple lying tightly entwined on the sand. They edged further away but there were other couples. 'I can't show you how much I love you here,' Ben said. 'It makes this seem furtive. Come and see my room.'

'What about your landlady? Will she mind?'

'I don't think so. She lets me do what I want.'

Within moments he was holding open a wide front door, the hall inside large and shabby. 'Cheers, Ben,' a young man greeted him, heading up the stairs with a steaming mug.

A plump motherly woman wearing a large apron had come to the kitchen door. 'Hello, you're home early tonight, Ben. Who is this you've brought with you?'

'My young lady, Lizzie Hardman,' he told her. 'This is my landlady, Mrs Philpin.'

'Pleased to meet any of Ben's friends. Come in and have a cup of tea,' she said, pulling out a chair at the well-scrubbed table. The kitchen was large, bare, and everything looked old-fashioned and well-worn. Lizzie knew Ben didn't want them to spend their time together talking to his landlady, but she sat down and made small talk over the tea.

Another young lodger came in for tea and biscuits, and Ben introduced her and then stood up. Lizzie did likewise. 'Where are you off to now?' Mrs Philpin asked, following them to the doorway. Ben was leading her towards the stairs.

'I thought I'd show Lizzie my room before seeing her home.' Ben gave her a winning smile.

'You know my rules,' she said. 'No young ladies in bedrooms, especially not at this time of night. It would get my house a bad name. Besides, I promised your grandfather I'd do my best to keep you out of trouble.'

'Oh, Philpy! Just this once.'

'Well, as my most trusted lodger and the one who's been here longest, I could as a favour let your young lady have a peep at it.' She followed them upstairs.

Ben threw back one of the doors. 'This is my place,' he said and Lizzie craned forward to look. Like the other rooms it was big, bare and shabby, but it was also tidy.

'Very comfortable-looking,' Lizzie said to please his landlady, though it was hardly that.

'Come in and sit down for five minutes,' he invited. She knew to sit on his bed would look wrong; there was only one hard chair in the corner so she headed for that, wanting the woman to go. They waited. Time seemed to stop.

'I'm not going to leave you here, my dear. It could ruin both your reputation and mine.'

'Just for half an hour,' Ben pleaded with his intimate pleading smile.

'Ben McCluskey, you're being naughty. Don't use your guile on me, it won't work.'

'Just this once. Please.'

'No! I've got my principles. I run a respectable God-fearing lodging house. There will be no sinning under my roof, or anything that might lead people to think there was. Now you see this young lady safely home, then I can settle down for the night.' Lizzie could feel her gaze on her back as she and Ben clattered back down the stairs.

'That was terrible,' he whispered once they were outside. 'I thought she'd let us, I really did. Usually she treats me like her favourite.'

CHAPTER SIX

Ben put his arm round Lizzie's waist and pulled her tight against him so she could feel his thigh moving against hers as they walked. They were close to the fair again. 'I could do with a drink,' he said. 'The Anchor is just round the corner, let's go there.'

Lizzie smiled. 'Father says it has a terrible reputation, one of the worst pubs in New Brighton. Fights breaking out, that sort of thing.'

'Most of its customers work in the fair and it's always been quiet when I've been there, but years ago there was a fight in the bar and a man was killed. It was closed for a while, but that's almost an historical event.'

Lizzie laughed. 'Yes, let's go, it sounds exciting. Father would have a fit if he knew you'd taken me there. He thinks I'll be tarnished for life if I step inside.'

'Nothing exciting about it.' Ben laughed too. 'Very ordinary, it's just a cheap pub.'

Lizzie agreed with him when she saw the Victorian tiles on the outside and the heavily frosted glass in the windows. It was dark inside and reeked of beer. 'Not in the bar,' he said, 'ladies not allowed in there.' He steered her into a small and comfortless room. 'They call this the lounge,' he said. Two middle-aged women turned to watch them. He led Lizzie to a seat as far away as possible. 'What shall I get you?'

'Lemonade, please.'

'Hey, McCluskey, tell Ted we want two more port and lemons, would you?' one of the women called.

Lizzie was surprised. Ben had not said he was well known here. That wouldn't please Father either. She watched the two women surreptitiously as they turned away from her to converse quietly together. Both wore hats pulled well down over their hair, and were rather plainly, even shabbily dressed.

Ben returned with the barman and their drinks. 'Who are they?' she whispered.

'Wife of the owner of the caterpillar ride. I think the other works on the roller coaster.'

The two women had settled back to their drinks when a young lad came in who looked under the age he should be to be inside a pub. One of the women cheered. 'Glad to see you, Jimmy.'

'Is he giving them money?' Lizzie asked.

'Yes,' Ben whispered. 'Jimmy Cox works on the boating lake, and augments his wages by acting as a bookie's runner. He's paying out on some bets they've won. Don't mention this to your family. It's illegal to bet, except on the racecourse.'

Lizzie had to ask him to explain further. 'There was horse racing at Epsom yesterday and Jimmy takes their bets. Looks as though they backed a winner.' Lizzie had heard Father's low opinion on betting and of those people who did. He didn't believe in anybody having fun.

Jimmy looked at Ben. 'It's the Oaks tomorrow – are you going to have a go?'

45

He shook his head. 'No thanks, Jimmy.'

'He's a bit young to be in here, isn't he?' whispered Lizzie.

'Yes, he's not long left school, but he works in the fairground, everybody looks after him.'

'Why?'

'Years ago, his father worked on the big dipper. Do you remember there was an accident? Anyway, his father was killed. Jimmy was only three or so at the time. When he was old enough to go to school his mother got a job. Luckily she was a typist, but they don't have that much. We all try to help a bit.'

'Poor lad.'

'Jimmy's happy enough. He tries to help his mother. Lizzie, I don't think I should have brought you here. Drink up and we'll go.'

Lizzie stood up and said, 'It is a bit shabby.'

Ben laughed. 'It's homely and I see my fellow workers from the fair, so I come quite a lot. We're quite a community.'

He walked her home. It was a lovely clear and balmy night and there were lots of people about. 'I reckon your lane might be the best place to get a bit of privacy after all,' he said.

They spent a little time there, with Lizzie leaning back against the high bank while he leaned against her giving her long deep kisses, but though her heart was pumping and she longed for more, she didn't feel safe and couldn't relax.

'This lane is so straight.' They both knew how any car turning in would light them up. 'There are other houses along here, our neighbours and Father's friends, so I'll be in worse trouble if we are seen by them.'

But Lizzie knew where they could have total privacy, and she wanted it badly so she led the way. 'Once our house was a farm so we have lots of old buildings, cowsheds and dairies.' She took him to the old stable. Last Christmas, Father had given both her and Milly a torch to light their way in the lane and she'd never needed it more. It was very dark inside.

'Just the place,' Ben enthused, but they soon noticed the sour damp smell and that the floor was of uneven cobbles.

'I used to play here once,' Lizzie said. 'There's a pile of old hay in that corner. It used to be my secret hideaway.'

'It could be again.' Ben chuckled, but the hay was white with mould and it stank.

'Perhaps the cowshed . . . ?'

Unable to wait any longer, Ben was kicking the worst of the mould away and pulling her down beside him. She welcomed him into her arms; she'd been waiting for his kisses since they set out from the fair and desire had built and built. Lizzie had not experienced love like this before and felt as though she was flying.

Afterwards, Ben was full of guilt. He felt as though he'd crashed into the bumpers. 'Lizzie, I'm sorry, I should never have let that happen.'

'Didn't you like it?'

'Of course I did, it was marvellous. But I could father a child on you. Think of the desperate situation we'd be in then.'

'Terrible.' Lizzie shuddered now. 'Father would go berserk if he knew we'd gone this far.'

'We can't do it again, not like this. It won't do for a girl like you, won't do for me either. We need to think things through.'

'What are we going to do?' Lizzie waited, hoping and half expecting him to say, 'Let's get married.'

His face was screwing with concentration. 'There must be

some way. Lodging with Mrs Philpin has been good up to now, but not any longer.'

Lizzie was trying not to panic; it sounded as though he didn't want to get married, only wanted her as a temporary girlfriend. 'I need a house of my own, for a start. I'll look for somewhere to rent, somewhere handy for the fair. And I need to get some of those French Letters from the barber, I'll go tomorrow morning.'

She had to ask. 'Don't . . . Don't you want to get married?' She knew she sounded half strangled, desperate.

'Of course I do, but we can't straight away. You're absolutely gorgeous, Lizzie. I've never met anyone like you before and I love you to bits. But getting married is a huge step for both of us and we have to be careful about making big changes like that. Get things in the right order. I've been saving up for some time.'

'What for?' She shivered. 'Is money more important than love to you?'

He thought for a moment; she sensed he'd flashed his impish grin at her. 'No, I'm aiming to have both. You are the girl I've dreamed of, one day I want us to live in a fine house with our children, but I will have to earn the money for that. Nobody is going to give it to me. I'm not going to inherit anything from my relatives, they have little enough for themselves. I'm saving to get a third sideshow or another roundabout to bring in more income. I need to go on doing that.'

He was deadly serious and Lizzie was taking in all he said. There was more to Ben than she'd realised; underneath, he was serious and cautious, more like Father than she'd supposed. She'd told him about Father inheriting his farm.

She said, 'So I haven't swept you off your feet? You aren't going down on your knee to propose and rush me into wedlock?'

He smiled. 'Yes, you've swept me off my feet and yes, I want to marry you.'

'That's marvellous.' She laughed aloud with relief and pleasure. 'I thought you wanted to put it off until you'd saved more.'

'No point if we've both made up our minds.'

'I think we have and I don't like waiting for what I want.'

'Nobody does, but I've had to learn to do that. You've told me it's your ambition to have a dress shop of your own one day. You're waiting and saving for that, aren't you?'

Lizzie laughed. 'I haven't saved anything. Just dreamed of it, I suppose.' All she earned she spent on clothes.

'That is where we are different. I've had to be practical, but don't worry, you are part of my big plan, I'll take good care of you. I promise we'll be married quite soon, and we won't be worried about making ends meet. Right now, we're young and we want to enjoy ourselves, so we'll put off having children for a while. We don't need responsibilities like that yet. How d'you feel about that?'

'That's exactly what I want too. It's an excellent plan.' She was proud of him; he was so sensible, so practical. 'I've never thought much about the future or about money either,' Lizzie admitted, 'but it sounds the best way to get what you want.'

'It is,' he said. 'My family have proved it. Gosh, this hay has made us both stink.'

'Nobody must guess we've been here.' Lizzie was panicking at the thought.

Ben was trying to pick stray strands off her best coat. He

shook it out of the door, picked some more wisps from her hair. 'Let's get out in the fresh air – that should help.'

It was moonlight now, and the breeze from the Irish Sea was as heady as wine. Lizzie was bursting with happiness. Ben was wonderful.

As Ben walked home through the starlit night he felt exultant. He'd made love to Lizzie for the first time, and with her it had been a bigger thrill than it ever had before. She'd been a virgin but more than willing. He could teach her to be a real seductress with a little more practice.

The major would not give his permission for her to marry him but he'd made Lizzie his. He felt triumphant; he was one up on her father. Now he wanted to live with Lizzie, make love to her every night, and spend all his spare time with her. He was blissfully happy, and felt he'd reached a plateau.

Lizzie would need a wedding ring on her finger because she'd been brought up to believe marriage was essential, so he wanted that too. She must have everything she wanted; he wanted to bond completely with her.

But it might not be easy. Lizzie was afraid her parents would be dead against her marrying him. They didn't like her coming out with him; they thought she could do better than a lad from the fairground, but what could he do about that?

By the time he was unlocking Mrs Philpin's front door, he knew he'd have to keep up the pressure on the major if he was ever to make this dream come true.

Lizzie let herself into the hall; she was later than usual but there was enough light from the moon to see Father's slippers in the porch. That meant he wasn't yet home, so no danger of a dressing-down from him. All the same, she crept upstairs to her room without putting on the light, her mind filled with Ben's declaration of love, her body glowing from his touch.

She took off her coat. It had a dirty mark on the back which she must get off; that old stable was filthy. She was reaching for her clothes brush when her bedroom door creaked open and Milly edged in. 'Hello.'

'Oh! Still up?' Lizzie was not pleased to see her sister; she wanted to get into bed and think about Ben. Then she noticed her cardigan neatly folded on her counterpane. 'Thank you for sewing that button on for me.'

'Mum did it, not me. Lizzie, I found these under it in your drawer.'

To see Milly spreading out the old creased and yellowing newspaper cuttings was a bit of a shock. 'Oh, goodness, Milly!' She'd read them herself many times to mull over those awful days.

'Dadda said Mum would explain it to me, but I can't get her to say anything. You tell me, Lizzie.'

It was the last thing Lizzie wanted to do, and certainly not now. 'I'm tired and it's late. Some other time, Milly.'

'Please, Lizzie.'

She could see that her sister was distressed.

'Why didn't you tell me your father took his own life? I didn't know. Mum said it gave you nightmares.'

'Gave her nightmares too, it was awful.' Lizzie didn't want to think about it. There had been blood everywhere. It was still dripping from him when she'd come home from school. 'He'd been fine the day before, bought me ice cream. It was so unexpected.' That was why she'd had those nightmares. She'd been terrified Mum might do the same thing and she'd be left alone in the world.

Lizzie sighed. 'Nobody wants to talk ill of the dead, though there's plenty we could all say about him.'

'Didn't you love your dad? Mum must have done.'

'I sort of did, but he was difficult. He upset Mum.' Lizzie was throwing off her clothes, reaching under her pillow for her nightdress. 'My dad was a rotter.'

'A rotter? In what way? What did he do? I want to hear all about him.'

'I'm cold, put the light out and come into bed with me. He stole things, told lies. He couldn't keep a job, was always getting the sack, so we were hard up. Really hard up. Mum had to find work and leave me when I was a baby.'

'That's when she became Dadda's housekeeper? Nobody has told me much about that either. Mum won't tell me anything.'

'She doesn't want to talk about it, Milly. They were hard times.'

'Your father looked after you then? What's so awful about that?'

'He was an alcoholic. Sometimes he didn't know what he was doing. He'd fall asleep and forget about me. Mum had to give him money to buy food and pay the rent, but he'd spend it on booze instead without telling her. That put us in debt.'

'Oh my goodness.'

'Then he was caught stealing from a shopkeeper and sent to prison. Mum cried when she found out he'd been to prison before. Twice before, in fact.'

She could feel Milly shivering. 'Then why did Mum marry him?'

'She didn't know what he was like, not to start with. She was taken in and thought he was romantic and lots of fun. She was in love with him, you see. He swept her off her feet.'

'Like you and Ben?'

Lizzie was indignant. 'No, Ben is completely different. He has a serious side, he's running his own business and he's careful with money.'

'He lets us have lots of free rides.'

'That's different; he's got a better grasp on money than Father has.'

'Has he? But surely, if your dad was that bad, it wouldn't have taken Mum long to see what he was like?'

'Yes, but by then it was too late. She was married to him.'

'And working for Dadda as his housekeeper?'

'Yes, when my dad died, your father let us come and live upstairs so Mum wouldn't have to pay rent and could pay off the debt.'

'You remember living upstairs? Was it nicer here?'

'We lived in the attic, the old servants' quarters. Not all that nice.'

'But Dadda must have been kind to you both, for Mum to fall in love with him.'

'Milly, I've told you what you wanted to know and I'm tired. Go to your own bed, there isn't room for both of us here.'

CHAPTER SEVEN

BY THE FOLLOWING WEEK Ben was all smiles when Lizzie went to meet him in the arcade. 'I've found a little house to rent,' he said. 'I'll just tell Duggie I'm leaving and we'll go and see it. I do hope you'll like it, I've been to see three places today and I think this one is the best. It'll give us a place of our own.'

Lizzie felt a surge of delight and she could see he was excited. 'I love the way you get on with things. There's no hanging about for you. Where is it?'

'Well, I'm a bit worried about that. It has to be handy for the fair otherwise I'll waste time going back and forth. I know you think it a bit slummy round here.'

'No I don't.'

'Your father will, I'm sure. It's a two-up two-down in Alvaston Terrace.' He was leading the way down a nearby back street. 'Here we are.'

Lizzie felt paralysed; she hadn't expected this. It was a mammoth shock. The street consisted of some nondescript buildings, warehouses or such, and Alvaston Terrace was ten stone-built cottages that had once housed fishermen but were now several hundred years old.

Ben grinned at her. 'Mine is number two at the far end. It's a bit shabby, I'm afraid.'

Lizzie thought that the understatement of the year. She could feel all her hopes spiralling downwards.

'Come on, I've got the key.' The front door opened into a small living room. 'I didn't like to tell you before you saw it but I've paid a month's rent.'

Lizzie couldn't get her breath. How could he think of living here? The wallpaper was peeling off the walls and it was as dirty as the cowsheds at home. There were dead flies on the window sill, grey ash falling out of the rusting fire grate.

Ben led the way into the room behind. 'This is the kitchen.' The only furniture was a cupboard, a small table and a broken chair. Lizzie looked at the stone sink and the dripping tap and felt sick. Bare stairs led up from here. She followed him to a tiny bedroom, which led directly to a larger one at the front. The ceilings were low and yellowing and had cobwebs in the corners. The whole place was cramped and smelled musty, dusty and of decay. It was awful. What was Ben thinking of?

'I can see you don't like it,' he said gently. 'You don't know what it is to live down in town. I can make this comfortable and it'll be cosy.'

'There's no bathroom?'

'No, but there's a lavatory and a wash house out in the yard.' He shot downstairs again and took the bolt off the back door. It was stiff to open and dragged along the floor. 'The bottom hinge has collapsed but I can fix it, don't worry about things like that.'

The back yard was ghastly: a rusting iron bed frame and a

zinc bathtub were propped against the wall; the lavatory was disgusting and lacked a seat. Lizzie shot back to the front living room, trying to find the words.

'Look, Lizzie, I know it isn't grand and it isn't what you're used to, but I can afford to live here and still save. One day, I promise you, we'll have a big house in a smart district. I've arranged for two men to come in and clean it up. I think a coat of white distemper all through should do it. That will make it lighter as well.'

'You won't get full daylight until you clean the windows.'

'Lizzie, I'm sorry. You don't like it, but it won't be for ever, maybe just a year or two.'

Lizzie was afraid it would be impossible to bring Mum or Milly here, and as for Father, he'd be appalled. 'Ben, I'll need my parents' permission to get married, and they won't like to think of me living here.'

'It will look quite different in a week or two,' he said with a confident smile, 'you'll see. I can furnish it from the auction rooms in Penkett Road. They hold one every fortnight. It's such a small house it won't take much.'

Lizzie spent the evening trying to dissuade him and went home feeling troubled. She couldn't see that he could make such a slum habitable. He'd rushed into taking out a tenancy on it before he'd even told her, and to think of spending money on it was beyond belief. She must say nothing to her family about this.

At breakfast the next morning, her mother said, 'Lizzie, you were very late coming home last night.'

Father looked up from his boiled eggs. 'You're spending a

lot of time with a boy your mother has never met. It worries her, Lizzie.'

'I'm sorry, Mum, but there's no need for you to worry about Ben. He has his head screwed on the right way.' Well, she'd thought he had.

'We do worry,' Father said. 'I think you should bring him here and introduce him.'

'You were very rude to him, Father, when you overtook us in the lane that night.'

He sighed. 'Yes, I was angry that you'd disobeyed me and kept Emilia out so late. I'm sorry about that.'

'I won't bring him here to be insulted again. Will you promise to be polite?'

Her mother protested. 'Lizzie!'

'I'll be on my best behaviour,' he said stiffly. 'Please bring him to tea on Sunday afternoon. Four o'clock.'

Lizzie went to meet Ben at his roundabout that evening and found he wasn't pleased by her news. 'So it's a formal invitation to see if my eating habits are acceptable?' he asked.

'They'll be looking at more than that.'

'Well,' he was resigned, 'I suppose it has to happen before they'll let me marry you.'

'Yes, I've told them you're in lodgings. Don't whatever you do mention that you're going to rent a house of your own or they'll forbid me to go near it. Don't let on you've been anywhere near the old stables either, and be prepared for embarrassing questions.'

'Right, what does Sunday afternoon tea consist of in your house?'

'Mum usually puts a cake in the oven when she's doing the roast for lunch, so just tea and cake. Possibly something more because you're coming.'

He laughed. 'We call our evening meal tea, but it's a bit more substantial. On Sundays there'll be meat left over from lunch with a salad, or a tin of something.'

'We have that too but we call it supper.'

'Right, so it'll be just a cup of tea. In the sitting room or the garden?'

'No, it'll be in the dining room. Father has only one arm and says it's easier for him to eat at the table.'

'Yes of course, sorry, I didn't think. What should I wear? I want to make a good impression.'

'Your best suit with a collar and tie.' He was wearing slacks with an open-necked shirt. 'Father wears a suit most of the time. He has lots of suits for different occasions.'

'Oh gosh, I'm glad I asked.'

'He's habit-bound, very old-fashioned – Victorian, almost.'

Sunday came, a day of heavy clouds and drizzle. Full of trepidation, Lizzie helped with the preparations, spreading a lace cloth on the table and setting out the best china tea service, as her mother directed. Together they'd cut tiny cucumber sandwiches, removing all the crusts, and Mum had made both a sponge cake and a fruit cake. Milly was quite excited because something different was happening. She hovered two steps behind them all afternoon, getting in the way. Lizzie waited in a fever of anxiety for Ben to come, and at five minutes to four he knocked on the front door.

She rushed to open it. 'Come in,' she said. He looked very handsome in a trilby and smart mackintosh.

'Hello, Ben.' Milly beamed at him. 'Let me hang up your coat.'

'Put the kettle on for tea,' Lizzie commanded.

Mum bustled out of the sitting room all wide awake and welcoming, but before the door closed Lizzie caught a glimpse of Father struggling to wake up from his afternoon nap. He came out to be introduced a few moments later. 'Good afternoon,' he said, shaking hands with Ben. 'I'm glad you could come, we've wanted to meet you.'

Lizzie sat stiff and uncomfortable while Mum poured the tea and Milly handed round the cucumber sandwiches. She could see Ben was sitting up straight and on his best behaviour. He said, 'I trust you are keeping well, Mrs Travis.'

'Thank you, yes.' That seemed to wake the major up.

'Such a dark afternoon,' he said, 'and the Sunday papers filled with doom about the threat of a coming war.'

'Nothing new about that,' Ben said stirring his tea. 'It's been threatening for some years.'

'Does it not worry you?'

'It's a concern, of course, but I'm engrossed in earning my living and my own affairs, and it still seems a safe distance away, and might never happen. I expect it worries your generation more than mine – I've never known war, while you have.'

'If it comes,' Father said sourly, 'it'll be your generation that has to fight, not mine.'

Lizzie was on edge but glad to find it leading on to what Father would consider a sensible discussion about what Hitler was doing, and they went on to talk about last year's Olympic Games in Berlin. Ben was holding his own and seemed to know what he was talking about.

Then Father smiled at her before saying the words she'd been dreading. 'Tell us a little about yourself, Ben. We'd like to know you better.'

Lizzie saw a flash of alarm cross his face; he managed a smile but there was nothing impish about it. 'What is it you want to know?'

'You've taken up with our daughter and her mother worries about her, so I'm afraid there are personal details . . . Are you Irish?'

'I was born and bred here in New Brighton, but of Irish extraction.'

'You went to school here?'

'Yes, to the grammar school.'

'So your family wasn't poor, they could afford school fees?'

'They are poor but I was put in for the scholarship exam and got a free place. I left at fifteen.'

Major Travis swallowed hard. 'Good gracious, after such a good start? Why on earth did you do that?'

'It felt like a waste of time, learning Latin and all that. I wanted to get on with life, earn my living.'

'A big mistake. A waste of the fine opportunity offered to you. So now you're employed in the amusement arcade?' Father's disapproval was showing.

'Not exactly employed, I'm running a small business of my own.' Ben told him about his roundabout and shooting gallery; and about his ambitions for the future.

'The funfair is lovely, Dadda,' Milly put in. 'Everybody thinks it's great fun.'

'I do not, Emilia. It causes a lot of trouble in the town. It

60

attracts young men who drink too much and run wild, and it brings in quite the wrong sort.'

'With due respect, sir, New Brighton brings in much of the revenue for the town of Wallasey. It draws people in not only from Merseyside but from miles around. It's a holiday resort that exists to provide fun, pleasure and enjoyment for families. The amusement arcade is the heart and soul of the whole district.'

'Possibly, but it isn't just the families it attracts, that's my point. What about the ruffians and drunkards who cause damage and trouble after dark?'

Lizzie was growing uneasy. Father was getting ruffled. She knew only too well he didn't seek fun, and that he thought her frivolous. He believed in doing his duty to God and the King, helping his community, but otherwise he wanted a quiet life.

'I'm afraid we blame the beer trade for trouble like that,' Ben said patiently. 'Any damage caused is often in the amusement arcade and we repair it at our own expense.'

Esmond grunted, 'They're louts who know no better.'

'I have some sympathy for them,' Ben said quietly. 'If they can't find work, their lives can't be orderly.'

'Sympathy?' Major Travis bit angrily into his fruit cake. 'They're fools to waste what little money they have on an excess of drink.'

'With due respect, sir, they have not had the same advantages in life that you have.'

Lizzie closed her eyes in horror; she'd never heard anybody argue like this with Father. She'd hoped he'd take to Ben but this must surely be putting him off. Still smiling, Ben changed the subject and began to show an interest in the history of

Oakdene Grange and its estate. It seemed to calm Father down to talk about it. Lizzie had heard it all many times before, but how had Ben known it was a subject close to Father's heart?

'From medieval times my family were engaged in the Liverpool shipping trade,' Father told him, 'and in the nineteenth century they chose to build a new house on this side of the river. Oakdene Grange was finished in 1845, a very large and grand house.' He sighed. 'Within a decade progress in the shipping trade meant new ships were being built of iron, were larger and needed engines. The family business could no longer compete and they found Oakdene Grange an expensive house to maintain. I'm afraid they let it fall into disrepair, and at the end of the century they moved here to what was once the home farm. Our land extended to over three hundred acres then. Now we have only ten acres left.'

'You still have a big solid house,' Ben seemed really interested, 'and they farmed the land? They turned their hand to a business that could earn them a living?'

'Yes, when I was growing up we kept a herd of seventy cows and were rearing their calves. We took the churns out on our own milk floats pulled by our own horses, and sold it all over New Brighton. Customers brought their jugs to be filled. Oakdene Farm was such a busy place in those days, but new methods took over once again and made it no longer profitable.' He took another slice of cake. 'The big dairy companies moved into the district and sold bottled milk, undercutting us on price.'

'Progress is inevitable,' Ben said. 'It's impossible to stop it. We have to change with it.'

Lizzie thought he was touching on quite dangerous ground and wanted to bring it to an end. 'Now we've finished tea,' she said, 'I'd like to take Ben to see round the garden and the buildings and then perhaps for a little walk.'

'Excellent,' Ben said, equally keen to escape. 'The rain seems to have stopped now.'

Lizzie leapt to her feet. 'I'll come back to clear away, Mum, don't you do it.'

'Hang on, I'm coming with you,' Milly said.

'No,' Lizzie hissed at her sister, 'no, be a real pet, Milly. Stay home. I'll take you out some other time.'

Milly bit her lip. In the silence that followed their voices could be heard in the hall, and when the front door slammed behind them, she said, 'Lizzie has no time for anyone but Ben.'

Mum and Dadda were staring at their plates. Mum said stiffly, 'He seems a nice enough boy, he has good manners.'

Dadda sighed, 'He's more intelligent than I expected but I have to question his lack of judgement. Leaving school at fifteen when he had a free place at the grammar school, the lad's a fool. Doesn't know which way his bread is buttered.'

Elsie Travis started to stack the dirty dishes together. 'It's far too late to worry about Ben's schooling now. We need to get to know him better,' she said. 'We must encourage Lizzie to bring him regularly. Milly, please bring what's left of the cakes to the kitchen.'

This first meeting with Ben had not settled Elsie's mind. He might not be all he seemed; what if he was lying about owning that roundabout? Jasper had told outrageous lies when she'd met him and she'd believed all of them. Lizzie was in love, that was clear by the way she looked at him; her attention had been fully on Ben throughout.

Her hands shaking slightly, she plunged them deep into the

washing-up water so they were out of sight. She couldn't help worrying about Lizzie; she was so beautiful. Even she felt dazzled by her daughter's slim and graceful figure, peaches and cream skin, perfect features and glorious golden curls.

Her father Jasper had been a very handsome man, and she'd inherited his good looks. Elsie had met him when she was sixteen: she'd gone to the pictures with a girl she'd known at school and he'd occupied the seat next to her. He'd been twenty-six, and had started what had seemed a polite and sophisticated conversation. She'd thought him a man of the world and as romantic as the hero on the screen. He was her first boyfriend and within days she'd thought she'd met her soulmate and had fallen wildly in love with him.

Her mother had been a devout churchgoing widow, and something of an invalid. She'd kept the corner grocery shop all her life, and since leaving school Elsie had been virtually running it. It had kept a roof over their heads and food on the table, though it would never have made them wealthy. She took Jasper home to meet her mother and he beguiled her too.

But as the weeks passed, Elsie began to doubt some of the stories he told her. Jasper said he was working in the local branch of Barclays Bank, but when she went to pay in the shop's takings and asked for him, they'd never heard of him. When she questioned him about it he laughed and said he'd been transferred to another branch, but that rankled, and afterwards she couldn't be sure anything he told her was true.

Esmond told her she had a nervous disposition and perhaps she had. He also said it was understandable that anyone who'd married a man as chaotic in his habits as Jasper would be racked by nerves. What made it worse for Elsie was that she believed she'd made a mess of her life and ruined her mother's. Now her main aim was to prevent her daughters doing the same thing.

She had been expecting men to run after Lizzie once she'd turned sixteen and had blossomed into the beauty she was. It had been a comfort when it didn't happen immediately, but now it had. She prayed that her Lizzie was not going to make the same mistake she had.

Milly asked, 'Mum, why are you washing up? Lizzie said she'd do it when she came home.'

'No point in putting it off, love, there's only a few cups and saucers here.'

Milly picked up the tea towel without being asked. 'I think I do more to help you than Lizzie does,' she said.

'You do, pet,' Elsie agreed, 'and I'm grateful.' She didn't have the same worries about Milly; if she turned out like Esmond she wouldn't go far wrong. With Lizzie she kept looking for signs that she'd inherited something of Jasper's personality and characteristics. Whatever happened, she must prevent her turning into the rotter her father had been.

CHAPTER EIGHT

B EN WAS MAKING HIS fifth visit to Oakdene Farm for tea on a Sunday afternoon, and they were both afraid he was making little progress. 'But you have to come,' Lizzie said.

'I know I need to show myself often enough for your father to accept me as a possible husband for you. Or we'll have to wait until you're twenty-one.'

'Don't forget you made a bad start by telling them you left school at fifteen,' Lizzie said.

'I want him to approve of me but I keep making the mistake of telling him things I should not.'

Elsie was taking the regular visits in her stride; she no longer thought it necessary to provide cucumber sandwiches, but she rarely said very much when he was there. Father had not relaxed; he was very much Major Esmond Travis and Ben had come to understand that to gain his approval he must converse sensibly. The major did not like inconsequential chatter.

Ben tried to come prepared to talk about something that would interest the major. This afternoon he planned to talk about business and he began by telling him his landlady Mrs Philpin could remember buying milk from the Travis milk float and that it had been pulled by a horse called Blossom. But that set Esmond off on another nostalgic trip into his family history, and he'd held forth all the time they were at the table.

'I was born just a couple of hundred yards further up the lane. There has been a manor house on the site of the Grange since medieval times, but my family added two large wings in Victorian times. I sold it with two acres twenty years ago. The new owner intended to make it more manageable by knocking down those two wings, but they found the whole building was riddled with dry rot and had to demolish it all.'

Lizzie couldn't wait to get Ben by himself, and as soon as Father had drained his second cup of tea she said, 'It's a lovely afternoon, I thought we could go for a walk round the land.'

'A good idea. Ben, I'll show you what we have left of the farm,' Father said, getting to his feet. 'Though there's precious little left of it now.' Lizzie's spirits sank.

'Perhaps I'll come too,' Mum said. 'I could do with stretching my legs.'

They all moved into the hall, and when Milly opened the front door, Ivor Coyne, the local vet, and his son Laurie were coming to their front gate. The Coyne family now lived in the modern house that occupied the site of the Grange, though they'd renamed it Oakdene House. Laurie's father was Dadda's friend and came round from time to time.

'We're taking Mutt for his walk,' he said, 'and I thought I'd return this book you loaned to me. Thank you, I thoroughly enjoyed it.'

At the sight of Laurie Coyne, Lizzie cringed: she felt guilty about the way she'd dropped him. She hadn't known how to tell him she didn't want to go out with him again without being hurtful, and so had avoided him instead. Now his baleful stare at Ben was making her feel worse.

Milly shot outside to make a fuss of Mutt and said, 'Ben, this is Laurie Coyne, he's training to be a vet like this father. This is Ben . . .'

Lizzie was near enough to kick her ankle; it made her wince but she could almost hear Milly continuing, 'he's taken your place as Lizzie's boyfriend.' Things were embarrassing enough without that.

Esmond took the book. 'Thank you. Ben, here, is a friend of Lizzie's and he's interested in the history of the estate.' Ben was patting the dog. 'Would you like to borrow the book?' he asked him. 'It'll tell you everything you want to know about this place.'

'I'd very much like to,' he said, with a show of enthusiasm, 'thank you, sir.'

'Good, it'll fit in your pocket, won't it? I've just been telling Ben that Oakdene Farm was my inheritance,' Esmond went on. 'My forebears built it up but it has been my lot to decimate it.'

They were all heading towards the farm buildings and the land sloped gently away from them. 'Now look at it, covered with small houses and the ten acres we have left will no doubt follow when we have need of more cash.'

'Surely there is something these buildings could be used for?' Ben said. 'Some little business you could run here? They look soundly built. It seems a waste of valuable assets.'

'The buildings are of little use without more land,' Esmond said irritably, 'and unfortunately the war robbed me of my ability to work at all.'

Lizzie thought Father was putting Ben in his place, but he hardly seemed to notice.

He was stroking Mutt, and the dog was looking up at him with melting brown eyes. 'He's a greyhound, isn't he?' Ben said. 'All muscle, did he race?'

'Yes, he's just retired after a brilliant racing career at Belle Vue,' Laurie said. 'They make splendid pets, very friendly. I'd been asking for a dog for ages.'

'As long as you never let them off their lead,' Ben told him. 'They'll go streaking after anything that moves if you do, squirrels, birds, rabbits, then they get lost.'

'You know about greyhounds,' Ivor Coyne said. 'Do you have one?'

'No, my father retired home to Belfast where his younger brother has a small farm and he's started raising puppies for the sport.'

'I believe many of the puppies are bred in Ireland,' Mr Coyne said. 'Amazing how dog racing has taken off in this country in the last few years.'

'Yes,' Ben said. 'Now, Major Travis, that's a little business you could run from your buildings: puppy breeding. You have the advantage of being closer to the dealers and the trainers than my uncle Jim.'

'And also near Manchester,' Mr Coyne said. 'Belle Vue was built only a couple of years ago, the first track in this country especially for dog racing. You couldn't be better placed for it.'

'What a marvellous idea,' Milly said. 'I'd love you to breed puppies, Dadda. I'd help you.'

Major Travis was wrinkling his nose with distaste. 'Puppy farming? I don't think I'd want to get involved with that sort of thing.'

'I'd love you to do it, Father,' Lizzie said, 'and Mum would too, wouldn't you?'

'Your mother has enough to do taking care of the family and the house,' Esmond said haughtily. 'Haven't you, Elsie?'

'Well, I don't know.' She looked hesitant, guilty at disagreeing with him. 'Would these buildings be suitable for greyhound breeding?' she wanted to know.

'Yes,' Mr Coyne said, 'after cleaning out and airing, but greyhounds feel the cold, so you might need to provide a little heat for them. Mutt will need a coat when winter comes.'

'But they must need a lot of exercise.' Lizzie could see that Mum was clearly thinking it feasible.

'No,' Laurie said. 'They're sprinters, not marathon runners. Mutt is very happy with one walk a day. He sleeps a lot.'

'A little business run from home,' Elsie pondered. 'It might be just the thing for us.'

'A source of income,' Ben said temptingly.

Major Travis drew himself up to his full five foot nine. 'I've heard some bad things about puppy farms. Dogs kept in poor conditions, not treated kindly.'

'Well there are good ones and bad ones,' Ivor Coyne put in. 'Some puppy farms may have put profit before the health and well-being of their dogs, but most don't.'

'We wouldn't,' Elsie said indignantly. They'd reached the door of the old stable. She sniffed. 'Gosh, this old hay stinks.'

'No, Elsie. We have no need to stoop to puppy breeding.'

Into the sudden silence, Ben said stiffly, 'Most of us have little choice. We have to earn a living where we can.' She was horrified to hear Ben go on, 'There's nothing wrong with puppy breeding. Most in the world would consider doing that more honourable than living on what their forebears hand down to them.' Lizzie froze; that was absolutely the wrong thing for Ben to say.

Esmond slammed the stable door shut and strode towards home without speaking. The rest of them followed politely.

As soon as they were alone, Lizzie burst out, 'Whatever made you say that?'

'I knew it as soon as the words were out of my mouth,' Ben lamented. 'Sorry, your father was being superior because he doesn't need to work. He's just being lazy when he says he can't earn a living. He can write, can't he, and telephone?'

'Yes.'

'He can do the organising and the women of the family could do the physical work, at least until the business gets started. My aunties love feeding and walking the dogs. Why, your father even has a friendly vet living up the lane if he needs medical help.'

'I think Mum feels hard up and would like to earn a little money. She loves dogs.'

'He could even have one of those fields properly fenced off so the dogs could run free. This should be good pasture land but he's let it lie idle year after year.'

'He sees it as potential building land,' Lizzie said, 'so it doesn't matter that the grass is waist high and full of weeds.'

Ben groaned. 'For me, Sunday is a busy and lucrative afternoon and I spend it trying to be polite to your father, but I keep putting my foot in it. Lizzie, could you not explain to him that as a working man, Monday would suit me better? It's a much quieter day for me.'

71

* * *

Milly was on the top deck of the bus that was taking her home and she'd never felt so free. She couldn't help chuckling to herself. St Monica's School for Girls had just broken up for over eight weeks of summer holidays. The end of the school year had been marked by a very long ceremony. She'd just sat through a speech from Sir Somebody or other that had been exceedingly dull, and an endless prize-giving, from which she'd won nothing.

She'd said, 'See you next term,' to her classmates, who all seemed to be anticipating family holidays in exotic places, while she would be staying at home. Dadda didn't like holidays so they never went anywhere but she didn't really mind. New Brighton offered every possible way of having fun and it was all on her doorstep.

The bus was coming to a halt at the Seacombe Ferry terminus and she caught sight of Laurie Coyne amongst those waiting to board. Would he come upstairs? She turned to watch for him, and laughed aloud. Yes! She waved as he appeared and called, 'Laurie, I've kept a place on the front seat for you.'

He came towards her. 'Hello, Milly, you're in good spirits.'

'Just broken up for the hols.'

'I did that last week,' he said. 'I've been over to Liverpool with Mum this morning, to Dad's outfitter to get new shirts. I've got new swimming trunks too. We're going to Le Touquet on Saturday.'

'Lucky you to be going away.' She knew that was expected of her. 'Where is Le Touquet?'

'France, but going away . . . There's never a right time to

go away, is there? I'm looking after quite a menagerie at the moment.'

'You've still got those two rats?'

'No, they've gone back to their owner, but I have a lamb that's broken its leg and there's Mutt. Then yesterday I found a sick rabbit in the lane.'

'I'll look after them for you,' Milly offered.

'Thanks,' he said, 'but there's no need. I take them down to Dad's practice.'

'In Wellington Street?'

'Yes, Dad's partner carries on the business as usual and the girls will take care of my animals there.'

'Very handy for you. Is the seagull better?'

'No, I'm afraid it died.'

'I'm sorry, after all the trouble you took to set its wing.'

'Dad said it was good experience for me, though nobody has ever brought a seagull to his practice, but he does get the occasional parrot. Do you want to come and see my lamb?'

She walked up to Oakdene House with him. 'Heavens, Laurie, this isn't a lamb, it's grown up. Almost a sheep.'

'Yes, the farmer said his shepherd was loading the lambs he'd picked out to go to the abattoir when this one was injured. He separated it from the other and shut it in a building so it wouldn't suffer, but then he forgot to put it in the waggon with the others.

'The farmer was cross that it didn't go to the abattoir. With a broken leg it would lose weight instead of putting it on. Dad went to the farm to treat his herd of cattle and brought the lamb for me; he said it would be good experience for me to reset its leg. Not that they usually bother to reset a lamb's leg.'

Milly said, 'Why not? What would they usually do?'

'Eat it.'

'Oh gosh, Laurie, no wonder Lizzie says you're a little strange.'

He grinned at her. 'I think Dad intends taking it back to the farm when it's well enough.'

It was several weeks since Lizzie had seen Ben's house, though daily he was describing every detail of the work he was putting in hand. He was a great one for making plans, and she knew he was making all these improvements with the intention that they would start their married life there. He frequently asked for her opinion, and she'd told him more than once that it wouldn't do, as Father considered the district a slum, and would be against her living there.

Today, he'd said, 'I want you to come and see it. I don't think there's much more I can do. I told you last week I'd given notice to Mrs Philpin and I moved in this morning. I need to know whether you could live there with me.'

Lizzie felt apprehensive; it would be even more difficult to convince him now. Nothing could improve the district.

'It's close to the arcade and I can walk home in a few minutes.'

Lizzie thought that would be the only good thing to be said about it.

They turned into Alvaston Terrace. 'You can see my house now,' he said. It certainly stood out against its neighbours: the paintwork shone and the windows sparkled in the evening sun; even the front step had been scrubbed. But all along the terrace the cottages looked scruffy. Two young boys were kicking a can along the street, and a stray dog had one leg up against the lamp-post.

The first thing Lizzie noticed when he opened the door was that the atmosphere smelled fresh. 'I haven't quite managed to get rid of the smell of new paint,' Ben said. The walls and ceiling were dazzlingly white. 'I bought the rugs and the easy chair at the auction house, and Mrs Philpin gave me the rocking chair and curtains. That picture hung in my old room.'

Lizzie hesitated. 'It looks – nice.' It was much better than she'd expected: the Victorian living room grate had been black-leaded and a fire was laid ready. 'I've tried cooking in the oven,' Ben said. 'I made a casserole, it all works.'

'You're going to cook in that?'

'Well, possibly, but I've got a gas cooker in the kitchen too. Sorry I couldn't do anything about the brown stone sink, it would cost too much.'

'I like the table and chairs.'

'So do I, they came from the auction rooms too. A Georgian mahogany dining table is a bit grand for this kitchen but we have to have somewhere to eat and I couldn't resist it.'

'It all looks fresh and clean,' she said cautiously.

'I had the cupboard painted inside and out.' He threw open the doors and she could see basic foodstuffs were already on the shelves. 'Mrs Philpin helped me get this organised.'

'She's been like a mother to you.'

'Yes. She said I'd have a lot more work to do now I've moved out and she's right, but it'll be worth it because here you and I will have privacy to do what we want.'

She was looking through the window. 'I see you've cleaned up the back yard too.'

'Yes, come out and see what I've done.' He'd had the blackened stone walls lime-washed, and a passageway built from the back door to the wash house. 'It's only a couple of zinc sheets but when it's raining we'll be able to go to the loo without getting wet.'

The lavatory was now clean and sparkling with a new wooden seat. 'It all looks much better,' Lizzie allowed.

'I've put two wardrobes in the first bedroom,' he said, 'and I found a lovely Georgian mahogany bedstead that was going cheap. I'm very pleased with that.'

'What about the mattress? Is that a couple of hundred years old too?'

He laughed. 'It came with a horse-hair mattress but I dumped that and ordered a new one. It was delivered yesterday. So what do you think of my place now?'

'I'm agreeably impressed.'

'But could you live here?'

'The outside loo . . . and Father will still say it's in a slum.'

'I wasn't planning to have him here.'

Lizzie laughed. 'Well, inside it looks cleaner and smarter than Oakdene Farm,' she allowed. 'That is much in need of repainting. And with you here . . .'

'We'll have fun, marvellous fun, Lizzie,' he said, and pulled her into a bear hug to rain kisses over her face. He lifted his head and she saw his impish smile. 'Is it too soon to set our wedding day? Now I have somewhere for us to live it can't come quickly enough for me.'

'Or me, but we need to spend more time working on Father. If I asked for his permission now, I think he'd say I haven't known you long enough.'

'But we could aim for a date, couldn't we? Let's say Christmas or the new year.'

'Yes . . .'

'Right, by January the first we'll try to have it all arranged.'

'If we can.'

'A winter wedding would suit me very well because business is always slow in the first weeks of the year when it's cold. Come on, Lizzie, cheer up, it won't be a long wait. The summer holidays are with us and it'll be autumn before we know it.'

'But this is between ourselves; we say nothing to my family now,' Lizzie cautioned. 'They won't like you having a place like this where I can come and we can be alone. It isn't something a young lady should do. Father would probably forbid me to come anywhere near here.'

'You'd better be careful Milly doesn't find out then. She'd broadcast the news everywhere.'

'I will be.'

'Right, and in the meantime we have somewhere that is very private to spend our evenings together. What could be better?'

'You and your plans,' she laughed, and raised her lips to be kissed again.

Chapter Nine

M ILLY WAS NOT SHORT of companions in the school holidays. Recently, she'd made a friend of Kathleen who had moved into one of the four big new houses further up the lane beyond Oakdene House. She didn't attend St Monica's school with her, but went to the Maris Stella Convent. Dadda shook his head and said, 'Wrong religion, probably better if you don't make a friend of her.'

Dadda was prejudiced against anything he thought was different, but Milly took to her; Kathleen was a chatterbox and told her lots of interesting stories about the nuns at her school, especially Sister Aquinas. She'd taken Milly home. It was a bright and smart house and her mother had been welcoming and provided lemonade.

Milly was walking past Oakdene House with Kathleen one day when she saw a bedraggled dog trying to hide under a bush. She recognised him. 'Mutt,' she called. 'Mutt, come here, boy.'

'That's Laurie's dog,' Kathleen said.

'He shouldn't be here, his family have gone away. Mutt, come and say hello.' He didn't move but he allowed Milly to go towards him and drag him out. He was wearing his harness and dragging his lead, which she took a firm hold of. 'What's happened? You poor old thing.' She put out a hand and stroked his head. 'You're all wet.' She saw him shiver. 'Come home with me and I'll dry you off.' Mutt dug in his heels and looked as though he didn't want to go anywhere.

'Perhaps he's hungry,' Kathleen said. 'I was saving this piece of fudge for later.' She took some crumpled silver paper from her pocket and opened it. 'It's melted a bit.'

'As if a dog would mind about that,' Milly laughed. He wolfed it down and licked hard at the wrapping. 'He's hungry. Come on, Mutt.' She shook the lead encouragingly, and after dragging him a few feet, he reluctantly walked with her.

Gladys, the woman who came every morning to help Mum with the housework, threw up her hands when she saw them at the back door. 'You can't bring that dog in here,' she stormed, 'he's filthy, just look at his feet. I've washed the kitchen floor this morning.'

'Will you get Mum then please?' Milly asked.

Dadda came too and said, 'Tie that dog up. I'll ring the vet's office and find out what's happened.'

Mum found an old towel so that Milly could dry Mutt off. 'I've cleaned his feet, Gladys,' she said. 'He won't make a mess now, but he's very hungry. What can we give him to eat?'

'There's lamb chops for your dinner tonight, miss,' Gladys said. 'You could give him your share now, he'll eat them raw.'

'Bread and milk,' Mum said slowly. 'It's all we have that's handy.' She set about making it and Mutt gobbled it down in seconds.

Dadda came back to tell them, 'They were delighted to have news of Mutt at the vet's. They've all been worried stiff that they'd lost Mr Coyne's dog. One of the girls took him out for his daily walk the day before yesterday, and he suddenly took off after a rabbit or something. She wasn't able to hold on to him and she's been very upset since. Apparently Ivor is due to return next Tuesday, so I told them we'd keep Mutt safely shut into one of our buildings until he comes back.'

'Mutt's allowed in their house,' Milly said. 'Laurie took him straight in without even asking when I was with him.'

'He's an animal, Milly, not a child.'

'Our buildings are filthy dirty.'

'You have plenty of time to clean one out.'

'But Mutt can't stay shut in on his own. Not for four days. They probably had him shut in a cage by himself at the vet's place and he didn't like it. He needs company, that's why he came home looking for Laurie.'

Dadda delivered his decision. 'Well, all right, he can come in the house during the day, but he must be shut in an outbuilding at night. We mustn't let him escape before the Coynes come back.'

'I'll clean a place up for him straight away,' Milly said.

Dadda came with them, bringing the dog. 'The stable is the best place,' he said, tying Mutt up inside. 'You'll have to clear out all this rubbish, especially this old hay. Dump it on the grass over there where I can burn it, then sweep the floor clean.'

'It'll need more than that,' Milly said. 'Just look at the windows. They're too dirty to let the light in. The whole place should be hosed down, and there's no clean hay we could use to make a bed for Mutt.' By lunchtime, with the work only half done, the girls were exhausted. Kathleen said she wouldn't be able to come back that afternoon because her mother was taking her out. Milly tied Mutt up outside the back door and he promptly went to sleep in the sun.

After a lunch of ham and salad Milly persuaded her mother to come out to see what else was needed to clean the stable. After one glance at the sleeping Mutt, she said, 'He'll have to be bathed before he can come indoors. His coat is matted with dried mud, he'll shed it everywhere.' She stood at the door of the stable frowning. 'It's not exactly clean and comfortable, even for a dog,' she said, pointing out several more things that needed doing. 'But you can't do everything, Milly, why don't you see if Clover will come and help you this afternoon?' Clover was Gladys's daughter; she was two months older than Milly but only half her size, a tough and wiry youngster. In the school holidays when they'd been younger, Gladys had had to bring her to work, and she and Milly had been friends ever since. Gladys and Clover lived at the end of their lane; the bus stop was outside their cottage and Milly had to pass it whenever she went out.

'Can I, Dadda?' she asked.

Dadda had strongly disapproved of their friendship and forbidden her to bring Clover home, but Gladys often gave her biscuits if she went there, and every school holiday they spent time together. Clover was a good swimmer so they often went to the fine new swimming baths or to the beach.

'Perhaps you better had,' he allowed. Gladys left before lunch, so Milly ran down the lane to see them and returned with Clover.

Milly said, 'What it needs now is hosing down, nothing else will clean this floor.'

Dadda decided he would do that, and afterwards that Mutt

must be bathed in the same way. He tied him to the garden gate and turned the hosepipe on him. The dog squirmed, making the girls giggle. 'He doesn't like it,' Milly said, 'that water is cold.'

'It's a warm day,' Dadda said, 'it'll do him no harm. His coat will be much cleaner after this.'

They laughed out loud to see the dog get his own back by shaking himself so vigorously that he drenched Dadda, who had to go in to change his clothes. Milly was surprised that he wasn't cross with Mutt after that.

By teatime the stable had dried and a large wooden box had been found to make a bed that would lift Mutt off the stone floor. Mum brought an old rug to put inside it and Dadda fixed a rope to Mutt's harness so both Milly and Clover could hold on to him when they took him for a walk. Mutt was placid and friendly and enjoyed being petted and stroked.

Lizzie came home from work and made a fuss of him too. 'He's lovely. Why are you so against dogs, Father? Mum would love to have one. In fact, she'd love to breed puppies as Ben suggested, and set up a little business. Milly would love it too and be ready to help.'

Lizzie had explained to her parents that Sunday afternoon was a busy time for Ben. She had to work in the afternoons so he was invited to supper on Monday evenings. Primed by Lizzie, that Monday he talked about his uncle's puppy farm.

Mum was obviously very interested and kept asking questions. 'Esmond,' she said, 'I really would enjoy looking after two or three dogs and rearing their puppies. We've all taken to Mutt, even you have.'

He turned to Ben. 'And you say it's possible to earn an income from doing that?'

'If you start with the right dogs it is. They have to be thoroughbreds, have shown form by winning races, and they'd have to be tested to make sure they're free from genetic diseases their puppies might inherit. My father is coming over for a short visit next weekend,' Ben said, 'to check on me. He knows a lot more about the trade because he's been helping his brother.'

Elsie's eyes were shining. 'Would you be able to bring him here with you for supper next Monday? I'd like to talk to him. Find out more about puppy breeding.'

'I'll try, Mrs Travis,' he said.

That evening, when he and Lizzie were alone, he said, 'I think your father's coming round to the idea of breeding puppies. It might endear me to him if I can get him more information about it.'

'I find it hard to believe,' Lizzie said. 'He's never changed his mind before. It's usually set rock hard once he makes it up.'

'Mutt seems to have persuaded him.'

'It's you who have done that,' Lizzie told him.

Milly was delighted that all her family had taken to Mutt. As soon as they sat down he would come and rub his head against their legs and look up with such friendly pleading that they'd bend down to stroke him. Mum was quite keen to take him out for walks. In fact, the dog had done more walking than usual because both Kathleen and Clover wanted to do that too. Milly credited Mutt with making Dadda more relaxed about accepting her friends, as once he'd seen Kathleen and Clover about the house, it seemed they were allowed to come again.

On Tuesday, Milly kept watch on the lane for the taxi bringing the Coynes home and once she'd seen it pass, she and Dadda took Mutt home and told them the story. They were delighted to see the dog again, safe and well.

'I rang your partner to find out what we should give him to eat,' Dadda said, 'and Elsie rang the butcher and got him to send up suitable meat and bones for him.'

Mutt was making a big fuss of Laurie. 'Did you have a good holiday?' Milly asked him.

'Le Touquet is a lovely place.' He smiled up at her. 'Lovely long sandy beaches and I was in the sea every day. That was lovely, but such a long walk out before the water was deep enough to swim. There was always a bracing breeze and big waves rolling in, but all Mum and Dad wanted to do was sit about the hotel and eat and drink.'

His arms hugged the dog. 'I could have done with you there, Mutt, to keep me company.'

That Sunday at mid-morning, Ben took Lizzie home for tea and biscuits. 'It's to meet my dad,' he said, 'and you know what parents are like, sticklers for the proprieties.'

Lizzie knew Ben had bought a sofa for the living room at a recent auction sale so that his father could stay with him. Ben planned to sleep on that so his dad would have a proper bed.

'I've told him I want to marry you, but don't let on you've spent much time at my place. Don't forget, I've told him you've been only once or twice and you've never been upstairs.'

Lizzie hoped her parents would approve of Mr McCluskey senior. He had an Irish accent, sucked at a pipe the whole time, and wore a thick tweed suit with a gold watch chain crossing his waistcoat. 'You've chosen a very pretty young lady, Ben,' he said, taking her hand and brushing his whiskery chin against her cheek in a token kiss. He talked a good deal, which meant she didn't have to. Ben made sure the visit was short, saying he had to go back to work.

'He looks even more old-fashioned than Father,' Lizzie said on the way back to the fair.

'It's that suit; he's had it for decades. Only wears it for funerals, church functions and formal visits.'

The next evening Ben brought him to Oakdene Farm for supper. He was wearing the same clothes, with the addition of a bowler hat, and looked positively Victorian. Mostly Monday night suppers were of cold meat, the remains of the Sunday joint, but tonight there was a casserole. Esmond asked for that if they were having visitors, because nobody had to cut his meat up for him. Ben and his father ate with gusto while Mum bombarded them with questions about dog breeding.

Ben had explained to his father what was needed, and he said, 'I can get you the names and addresses of the dealers that my brother uses. They will have thoroughbred dogs for sale of the sort you'll need to breed from. Mostly they have been put out to stud by four or five years of age. Ben could take you to see them; there are several dealers in the Manchester area. Frank knows all the trainers too who are always keen to buy puppies of the right sort.'

Lizzie thought her parents rushed him out rather too hurriedly to assess the stable for suitability as a kennel. The rest of the family trailed behind them.

Elsie threw open the door to the stable. 'Excellent,' he told them, going inside, though the gathering dusk made it impossible to see much. 'Plenty of space to store all your equipment, and to make a playroom for the puppies in here.'

'Would we need a lot of equipment?'

'No, Major,' Mr McCluskey went on, 'and you could start with the minimum, but of course, you would need to provide some heating for them, greyhounds have a thin wiry coat and little spare flesh. They really feel the cold.'

'What sort of heating?' Elsie asked. 'They'd knock an oil heater over, wouldn't they?'

Mr McCluskey was staring up at the dark ceiling. 'You don't have electricity over here?'

'No,' Esmond said, 'not in the outbuildings.'

'It would be easy enough to run a line over from the house.'

'At a cost,' Esmond said hollowly. Lizzie guessed he'd baulk at that.

'There are always costs to set up a business and costs to run one,' Ben said easily.

'Yes,' his father agreed, 'but my brother says he finds puppy breeding profitable.'

Esmond brooded silently.

'Ben, why don't you take them to Belle Vue so they can see the dogs racing? I'm sure you'd enjoy that, Major.'

'I know I would,' Milly and her mother said together.

Chapter Ten

LIZZIE WENT INTO THE kitchen one evening when Milly and her mother were preparing dinner. She pulled out the grill pan. 'These chops look cooked,' she said.

'Your father likes them well done,' Mum said, 'and the potatoes need another minute or two.'

'Can I do anything to help, Mum?'

'No, dear, you'll just have to be patient.'

Later, at the table, Milly had cleared her plate, and said, 'You're always going out these days, Lizzie, you don't have time for me any more.'

'Of course I do.' She knew that wasn't true.

'You used to take me to the pictures or to your shop, but now you're always out with Ben. Where does he take you?'

Lizzie was caught on the back foot. She spent most of the time in Ben's house now, the existence of which she'd kept secret from her family. 'To the pictures,' she said guiltily, 'or to the Tower to dance, or for walks, and to this café or that for a cup of tea.'

'You're out very late almost every night,' Mum said gently, but her eyes were reproving.

'I hope he isn't taking you to pubs and bars.'

'No, Father.'

'I'm surprised you can do a decent day's work on so little rest,' he told her. 'You must come home at a reasonable hour tonight.'

One Monday several weeks later, Ben told them that his father was bringing his uncle Frank over at the weekend. 'He's thinking of buying more bitches and wants to visit some of the dealers to see what they have. He's quite friendly with the trainer who buys his puppies so he plans to visit him. And that Friday,' he went on, 'some of the puppies he's reared and sold on will be racing at Belle Vue. He's quite keen to see how they get on.'

Lizzie was already bubbling with excitement. 'They've promised to take me and Ben, and suggested that you all come. Then you'll meet people who can start you off and see what you would be rearing puppies to do.'

'Oh, I don't think so,' Esmond said.

'Dadda, you must,' Milly wailed. 'I would absolutely love to go. So would Mum.'

'I think we should, Esmond,' Elsie said. 'Didn't you say we'd need to find out all we can about the business before we think of going further?'

Ben told them more: 'If you come, you will meet Uncle Frank's dealer and see the dogs he has for sale. He will be able to show you the dogs' histories and pedigrees. As I said, my uncle is thinking of buying more. You might see some you like.'

Esmond was reluctant. 'Perhaps later on, when we've had more time to think about it.'

'Father,' Lizzie said sternly, 'you don't need time to think about this. It's an opportunity to see several dogs of the right sort, and meet the people you need to know if you do decide to let Mum do what she wants.'

Milly's eyes were sparkling. 'And best of all, we can all see them race.'

'Dog racing.' Esmond shook his head. 'Going to the dogs? It isn't respectable. Not a place to take a family.'

'But it is, Major,' Ben assured him. 'It is the fastest growing sport at the moment and hugely popular both here and in Ireland. Stadiums are being built up and down the country. The one at Belle Vue is new. This is your chance to learn all about it. Nobody will force you to buy. You can come home to think about it afterwards.'

When Lizzie went to the door to see Ben out later that evening, he said, 'I'm bending over backwards to make your father see me as a suitable husband for you. I'm showing him how he can start a little business to bring in income, and at the same time really please Elsie and Milly, they'll love it. But it would be easier to move heaven and earth than get him moving.'

'I've never known him change his mind,' Lizzie said.

'But we have to keep trying.'

Milly was over the moon when her mother told her she'd persuaded Dadda they should all go to Belle Vue to see the dogs race. 'It'll be a great day out,' she said.

On Friday the following week she was still in high spirits when her family met Ben, his father and uncle, and took the train to Altrincham to visit the man who trained Uncle Frank's puppies. 'He'll be able to tell you how to rear puppies from birth if they are to win races.'

Uncle Frank wore smart country tweeds and seemed prosperous, more alert and in tune with the times than Ben's father. He was more than a decade younger and a different personality altogether. Like Ben, he was good at talking to Dadda.

In Altrincham he seemed on friendly terms with the trainer who bought his stock, an athletic young man who showed the Travises round his premises. 'The puppies come to me at around eight to ten months of age,' he said. 'At that age they have to be able to gallop, and we've found out which ones appear capable of winning races and which are slower. They are twelve to fourteen months old before they start to race.'

Milly had already heard that he charged nothing for their keep or their training, but he took 50 per cent of the dog's winnings. She squealed with delight when she saw all the squirming pups playing together, and was sure this would open up a new world to her parents. Mum was hanging on to every word he said.

'Almost from birth they will enjoy a short training session followed by a play time. They need to get used to close confinement for short periods in a portable dog crate, so they become used to being shut in the starting trap before they race.

'You will need to confine them in a puppy playroom, a small area with a comfortable bed for them, a bowl of fresh water and some toys to chew, and I want them to be toilet trained before they come.'

'How do we toilet train a puppy?' Mum looked astounded.

'As you would a child,' he said. 'You will need to provide them with a suitable toilet like this one, praise them when they use it and give them a food treat afterwards.'

He provided a lunch of sandwiches and coffee in his house

before taking them back to the station. From there they went north of Manchester to visit Uncle Frank's dealer, where he was hoping to buy two or three more bitches from which he could breed.

Milly nudged Lizzie. 'Bitches?' At school that was what they called teachers they didn't like.

'Female dogs,' she said impatiently.

The dealer was also young and enthusiastic and showed them what he had for sale. 'I have these recently retired dogs to sell on,' he said. 'They have good histories.'

Uncle Frank was down close looking them over one by one, asking to see their papers. Milly was totally beguiled by their big brown eyes, and she could see her mother was too. They were all friendly but one in particular caught Mum's eye. Dido was a lighter brown than Mutt. She had the softest ears and when she was spoken to, she had a way of lifting them together on top of her head as though listening. Even Dadda bent to stroke her.

'Mum would love to have her,' Lizzie said, 'even just the one as a pet to start. We could take her for walks.'

The dealer looked out her paperwork for them, and said, 'Dido comes from a long line of thoroughbreds that have competed at Belle Vue over the years and won. She has been the star of the track. She's won the English Greyhound Derby twice, the Northern Flat and the Laurels three times, and the Northern 700 twice. She's also come second in races, time and time again. She's top class, and any pups she has are likely to inherit her talent.'

Uncle Frank had chosen two bitches and was looking for another. He was in close consultation with the dealer, who was showing off one bitch after another, and reading through their genealogical and medical records. The Travis family were left to their own devices. 'Please, Dadda – please, please, please let us have this one,' Milly pleaded.

'Dido is gorgeous,' Lizzie said, and it was obvious Mum was of the same opinion.

'He wants a lot of money for her,' Dadda said. 'She's very expensive.'

'Yes, but look at her track history,' Ben said. 'Her puppies will have great potential, and you'll soon recoup her cost by selling them to a trainer or back to a dealer.'

It seemed Dadda was persuaded to buy Dido because Uncle Frank was choosing three. He was arranging for them to be shipped to the docks in Liverpool when he'd booked transit for them. Dido could be dropped off on the way.

Milly felt she'd never been so happy. With everything settled, they were taken to the dealer's house and tea and cakes were served. Milly bit into her Victoria sandwich and savoured the thought of taking Dido for walks with Laurie and Mutt.

Greyhound racing was held at Belle Vue Stadium on Friday and Saturday evenings. 'We have more than an hour before the first race,' Uncle Frank said, 'but the bar and restaurant will be open. We could do with a drink and something solid to eat.'

They went by taxi, and Milly could see her family were very impressed. The stadium had a huge glass-fronted grandstand, the restaurant was luxurious, and it was rumoured to have the longest bar in Manchester.

She devoured a plate of fish and chips. 'The best I've ever

tasted,' she told Uncle Frank. He went alone to see the dogs he'd brought up from puppyhood before they were brought to the starting pens. She couldn't help but notice that around her the clatter of cutlery, the chatter and laughter from fellow customers was rising steadily in volume, as did the atmosphere of excitement and anticipation.

Uncle Frank returned with a race card for each of them and said, 'I want you to study form. To get the most enjoyment from this experience you should decide which dog you think will win and put a bet on. One of the pups I reared is competing in the first race under the name of Miss Muffet. She's said to be pretty good so I shall bet on her.'

'I don't bet,' Major Travis said haughtily.

'Your choice.' Uncle Frank beamed at him. 'I'm just saying it's more fun if you do.'

'I don't know how to bet on a dog,' Lizzie said, and Ben's father explained the system.

She seemed to grasp it instantly but Milly thought it complicated. 'I don't have any money to bet with,' she wailed. Ben gave her two shillings while Uncle Frank slipped her half a crown.

Ben volunteered to place their bets. Most decided to back Miss Muffet, but Lizzie had formed her own opinion and decided her money would go on Jake the Rake to come first or second. Knowing how lucky her sister could be, Milly followed her lead and put two shillings on.

They found their places in the grandstand, and Ben's father told them what to expect. 'Only six dogs run in each race and they chase after a lure.'

'What's that?' Milly asked.

'A stuffed object such as a bone or a rabbit attached to an arm. It is driven by electricity and always kept at the same distance from the leading dog.'

Milly was enthralled to see the dogs being put into their individual starting traps. Miss Muffet had drawn trap number four, and Jake the Rake number six – they were wearing their numbers on brightly coloured racing jackets. The noise had died to an expectant hush and the excitement had risen to fever pitch. 'Keep your eye on number six,' Ben's father whispered.

Milly held her breath; she had a good view of the oval track and meant to do just that. The bell rang and the dogs were off. Lizzie leapt to her feet, as did some of the crowd in front of her. Milly was deafened by the screams of encouragement, run, run, run, and within an instant it was all over. Most of the crowd flopped back into their seats, but Lizzie was jumping about, waving her arms, her face radiant. 'We've won,' she screamed at Milly. Ben's father was congratulating her. 'Jake the Rake came first.' Milly felt it had all passed her by. She'd had one glimpse of the winner in his green racing jacket sporting number six before it was all over.

The crowd was silent again as the results were announced over the loud speaker: 'Jake the Rake first in 28.6 seconds.' She heard then that Miss Muffet had come in fourth and taken 29.68 seconds, and understood why Uncle Frank looked glum. Only she and Lizzie had bet on the right dog.

'How did you know?' they were asking Lizzie. 'How did you pick the winner?'

She held up her racing card. 'He won last week.'

'The race lasted less than half a minute,' Milly marvelled, 'and only a second separated Miss Muffet from the winner.'

'Yes,' Ben's father said. 'The distance is worked out in yards but it's about a quarter of a mile. They run at about forty miles an hour.'

'Like a car,' she said, but they were all consulting their racing cards again and thinking about the next race, all except the major.

'I see the last race doesn't take place until ten thirty,' he said. 'That's far too late for Milly to be in a place like this.'

But everybody was in high spirits, even Elsie. 'For once it won't matter,' she murmured. 'It is school holidays, after all.'

'It's a sport for the working classes,' he said disdainfully.

They were waiting for Lizzie to make her choice. 'Bella's Hope,' she said, and this time they all followed her.

Ben was going down to the bookies' stalls to collect their winnings and place their new bets. 'Milly,' Uncle Frank said. 'To stay in control, it is considered better not to spend your winnings on another immediate bet.'

'Lizzie's going to,' she said, 'so I will too.' It happened all over again and this time she saw Bella's Hope flash round with the pack and was as thrilled as her sister to find she'd come in first.

Lizzie lost her stake in the next two races, but went on to pick the winner in the following one. Uncle Frank explained more complicated ways to bet, involving two or more dogs and two or more races.

For the last race, Lizzie considered her racing card for a long time. 'What d'you reckon?' Uncle Frank asked. 'Flash of Gold is another from my farm, I think he'll do well.'

'So do I,' she said, 'he's my choice.' The rest of the party decided to do the same, and again she'd picked the winner.

'I can't believe your luck,' Elsie said. They were all clapping her on the back; her cheeks were flushed, her eyes danced and she couldn't stop laughing and chattering. It was all over and Milly thought they all looked as deflated as she felt. After they'd collected their winnings they had to wait in a long line to get a taxi to the station. Father had been looking sour for some time and now complained.

Uncle Frank laughed outright. 'Major, this lass of yours has the golden touch. If you'd laid on a few bets you could have bought that bitch out of your winnings. I've recouped the cost of the day out.'

Lizzie hugged her handbag to her, gloating that it now contained a sum equivalent to seven weeks' wages, and that she'd earned it in such a thrilling way. 'Pity about Miss Muffet,' she said to Uncle Frank.

He smiled at her. 'Flash of Gold coming first more than makes up for that. He's won me an excellent payout and a gold trophy.'

Elsie said, 'I can't remember ever enjoying a day out so much. I think I'll treat myself to a new dress with my winnings.'

'Come to the shop,' Lizzie said, 'I'll help you choose.' She looked ecstatic at the grateful praise. Ben and his father were relishing their betting success too. 'It was a great day out.'

Milly was thrilled with the two pounds eight shillings now in her pocket; she considered that riches.

CHAPTER ELEVEN

LIZZIE KNEW THEY WERE all relieved to get on the last train home, as they were now very tired and the excitement of the day had worn off.

'We won't need much when we get home.' Uncle Frank settled into his seat. 'A cup of tea perhaps.'

'I bought some ham in case you wanted a sandwich,' Ben said.

'No thanks, not for me,' his father said. 'Neither of us will need much rocking tonight. I didn't think I could sleep in the same bed as Frank. We've both expanded a bit since we've done that, but your bed is very comfortable.'

Lizzie held her breath; she was sitting next to Father and hoped he was too tired to pick up on that. She felt him stir. 'I thought you were staying in a hotel,' he said.

'No, Ben has put us up.'

Father was glaring at Ben. 'I understood you were in lodgings.'

'No, I moved out to rent a place of my own.'

'When? How long ago?' he demanded.

Ben looked as though he'd been beaten. 'I moved in in August.'

'That's three months ago.' Father's jaw dropped. He turned

on Lizzie and thundered, 'You've deliberately kept this from us. Why? Well, I know why, because you've been spending every evening alone in his house with him. You knew your mother and I would be very upset about that, but you gave no thought to us, or to your reputation.'

'Oh, Lizzie!' Her mother looked near to tears.

The mood in the carriage sank like a stone from triumphant and pleasurable joy to razor-like guilt and anxiety. A defeated silence settled on them for the rest of the journey.

Elsie knew she mustn't forget her manners and when they were getting off, she said, 'Thank you, it was a really wonderful day out. Wake up, Milly, it's time to get off.'

Milly knew Mum was talking to her but it took her a moment to realise she wasn't in her own bed. She was a little embarrassed but Uncle Frank patted her arm sympathetically. 'You fell asleep as soon as we got on the train,' he said. 'You were dog tired. We all are. Goodnight.'

Knowing there'd be no taxis around at this hour, Father had arranged for a hire car to meet the train. Once separated from Ben and his family, Lizzie felt a more ominous silence descend. She'd felt Father fuming since Ben had let the bombshell fall; his face was twisting with rage.

She knew Ben had warned his family to keep quiet about him having a place of his own, but they were all exhausted by that time so she couldn't really blame them. Uncle Frank had given them a marvellous day out, but for her it looked like ending in disaster.

Father erupted as soon as the front door closed behind them. 'Go to your bed, Milly,' he stormed, 'this is nothing to do with you.' Obediently she turned to the stairs. Lizzie knew

Milly liked to know what was going on. She'd probably leave her bedroom door open and hear every word. She'd have no difficulty since they were below her in the hall and Father was white-hot with fury.

'I find this hard to forgive, Lizzie,' he stormed. 'It's deceitful behaviour. You've been going to Ben's house regularly. We see little of you at home. No decent young man would allow a lady friend to risk her reputation in this way. I do blame myself for encouraging him to come to our house. We can all see now how totally unsuitable he is. You should have nothing more to do with him.'

Her mother said quietly, 'Esmond, we're all dead on our feet and it's very late. Let's leave this until morning.' She took his arm to lead him to the stairs.

Impatiently he shook her off. 'I'll get myself a nightcap,' he said, striding towards his study.

Lizzie had run upstairs. Mum came to her bedroom door. 'Lizzie, dear, we can't help worrying about you and Ben.'

'He's lovely, Mum. His family are very kind and generous. We had a great day out, you enjoyed it. You know you did. And they persuaded Father to buy a dog.'

'Yes, but the life Ben leads is very different to ours. He could find himself in difficulties. I fear for you.'

'You don't need to, Mum, honest. Ben is very organised, he plans everything, he knows what he's doing.'

'Yes, but I can't help worrying about you.'

She could see tears in her mother's eyes. 'I'm sorry.'

'Oh, Lizzie.' Mum's arms came round her for a huge hug. 'Goodnight, love.' She went, closing the door quietly behind her.

Tears gushed from Lizzie's eyes as she threw off her clothes and got into bed. Damn, damn and a thousand damns. Ben had been doing so well in his effort to get into Father's good books. It had all been going so well until Uncle Frank said the wrong thing.

Christmas was getting closer and they'd decided that would be the time to tell her parents that Ben had proposed and she'd agreed to marry him. It would soon be time to ask for Father's blessing to their union, and a week or so later, she'd intended to ask formally for their permission to marry. Now their plans had gone horribly wrong.

Lizzie had to get out of bed to find more handkerchiefs. She must stop crying or her eyes would be sore and red in the morning, and there were precious few hours left before she had to go to the shop. She blew her nose, but it didn't help. She couldn't stop the hot tears running down her cheeks.

The alarm woke Lizzie at the usual time the next morning. She had to go to work as Saturday was the busiest day in the shop. A swift glance at her face in the dressing-table mirror shocked her; nobody could doubt that she was in trouble and had been crying. She applied a lot of make-up and hoped that customers wouldn't comment on it. She felt like a zombie.

She was glad nobody else was up, though her family usually ate breakfast with her. She wanted only tea this morning.

The house was silent when Milly got up; she found Gladys was doing the ironing. 'I'll put the kettle on,' she said. 'What do you want for breakfast? Where is your mother? Is she not well?'

'She was all right last night. But it was very late when we came home and we've all slept late. They are awake though, I've heard them.'

'Run up to their bedroom, Milly, and ask if they want a cup of tea up there.'

While Gladys prepared a tea tray to take up to her parents' room, Milly went to the cupboard and took out a packet with a picture of a spritely Yankee Doodle Dandy on it. Milly loved the new American breakfast food called Force that was all the rage with her school friends. Usually Mum made eggs or bacon or something, so this was a treat.

She decided then that she'd walk up the lane to see Laurie. She needed his advice. She rang the doorbell and found he was about to come out; he had Mutt already on his lead. 'Dadda has bought a dog for Mum. She'll be here in a few days.'

Laurie was immediately interested when he heard that Dido had raced at Belle Vue. 'You're having just one bitch?' he asked. 'Your Mum talked of puppy breeding.'

'She did, but Dadda bought only one for now. He's really against it but he bought Dido to please her. The thing is, I want to get things ready but we don't know where to start. What will she need to sleep on?'

'Come in and I'll show you Mutt's bed. It's just a large basket with straw at the bottom. An old laundry basket or even a shallow wooden box would do.'

'Where do I get the straw?'

'Dad brings it home from the practice but an old blanket would do; or an old rug or cushion just to make it comfortable.' They were in a sort of porch off the back garden, a place the

Coynes used to store firewood, gardening shoes and wellies. Old coats hung on one wall. 'Mutt chose this place himself,' Laurie said. 'He kept coming in here. Our hot-water boiler is the other side of this wall, so it's always warm here, that's what he likes.'

'We've nowhere like this. Dadda thinks she should be shut in the old stable at night, though everybody is telling him it'll be too cold for her. Will you come and help me choose the best place for her?'

'OK, I was just about to take Mutt out for a walk anyway,' he said. 'Dido'll need to sleep inside your house. Do you have her racing history?'

'It will come with her. She's won lots of races. At one time she was the star of the track.'

'Mutt was too in his day.'

They reached the back door and Milly threw it open. Gladys surveyed Mutt with hostility. 'I'm not having any dogs in here,' she said.

Milly laughed. 'I have to tell you Dadda bought one yesterday. It'll be living here in a day or two.'

Gladys glared at Mutt. 'A dog like that? How will I ever keep the place clean? A child like you is bad enough.'

'I am not a child,' Milly said indignantly. 'I'm as tall as you.'

'I'll tie Mutt to the gate,' Laurie murmured, and went to do so.

'I can't believe your father's bought a dog for you.'

'Mum wanted one. She wants a lot of dogs to breed from, so soon there'll be lots of puppies here too.'

'Heaven forbid. Not in the house?'

'It's the only possible place for a greyhound,' Laurie said. 'Now, where's the best place for her bed? Somewhere warm.'

'The kitchen,' Milly said. 'The Rayburn stove keeps it warm.'

'You can't keep a dog in the kitchen. Not near food.' Gladys was adamant. 'Your father won't want that. It wouldn't be hygienic.'

'Gladys, you'll love Dido, there's a lot of white in her coat and she has pale brown brindle patches. Brown ears too.'

'I don't care if she's sky blue and pink.' Gladys's voice followed them as Milly took Laurie round their kitchen quarters.

'This is the old dairy which we don't use much any more,' Milly said.

'It won't do,' he said, 'it's cold in here, it faces north. Do you have a small room on the other side of the house?'

She took him there. 'Yes, the parlour. We use it a lot because it gets all the sun.'

'Can't use it as a kennel then,' Laurie said, 'and it's not all that warm anyway.'

'It's overcast today.' They giggled and returned to the kitchen. 'It'll have to be somewhere here. It is noticeably warmer.'

The house was over two hundred years old and had extensive kitchen quarters: a storeroom, pantries and a laundry room. Laurie said, 'The laundry room comes next to the kitchen.' Milly looked round at the two big sinks, a wash tub and an enormous mangle. 'The ironing is done in here and the airing cupboard is here too.'

'Just the place,' Laurie said. 'Dido will be very comfortable if you make a bed for her in here.'

'No,' Gladys protested. 'I don't want a dog around here amongst my washing.'

'Laurie is training to be a vet,' Milly told her. 'He understands how dogs should be treated.'

'Yes, I can see that. He wants dogs to be treated better than human beings.'

Chapter Twelve

WHEN HER WORKING DAY was over, Lizzie went straight to Ben's house. She knew he'd be alone, and his father and uncle would have returned to Ireland. He too was in a low mood and Lizzie was near to tears again. 'Father went for me as soon as we got home. Mum stopped him last night when he was in full flood, and I didn't see them this morning, so he'll no doubt start again as soon as he sets eyes on me. He and Mum are dead against you now.'

'I'm sorry, Liz. It shouldn't have happened like that. I was too tired to watch what I was saying.'

'Our first mistake was to take Father to Belle Vue; I should have known he'd take the moral high ground and refuse to bet. He's a miserable old thing.'

'I thought it would show him what my family do, and that there's nothing wrong in having a flutter on the dogs. I thought I could help your mum get the dog she wanted.'

'You did, she'll have her dog. And I found it all absolutely thrilling, and ended up with extra money in my pocket. Betting is a divine way to get money instead of working for it. Milly will be over the moon too about that. It was a red-letter day until Father found out about you having your own house.'

'That has done the opposite to what I intended. He thinks I'm a rotter now.'

'This has ruined everything. Can I stay with you tonight instead of going home?'

Ben groaned. 'No, I'd love you to move in with me permanently now, but it's the last thing you must do. I've been trying to think of the best way forward all day and it's difficult. If you stay here tonight it would really put his back up and you'll never get his permission to marry me. I think I should take you home quite soon so you can get an early night.'

'Face him, you mean?'

'Yes, sometimes it's the best way. We've both worked all day; you must feel spent, I know I do. Let's go out and get fish and chips, I haven't the energy to cook. Then I'll walk you home. Do you want me to come in with you? Talk to him?'

'Do you think that would be a good thing?'

'I'm afraid I might be like a red rag to a bull, but I want you to feel I'm behind you on this.'

Lizzie felt shattered. 'I know you're behind me. I suppose it would be better if I faced them alone.'

'It would. I want your family to like me. I don't want them to cut you off, which might happen if you stay. I'm afraid they'd see it as a fight, a battle, or even a declaration of war between me and them.'

'We'll do that then,' Lizzie said. 'You're quite wise, you really do think long term, Ben.'

'Sometimes,' he said.

Later that night Ben kissed her goodbye and paced back to town deep in thought. He felt he was always on his best behaviour with Lizzie's parents, and bending over backwards to please them. If Elsie wanted to breed greyhounds he was happy to show her the way. He knew the major wouldn't consider his father and uncle his social equal, but they worked hard and had made comfortable livings by using their wits as well as their brawn. They were enjoying their lives.

By contrast, he thought that the major, by inheriting property from his forebears, had a huge advantage. He should have added to it but instead he'd kept selling bits off to provide money to live on and support his family. Ben thought him lazy because he did nothing to earn his own living, and he was far too ready to call for help from others instead of standing on his own feet. He was also cantankerous, and far too high and mighty to relax and have a bit of fun. He saw him as a very difficult man.

But his own family had loved Lizzie as soon as they saw her, and thought her a real live wire with the luck of angels when it came to betting. Uncle Frank couldn't believe she was new to it and that she hardly understood the basics of what she was doing.

Lizzie heard the grandfather clock strike nine o'clock as she let herself into the hall. Her heart was pounding, and as she went into the sitting room all the family turned to look at her. Milly was doing a jigsaw puzzle on the floor.

'Lizzie!' Mum exclaimed. 'I was worried that you didn't come home for your dinner. I've saved it for you; shall I warm it up now?'

'Thank you, Mum, but no. I've had fish and chips.'

Father had put his newspaper aside. 'Is it too much to let us know when you don't intend to come home for a meal?'

'I should have, I'm sorry. Ben doesn't have a phone.' By the time they'd gone out for chips, dinner here would have been long since over.

'Milly, will you leave us? This has nothing to do with you.'

'Dadda, I don't want—'

'Please go when I ask you to.' His tone was cold with fury. Milly leapt to her feet and rushed out. He got up and closed the door after her.

'Elizabeth, your mother and I are shocked. We want you to be a respectable young lady and that's the last thing you are if you're going to Ben's house to be alone with him. Your reputation will be gone if that becomes public knowledge. It's got to stop, you mustn't keep going there.'

She was backing silently towards the door. 'Elizabeth,' he went on sternly, 'I want you to promise that you won't go there again.'

'I can't promise that,' she said.

She saw his face go an even deeper crimson. 'I forbid you to go there alone ever again.'

'You can't stop me.'

'Lizzie.' Mum looked desperate. 'I want you to ask Ben to come here so we can talk to him about this.'

'Right, I will.' The door slammed behind her and she went straight to bed.

Elsie burst into tears. 'Esmond, please don't be so strict with her. I'm afraid she'll cut herself off from us completely.'

Milly had everything ready for Dido: Laurie had seen a shallow wooden box in one of their outbuildings that he said would do for her bed, and he brought her a bag of dog meal and a couple of tins of dog food from Mutt's supply, 'To get you started,' he said. 'You can give her household scraps too, but she should have only one meal a day, in the evening.'

Mum had helped her pick out two large bowls from the kitchen cupboards, one for her water and the other for her food.

The following day Laurie knocked on the kitchen door; Milly had helped her mother make a rhubarb pie and it had just gone into the oven. 'My dad asked me to deliver these for your new dog,' he said, handing over two large carrier bags. 'It's mostly straw for her bed, but there's a lead and a harness which should fit her.'

'Thank you, and thank your father too,' Elsie said. 'You've been very kind.'

'I've been helping down at the practice and that's where they're from. Second-hand, of course, but none the worse for that.'

'I bet they belonged to a dog you've put down,' Gladys said. 'Some people want to get rid of them.'

Laurie grinned at her. 'They did,' he admitted, 'but we usually put dogs down because they're ill and in pain and we've tried everything else.'

'They look almost new.' Milly was delighted, and when she saw he had Mutt with him she said, 'Are you taking him for a walk? I'll come with you.'

Dido was expected late the following afternoon, and all the family were looking forward to her arrival. When the van arrived and she came out of her crate she looked a little dazed, but she shook herself and put both her ears on top of her head to look at them, then she licked Elsie's hand.

She was accompanied by a large brown envelope which contained her medical reports since puppyhood, a genealogy chart showing her breeding, her vaccination certificates and her racing history. Esmond took them to his study to read later.

Dido was wearing a scarlet collar. Milly clipped the lead on and led her round the kitchen to see her bed. 'Let's take her out,' Elsie said. 'She'll need to stretch her legs after being cooped up in that crate.'

'You must be careful that she doesn't pull away from you,' Dadda said. Milly slipped on the harness Laurie had given her and attached another lead to that. She and Mum led Dido while Dadda walked up the lane beside them to show the dog to Laurie and his father.

Dido had a lovely prancing walk; she almost seemed to dance. Everybody but Gladys loved her.

The following week, as Father had an engagement on Monday evening, Ben's invitation reverted to afternoon tea on Sunday. Lizzie was dreading it, knowing that the major would grill Ben this afternoon.

'Don't worry,' Ben said. 'I have to come and it's high time we got this out in the open. We're both free to marry, aren't we? We'll hide nothing, I'll tell them straight we're in love. They must have been in love themselves at one time, mustn't they?'

'That's hard to imagine,' Lizzie said caustically. 'I'm sure it's because of him that Mum suffers from nerves, and she says they've been playing up all week. He's almost sending her over the edge. We should give thanks that he bought a dog for her.

I do believe it is only Dido and Milly that are keeping her sane at the moment.'

Mum had made a seed cake for the occasion. Father was fond of it though the rest of the family were not. Milly hated caraway seeds. Lizzie put it on their cut-glass cake stand and took it to the table. 'Mum, shouldn't we have biscuits or something as well?'

The front doorbell rang and Milly scampered down the hall to let Ben in. Lizzie thought he looked subdued as she brought him to the sitting room to see Father. Dido had given one bark and moved towards him. 'Hello, Dido,' he said and put out a hand to stroke her. 'Good afternoon, Major Travis, I trust the dog is settling in all right?'

'Yes,' he said putting his newspaper aside, 'she seems quite at home with us already and happy with her quarters. She's no trouble really.'

Thank goodness she's here to break the ice, Lizzie thought, perching on the edge of a chair. Father was no longer furious, either; his heavy Sunday lunch and a nap afterwards had had a calming effect. 'She's very friendly towards everyone.'

Dido had gone over to Father and he was stroking her now. He said, 'I'm glad you feel able to come and see us, Ben. We have something to discuss. I think—'

The door crashed open and Milly came in. 'Mum says you can come to the table, everything is ready.'

'Oh, for heaven's sake.'

Lizzie was on her feet. 'We'd better go.' The dog followed them. 'Not in the dining room, Dido,' Father said, 'out of bounds for you.' He shut the door in Dido's face.

'Dadda!' Milly said. 'I thought you agreed that she could.'

They sat down in an awkward silence. 'Emilia, she watches every morsel I put in my mouth, it won't do.'

Mum's hand was shaking as she poured the tea. Cups were handed round. 'That one is for your father, Milly.' She took up the knife to cut the cake.

Esmond accepted a large slice. 'Excellent, my favourite seed cake. As I was saying, Ben, I think it very wrong of you to encourage a young girl like Elizabeth to come to your house alone. It has upset her mother. We are both worried. I know you understand that.'

'Sir, I did know it was wrong and I apologise.'

'That's a start, but apologies are no use unless this behaviour changes. What we find very hurtful is that we only know now that you have a house because you and your uncle forgot it was a secret and let it out.'

Ben's cake was untouched. 'I can assure you my intentions are honourable. I love Lizzie; I'd never do anything to harm her—'

'But you have, don't you understand what I'm saying? Allowing her to come to your house is harming her.' Esmond was getting agitated.

'Father, I—'

'Be quiet, Lizzie, when I'm talking. Where is this house you've rented?'

'Alvaston Terrace, do you know where that is?'

'The Terraces, yes,' Esmond said. 'They were fishermen's cottages originally. Behind the Tower and the Gardens, a bit unsavoury down there now, isn't it?'

'Ben has done it up beautifully. He's redecorated every-where.'

'That's not the point, Elizabeth. When the pubs close those backstreets are thronged with drunken louts. It must be noisy. The police are often called to places down there because they make trouble. We've discussed in the council chamber the need for an earlier closing time for public houses. And you don't need me to tell you that, we all read about it in the local paper. I'm not sure it's safe for a girl like you to go down there.'

'There's no danger, I assure you, sir.'

'Esmond, it isn't that bad.' Her mother looked fearful.

'Elsie, leave this to me. We do not want you to go there, Elizabeth. No young girl can go alone to her boyfriend's house and not lose her reputation.'

'Can I speak frankly, sir? I love Lizzie and I've asked her to marry me. She has agreed.'

Esmond said frostily, 'She's under age and cannot marry anyone at the moment. And do you think that makes it any better? I'd say it makes it more dangerous for her.'

Ben was stiff and serious. 'Lizzie and I would like to get married. I'm in a position to support a wife and we were about to ask for your approval.'

'I really do want to get married, Father. My mind is made up. What is the point in making me wait?'

'No, Elizabeth. Haven't I just made my position clear? No, I cannot give you permission.'

'Mum,' Lizzie implored. 'Mum, please . . .'

Elsie was biting her lip. 'What is the hurry?'

Father spat the words out. 'You will have to wait until you're twenty-one.'

'Much the safest thing,' Mum said. 'Really it is, Lizzie.'

'You'll probably change your mind half a dozen times

before then as you come to your senses. As the law sees it, you are still a child in need of parental guidance. In my opinion, Ben would not be a suitable husband for you.'

'That is outrageous, Father.' Lizzie was on her feet. 'I won't change my mind. Come on, Ben, let's leave them to it.'

Elsie leapt to her feet. 'Ben, we don't want you to stop coming here. I don't want you and Lizzie to cut yourselves off.'

'Mum, don't expect me home tonight.' The door slammed behind them.

'Dadda,' Milly leapt to her feet, 'that was very unkind to Ben. He's lovely, really he is. You don't know him. Lizzie loves him, she won't change her mind.' She turned to rush out after them. 'She can be as obstinate as you.'

CHAPTER THIRTEEN

ELSIE HAD BEEN FIGHTING tears for some time; now they came flooding out. Ben reminded her painfully of Jasper, Lizzie's father. She'd made a tragic mess of her life by marrying him. He'd brought terrible worry and financial problems to her and had blighted her mother's life. Marriage to him had been a disaster.

'What I fear more than anything else is that Lizzie will follow in my footsteps,' she said. 'Now she's in love with Ben, it seems her feet are already on the same downward path.'

Esmond got up from the opposite end of the table to put an arm round her shoulders. 'I don't want Lizzie to cut herself off from me,' she cried. 'You were too heavy-handed with her.'

'If you don't want her to marry Ben it had to be said. Elizabeth has been spending a lot of time alone with him at his house. Nothing could be more dangerous for her than that.'

'I know, I know,' she said, 'and it frightens me.' But Esmond's manner could put people off him. He didn't understand that and she couldn't tell him. He had a way of issuing orders and expecting them to be obeyed without question, a typical military commander.

'Let's go to the parlour and have a talk,' he said.

'The washing up . . .'

'That can wait until Gladys comes in the morning.' They sat down side by side on the parlour sofa. 'We need to decide on the best way to handle this,' he said gently.

'I don't trust Ben,' Elsie wept, 'and Lizzie is very young.'

'I don't trust him either, but Elizabeth is determined to have her own way. How do we persuade her that to wait would be sensible?'

'I've been thinking of nothing else since she met him,' Elsie said, 'and I don't have an answer.' Dido had followed them in and she put her head on Elsie's lap. Automatically, Elsie's hand reached out to stroke her. 'Oh, Esmond, what I want most for Lizzie is that she has a better life than I had, but this is like history repeating itself.'

'Did you go against your parents' wishes?' He remembered that her father had died when she was a toddler. 'Well, your mother's?'

'Yes, I suppose I did. She brought me up alone in a corner shop. I met Jasper Hardman when I was sixteen and fell in love with him.'

'Younger than Elizabeth then?'

'Yes.' Elsie had never told him the full story – bits of it, yes, but not all. 'My mother only gave me permission to marry because I was pregnant with Lizzie. I'm so afraid that is going to happen to her. If it does, she'll feel trapped as I did. My mother did her best not to show her deep disapproval; I think she assumed marriage was what I wanted. I never dared tell her I'd already found out Jasper was not trustworthy.'

'But you still married him?'

'I was brought up to believe there was no greater sin for a girl than to have a baby before she had a husband. I was embarrassed to find it was happening to me.' He squeezed her hand. 'So I went ahead. After a hasty church wedding, Jasper moved in with us. He earned his living as a gardener at one of the big houses in Sandfield Road, though he'd only started that the month before. When he was at home he helped in the shop and made himself useful where he could. He was kind and concerned during my confinement, but my mother was troubled with arthritis. Jasper persuaded her that the shop would be too much for us with the baby to care for as well, and the best thing to do was to sell it and let him take care of us.'

Elsie paused to wipe her eyes and blow her nose. 'I was such a fool to believe him! It wasn't as if I hadn't seen warning signs. Marrying him, tying myself legally to him, was the worst thing I could have done. So was selling the shop that had provided a living for our family for thirty years. The property was rented and our little business sold for a modest sum. Of course, we had to move out of the flat above it, and Jasper found a pleasant three-bedroom house for us to rent.'

'That was all right, wasn't it?'

'I thought so at first. He soon persuaded my mother to part with her cash for a variety of what he called "sure income earners". It was soon gone; then the real problems began to bite. I'd always known he enjoyed a drink, and by that time I thought of him as a heavy drinker. He was spending a lot of time in the local pub.

'A theft took place from the house where he was employed. That worried us sick as it seemed he was suspected. He protested his innocence and nothing was ever proved, but the police came round to question him more than once and he got the sack from his gardening job.'

'Oh dear.' Esmond's fingers tightened round hers.

Elsie took a deep breath. 'It came as a real shock to hear him admit he'd served two prison sentences for theft and fraud.'

'What? Elsie, you haven't mentioned anything like this before.'

'I was ashamed.'

'But it wasn't your fault, nothing for you to be ashamed about.'

'No,' she sighed. 'Well, he looked for another job but he had no recent reference and jobs were impossibly scarce at that time. With our nest egg gone we had no money to buy food and pay the rent. That's when I knew I'd have to find work and I answered your advert for a housekeeper.'

'Elsie, you gave no sign that you had such troubles.'

Her laugh was mirthless. 'I couldn't, could I? You wouldn't have given me the job. It wasn't easy to run two households with my mother getting increasingly frail. She was able to look after Lizzie during the day when she was a baby, but I had to do a lot for the baby when I got home.'

'I demanded a lot from you while you were here. I had no idea you had problems like this, not at first.'

Elsie wiped her eyes again. 'That's not the end of my problems. Jasper had suggested that my mother and I rent the house in our joint names, and every week I put the rent money under the clock on the mantelpiece. He was often in town and I asked him to pay the landlord at the end of each month.

'By the time I found out he wasn't paying it, he'd run up quite a debt and it was at this point we realised Jasper was not just a heavy drinker, he was an alcoholic. He would go on a four-day bender and get drunk and aggressive, then be filled with remorse that he'd spent money that should have gone on food or shoes for Lizzie. He promised many times to give it up but he couldn't, every penny he could get his hands on went on whisky.' Elsie sighed again. 'But you knew about my debt.'

'Not at first and you said very little about it later. I should have seen that you had major problems,' he said. 'Things went on like that for years, didn't they? You should have told me.'

'Yes, it was a struggle to keep going. I felt I'd caused the problems and was filled with guilt to see my mother becoming more and more infirm with rheumatism. Lizzie was a vigorous toddler and very hard work. I thought life couldn't get any worse but it did. My mother caught pneumonia and was dead within a week.'

'I remember you being absolutely stricken by that. I was sorry for you.'

'You sent flowers for her funeral.' She managed a half smile. 'The cost of that had loomed frighteningly, but I found Mum had been paying sixpence a year into an insurance policy since the turn of the century and it paid out. However, the landlord was asking me to repay the debt Jasper had built up.

'Lizzie was nearly five by then and it was a relief when she was given a place at the local primary school. I could take her there in the morning before I came to work. Jasper promised to fetch her home at quarter to four, but soon there were times when he forgot about her, and times when he was too drunk to care.'

'Yes, I remember you had to ask an acquaintance who lived in the same street if she'd collect Elizabeth from school and take her home with her own child,' he said. 'She looked after her until you got back from work.'

'Yes, and you raised my wages so I could pay her a few shillings for doing it. That brought me peace of mind, until my friend moved house to the other side of town. Jasper promised again that he'd collect Lizzie and take good care of her, and said there was no need for me to spend money on paying someone else to do it.

'He did meet her for a while, but then the same thing happened. Lizzie was six by then and had learned to come home on her own when he didn't turn up. I left a key under the doormat for her in case he wasn't at home when she got there.

'We managed like that for a time and then I heard from my next-door neighbour that the police had been round questioning Jasper again.'

'Elsie, don't upset yourself further,' Esmond said. 'I know what happened after that. Can I get you another handkerchief, a big one of mine? Those bits of lace aren't very practical. You've had some very hard times and you're a real stoic but all that's behind you now.'

Elsie shuddered. 'I'm very much afraid it won't be, if Lizzie is about to go through the same experience.'

She heard the door close behind him; he'd left her alone with Dido on the comfortable sofa with the searing memories she couldn't erase. She fondled Dido's ears and the dog's big brown eyes seemed full of sympathy.

Elsie remembered how she'd been facing the worst crisis of her life, one she and Lizzie could never get over. She recalled coming home from work to find Lizzie alone and playing contentedly with her doll. It was one of those days when Jasper had not met her from school and wasn't at home when she got there.

The house had been cold but Elsie had not had Jasper to cope with. She soon had a fire going and a hot supper for them bubbling on the stove. As he still hadn't come they had second helpings of stew and ate his share too. She'd put Lizzie to bed and was getting ready to go there herself before he came home.

He was in a very strange mood, jumpy, and adrenalin seemed to be racing through him as though he'd had to run. He'd torn his trousers and grazed his thigh and complained mightily about the pain. 'What have you been up to now?' she asked with sinking heart, afraid it would mean more trouble.

For once he seemed stone-cold sober. 'Better if you know nothing about it,' he'd said. She bathed the graze and washed away the dried blood. He wanted her to dress and bandage it, but she had nothing but Vaseline; she smeared that on hoping it would calm him.

Jasper was on his feet again and put the morning sticks on the dying fire despite her protests. Then he rolled up his torn trousers and added them to the blaze. The acrid smell of burning cloth made her open the back door, but he came behind her and slammed it shut again. 'We don't want the neighbours to notice,' he said. 'It'll be gone by morning. Come on, let's go to bed.'

'What have you done?' Elsie had felt rising panic. 'I hope you haven't been robbing somebody.'

'Come to bed,' he said, calmer now. 'I feel so guilty, I've been a rotten husband to you, and a rotten father to Lizzie.'

Elsie had been exhausted but now sleep felt miles away. 'Are you feeling a bit depressed?' she asked. He always was when in need of another drink, but she couldn't smell whisky on him. Then he got up and put the light on again to look for the half bottle he'd hidden in one of his drawers.

'You'll be better off without me,' he'd said, and it hadn't occurred to her then that he intended to kill himself, but that must have been what was on his mind. Instead she thought he was in trouble with the police because he'd committed yet another criminal act, and he needed a drink to face it.

He was asleep when Elsie got up in the morning. She'd found the bottle empty on the floor beside him and the living room still stank of burned cloth. She cleared the grate and opened both the front and back doors to clear it, while Lizzie went upstairs to take Daddy some tea. Then Elsie had eaten breakfast with Lizzie and taken her to school.

When Elsie had come home that day she could hear Lizzie screaming and crying at the top of her voice before she opened the front door. She found Jasper had cut his wrists and was lying inert in an armchair. She knew Lizzie had come home from school an hour or so earlier. Poor child, she'd been alone with him all that time; her cheeks were wet and shining, even her jumper was damp, and her eyes red and swollen.

Elsie had thrown her arms round her and hugged her close. To find Jasper had killed himself came as an almighty shock to her and she'd sat cuddling Lizzie and trying to soothe her. Between sobs Lizzie had said, 'Look at all this blood that's leaked out of Daddy. What's happened to him? He can't be dead, can he? Not really dead? Not when he was all right this morning?'

Elsie had been unable to drag her eyes from Jasper's face; it was distorted with pain and death. He'd bled all over himself and the chair; even the hearth rug was soaked, and the stench of blood hung in the air.

Eventually, Lizzie began to quieten down, though she still gave an occasional shudder of distress. The need to do something about it had been pressing on Elsie but her head felt fuzzy. She pulled herself to her feet and carried Lizzie next door to seek help. The neighbours she'd hardly spoken to were kind, made her a cup of tea and sent for the police.

Elsie could remember very little of what happened then except the policeman showed her a letter they'd found on the table that Jasper had written.

Dear Elsie,

I'm a loser but you know that already. I've always worked hard and done my best for you, but I've not been a success at anything and it's all got too much for me. You and Lizzie will be better off without me. Sorry to do it this way.

I do love you both,

Jasper

As far as Elsie could remember, Jasper had never made the slightest effort to do his best for anybody. He'd defied authority, did what he wanted and took what he wanted. She'd thought the sun shone out of him until she'd married him and realised he was a fantasist who told everybody lies. He'd hidden so much from her, that she'd never quite understood him. She'd thought him the least likely person to commit suicide. Right up until she saw that he had.

Elsie continued to stroke the smooth, straight fur on Dido's head; to have her company was soothing, and went some way to comfort her. Lizzie had been terribly distressed, and it had taken months for her to forget her fears. For years afterwards she'd had nightmares about it and occasionally woken up screaming in the middle of the night. She'd thought Lizzie was reliving what had happened, but it seemed there was more.

Months later Lizzie sobbed out, 'I was afraid you would die too. Gran did and so did Daddy,' and Elsie understood that she was terrified she'd be left alone in the world to fend for herself.

CHAPTER FOURTEEN

ESMOND CAME BACK WITH with one of his handkerchiefs and two cups on a circular tray that he could balance with one hand. 'We didn't finish our tea, did we? I thought I'd make some more.'

'Thank you.' She took the hanky and mopped her face but she'd no more tears to shed. Jasper's suicide and the aftermath had left her in the depths of despair, but she'd had to pull herself together to take care of Esmond's home and his needs; and at the same time look after Lizzie. And still the landlord was pressing her to repay the debt that Jasper had run up in her name. She tried to put a few pence on one side each pay day for that, but she could see it was going to take years.

Esmond had been unfailingly kind. 'You could move into the rooms upstairs,' he'd suggested one day. 'Bring your child with you. Have you ever been up to the attics? In the good old days they were the quarters for servant girls and milkmaids. Go and take a look at them, see what you think. Of course, nobody has lived there for years, they'll need doing up, but that can be done. Let's take a look now.'

She'd had a peep into them when she'd first come to work for him, just to see what was there, but she'd been glad he no longer used them or required her to clean them. Now he too found the rooms airless and dusty, the soft furnishings rotting and dirty. Elsie tried to open a window, but it was too stiff to move.

'I could get somebody in to give the place a coat of paint,' he said, 'do it up a bit. What d'you think, would you like to live here?'

The advantages were obvious to Elsie: it would cut out her journey to work and cut down her workload. 'You wouldn't mind me having Lizzie here?' For her that was the big question.

'She's at school all day, isn't she?'

'Schools have holidays,' she said slowly, and he might scare Lizzie. She was more nervous than she used to be and he wouldn't have much patience with young children. They'd have to be kept apart. 'Lizzie would take some of my attention.'

He had a rare and distant smile. 'She takes some of your attention now. If she were here, she might take less.'

Elsie's mind was flying ahead. 'You'd have to feed both of us then.' That would be a big saving for her. 'And what rent would you want?'

'None, of course, I want to make it possible for you to repay that debt.' And, of course, she had managed to do that.

It had taken Elsie a very long time to realise she'd pay him in ways that didn't involve money.

Milly continued to miss Lizzie's company. Family life had thrown them together, and from an early age her sister had taken her out and about. Milly knew every part of New Brighton as well as the quickest routes to return home.

On wet afternoons Lizzie had taught her to dance. Most of their rooms were furnished with carpet squares and heavy furniture which made dancing impossible, but in the dining room there were carpet runners round the table which were easy to roll so they could dance on the parquet beneath. Lizzie had discovered an old wind-up gramophone in an attic with some very strange records – Edwardian ballads for the most part but also a few jollier ones of Gilbert and Sullivan. She had bought a few records they could dance to – Ambrose, and Harry Roy and his band – but there was a wireless on the corner of the sideboard and sometimes they were lucky enough to get some really modern dance music on that.

They'd taken the chairs away from the table and practised round and round the table until Milly felt she could waltz, quickstep and foxtrot with the best of them. Once she'd learned, she wanted to go to a dance at the Tower Ballroom. Dadda forbade it, saying the local girls went there to pick up men; Lizzie had been many times and said it was wonderful. It would hold two and a half thousand dancers, and had a big ball on the ceiling that cast fragments of coloured light over everyone. There was a big band there playing all the latest tunes.

Lizzie had also taught her to knit and play simple card games, and she'd given her lots of clothes and dolls and books and jigsaw puzzles as she'd grown tired of them. Milly thought there was no better big sister in the whole world and wanted her here with her.

But all Lizzie could think about was getting married to Ben.

Ben continued to join them for supper on Monday evenings but none of them was at ease any more. Elsie tried to pretend there had been no falling-out, though Lizzie still went to his house just as often and made no secret of it.

Christmas came and brought the party season. It was the one occasion on which the major indulged his family. He booked a pantomime performance on Boxing Day and Elsie made all manner of cakes, pies and puddings. In the week before the big day, they invited the Coyne family, and sometimes other friends, to a festive supper, and were invited back to their homes in the week before New Year.

Milly saw a lot of Laurie during the Christmas holiday; often they walked their dogs together. 'I'll be sitting my finals this summer,' he told her.

She'd known that was coming. 'And if you pass you'll be working in your father's practice afterwards?'

'Not straight away. I'm thinking of applying for a post-graduate course in veterinary surgery at Leahurst.'

'Haven't you done enough book learning?'

'There are two working farms at Leahurst and this course concentrates on the practical side and it's only for one more year. It's part of the vet school and Dad recommends that I do it.'

'I remember you being there before. So then you'll join his practice?'

'That's the plan eventually, but he thinks I should work for a year somewhere else for the experience. That should give me a year in his practice before he retires. Then I'll take his place.'

'You should know everything about animals by then.'

'It's hard to know when you know enough.'

Laurie took both her and Lizzie carolling on Christmas Eve and they had a great time. To please Father, Lizzie went with the family to the midnight service at church. Ben had asked her if he should join them, but she'd said no. He was invited to lunch on Christmas Day and came bringing small gifts for them, but his presence caused unease to all except Milly. She thought Christmas 1937 the best ever and she was enchanted with all the old traditions and thrilled with her presents.

Lizzie thought the standoff with her parents took the gloss off Christmas and hoped it would be sorted out soon. After all, she would be twenty years old at the beginning of March.

On one of the cold days towards the end of the holiday, Milly, wrapped up in scarf and gloves, led Dido out for her walk and found Laurie was just passing her house with Mutt. 'Hello,' he said, 'we've timed things well. Our dogs always seem pleased to see each other. Dad wants me to go down to the practice. He isn't feeling well and wants me to collect some paperwork he can do at home.'

'Can I come with you? I usually take Dido round the fields, and it would be a change to go into town.'

'Of course, Milly.'

'I'm sorry Christmas is over, it's all gone a bit quiet now.'

'Flat,' he said. 'I know what you mean; it's all over for another year, but I've got plenty of revision to do and Dad thinks I should offer to help if the practice is busy.'

'I've never been inside. Is it a hospital for animals?'

'Sort of, come in and see it for yourself.'

Outside the New Brighton Veterinary Practice an iron bar had been let into the wall. 'I'm going to tie Mutt up outside,' he said. 'He's healthy, no point in taking him in.' He did so, and then tied Dido up at the other end of the bar.

They were turning to go in when Mutt mounted Dido. 'Oh my goodness,' Laurie cried. 'She's not in season, is she?'

'What's that?' Milly asked. 'He's not hurting her, is he?'

But Laurie was trying to prise them apart and finding it difficult. 'On heat,' he grunted.

When he finally managed it, Laurie said, 'There's another dog coming, we must take Dido inside. Come quickly.'

'Why?' Milly wanted to know as he slammed the door on them. She looked round – the place seemed starkly bare and smelled strongly of disinfectant.

'Did your father not say you must watch out for her coming into season?'

'No, what is that?'

'I think Dido might be ready to have puppies.'

'Is she?'

When Milly was introduced to Raymond Metcalf, Ivor Coyne's partner, he asked her, 'Will your father be cross if Dido has puppies?'

Milly shrugged. 'I don't know about Dadda, but Mum will be pleased. Ben and his uncle talked to her about that and she wanted half a dozen dogs to start a puppy farm.'

'Well that's a relief.' Laurie was quite upset. 'Embarrassing if she is and I let it happen here. Thank goodness Mutt is a thoroughbred and a good match for Dido. Much worse if it had been that nondescript terrier we saw sniffing at her outside.'

Raymond Metcalf was supportive. 'I remember Ivor taking his copy of the *Dog Breeders Handbook* to give to the major. He said he'd explained the signs he'd need to watch for.'

'I'll go home with Milly and tell her parents what's happened,' Laurie said.

Milly was intrigued. 'So is Dido going to have puppies?'

'Well, we can't be sure yet, that depends on which day she ovulated. We'll have to wait and see.'

Laurie showed Milly round while his father's partner sorted out the paperwork for him to take home. She was very interested in a spaniel, still unconscious in his cage but recovering from an operation he'd had that morning.

Laurie was worried as they walked home. He had to keep a very firm hand on Mutt's shortened lead to keep their dogs apart. 'Oh lord, Milly, I hope I'm not in trouble because of this,' he said as he tied Mutt to their garden gate. They took Dido indoors with them.

Dadda said, 'I've read half of the book your father loaned to me and found it very interesting. I'd told him Elsie wanted me to buy half a dozen dogs to breed from and I thought he was giving me information to prepare me for that.'

'Keep Dido away from other dogs for the time being,' Laurie advised Milly.

After Ben's next visit, he and Lizzie took Dido for a walk round the fields and Milly went with them. 'Dadda says Dido is named after the first Queen of Carthage,' she said. 'He told me a whole lot of Greek legends and myths about her this morning; and thinks because they name greyhounds after her now it shows how educational standards have fallen.'

Ben laughed; he'd already heard what had happened when Milly and Laurie had taken the dogs out together. 'He thinks I should have stayed on at school until I was eighteen and if I had that's exactly what I'd have learned, Greek legends and myths. Your father's head is stuffed with what he reads in books; he's an academic without an ounce of practicality in

131

him. He lives in a world of his own, thinking the information he'd been given was interesting but failing to apply it to Dido's care.'

'Mum hopes Dido will have puppies; she's quite excited at the prospect. So am I.' Milly beamed at them.

Afterwards, Lizzie went home with Ben for a few hours. She hated going home to bed every night, when what they both wanted was to stay together. 'I wish we could get married,' she said.

'So do I,' Ben murmured, 'but only fourteen months until you're twenty-one, and then you can do as you like.'

'It's fourteen wasted months. I want us to be married now.' Lizzie could think of little else. 'I don't want a big wedding and a lot of fuss. I don't care about a white dress, Father will think I'm no longer entitled to wear that anyway. They know I'm going to bed with you, we haven't hidden that. This is bullying on Father's part. He's even forbidden Milly to come here in case I lead her astray.'

'But she comes to the shop to see you.'

'Yes, occasionally on the way home from school. She loves to watch what goes on there. Father doesn't approve of that either in case she decides to do the same. But I can't concentrate on her when she comes to the shop. I have to keep breaking off to serve customers. It would be easier if she came here once in a while, and why not?'

CHAPTER FIFTEEN

1938

THE WEEKS WERE PASSING. Laurie decided Dido was pregnant and his father came down the next day to confirm it. 'Only nine weeks for a dog to wait?' Elsie marvelled. 'Dido, you don't realise how lucky you are.'

'That means about the middle of March,' Laurie said, and told them what preparations they needed to make and what to expect. 'You need to provide a whelping box for her,' he said, but he brought them an old tea chest and turned it on its side in the laundry room. 'She can have her pups in this,' he told Elsie. He placed it next to her bed. 'She'll be warm here, and you'll have plenty of space if you have to pull one of her puppies.'

'Pull them?' Milly and her mother chorused together.

'It's hardly ever necessary with a greyhound,' Laurie said hastily. 'They give birth easily because they have small heads and lean bodies.'

'I hope we'll be able to manage,' Elsie said nervously. 'We don't know anything about dogs, or what to expect.'

'Dogs are mammals, like we are. They have contractions when they give birth.'

'And pain?' Elsie asked.

'Most dogs do it entirely on their own without any help,' Laurie said. 'If you need me I only live up the lane. I'll be very happy to help, and if anything should go wrong I can always call on Dad. There's nothing to worry about.'

'So what else do we need to do?'

'Collect together any old towels or rags of any sort and put plenty of bedding in the tea chest so Dido can be comfortable.'

'I get shivers running down my spine every time I think of her having puppies,' Elsie said.

'Yes, excited as well as nervous,' Milly agreed.

'Absolutely no need to worry,' Laurie assured them. 'Dido will be fine.'

Elsie and Milly watched Dido closely as the time for giving birth drew closer. She lost interest in her food and didn't like being left alone. Milly had found an old carriage rug in the stable and Dido had had it on her bed for a while; now they discovered she'd dragged it into the far corner of the laundry room behind the mangle and the zinc tub.

Laurie smiled when Milly told him and said, 'She's decided she's going to give birth there. She feels safer in the far corner. Give me a hand to move the tea chest and we'll put her rug on top of the bedding. The pups will be out of all draughts in that, and we can move the old mangle further back to give us room once things begin to happen.'

One wet day, Lizzie hurried round to see Ben straight from the shop, and no sooner had she closed the front door than the bell rang and there was an urgent rat-a-tat on the knocker.

She opened it to find Milly on the doorstep. 'This is Ben's

house?' She shot across the room and into the kitchen, gazing round, entranced. 'It's lovely, just like a doll's house. No, a playhouse, I'm so glad I've found it.'

Lizzie took off her mac. 'How did you?'

'Well I was coming to your shop but I was late because I went round Woolworth's with Maggie Jones from school. As I turned the corner I could see your shop was being locked up and you were all coming out. I did call but you didn't hear me, so I thought I could follow you home and find out where you lived. Are you cross with me?'

Lizzie laughed. 'Take off that wet coat so I can hug you. Of course I'm not cross. I'm pleased – it's lovely to have you here.'

'But what do I tell Dadda?'

'Exactly what you've told me.'

The fourth of March approached, bringing Lizzie's twentieth birthday. Ben said, 'I want to take you out to choose a ring. I don't want to spend the earth on it because, well – precious stones are pretty but there isn't much you can do with them except look at them. But you need a ring to show that we are engaged, officially engaged.'

She chose a Victorian ring shaped like a belt with two tiny diamonds in the buckle. 'It is pretty,' Ben said, 'though I think it's meant to be a dress ring.'

'I love it,' Lizzie said, 'and to me it is an engagement ring.'

He took her to the Albion Hotel for dinner that evening to celebrate. Her parents had gone to bed by the time she got home, they often did these days, but the next morning they admired her ring. 'There's quite a lot of gold in it,' Father said, as though he expected it to be made of tin.

'It's an antique,' she told him. 'I thought you'd like it.'

'It's a sensible choice, Elizabeth, I do like it,' he said, but neither he nor Mum was smiling.

Ben took time off and arrived at Oakdene Farm to find Elsie had laid on a birthday cake and a celebratory spread. It took Lizzie three attempts to blow out all the candles, and as the family clapped she collapsed breathless and laughing to say, 'We only have one year more to wait, hurrah.'

That was met with a stony silence. Then Elsie said, 'Do you want to cut the cake, Lizzie, or shall I?'

Lizzie wasn't laughing now. 'Mum,' she said, 'Ben and I are officially engaged; we want to get married soon. Please will you give me permission? I'm not going to change my mind, neither will he. What is the point in making us wait? Please, Mum.'

Milly gasped; even she felt the sudden tension. It was her father who answered, 'You've heard what we have to say on that, Elizabeth. We aren't going to change our minds either. You will have to wait.'

Lizzie could see Mum's eyes were filling with tears. She said, 'Come on, Ben, we're wasting our time, let's get out of here.'

They went without even tasting her birthday cake.

The next morning, Milly found that Dido was more restless than usual, getting up and lying down, unable to settle anywhere. She didn't want to go for a walk. Mum said, 'I think she's near her time, you'd better go up and tell Laurie.'

But ten minutes later he rang to ask how Dido was. 'I'm just taking Mutt for a walk,' he said. 'I'll call in and see her on the way back.'

He did, leaving Mutt tied to their garden gate. Dido was settling in the tea chest when he came. 'Good, she's decided it is more comfortable in that than on the stone floor,' he said. 'I think you're right, she won't be long now. Ring me if anything changes.'

'We're getting excited, Mum and me,' Milly told him. 'Well, we're a bit nervous too.'

'No need to be.' He smiled. 'If I don't hear from you I'll come back to see her before I go to bed.'

Dido was no longer padding behind Milly, now she didn't want to leave her tea chest, hidden behind the mangle. Elsie and Milly were up and down all evening to make sure all was well. Milly begged to be allowed to stay up with Dido.

It was nearly eleven when Laurie brought his father down to see the patient, and Milly was having trouble hiding her yawns.

'Dido is fine,' Ivor Coyne assured them. 'What's happening is perfectly normal. The first pup will come at any moment. Laurie will stay with her, he needs the experience, and he's brought my whelping bag with him so he has everything he might need. I'd go to bed if I were you, Elsie. You have nothing to worry about.'

'I want to stay up,' Milly said, afraid she'd be sent upstairs. 'Dadda, you agreed that I could.'

'All right, it is Sunday tomorrow,' Mum said, getting out the tin with Lizzie's birthday cake inside. 'You've eaten quite a lot already, Milly.'

'Nobody else wanted any but me.'

'No.' Mum was tight-lipped. 'Lizzie is very late tonight.'

'Will she be coming home?' Milly asked. 'I don't think she'll want to.'

Dadda said, 'Come on, Elsie, let's go to bed, you must try and have a better night. Goodnight, Laurie, this is very kind of you.'

'Goodnight, Milly,' her mother said. 'You could make a cup of tea for Laurie while you're waiting.'

'Lizzie's in dead trouble,' she told Laurie as soon as her parents had gone. 'She stayed out all last night with Ben and they think she's going to do the same tonight. Nobody's talking to me about it, but now they think she's left home altogether.'

'Oh!'

'Mum's very upset and I'm forbidden to go near them, but I do. Ben has a lovely little house. Lizzie keeps asking for permission to marry him but they refuse. They don't like him.'

'Milly, I wouldn't talk about this to your friends if I were you. Your parents won't want that. Neither will Lizzie.'

'I wouldn't mention it to anyone but you,' she said. 'You're different.'

He grinned at her. 'In what way?'

'Well, you know . . .'

Laurie was laughing as picked up the bag he'd brought and said, 'I'd better take a look at Dido.' He put on the laundry room light and went in. 'Come and help me move this mangle and all the other bits out of the way,' he called. Dido watched them uneasily.

Laurie got down on his hands and knees and crawled up to examine her more closely with his torch. 'She's having contractions, I can feel them, so she's started in labour. They're quite strong and close together. I think I can feel the first pup in the birth canal. It won't be long now.'

'Is there time to have a cup of tea and some birthday cake first?' Milly asked in her best hostess manner.

'If we're quick,' he said. 'So Lizzie's had her twentieth birthday?'

'Yes, hardly seems worth all this trouble to stop her getting married, does it?'

They were sitting one each side of the kitchen table. 'Scrumptious cake.' Laurie bit into his second slice. 'We could do with something to sit on in there so we can stay with her.'

Milly pulled out two of the basket chairs Mum used for sitting in the garden on sunny days. Laurie placed them in front of Dido's box: 'Not too near, we don't want to upset her but we need to see what she's doing. Do you have a small table as well, Milly? Something I can write on?' She produced one from the parlour. 'Excellent, now we can wait in comfort for something to happen.'

At twenty to twelve Dido pushed the first pup out. 'Without any help from me,' Laurie said, but he got up to help her pull away the amniotic sac so the pup could breathe. Dido was up on her feet and doing the same and eating the sac and all the other birth products. She was excited and licking the pup clean.

'It's a boy.' Laurie quickly tied off the cord and cut it, slid a red band round the pup's neck and weighed it on the spring balance scales he'd brought with him. He pushed an old towel towards Milly. 'Help her dry it,' he said, and started his records with the date and time of the first pup, together with his weight.

Milly was in raptures. 'He's lovely but his fur is awfully thin.'

Dido was out of the tea chest in seconds. 'Give him back to her, Milly, she's afraid you're going to keep him. Just put the puppy back inside and she'll go after it.'

'Oh gosh, I didn't think she'd come right out. We'll have to think of names for them.'

'Right now he's Red. You can take your time thinking of something fancier.' But already Dido was lying down again and they could see the strong contractions she was having.

'Right, here's puppy number two at twenty past midnight, a girl this time.' Laurie went through the same procedure and slid a green band on her neck. Milly was trying to dry this one off as Dido excitedly licked at her too.

'Let's see if Red pup knows how to feed.' Laurie put the pup's nose on to one of Dido's nipples and within moments he had latched on and began to suck. 'Excellent, he'll be fine.'

'Isn't this miraculous?' Milly was starry-eyed. 'But they can't stand, they're just rolling and sliding round on the straw.'

'Yes, if we were not here they'd roll out of the tea chest and soon be too cold on this stone floor. Can you find something heavy to put in front of it to keep them in?'

'There's an old fender in the dairy that used to be in the parlour until Dadda got that new one with a seat at each end.'

'Just right,' Laurie said when she put it in position. 'It's high enough to keep the pups inside and Dido can still get in and out easily. Newborn pups can't see or hear for the first few weeks.'

'They aren't as attractive as I thought they'd be.'

'Wait a couple of weeks and you'll think they're beautiful.' Laurie smiled. 'All it takes is time. There are more to come, I can feel two at least, possibly more. Could you get Dido a drink of milk? That's said to be good for a dog when she's giving birth.'

Milly produced it but Dido gave it only a half-hearted lick; she was more interested in her pups. They had to wait until quarter past one for the next and Laurie helped her by pulling it out. 'Another boy, this one can be Yellow.'

At quarter to two Dido had another, and half an hour later another followed. 'This must be terrible for her,' Milly said.

'She isn't complaining.'

Laurie decided there was another still to come. They had to wait some time for it. Milly suggested another cup of tea to drink in their basket chairs and they finished off Lizzie's birthday cake.

'Dido's had six healthy puppies.' Laurie was high on the excitement. He wrote up details of the last puppy and Milly made sure they were all clean and dry.

'Dido appears to be delighted with her brood. She'll be all right on her own now. I'm going home. Thank God we saw Mutt humping her because if it had been any other dog her pups wouldn't be thoroughbred and would be no good for racing. I feel I had a stroke of luck there. Dad said I should have recognised that Dido was in season.'

'So should Dadda, especially since your father gave him a book about what to look out for.'

'We've had a good night, haven't we?' he said as she saw him out.

Milly was euphoric. 'Thrilling, that's the most amazing thing I've ever seen.'

She was so excited it took her ages to get to sleep.

CHAPTER SIXTEEN

MILLY WAS ALMOST ASLEEP when she was roused by a strange sound. It took her a few moments to recognise that it was her mother sobbing and in deep distress. She was being comforted by Dadda. 'Lizzie hasn't come home again,' she wept. 'This means she's planning to stay there with him, live with him. And now they're engaged. What could be worse than that?'

'Pig-headed girl,' Dadda exploded. 'I'm horrified, though we knew she was sleeping with him. She's determined to get her own way on this. Come back to bed, Elsie, you need your rest.'

The house was silent again after that. Milly thought they should let Lizzie marry Ben and then all the arguments would stop. She pulled her blankets closer; her bedside clock was telling her it was twenty minutes to four.

It was almost time for lunch when Milly woke up the next morning. She was ready to go downstairs when she heard Mum let Laurie and his father in. She ran down to find they were all in the laundry room and Ivor Coyne was checking over Dido's pups.

'They're all fine,' he said. 'They've got full tummies so Dido is mothering them well.' He clapped Esmond on the shoulder and said, 'You're very lucky to have thoroughbred pups.'

'I know, I'll bear in mind all you tell me in future.' Esmond looked repentant. 'And I'll watch Dido for the signs.'

'Milly and Laurie did well last night, didn't they?'

'Yes, thank you, Laurie, I'm very grateful for your help.'

'It was good for him,' his father said. 'You can't beat practical experience.'

Milly said, 'Laurie, I wouldn't have missed last night for anything. It was wonderful.'

'It was,' he smiled. 'Everything went well.'

Elsie seemed to have recovered from her distress of the middle of the night. She said to Ivor Coyne, 'I want you to know I'm thrilled with these six puppies. It suddenly seems feasible for us to have half a dozen bitches and set up a puppy farm. I really think we could do it.'

'Oh yes,' Milly breathed, 'we could.'

'These pups will be worth a lot of money in six months or so but they'll need special training in puppyhood if they're going to win races.'

'I don't know if we'll bother . . .'

'Esmond please,' Elsie implored. 'Both Dido and Mutt have been big winners in their day. The trainers will want them.'

'You should talk to Ben about them,' Milly said. 'He knows a lot about racing dogs and will want to help.' She saw her mother's face change and knew she shouldn't have mentioned Ben. It had reminded her that Lizzie had gone to live with him.

'You'd have to have a better place for them than here in the laundry room,' Laurie said. 'Not enough space.'

'It would be too expensive to put heaters in the old stable.' Esmond frowned.

Ivor was striding round. 'You've got plenty of space through here. What is this place?'

'The old dairy, and it faces north to keep it as cool as possible.'

'It would be cheaper to put electric heaters on the wall here, and more convenient to have the dogs in the house,' Ivor Coyne said. 'And very soon you'll have to move all the stuff you have stored here as you'll need more space for these six pups.'

'I'll help you move it all to the old stable, Mum,' Milly offered.

On Monday Milly went to school and told her friends about Dido and what a miracle it had seemed when she'd had six pups, and how clever Laurie Coyne was already, even though he still had another year of studying ahead of him before he would be a real vet.

Elsie said, 'I wonder if Ben and Lizzie will come to supper this evening.'

'At least Dido and her pups have stopped you worrying yourself sick about them,' Dadda said. Suppertime came and although Elsie had cooked a meal for four, there was no sign of Lizzie and Ben.

Milly felt she was walking on eggshells. 'Mum, you must invite them to come to supper next week so they know they're welcome. You need to talk to Ben about getting more dogs if you really want that. Honestly, Dadda, I'd love to have lots of dogs here and so would Mum. It would be good for us both.'

'You do it for us, Emilia, if that's what you want.' Dadda was half-hearted, so the following day she called at the shop where Lizzie worked and told her about Dido's pups. 'I'm told to say, "Please will you both come to supper next Monday." They want advice from Ben about training puppies, and you'll be able to see Dido's brood then.'

Lizzie had been upset after the tiff with Father at her birthday celebration supper. Her conscience had been troubling her because she hadn't been home since then. She'd always felt close to her mother and knew how bad she'd be feeling about her staying away. 'Thank her, Milly, and tell her that we'll come.'

'Ask them again for permission to marry,' Ben advised when she told him. 'Although they'll accuse you of living in sin and blame me for it, it is they who have put us in this position. But don't say that, it'll only put your father's back up.'

Lizzie laughed. 'Of course I won't.'

Ben did his best to cheer her up. He'd promised they would have a good time while they were young, and for the last few months he'd set about doing his best to provide it. He was now taking her out regularly for drinks in a bar, to the theatre, music hall and cinema, and occasionally for dinner at a leading restaurant. Every few weeks there was a big dog race on at Belle Vue and they went to that. Lizzie really enjoyed betting and usually she came home delighted with what she'd won.

One evening, Lizzie lost several times in the early races, and when the big race was looming, she looked up from her race card and said, 'I'm going to double my stake on Flash of Gold.'

'No,' Ben protested, 'just keep to your normal amount.'

'I'm certain he'll win,' she said, 'I have that gut feeling.'

'You can't be certain.'

'I am about this one. Flash of Gold has won pretty well all his races recently. A bigger stake means it's more thrilling and I'll win more.'

'I had noticed that you're no longer interested in old Bill's roll-a-penny stall.'

'Pocket money stuff,' she scoffed.

When Ben was ready to put their bets on she gave him her stake. 'Please,' she said, 'if you don't put it on, I'll be disappointed if he wins.'

Full of anticipation, Lizzie waited for the race to start. She loved the lure of the lights and the smell of the place, all sweat and dogs and tobacco smoke. When the dogs burst out of the starting traps in their brightly coloured jackets and were round the course in a glorious flash, even she wasn't sure until the official announcement was made.

Flash of Gold was first! She'd won again, just as she'd known she would.

Ben was pleased for her. 'You have tremendous luck. I can't believe you've done it again.'

Lizzie laughed. 'I told you so.' She felt high on success; this was absolute bliss. She and Ben had a marvellously indulgent night of it.

Over the weekend the joy of that faded; as they walked up to Oakdene Farm on Monday evening, she felt anxious about their reception. Should she ignore the rift and the two weeks she'd stayed away? Should she ring the bell? Or use her key and walk in as usual? She did both, calling, 'Hello, Mum, we're here.'

There was no answer but Milly shot into her arms and

146

hugged her. That helped to dispel her unease and they were both led immediately to see Dido sitting amongst her six writhing pups. 'Look at her face,' Ben said. 'Doesn't she look the picture of proud motherhood?'

Milly said, 'Mr Coyne says they'll have to be trained in puppyhood if they are to be the best at racing.'

'They will,' Ben confirmed.

She was dragging him to see the old dairy. 'He thinks this—'

Lizzie stopped her. 'Mum doesn't know we're here, she'll want to know what Ben says about this, won't she?'

But Elsie had heard the doorbell ring and was bringing Father too. She looked a bit tearful and hugged her so fiercely that Lizzie felt she was being crushed. 'Lizzie, love, don't stay away like this again.'

Father was glaring at Ben, his expression warlike. 'Nothing upsets your mother and me more,' he said stiffly. 'Please don't estrange yourselves in future.'

Again it was Milly who eased the tension. 'Mr Coyne says we should get some heaters fixed up on the walls in here, and if we move all this stuff out we could use this room for Dido and her pups.'

'Yes.' Ben looked round. 'It would give you all the space you'd need.'

Milly said, 'I'll get Clover to help me take all this stuff over to the old stable next weekend. Ben, we want you to tell us what we'd need to do to this dairy to put the pups in here.'

'Mr Coyne has told you, the main thing is to get some heat in,' he said. 'It's warm enough in the laundry for the time being, and if you move the mangle and tub to the back of the room and take the garden furniture out you'd have enough space here for the first few weeks.'

'I'm a bit worried about that,' Elsie said. 'Gladys normally does the washing in there on Mondays, and when she saw the pups I thought she was about to refuse. I don't think she shares our pleasure in Dido.'

'Oh dear.' Ben hid his smile. 'Better make all speed on getting some heating in the dairy then.'

'Is there anything else we'd need to do to start training these pups for racing?' Elsie asked.

'Oh yes, quite a lot. I've seen Uncle Frank's set-up – let me think for a minute about what he does. Yes, the pups stay with their mother for about ten weeks until they're weaned, but it can take longer. Then he keeps them in what he calls his puppy playroom, they have their bed there, and they have to be toilet trained, so you'll need to provide a litter box for that. They have toys or something they can chew, and a bowl of water. You could fence an area off in the dairy for that. That's about it but I'll write to him and ask for full instructions in case I've forgotten something.'

'I'd be grateful if you would,' Father said through gritted teeth.

Later, over supper, Ben said, 'I remember he has a portable dog crate and every day he shuts them in that for a short time.'

'That doesn't sound very kind,' Milly said.

'It's to get them used to being shut in the starting trap. They use starting traps on all the courses to make sure all the dogs can get away at exactly the same moment. If you begin when they're young they get used to it, and they'll be no good at racing if they can't make a good start. The pups should be ready to race by fifteen to eighteen months and they love it.'

'And that's all we need to do?' Milly asked.

'Oh no, they'll need to be housed outdoors when they're older. You'll need to build a long fenced-in run outside in a field, where they can play, dig into the ground and run about. They'll have to have a shelter with lots of straw they can burrow in to keep warm. Later, you have to divide them, have three in one pen and three in another running parallel so they can see each other and run races up the dividing fence.'

Esmond's cup crashed onto his saucer. 'All these kennels and fencing will be expensive,' he said.

'It needn't be,' Ben told him. 'You could put roofing felt on a box to make a kennel, and a couple of rolls of chicken wire is all you'd need to make the runs. Of course you couldn't do it yourself,' he added hastily, 'but I know a reliable lad who would do it for you quite reasonably.'

'You see, we could do it, Esmond,' Elsie said.

'Possibly.' But he looked a little sour.

'You're changing your mind about having dogs,' Lizzie said. 'I wish you'd change your mind about giving me permission to get married.'

That brought her father's gaze down on her. 'Elizabeth, what you've done is very wrong. You're living openly with Ben, how do you think we feel about that? It really has upset your mother.'

'If you won't let me marry him, it's the next best thing,' she retorted.

'Don't start quarrelling about that again,' Milly said. 'Mum and I want to talk to Ben about these puppies.'

* * *

As they walked back to Ben's house Lizzie fumed, 'They're being unreasonable, I knew they would be.'

'There's only one way we can change that,' Ben said. 'We can carry on like this for another week or so, and then I could tell them you're pregnant. Ask them again to give you permission to marry. That would probably persuade them.'

Lizzie was thoughtful. 'It probably would, but it would be an out-and-out lie. You're very well organised on contraception, as well as everything else.'

'But they don't know that. Nobody spells that out, it's private. I want children but not yet, we aren't ready for them. We need our own house and a bigger business before we can afford a family and anyway we're too young to be pinned down by babies. I want us to have fun before we take on more responsibilities.'

Lizzie agreed with all that but said nothing.

'They're probably half expecting I'll get you pregnant. They think that's what living together is likely to lead to.'

'It would still be a lie.'

'They needn't ever know that. You can always tell them later that you were mistaken, that it was a false alarm.'

'But we'd know it was a deliberate lie,' Lizzie said. 'Mum was always strict about us being honest and truthful, and I've always tried to be.'

CHAPTER SEVENTEEN

THE WEEKS WERE PASSING, and Milly knew all was not well in her family. She could feel the tension between her parents when they were only three at meals, and it felt so much worse every Monday evening when Lizzie and Ben came. She knew Lizzie passionately wanted to be married and that she blamed Dadda for withholding permission. She'd said, 'He thinks Ben isn't a good enough husband for me and I could do better. But I love him and he loves me.'

Milly had told her father about following Lizzie home from the shop, and now he forbade her to go to see Lizzie at the shop. Milly had dissolved in tears at that; Lizzie was not only her sister but the friend she loved most. She got round that by going to see Ben; it hadn't occurred to Dadda that she'd do that. He would send somebody round to ask Lizzie to come and join them, and give her free rides on his roundabout while she waited.

'Mum is afraid you'll catch my wild ways and in another year or two follow my bad example,' she said.

'I won't,' Milly said.

'And Father would be furious if he knew you were coming to the fair to meet me. He'd see that as worse than coming to my house.'

'Mum is upset about you, I know, but we spend more and more time with Dido and the puppies. They're absolutely gorgeous now, very playful. Clover and Kathleen come to play with them every day because Laurie says it's good for them to get used to being with people. Oh, and we have the first pens ready in the field. I took Dido to see them and when it gets a little warmer the puppies will be going out. Mum is still talking about getting more dogs and setting up a puppy farm.'

'She'll never persuade Father.'

'I think she might. He'll do things for Mum that he won't for anyone else.'

Monday evening came round again, and as usual Ben and Lizzie went to have supper with her parents. They said little throughout and looked miserable. Fortunately Milly couldn't stop talking about the puppies and now the lighter evenings were here she took them outside to play with them. Otherwise it would have been a ghastly visit.

'I'm fed up with going there,' Lizzie told Ben later when they were home. 'They ask us to go, to stay in touch, but it's getting us nowhere.'

'It's now a question of deciding whether to wait until this time next year, or I tell them you're expecting and we could plan a wedding in May or June followed by a summer honeymoon.'

'I thought you couldn't leave your business in the summer?'

'Shouldn't really, but before the school holidays start, perhaps for a few days. Where would you like to go?'

'Well, not another holiday place.'

'What about London?'

'Marvellous.'

'Shall I go and tell them now that you're in the family way? Get things started? Do you want to come with me?'

'That's the last thing I want,' she said. 'You'll be more convincing on your own.'

It was Tuesday evening and Elsie had felt low all day; she'd sensed over supper last night that Ben and Lizzie had been more on edge than usual. It had been an unsatisfactory visit, but she didn't know what to do about it.

They'd just finished eating supper when the doorbell rang. Elsie was crossing the hall with the used plates in her hand and went to open it. When she saw Ben was alone the cutlery slid noisily to the floor and she only just saved the plates. 'Is Lizzie not with you?'

'Not this time. I'd like a quick word with you and the major.'

Her heart seemed to turn over; this could only mean trouble. The crash had brought Milly shooting out of the kitchen. She helped Ben pick the cutlery up and asked, 'Has something happened? You were here only last night.'

Elsie pushed the plates onto Milly. 'Come to the sitting room, Ben, will you?' She could feel her heart thumping as she led the way.

Esmond looked up from his newspaper. 'Ben, you've come alone? Come and sit down.'

'I won't, thank you, Major. 'I just want to—' The door opened and Milly pushed in behind him.

'Milly, please . . .' Elsie collapsed on an armchair with tears burning her eyes.

'Emilia, dear, would you please leave us?' Elsie heard the door click behind her.

Ben said, 'I've come to ask you to reconsider giving Lizzie permission to marry me. We are embarrassed to have to tell you she is with child.'

'Good God!' Esmond lost his temper. 'This is what happens when you take the privileges of marriage without the responsibility. I could have told you it would, but any decent man would understand that. You said you would never hurt Elizabeth but now, even you must understand that you have.'

Elsie was weeping openly.

'I do, sir, but will you please give her this permission so I can rectify things?'

'I can't say it's unexpected and of course it alters everything.'

'No,' Elsie shouted. 'No, never. Lizzie may think this is harsh now, but it could save her from far worse. Tell her no. She needs time to think this through. I will never change my mind about this.'

Elsie was struggling to hold back her tears and was glad to see Ben go.

'All I ever wanted for my girls was a better life than I've had,' she said, 'but now Lizzie is making exactly the same mistake I did.'

Esmond came to give her a hug. 'Well, perhaps we should reconsider . . .'

She collapsed against his shoulder in a fury of tears. 'No,' she wailed. 'I'm afraid for her. Isn't this part of my history? Marriage could be her worst option. With hindsight, marrying Jasper brought problem after problem and they grew worse over the years. I'd have been far better bringing up Lizzie on my own. I had a home with my mother and a means of supporting us all. By marrying him I lost everything. It was the worst mistake I ever made.'

'Elsie, my dear, Ben is not an alcoholic and he's not without common sense. What happened to you will not necessarily happen to Lizzie.'

'I don't trust Ben. I don't know why but I don't. There's something about him . . . You don't like him either, I know.'

'I don't like what he does or where he lives.'

'Though you won't go and see his home, so you don't really know . . .'

'Have you been there?'

Elsie mopped at her eyes. 'I went one day to look at the outside.'

'And did you like what you saw?'

'It was a simple terraced cottage. Lizzie asked me to come down and see round it, she said I'd like it, that Ben had set it up beautifully. But I didn't go in.' She burst into another torrent of tears.

'Elsie, I'm afraid Elizabeth is going to cut us off if we refuse to let her marry him. You need to think quietly about this on your own.'

'You think we should let her do it? Sign that form for her?'

'It can often be a lesser evil than having a child while un-married. The shame of that reflects on the whole family, on Milly. Think carefully, lots of girls marry before they're twenty-one.'

Elsie couldn't stop her tears. It would reflect on Esmond's position in the council too – clearly he didn't want that.

'I'm going to take you upstairs, and I want you to get into bed even though it's early. This has been a shock to us both and we need to think about the consequences now. I'll ask Emilia to make you some cocoa and bring it up to you.'

Elsie washed her face. Esmond was right; she would be better on her own with time to think about it. Milly came and went. What a bad example Lizzie was for her, but how could she blame her? She'd been a terrible example to both of them. It was as much her fault as Lizzie's.

She was glad to get into bed, but what must poor Lizzie be going through now? Elsie would never forget the paralysing shock when she'd realised she was pregnant. She'd been distraught and unable to tell her mother, who was a devout churchgoer and found comfort there. But the church expressly forbade what she had done. Elsie had said nothing to anybody, and just hoped she was making a mistake, though each passing week confirmed that she was not. That had been the most agonising two months in her life.

She'd broken down and told Jasper first, half dreading he'd walk away and she'd never see him again, but he'd said, 'We'd better get married, hadn't we? Why not?'

At the time that had come as a blessed relief; it was what she'd hoped he'd say. For her, at that moment, there was no other way round her problem, though she'd known even then that her love for him was on the wane. It was Jasper's support she'd craved.

Lizzie would be in that same dreadful state now.

Lizzie was waiting eagerly for Ben to return. 'It hasn't worked,' he told her. 'They were shocked and your father was angry.'

'He would be,' she fumed. 'And Mum? Of course she goes along with everything he wants.'

'No, Elsie was in tears, but she's the one refusing permission. I think he was on the point of changing his mind and saying yes.'

'Oh heavens, are you sure? I was certain it was Father's idea. He refuses to let me and Milly do anything we want.'

'No, it's definitely your mother this time, Lizzie.'

'Oh, surely not. I could always persuade her to give me what I wanted. We must really have upset her then. I thought she quite liked you and your talk about dogs. Why doesn't Mum want me to marry you? Oh lord, what am I going to do now?'

Elsie slept little and agonised in her long periods of wakefulness. She should never have gone against her mother's ruling and risked having a baby before they were married. Despite all the trouble that had brought her, she'd done exactly the same thing with Esmond.

With Jasper, at least she could say she'd been very young and at the time she'd loved him too well. With Esmond she should have had more sense.

He hadn't rushed her into it; he'd told her he loved her and suggested marriage. She'd deliberated long and hard about what she felt for him, and knew it wasn't love. He'd been kind and generous and had removed the spectre of poverty from her door. Marriage to him would banish that for ever, and her children would not lack the basics of comfort.

It was gratitude she'd felt for him, and that had made her unable to refuse him when his love-making went too far. She hadn't wanted to say no, couldn't say no, she'd been scared that might put her out of the job and therefore her home too. So she'd found herself in the same position as before, pregnant with no husband and with the responsibility of looking after Milly as well as Lizzie.

Now Lizzie had grown up, she was telling her she waited on Esmond hand and foot and anyone could see she'd been his housekeeper, though he didn't treat her as such. It was habit developed over the years that made her give in to his every wish, and made her feel inferior when she met the wives of his colleagues on the council.

Once she'd realised she was pregnant she'd told him. She knew him well enough to know what he'd say. 'A bit of a shock, I have to say.' But he'd smiled. 'You know I love you and I've proposed marriage. Perhaps this will persuade you to agree.'

It did and she told herself she liked him well enough, and hoped that in time she'd learn to love him. She'd had to school herself not to flinch at the sight of his amputated arm and the terrible scars on the left side of his body. A bullet had grazed his lung and a piece of shrapnel had been removed from the flesh round his hip. He'd kept that as a souvenir and proudly showed it to her. He said he was lucky to be alive when so many had died of their wounds. Esmond was a war hero – she had to admire his gallantry and the sacrifices he'd made for the country.

With hindsight, Elsie thought she'd made another mistake. Anyone could make one mistake but to make it over again, she had to be a complete idiot. Marriage to Esmond had not changed her day-to-day life all that much, except now she was the lady of the house instead of the housekeeper. Common sense said she was better placed, but now she shared his bed and he wanted to make love to her once or twice every week.

She had to pretend to enjoy it, and if possible she had to make herself show enthusiasm. The truth was, she couldn't rid herself of the instinct to shrink from him. She couldn't bear the sight of the scars on his withered body and his amputated arm when it was devoid of its false extension and its inert leather glove. Every night he took that off and laid it on a chair with his clothes – his prosthesis, he called it.

Esmond deserved a loving wife, and there was a great deal to love in him, but she just couldn't. He must never guess she'd married him for the comfortable life he could provide for her and Lizzie. Now there was Milly to think of too, so she had to keep him believing she loved him. It would make him feel absolutely awful if he knew the truth. This was something she had to hide from everybody if she was to hold her family together, but now holding on to Lizzie was proving difficult.

She slept late the next morning. Gladys brought up a breakfast tray to her room. 'The major's had his egg and bacon and has taken Dido out for a walk,' she reported, 'and Milly's gone to school.'

Elsie had deliberated half the night and decided she must pull herself together and put Jasper Harding out of her mind. She got up and walked down the lane to meet Esmond and Dido. She knew that later he'd be going to a council meeting, and once he'd gone she changed her dress and took the bus into town to arrive at the shop where Lizzie worked shortly after twelve o'clock.

She saw her immediately as she went in, tidying dresses on

159

a rail. 'Come to the café round the corner,' she said, 'and have a sandwich for lunch. We've got to talk.'

'Mum, are you ill?'

Elsie knew she looked heavy-eyed and exhausted. 'I didn't sleep too well last night,' she said. 'Ask if you can come now.'

Mrs Field, the owner of the shop said, 'Yes, we aren't busy, you go now, Lizzie, and you don't need to rush back.'

'Lizzie is very willing,' she told Elsie, 'and good with the customers. She's got good fashion sense too.'

Once outside, Lizzie took her arm and said, 'Mum, I feel dreadful about this. Come home with me, I usually go home for lunch. We've got soup; it won't take a moment to heat it up.'

'Will Ben be there?'

'Yes, he comes home for lunch.'

'I'd like us to be alone.'

'Right, we'll go to the fair first, and I'll ask him not to come home. He'd worry if I went to a café with you without saying anything. Here we are: this is his roundabout, but that's Duggie Bennett in charge.'

'You'll find Ben at the shooting range, Lizzie,' he called, and lots of other people greeted her. It seemed everyone knew her here.

'He seems to be doing a reasonable amount of business,' Elsie said, 'although it's a cold day.'

'That's because his sideshows are in the covered part, but he's not very busy. Wait till summer comes, the fair is quite different then.'

Ben was setting out prizes on the shelves of his rifle range. 'I'm impressed with all this,' Elsie told him and had to decline his offer of a gun to try her skill.

'I'm glad you've come to talk to Lizzie, it'll set her mind at rest,' he said. 'Don't worry about me. I'll get myself some chips today.'

'Our house is only three or four minutes' walk from here,' Lizzie said. As they turned the corner into Alvaston Terrace it stood out; it was the only one that had been recently painted. She could understand Esmond not liking this district, but she and Jasper had lived in worse.

To Elsie it felt cosy and welcoming as she went in. It was spotlessly clean, though she hadn't been expected, and a fire had been laid ready in the grate. 'We usually light it when we come home in the evening, but as you're here I'll put a match to it now.'

'No, love, you'll have to go back to work.'

'Are you sure? We'll have this then.' She brought out a new electric fire, and she had the latest electric cooker in the kitchen too. Elsie was surprised and pleased. Her home with Jasper had never been anything like this; she'd had no energy to keep it tidy and no money to replace anything, not in all the years they'd been together. This cottage was small but it was lighter and fresher and smarter than she could ever have imagined. Really it was much smarter than Oakdene Farm.

Had she misjudged Ben? Lizzie seemed happy with him, and if she were to be honest, he was nothing like Jasper. Ben was organised and running his own business.

Lizzie did not ask her again for permission to marry, but before she left, Elsie said, 'I want you to know that I was expecting you before I married your father, and I would have been wiser not to.'

'Mum!' Lizzie was shocked at that. 'You seem to have a life without upsets and worries.'

'At that time I had plenty of both. I legally attached myself to a man who brought me nothing but poverty and one problem after another. I should have known that Ben is nothing like Jasper. I'll give you permission to marry him. You have my blessing.'

'Mum! Oh, that's wonderful.' She felt her daughter's arms come round her in another hug. 'Thank you.'

'Lizzie, love, nothing must come between you and me. I couldn't stand us being estranged.'

CHAPTER EIGHTEEN

LIZZIE'S CONSCIENCE TROUBLED HER all afternoon. She was ashamed of living in sin. She'd told nobody about that at the shop, as nice girls just didn't do that, and she'd let Ben tell Mum a deliberate lie to trick her into giving her permission. She'd reduced her to a nervous wreck. Mum deserved better.

Ben said when she told him, 'It had the right effect, though, didn't it?'

A week later, when they went to supper on Monday evening, Lizzie had to take her mother aside to whisper that she'd made a mistake about expecting a baby. It made her feel awful to tell yet another deliberate lie. 'I'm fine, Mum, sorry I caused you worry. We both very much want to get married and I hope we still have your permission.'

Her mother looked taken aback, a little shocked even. Did Mum suspect it had all been a ruse? She was almost overcome with embarrassment.

Silently Elsie nodded and squeezed her hand. 'You'd better let your father know. It worried him that you were to become an unmarried mother. He was afraid you'd have a hard life as a result.'

Lizzie closed her eyes in relief. To tell Father was even more embarrassing but she managed to get the words out at the table. She saw Ben cast his eyes to the ceiling but her parents accepted it and it had got them what they wanted.

Ben thanked them and said, 'We're going to arrange our wedding just as soon as we can. This year Easter falls on April the seventeenth, and the fair will be busy by then and throughout the summer. I want us to be settled before that happens.'

'Can I be your bridesmaid?' Milly piped up.

'It isn't going to be that sort of a wedding,' Lizzie said. 'We thought in the registry office.'

'Oh, Lizzie no,' Esmond said. 'In church please.'

Not to cause any further strife, Lizzie and Ben immediately agreed to a church wedding. 'We want it to be quiet, without fuss, no white gown with veil, no choir, in fact no music, and on a weekday morning very soon,' Lizzie said. 'That's the way we want it to be, and if you want to be my bridesmaid, Milly, then I'd love to have you with me.'

'Of course I want to. It'll be your wedding. I don't care that there'll be no fuss.'

'Easier to arrange that way,' her mother said. 'We'll have the wedding breakfast here.'

'There won't be many guests,' Ben told her, 'perhaps just my father and uncle.'

'I'm glad you don't feel you need to invite a lot of friends from the fair,' Esmond said.

When they'd gone home and Milly had gone to bed, Esmond poured himself a nightcap of whisky and sat down on the opposite side of the dying fire. He said to Elsie, 'Do you think they were telling the truth, that Elizabeth really believed she was pregnant?'

'Don't you?'

'It got them what they wanted. I wouldn't put it past Ben to organise that.'

'Lizzie would never tell a deliberate lie. As I brought the girls up I emphasised that they must always tell the truth. After being married to Jasper I didn't want them to grow up like him. I've always found Lizzie to be truthful.'

With mounting excitement that at last she was allowed to marry, Lizzie bought herself a blue dress and a matching hat. Milly was in paroxysms of delight when Lizzie invited her to come to the shop to choose her bridesmaid dress. Together they chose a dress of a different design but of a very similar shade.

It was decided that Monday the eleventh of April would be their wedding day, and that they'd have a short honeymoon in London and be home by the Easter weekend, which was always Ben's busiest time.

When the day came, Lizzie was thrilled and excited and found Ben equally so. There was no question of wedding nerves, how could there be when they were getting ready in their own bedroom? Ben had bought a new suit and she'd gone with him to choose one that was not too formal.

As Lizzie walked down the aisle on Father's arm, Mum smiled at her as they passed her but there were tears in her eyes too. She couldn't understand why they were so suspicious of Ben. He turned to give her a half-smile as she reached his side; she could see love for her in his eyes and she knew he was dependable and absolutely rock solid.

The church was almost full with the people from the fairground. His best man was Steve Docherty, who ran his rifle range for him. Milly was in a dreamy state and almost dropped the bouquet of spring flowers when Lizzie handed it to her, but Lizzie had no doubt that marriage to Ben was right for her.

Not many came to the reception afterwards. Ben's father came, but his best man had to return to the rifle range. There were two girls Lizzie worked with and one friend from school. Esmond had invited some of the neighbours, and Milly said she was disappointed that Laurie Coyne had said he wouldn't be able to come, but his mother did. His father came to the ceremony but went back to work afterwards. All Lizzie wanted to do by then was to get away, and the taxi arrived to take them to the station before too long.

Ben believed in enjoying himself and they had a marvellous time in London. They ate at the best restaurants and went to two theatre shows, but most of all they enjoyed the evening they went to the dog track at Walthamstow. Lizzie felt intoxicated each time she'd put her bet on the winning dog. Ben knew some complicated system of betting on several dogs at once, and that bet came up too. They'd never had a more thrilling time.

On the strength of that, Ben said, 'Let's go to Cheltenham tomorrow and try our luck on the horses. It's on the way home, after all.'

Once there, they had difficulty finding a bed for the night but at the racecourse they were both in great form. 'Your lucky star is truly shining on you at the moment,' he told her, and she suggested betting larger and larger sums.

'You're risking your winnings from the dogs,' he warned. 'Are you sure?'

'I feel lucky,' she laughed, 'and isn't it thrilling?'

'It will be if you win again. Come on, let's do it then.'

Lizzie enjoyed the horses more than the dogs, because their races took longer and she had time to see how they performed. She lost on two races, but Ben's horse won one of them. When they totted up their winnings they were both ecstatic to find they had won more than they'd spent on travel, hotels and entertainment during their honeymoon. 'Everything for us is turning out right,' she laughed again. 'I count this as the best week of my life.'

'So do I.' He hugged her. 'Your eyes are like dancing stars. The future is set fair for us.'

Elsie invited the newly-weds to supper on the first Monday after their return from honeymoon. 'We'll want you to come every Monday just the same,' she told Lizzie, and seeing her and Ben together they certainly seemed happy. Lizzie was fizzing with high spirits and as usual had plenty to say about the latest shows they'd seen, the restaurant meals they'd enjoyed and the lovely hotels they'd stayed at.

'I hope you aren't spending more on enjoying yourselves than you can afford,' Esmond said dourly.

'No,' Lizzie smiled broadly, 'Ben has great plans.'

'A husband has obligations to his wife,' Esmond went on. 'You do realise, Ben, that marriage means you need to make a new will?'

'A new one?' he laughed. 'I haven't ever made one.'

'Then now you I suggest you do. A married man has responsibilities and you should take them seriously. You should see your solicitor next week. You do have a solicitor?'

'Yes, I've used one to buy a business . . .'

Lizzie pulled a face. 'Father, surely there's no hurry for things like that?'

'I think there is. If war comes, and there are plenty of rumours that it will, then none of us knows what will happen.'

'I'll make a will, sir,' Ben said. 'I mean to take care of Lizzie.'

'I can take care of myself,' Lizzie said. 'I enjoy my job but I'd love to have my own dress shop. I've started saving my wages for it.'

'You've been saying that for a long time,' Milly said.

Ben smiled fondly at his new wife. 'I have my ambitions too,' he said. 'The current owner of the caterpillar ride wants to retire, so I've decided to buy it. I shall keep on his assistant to run it and as it's not far from my roundabout it won't be difficult for me to keep an eye on it.'

'I'm impressed,' Esmond said when they'd gone home. 'Ben seems to have a good business sense. He knows how to earn his living. Elizabeth might be all right with him after all.'

Elsie and Milly were enjoying looking after Dido and her pups and when they were nine months old, Ben contacted the trainer whose premises they'd visited with his uncle. He came to Oakdene Farm to see them. 'Top class, all of them. Do you want to sell?' he asked Esmond. 'Or do you want me to act as your agent? Either way I will continue their training and eventually race them at Belle Vue.'

Ben had explained how his uncle handed over his pups to be trained by this man who charged nothing but took 50 per cent of their winnings when they raced.

'Sell,' Esmond said, and was offered a sum that surprised and delighted him.

A LUCKY SIXPENCE

Elsie wanted more bitches to bring her dream of breeding puppies closer, and Esmond finally agreed that some of the money from the sale of the puppies could be spent that way. So on their behalf Ben contacted the dealer from whom they'd bought Dido and took them to see his stock. He helped them choose two with the right breeding and right racing histories.

The first, Miss Muffet, was five years old. In 1937 she'd won the Golden Collar in record time and had been a star at Belle Vue ever since. Liverpool Lady was six months younger, and at home she answered to the name of Wuffie. Both were brown brindle and each had a very sweet nature.

'These two will be ideal to breed from,' Ben told them, 'and you already know that agents are keen to buy your puppies and train them for racing.'

Elsie was thrilled. She knew where to go for advice when she needed it and felt things had never been so good for her.

CHAPTER NINETEEN

I T WAS NEW YEAR 1939 and Milly was in her father's study. 'I'm afraid war is getting closer,' he said. 'I'm going to buy another wireless for your mother so she can hear the news bulletins in the kitchen.'

Milly had noticed that her parents were watching what Hitler was doing and were increasingly concerned. 'Hitler now has absolute power in Germany and he is seeking to expand his frontiers. He's unified Germany with Austria and he's building up his fighting forces. It looks very much as though he's preparing for war.'

Milly knew Dadda was worried but for her everything seemed to be going along as usual. Her mother was happily caring for her dogs. In the first months of the year Miss Muffet had seven puppies and Wuffie had five. In March, she was thrilled to hear that her mother had become a licensed breeder of greyhounds.

The months were rolling on. Lizzie found Ben was as good as his word; he took her out and about to enjoy the attractions of New Brighton, and she felt she was having a great time. She wanting to go to Belle Vue every week and kept asking him to take her. It was what she enjoyed most, but Ben was losing his enthusiasm for it.

'Lady Luck has deserted you,' he told her when for a second time her betting lost them money.

'Next time we go, I'll win it all back,' she laughed. 'You know I will.'

A few weeks later at a race meeting, she lost on the first two races but redeemed her fortunes by winning on the big race of the evening; between them they'd ended up with a little profit. On the train going home, Ben said, 'It bothers me that you're so keen on betting.'

Lizzie laughed. 'Why shouldn't I be? I can win money that way and I like it much better than working for it. You do too, admit it now.'

'Of course I do, but a business is a more reliable way of earning money. Even you don't always get it right.'

'Most of the time I do,' she laughed again, 'and it gives me a real thrill, a buzz that I don't get doing anything else.'

But their pleasures were pushed from their minds because the talk of a coming war had become more pressing. Those who'd lived through the last war admitted to being frightened, and everybody hoped that Hitler would be appeased. One day in April, Ben and Lizzie were eating a sandwich at lunch time and listening to the one o'clock news on their wireless, when they heard that conscription into military service for unmarried men aged twenty and twenty-one would start immediately.

'Oh my God!' Ben exclaimed. 'Conscription, how could I possibly cope with that?'

'You're twenty-four,' Lizzie said, 'it doesn't apply to you. Not yet anyway.'

'But call-up will be by age for all men between eighteen and forty-one, they've just said so. It won't take long for my turn to come.'

There were a lot more details about Britain needing a bigger army if war should come, and a list of essential tradesmen who would never be called up, 'But fairground operator is never likely to be on that list,' Lizzie said.

Ben was shocked. He'd made his life plan and it was working out well. All he'd have to do was carry on in the same way, and the large comfortable house with sufficient income to provide a clothes shop for Lizzie, holidays, a car and the family they both wanted would be his. He'd heard little mention of conscription, and forgotten that it might come and prevent him staying here to look after his business. He was worried now. He couldn't possibly leave New Brighton.

'Lizzie,' he said, 'if I have to join the army, could you take over my business? I could show you how. Teach you all you'd need to know while we still have time.'

'No.' He could see the idea terrified her. 'Not the rifle range, I know nothing about guns.'

'Steve might not be called up. I can't remember how old he is, but he must be more than forty. He'll manage the rifle range and help you. He's a good sort. You could manage the roundabout and the caterpillar ride, collect the fares?'

'No, Ben, I couldn't possibly.'

'It's not hard, you know where I bank the money, we've done that together, haven't we?'

'No, Ben, I couldn't work in the arcade. I know nothing about what you do.'

He didn't talk about it again to Lizzie; the last thing he

wanted to do was frighten her. But he was not the only man
working in the Palace Amusement Centre, the boating lake,
the cafés and the gardens surrounding it, who was worried.
Those most worried owned and operated the rides and
sideshows.

There was no let-up after that. The coming war seemed to
press on everything. Milly went to her father's study to find out
more; he'd always encouraged her to come and talk and she
often did. 'Identity cards are going to be issued to everyone and
plans are being made to evacuate the children from Merseyside.'

'Does that include New Brighton?' Milly wanted to know.

'Yes,' Dadda said.

'Will I be going?'

'We haven't decided yet, I'll have to talk that over again
with your mother.'

'Where would they send us? It sounds a great adventure,
but I don't want to leave Dido and the other dogs. And you
too, Dadda, of course, I don't want to leave you.'

At school, Milly found they were digging air-raid shelters at
the far end of the playing field, and gas masks were being
issued. They received theirs the following week and they
practised putting them on in class. They were horribly tight
and stank of rubber.

A leaflet was delivered instructing all householders on the
possible need for a blackout and how it could be achieved. The
windows in the sitting and dining rooms at Oakdene Farm
were sash windows that went from floor to ceiling in a style of
bygone days, and they were already fitted with wooden shutters.
Before they went to bed one night, Dadda closed them and

switched all the lights on. Then they all trooped outside to look and found that there were plenty of cracks that let through slivers of light. Many shops were stocking dense blackout material, so Elsie measured up and started to sew.

Once completed, Milly and Dadda were helping her to hang them when Elsie said, 'What if we're invaded?'

'We won't be,' Dadda said confidently. 'We control a huge empire and we haven't been invaded since William the Conqueror. Hitler isn't strong enough.'

'But there will be terrible food shortages.' Elsie had been about Milly's age when the Great War had started. 'I remember them, though I didn't go hungry because of our shop. When our supplies ran out our customers begged and pleaded for food which we couldn't give them.' She started stocking up with tinned and dried foods and advised Lizzie to do the same.

More fearsome than anything else, the public were advised to provide themselves with a personal air-raid shelter if they could, and Anderson shelters were being designed for use in back gardens. Otherwise they could use underground railway stations as public shelters and more were being dug in all towns and cities.

'What do you think we should do about a shelter?' Elsie wanted to know.

'I think I'd better buy one of those Anderson shelters,' Dadda said. 'In the absence of a cellar they sound the best bet.'

When it had been delivered, Ben brought up Jimmy Cox, who was always looking for extra work to increase his income, and together they dug out the hole for it, put it together and covered the top with grass sods. Elsie bought sleeping bags and a hurricane lamp to fit it out.

'It looks as though war really will come,' Milly said. 'Am I going to be evacuated? Nobody much from my class seems to be going.'

'No,' Dadda said, 'not now. Your mother has decided she couldn't bear to send you away. We'll have to see. We might have to think again about it.'

Summer came, bringing warmer days and lighter evenings. Milly sympathised with Laurie because he was working hard for his exams. 'I could take Mutt out for his walk if it would give you more time,' she offered. 'After I've walked Dido.' She knew she wasn't thought strong enough to control two dogs at once.

'No, Milly,' he smiled, 'you've got Miss Muffet and Wuffie to walk too.'

'Mum mostly does them.'

'No, it gives me a break to come out with you and the dogs. I need that – besides, I enjoy it.'

'Good,' Milly said; she felt she was getting somewhere with Laurie at long last. 'I enjoy it too.'

For Milly the long-awaited summer holidays came, and Lizzie took her to the cinema as Dadda allowed late nights when there was no school. She was late getting up on the first morning and as she came down she pulled the Wallasey *Gazette* from their letter box. It was delivered every week as the editor John Thornley was a friend of Dadda's. They shared a passion for chess, met to have practice games and in the past had entered national competitions.

The house was quiet. Mum was busy sewing blackout material, so Milly took the packet of cornflakes from the cupboard, sat at the kitchen table, and started to read while she ate.

'Gosh, Gladys,' she said, 'listen to this. "A new traffic round-about was being constructed on New Brighton Promenade and workmen discovered some unmapped caves. The owner of the land is having them dug out and is said to be constructing blastproof rooms in the caves so that a munitions factory can be set up in them."'

'I've heard about that before.' Gladys was preparing salad at the sink for their lunch.

Esmond came in with Dido at that moment; he'd taken her out for her walk. Gladys hastened to wipe her paws.

'Dadda . . .' Milly told him about the unmapped caves and continued reading the newspaper report.

'I wouldn't fancy working underground every day,' Gladys said, 'but our Clover says she wouldn't mind because she's heard they pay well and it would be safe from any bombs, wouldn't it?' They'd all heard that munitions factories were being set up everywhere and were working hard to stockpile for a war. Clover had left school and was working in a café on the seafront.

'There's a huge network of caves and tunnels and cellars under Wallasey and New Brighton,' Dadda said. 'I've told you about the reputation we had for smuggling and wrecking, and because of that the exact location of these caves was kept secret.'

'Our Clover fancies a job there,' Gladys said.

Milly said, 'I thought Clover liked her job?'

'She does, but it's a summer job. She'll have to find something else in the winter,' Gladys said. 'She says it'll be warm in a cave, and if there is a war she wants to do all she can to help win it.'

'I could do that too,' Milly said. 'I'd like to do something positive to help win the war if it comes.'

Dadda said, 'You need a career for life, Emilia, not just for a war that might or might not come. You must take the long-term view. Think of what you'd be good at and what you'd enjoy doing.'

'Well . . . I think I could write things like this.' Milly waved the Wallasey *Gazette* at him. 'I wouldn't mind being a reporter.'

'A journalist,' Esmond said. 'Are you serious?'

'Yes, I've been thinking about a career. I really would like to be a journalist.'

Dadda looked thoughtful. 'Your school reports say you are good at essay writing and English.'

'Yes, it's something I could do right away.'

'No, it isn't, I'll have a word with John Thornley. See what he suggests. I'll see him on Saturday.'

'That would be wonderful,' Milly said. 'Ask him if he would take me on as an apprentice. That way I could learn on the job.'

'Perhaps he wouldn't want you,' Gladys said.

Milly waited up to talk to Dadda when he came home on Saturday night, though he'd warned her he'd be late. 'What did Mr Thornley say?'

'He said you'd need to stay on at school and pass your exams, and you'd certainly have to learn shorthand and typing first. And if you do that, and he has a vacancy at the time, he might think of taking you on.'

'That's going to take years,' Milly complained.

CHAPTER TWENTY

LIZZIE WAS GETTING BUTTERFLIES in her stomach at the thought of Ben being called up. The future was beginning to look ominous. All these preparations, and everybody coming into the shop aired their fears about a coming war. At the same time, Ben was no longer seeking pleasure or keen on taking her out. There were no more extravagant restaurant meals or trips to the theatre. 'I'm worried about having to leave my business,' he said.

'I thought you'd decided Steve could keep an eye on everything for you as well as run the shooting gallery.'

'He's told me he'll be forty next month, so the time might come when he is called up too.'

'Well, no point in making us all miserable about it,' she told him more sharply than usual. If she said she wanted to go out, he'd take her to the Anchor Inn for a quick drink, but she didn't like the place and the only topic of conversation there was the coming war.

She suggested another trip to the dog races, but he said, 'No, Lizzie, it means a very late night on Friday and then I'm shattered all the weekend, and you're far too intense about it. I think we should give it a miss for a while.' Lizzie had really missed not being able to have a flutter. The rumours about a coming war were ruining everything.

One day, she'd been to see Ben and was walking home through the fairground alone when she met Jimmy Cox. He always treated her like a close friend. 'Is your father pleased with the Anderson shelter I helped to build?' he asked.

'Yes, though he hopes we'll never have need of it.'

'Racing at Epsom this week, Mrs McCluskey,' he said to remind her of another line by which he added to his income. 'Are you game?'

Lizzie hesitated, but why not? It would really cheer her up, and if Ben no longer wanted any fun it would be one in the eye for him to see she could place the occasional bet without his help. She said slowly, 'I might be if I had a race card.'

'Come to the boat house.' He smiled. It had a window where he sold tickets for boat hire. Jimmy kept the race cards under the desk.

'I'll need a newspaper, a racing paper.'

She saw him feeling for his own and then changing his mind. 'You'll have to buy your own,' he told her with a cheeky grin. 'Any bet you make with me must be written down with the date and time of the race. And I must have your stake money in advance.'

Lizzie walked home via the newsagent and bought a racing paper. After studying the runners she gave Ben's sideshows a wide berth and went to the boating lake to give her bet to Jimmy Cox.

That gave her such a thrill, she felt on top of the world for the rest of the day. She didn't tell Ben.

The following afternoon she rushed home from work and switched on the wireless to find her horse had won. When Ben came home she told him and was so full of joy she could hardly get the words out. 'How much will the prize money be?' she asked him.

'That depends on your stake.' When Lizzie told him, he was shocked. 'Goodness, Lizzie, that's more than I'd ever risk – a whole week's wages for you.'

'Yes, but I've won.' When she'd dished up their dinner she almost danced their plates to the table.

'Let's go to the pictures.' Ben seemed to have cheered too. 'There's a film called *Test Pilot* on at the Regal. Everybody in the arcade is saying it's good.'

Lizzie went, though it meant she wouldn't be able to see Jimmy Cox that night.

She went home from work the following day to find Ben was already there and had put a pile of banknotes on the table. 'Jimmy Cox gave me your winnings,' he said.

It was the equivalent of two months' wages. 'Marvellous, isn't it?' She was exultant.

'Yes, but please stop while you're ahead. You don't always win. You're overdoing it and staking far too much. It bothers me.'

'Milly doesn't call me Lucky Lizzie for nothing,' she laughed.

That confirmed to Lizzie that Ben wasn't nearly so much fun as he used to be, a bit of a spoilsport really. She loved having extra money, and betting was such a lovely way to get it. She treated herself to a new outfit and bought Milly a new dress and hat, and then added a pair of new sandals. It was great to be able to be generous in this way.

She didn't want to stop betting. She had her own wages which Ben wanted her to save towards buying her own shop, and there was a convenient post office in the newsagent on the corner where she bought her *Sporting Life* for racing information. She could make her transactions direct with Jimmy Cox with ease and Ben didn't have to know. In June and July she bet on horses running at Ascot and Newmarket and wished desperately that she could be there to watch them.

When it came to regular betting Ben thought pretty much as Father would – don't do it – and if she did dare, he thought she should risk only small amounts. Lizzie thought that pointless because when she did win there was little satisfaction because the winnings were small too. For Lizzie to get anything like the buzz she used to, the sums had to be big. Anyway, her bank balance was showing a profit. Why stop when she was winning much of the time?

Lizzie felt much better now she had a little hobby and she was able to amuse herself.

One Saturday morning, when all their dogs were waiting for their walks, Milly was in the kitchen and saw Laurie and Mutt coming down the lane. She ran out to say she wanted to walk Dido with him and asked him to wait a moment while she put Dido's harness on. Only then did she see he was not alone. His father and another girl were walking behind him. 'Hello, Milly,' he said. 'Of course we'll wait.'

'What about your other dogs?' Ivor Coyne asked. 'We can walk them all at once. We'll each take a dog.'

Laurie went in with her to help harness up Miss Muffet and Wuffie while the others patted and stroked Dido, who as usual was lifting her ears up on top of her head as though listening to them. When they brought the other dogs out it was to find Ivor

Coyne and the girl were laughing and making a real fuss of Dido.

Milly said, 'She recognises Laurie now. Nobody can resist Dido when she does that.'

Laurie was lifting the dogs' tails, to examine them. 'I have to be careful,' he said. 'Your parents won't be pleased if these bitches have another litter now, but none seem to be on heat.'

'They aren't,' Milly said indignantly. 'I'm keeping an eye on that and so is Dadda.'

'I'm glad to hear that,' his father said. 'Gina, this is Milly Travis, our neighbours' daughter and a keen dog owner.'

'Laurie has been very kind to us.' Milly smiled. 'He delivered Dido's pups for us, and I stayed up for most of the night to help him. He was marvellous.'

'Milly, this is Gina Flowers, Laurie's fiancée, they've just become engaged.'

'Pleased to meet you, Milly.' She smiled at her.

Milly's mouth dropped open; she was shocked. 'Just got engaged?' She didn't want to believe that; she knew Laurie went out occasionally and understood he sometimes took a girl, but he'd never mentioned having a special girlfriend. Gina was tall and slim with a sophisticated coat and hat, but she wasn't as beautiful as Lizzie, though her hair was pale yellow and Laurie liked blondes.

'Yes . . .' Laurie was smiling at everybody, 'we've made the big decision.'

'Though with all this talk of war it's difficult to say when we can be married.' The girl was not beautiful but she was good-looking, far too attractive.

Laurie said, 'We've come through vet school together. Like me, Gina's just passed her finals.'

'But I've got a job,' she said.

'At a small-animal practice like ours in Liverpool,' Ivor Coyne added.

Milly's mouth felt dry; she ought to say congratulations or something like that but the words stuck in her throat.

'We're both of us exhausted,' Gina went on. 'We're so relieved all those exams are over and we can enjoy ourselves without worrying about them any more.'

Laurie smiled at her. 'You're forgetting I shall be doing it all over again next summer,' he said. 'I've been accepted for a postgraduate course at Leahurst. So I'll be going there in September.'

When they started to walk again, Milly found she was behind the engaged couple and walking alongside Mr Coyne. She felt rejected by Laurie but the last thing she wanted was their pity – she had to make a huge effort to pull herself together.

'So will Laurie be a qualified vet like you now?'

'Yes, he is, but this postgraduate course will take him another year.'

'And then he'll be working with you at your practice?'

'No, that was the plan once, but now . . . I think he'll be called up pretty soon after he finishes his course.'

'Oh!' Laurie hadn't shared that with her either. She'd walked Dido with him and Mutt only last week. 'Will they need vets in the army? Well, they won't in the navy or the air force, will they? Are animals used much in the fighting forces these days?'

'Not as much as they were in my time, but they still have

some. In the last war I was sent to France,' Mr Coyne told her. 'There were horses on the front then, and so many got injured. It was dreadful to see them suffer, cruel. I'm glad we're more mechanised now.'

Milly couldn't take her eyes off Gina as she laughed over some private joke with Laurie. Her fawn and blue checked coat swung beautifully round her legs; Lizzie would love it.

As soon as they'd left her, Milly took the dogs out of their harnesses and ran up to her bedroom. This was the death knell to all her hopes. She'd thought Laurie was her special friend but he'd asked somebody else to marry him. Gina had taken Laurie from her. Milly was burning with resentment and disappointment. Tears prickled her eyes.

On 3 September Ben went to work as usual knowing that already the evacuation of children was under way. Summer Sundays were a busy time for him, but like everybody else in the country he'd been listening to every news bulletin on the wireless over the last week or so. When he heard that the Prime Minister would speak to the nation at eleven o'clock that day, he knew what he was about to announce.

So did Lizzie: she stopped cleaning up and sat down to listen. For months she'd been dreading what the Prime Minister would say, but it was what everybody was expecting. He told them the country was at war with Germany. Lizzie had barely taken that in when he went on to say that all theatres and places of entertainment must close immediately. Lizzie sank back in her chair in consternation.

All places of entertainment? Wouldn't that include the amusement arcade?

She was still sitting there when Ben came bursting through the door. 'The amusement arcade has had to close,' he said. 'I can't believe it. This will be ruinous for me. It took time to close the doors, nobody wanted it, though for once there weren't many customers.'

'Everybody was at home listening to the wireless,' Lizzie said.

'Yes, and I hear conscription rules have been tightened up. Now it's for all men married or unmarried between the ages of eighteen and forty-five. This is black Sunday. Everybody's in a panic, they're expecting bombs to start dropping and guns to start firing at us right now.'

Later, Ben went back to a hurriedly called meeting with his fellow sideshow owners in the fairground, and Lizzie went to see her family at Oakdene Farm. Milly was out playing with the dogs and her parents were sitting each side of the empty fire grate, clearly worried.

Father said, 'It's very frightening that war has been declared, but reason tells me that if Hitler's planes are busy dropping bombs on Poland, they won't be coming here today.'

'Then why close all places of entertainment?' Lizzie demanded. 'Ben's furious at the loss of business.'

'To keep us safe,' Elsie said.

'The government has panicked,' Father scoffed. 'Nothing can happen straight away; it takes time to draw up strategy and move an army, but Hitler will turn his attention to us soon enough.'

Elsie sighed. 'Can bombers come this far north? My mother told me they couldn't in the last war.'

'That was twenty years ago,' Lizzie said impatiently. 'They

probably can now, but this government has closed down the amusement arcade, dog racing, cinemas, horse racing, football and everything else that could attract a crowd.'

'Dog racing?'

'Yes, Father, that is entertainment, isn't it?'

'They can't close all entertainments. What are they thinking? What is Joe Public going to do if they can't go to a football match or the pictures?'

That didn't ease Lizzie's worries but Ben came home and said that the boating lake had not closed at all. Alec Hooper said rowing was not an entertainment, and the tea rooms had done a brisk trade all afternoon.

It had been a warm autumn day and the sky was full of barrage balloons which would stop enemy planes flying low. During the afternoon some of the outdoor roundabouts and sideshows opened up. Ben, together with some of those in the covered arcade, decided they would start up in the morning. It made no sense to close down on a fine weekend. After the bad news they'd had, surely it would do people good to spend the rest of the day at the seaside, enjoying all the fun of the fair?

By the end of the month almost all cinemas and theatres and places of entertainment were fully functional again, including the fairground.

The thought of conscription was haunting Ben and he'd been sounding out the other men in the Palace Amusement Arcade. Steve said he had the name of a man with a guaranteed heart problem who was willing to stand in for others at the army medical exam, so they would be officially classed as unfit for military service. It was of course illegal, and because of that expensive, but Ben thought it might be worthwhile. He was the youngest of the owners and expected to be the first one to receive his call-up papers. He knew they were all waiting to see what he would do.

He still didn't like going to the Monday night suppers he had to eat with Lizzie's family. He thought them stiff and formal. The major expected him to discuss things that were of interest to him, and under his gaze, Ben felt uncomfortable. He knew he had the major's full attention on him, and it made him anxious. He distrusted him and knew the feeling was mutual.

Milly's chatter usually helped to make it seem a more normal family meal. Tonight she said, 'The country may be at war but nothing seems to be happening. Certainly nothing in my life has changed. It's back to school for the autumn term. Mum and I went into Wallasey today to buy more school uniform.'

'You really must take more care of your belongings, Emilia. You've lost your school hat?'

'Sorry, Dadda, I have. My winter velour, but that was the end of last winter, so I know I'll never find it now. I needed the new tie and pullover, didn't I, Mum?'

Ben couldn't help liking Milly – she was so open about everything; he could understand how her mind worked.

'Ben . . .' she turned to him, 'what I was about to say, was Mum and I were coming home on the bus when we saw you coming out of that garage in Broadway. Are you going to buy a car or something? They have a lot for sale there.'

Ben couldn't swallow his mouthful of steak and kidney pie; he felt catapulted into a blue funk. 'No, Milly, no, nobody wants a car now because petrol has been immediately rationed; no, nothing as exciting as that.'

Her face was eager, expectant, as she waited for him to tell her why he'd been there.

'A friend asked me to call in there on his behalf when he knew I was going into Wallasey.'

Ben held his breath, waiting for her to ask why he'd gone into town in the first place. She didn't, thank goodness. He and his circle of friends could now see that war would bring new and different opportunities to earn money, and they often talked about it, but he did not wish to be associated with the proprietor of that garage, certainly not in the major's mind. Steve Docherty was engaged in some nefarious scheme with him, and Ben had delivered a big envelope on his behalf. He understood they had spent time together in jail.

Ben was only too aware the major was listening, and he was afraid his explanation sounded inadequate. He felt embarrassed yet again.

CHAPTER TWENTY-ONE

To MAJOR ESMOND TRAVIS the declaration of war was a call to him and all British men to do their duty. His main regret was that he couldn't return to active service. Instead he thought about what he could do and volunteered to be an air-raid warden and also a fire-watcher.

Over supper on the following Monday, he told the family about it and said, 'I'm glad I can be useful again, but there's no point in you signing up for these things, Ben. You'll be called up for active service before much longer.'

'Yes, sir.' Ben was worried enough about that and felt it gave him a dig he could have done without. In bed that night it seemed unsurmountable; he needed some plan in place to deal with his conscription before it came.

The next morning started as it usually did: he got up and went to work. He found Duggie Bennett there before him, who said, 'I've received my calling-up papers.'

That shook Ben up; he'd employed Duggie as a helper on his roundabout since the day he'd bought it, and found him reliable and willing. He counted him a friend. Duggie wasn't pleased about it either. 'I've just met this smashing new girlfriend and now I'll have to leave her.'

While Duggie was letting out all his anguish, Ben realised he was only three weeks older than him. That sent shivers down his spine. It meant he could expect his papers any time now. And Duggie had been given only ten days' notice to attend the army recruitment centre to sign on and have his medical examination.

That gave Ben another difficulty: where would he find a lad to replace Duggie? Well, summer was almost over and they'd be less busy in the winter, when everybody hugged the fire. Could the lad who helped on the caterpillar ride relieve him too for breaks and meals?

It had been a dark wet day and the footfall through the fairground had been light. By late afternoon he was sunk in misery and generally fed up. He'd go home and check his records because he couldn't remember how old Steve was either, and he couldn't afford to lose another man just now. He often went at this time because Lizzie would soon be home from work and they'd share their evening meal.

He told Duggie he'd be away for an hour or so. The rain had stopped but it was cold for September. He let himself in and found he was home first. He picked up several envelopes that had come through the letter box in the mail and put them on the table. First he must light the fire to warm the place up a bit. Lizzie felt the cold. He always laid it in the morning before he went to work, and brought in a big bucket of coal.

He struck a match and as the fire began to catch, he turned back to open his mail. There was yet another government leaflet about air-raid precautions, a catalogue from the firm where he bought prizes for his shooting gallery, a bill for electricity and . . .

Oh my God, it couldn't be? Yes, it was his call-up papers!

He had the same date as Duggie to report to the army barracks and have his medical. He went hot and then cold. Hell and damnation, what was he going to do now? It put him in an impossible position. He'd do almost anything not to have to go to war! His head was spinning.

At that moment he glimpsed Lizzie through the window coming to the front door. Hell! He hadn't had time to think. He dropped the letter into the fire and when he noticed the torn envelope still beside him he flung that into the flames too. When Lizzie came in he was placing small lumps of coal over the paper. Would she notice the burning paper on top and that he was shaking like a leaf?

'Hello, Ben, had a good day?' She took off her coat and came over to kiss his nose.

'No. Duggie's got his call-up papers.'

'Oh, how old is he?'

'I don't know,' he lied.

'But doesn't that have a bearing on when you'll get yours?'

'Yes.' Ben loathed having to talk about anything to do with conscription. 'I need to find another lad and they're all being called up.'

'Go for a younger one, a fourteen-year-old just leaving school. There must be plenty of those around, and they'll jump at a job in the amusement arcade.'

How could he tell Lizzie he'd just burned his own papers? Ben was sweating; hadn't he heard somewhere that men would be sent to prison for that? Lizzie had been brought up to be as honest as the day, and to do her duty to King and country.

'Yes, good idea,' he said. 'What's for dinner?'

'We made a pan of scouse last night, enough for two days,'

she said. 'How could you have forgotten that?' She lit the gas in the kitchen to warm it up.

Ben sank into the armchair and then bounced to his feet again. He mustn't give Lizzie any reason to think anything was wrong. He spread the tablecloth on the table, got out the cutlery and the jar of pickled onions. He must do what he normally would; she mustn't suspect.

His mouth felt dry. He couldn't possibly join the army. He had to stay here and run his business, stay with his plan, but what would happen now? At least he'd delayed things for a time.

He ate his scouse in a fog of fear and guilt, turning over and over in his mind what he'd done. The postman might remember delivering his call-up papers – he'd surely recognise the envelopes by now, he'd be handling lots of them – but there had been other post today. Ben had no idea what would happen next and that was half the problem. Probably he'd be sent another set of papers when he failed to show up with Duggie.

'What is the matter with you?' Lizzie asked. 'You're lost in gloom tonight.'

He sighed guiltily. 'Duggie being called up,' he said. He hated telling lies to Lizzie, keeping things from her.

'How about going to the pictures? That would cheer you up.'

'I need to go back to the fairground tonight.' He'd probably get another set of conscription papers within the next week or so. He had to tell Steve he had an urgent need for this person he knew with a heart problem who would stand in for others at the army medical. It would solve it if he could be classed as unfit for military service. He felt desperate.

A LUCKY SIXPENCE

* * *

It took Milly some weeks to accept that Laurie saw her just as a friend, someone to chat to as they walked their dogs, almost like one of his family. She decided she'd been too close to him for too long, and her family was too friendly with his.

She'd expected more from him. She'd looked at him with stars in her eyes. She'd been half in love with him since he was taking Lizzie out. He still called in, mostly when he was walking Mutt, and she still saw a lot of him, and he was always friendly. She found it hard to believe he didn't think of her in the way she thought of him.

She had to admit he'd never done anything to rouse her hopes; in fact, years ago he'd told her she was too young for him. That had been hurtful and perhaps it had been true then. But now she was nearly sixteen and plenty old enough to have a boyfriend; lots of girls at school were boasting that they had them.

But Milly had come to realise that if Laurie preferred Gina Flowers there was nothing she could do about it. It took her another week or two to decide she'd give up all thought of ever getting married. Instead she'd have a career as a journalist. She'd concentrate on that. One day she'd live in London and work for one of the big daily newspapers.

Dadda had told her only the other day that Mr Thornley was coming to have a game of chess with him on Wednesday evening and he'd probably have a word with her then. She knew him, of course, he'd been before. He might ask to see something she'd written so she looked through her schoolwork for a story her teacher had praised last term and asked her to read out to the class.

193

When Mr Thornley rang the front doorbell, she ran to open it. 'Hello, Emilia,' he said. 'Goodness, how you've shot up, quite the young lady now.'

'I'm fifteen,' she told him as she led him to the sitting room.

'I hear you want to be a journalist,' he said. 'I've found it a satisfying life, and if you like writing you probably will too.'

'I do,' Milly said.

'She's very keen,' Mum confirmed.

'And she has a good writing style.' Dadda beamed at her. 'I've told her that if she could write little snippets of news you'd consider publishing them.'

'Of course I would . . .' he smiled at Milly, 'if it suits the paper. What you really need is training. I take on an apprentice from time to time. I'll have to see how I'm placed when the time comes. Right now my paper is being reduced in size because of the paper shortage so that means I need fewer staff. What sort of things are you writing?'

'Stories for children; I've written one about dragons that—'

'I don't want anything about dragons,' he said. 'I only want true stories about real people, and things that are happening here and now.' He sighed, 'With this war I don't know how I'll be placed.'

Milly was taken aback, 'You mean you won't want an apprentice until the war is over?'

'Well, you'll be going to college in the autumn,' Dadda pointed out, 'and then you'll need another year to become competent in shorthand and typing, so we aren't talking about any time soon.'

Milly watched with a sinking heart as Dadda led his friend

to his study for a game of chess. For her, everything meant waiting and being patient.

Mum used to make them cakes with a pot of coffee and Milly would take it in before she went to bed, but now the only coffee available was Camp coffee, which Dadda said had a flavour that bore little resemblance to the real thing; he preferred to have whisky. Although that was in short supply too, Dadda's drinks merchant kept a few bottles under the counter for him because he used to order it by the case before the war.

Dadda said whisky called for something savoury and had suggested biscuits and cheese but they were rationed now. Mum took Milly with her to the kitchen to cut small sandwiches. She bought something called sandwich paste to put in them. Bloater paste was thought the best sandwich paste because it had the strongest taste but Milly hated the stuff.

As the months rolled on there was little sign on the home front that they were at war, though the British Army was retreating in France, and German submarines were sinking British ships in the Atlantic. Much of the food Britain needed was imported through Liverpool, the second largest port in the country. Esmond was afraid Hitler was trying to blockade them and starve them into submission.

Parents who had agreed that their children should be evacuated now began to bring them back. Some older children got fed up at being away from home and walked back to Merseyside along the railway track from Wrexham to Bidston.

Elsie's puppy farm was thriving. Miss Muffet's puppies were now eight months old and were reaching the point when a trainer would be glad to take them over. One day, she rang the trainer she knew who had bought Dido's pups. He spent a few moments praising the progress the pups were making, but when she told him she had more, he said, 'I'm not buying at the moment, I'm waiting to hear what's going to happen at Belle Vue. I've heard a rumour that they're going to stop racing dogs for the duration.'

Elsie gasped, 'Stop racing dogs for the duration? That could spell disaster for my little business.'

'It will have some effect, I'm afraid, but that doesn't mean dog racing will stop in the rest of the country.'

'When will you know definitely?'

'You know what committees are like. Who is to say when a decision will be made?'

When she told Esmond he was cross. 'When we've spent all this time and money setting things up.' He carried on grumbling about it over the following two days until Ben and Lizzie came to supper again.

'I knew it was a silly idea from the beginning,' he told Ben. 'Just a waste of time and money.'

'Well,' Ben said, 'with all due respect, Major, it seems the fate of dog racing hasn't yet been decided, and even if it stops at Belle Vue, it may not stop down in London. Have you tried to find out more about this?' He had not and that increased Ben's irritation. 'Don't start worrying yet,' he told Elsie.

'There's going to be a huge shortage of food,' the major grumbled on. 'Nothing will be imported for dogs, and we are going to end up with fifteen of them to feed because we can't sell them. There will be no financial gain for us, quite the opposite.'

'You haven't really tried to sell them yet,' Ben said. 'I'll have a go for you when the situation is clearer.'

'Thank you,' Elsie said.

The major was not appeased. 'So you should. You got us into this; you should help to get us out.'

As they walked home afterwards Ben said, 'He does nothing but complain about it. Why can't he try ringing round other trainers?'

'That's not Father's way.'

'No, he puts pressure on others to work for him. Oh dear, and I thought I was getting into his good books by helping your mother to buy those dogs.' Ben sighed. 'The best that could be said is that it's taken my mind off my own problems for a while.'

'New Brighton doesn't seem the same in the blackout,' Lizzie said. 'We always used to see the lights from the town and a coloured glow in the night sky – now we could be in the middle of nowhere.'

'If the wind was in the right direction we used to hear wafts of hurdy-gurdy music from here.'

'Now it closes when it gets dark. We can't see in the blackout.'

'I can see the vague shape of a barrage balloon over there,' Ben said, 'but I wish it was all over.'

Ben felt as though a sword was hanging over his head; he'd been stiff with fear since he'd burned his papers. He broke out in another sweat as he remembered the major was waiting and watching for his conscription papers to come too. That was giving him wakeful nights filled with dread, and even at work there had been times when he'd felt his nerves were getting the better of him.

When next they went to Oakdene Farm for supper Ben found the major was still bristling with aggression about Elsie's puppy business. 'Have you found a trainer to take these puppies?' he asked. 'You said you would.'

'Have you heard anything more about it?' Ben asked. 'I said I'd try when the position was clearer.'

'It's patently clear to me,' Esmond said, 'that the bottom has dropped out of the business. It was a big mistake, Ben. I should never have listened to you. All that time and money spent setting it up, and now we've got all these dogs on our hands.'

'I've loved having the dogs,' Elsie said, 'and I know it's the war that has caused this. I'll be sorry to see the pups go, but it's time Miss Muffet's six did. They're now nearly nine months old.'

'Exactly the right age to go to a trainer,' Ben agreed, trying to sound affable. 'How old are the others?'

'Liverpool Lass's are six months old, eating solids and toilet trained. All are healthy and playful. Will you try to arrange something for them? You'll be better at that than we will.'

'The trainer who took Dido's might yet take them,' Ben said, 'when he knows more about Belle Vue.'

'But can we afford to wait? Won't these pups get too old?'

'No, not as long as their training continues.' Ben wasn't sure but he hoped that was true.

The younger members of the family cleared up after the meal, and they had had an hour in the sitting room trying to calm the major down when the doorbell rang again. Milly went to answer it and found Laurie Coyne on the step. 'I'm taking Mutt for his walk and I've tied him to the garden gate, is that all right?'

'Yes, that's fine, our dogs are all in for the night. Come in, Lizzie and Ben are here.'

Once in the sitting room Laurie said, 'I've just stopped by, Mrs Travis, to give you some bad news. There will be no more greyhound racing at Belle Vue for the duration. It's just been confirmed.'

'Oh! Well, I suppose I've been expecting it.'

'This is terrible news,' Esmond burst out. 'Elsie, you take everything lying down. I knew spending all that money on dogs wasn't the right thing to do, and what are we going to do now? Terrible advice you gave us, Ben.' He was loud in condemnation.

'I could hardly have foreseen this, sir,' Ben said.

The major's face was crimson. 'I did,' he said, 'and now it seems we can't sell the pups.'

'Hang on,' Laurie said, 'it's only at Belle Vue that dog racing has stopped. It's still going on in London and everywhere else; in fact, it's been announced that the English Greyhound Derby will be held in Harringay Stadium next year.'

'There's no need to close your puppy farm down,' Ben said coldly. 'You'll be able to sell the puppies to trainers in the south. If you can't manage that, I'll help you.'

'That will be more difficult, won't it? The costs will be greater because of the distance, and what happens if dog racing is stopped there? No . . .' the major was adamant, 'I've gone along with this nonsense long enough. I'd like to see the whole lot sold off.'

'Well if you've changed your mind because we're now at war, Jimmy Cox and I could easily convert those kennels and wire runs so you could use them for hens, or even rabbits. Chickens would provide you with eggs and help with the rations. What you've spent need not be a dead loss.'

'Will you try and sell them now?'

'Look, Major, it's getting on for eleven, a bit late to do anything tonight.'

'It's time we went home,' Lizzie said hurriedly. 'We'll walk part of the way with you, Laurie, if you're going our way.'

'I am,' he agreed.

'I thought I'd go out for a walk with Laurie and Mutt,' Milly protested.

'You could come too, Milly,' he said.

'No, Emilia, it's time you were thinking of bed, not going out again.'

Milly fumed while Lizzie kissed her mother goodbye.

'When can we expect some action?' Esmond wanted to know as he showed them out.

'As soon as possible,' Ben said, trying not to lose his temper. 'I'll need to have a word with my uncle. He might know some of the trainers in the south.'

By the next evening Ben said to Lizzie, 'I've had enough of your father, he's a pain in the neck. I've got some phone numbers for trainers I could ring but it's long distance. It's so easy to run out of change in a phone box.'

'You could go up and use his phone,' Lizzie said. 'No reason why not.'

'We could leave it until next Monday and get up there early.'

'No, I'll come with you. He's driving Mum berserk over this and she's worried some of the pups will get too old. I'll ask if I can leave work early tomorrow and we'll get it over with. That's if you'll take me out for a meal afterwards.'

'All right,' he said. 'You fix this and let your mother know we're coming, and that we can't stay.'

The following evening Ben was ushered into the major's study and left alone. He looked round and decided that one day he'd like to have a room like this to call his own. He then got down to the job.

He returned to the sitting room to report, 'I've managed to interest a trainer with premises near London. He's agreed to come up and look at the puppies and he'll take back with him those he buys.

'You also have three valuable breeding dogs,' Ben went on. 'If you don't want to keep them, see if this man will take them, or ask if he knows anybody who'd be interested.'

On the way back into town Lizzie told him that he'd spent so long on the phone that her father grew agitated and muttered to her mother about the expense of allowing him to use it.

The trainer came ten days later and took both Miss Muffet's brood and Liverpool Lass's, but he said he wasn't interested in adult dogs. Elsie thanked him and said they were pleased with the price he'd given.

Ben had another word with his uncle, who agreed he'd have them when he could arrange a sea passage for them. It took a while because of the war, and by then Elsie had convinced Esmond they should keep Dido as a family pet.

'We did make a little money out of the dogs,' he finally admitted to Ben. 'But now there's a war on it might be more patriotic to have a few chickens and then we'd have eggs. You know more about these things, could you get some for me?'

'Yes, but they wouldn't be safe in those kennels you have in the field,' Ben said. 'A fox could break through that wire netting and kill them. So first you'll need a proper henhouse you can close up at night.'

'All right, I'd like you to get rid of those puppy shelters, they are such an eyesore, all that wire netting too.'

'Well, you could fix those to the hen house, though it would be better to give them free run of the field. They'd pick up a lot to eat there for themselves.'

'Oh no, we can't go chasing round the field to catch them. They'd be safer and more controllable within a run.'

'I take it you'll be happy to pay for a lad to help me do all that?'

Ben brought Jimmy Cox up when they had a few hours free. He found Jimmy a mine of information about anything that might lead to earning an extra penny. He heard of several people who had proved both helpful and reliable to Jimmy in somewhat shady circumstances. Together they procured a second-hand hen house and a dozen point-of-lay chickens at a very reasonable price.

Ben suggested the rest of the wire netting, of which there was a lot, be taken into one of the buildings, and cages made where he could keep rabbits, but the major didn't take him up on that. Instead he wanted it sold and, since like everything else it was probably going to be in short supply, Ben got a good price for him.

He told Lizzie several times that he was bending over backwards to keep on good terms with her family, and particularly the major.

Lizzie was in buoyant spirits. Ben knew she'd won on a bet she'd placed through Jimmy Cox, and though she never mentioned betting to him these days, he guessed she was doing it and having a good run of luck.

Ben felt she was heading for trouble, and though he'd tried to stop her he couldn't. He felt guilty that it was he and his family who had introduced her to betting. It had come between them. Lizzie was going out without him more and more, either to the pictures or the music hall, with the girls from the shop or with Milly.

He was not displeased about that because he no longer had the energy to take her out and she didn't fit in with the crowd at the Anchor Inn. But he wished he'd never tried to help Elsie get her dogs. Even more, he wished they hadn't gone to Belle Vue with his uncle and introduced Lizzie to betting.

He'd never dreamed it could harm anyone like this, and it hadn't made the major look more kindly on him.

CHAPTER TWENTY-TWO

THE FIRST CHRISTMAS OF the war came and passed quietly, and as most housewives had stockpiled, they were still able to provide all of the traditional delicacies. There was less entertaining as fewer luxuries were in the shops. Everybody agreed that Christmas had not been the same; they were all on edge and a little apprehensive as they waited to see what the New Year of 1940 would bring.

In January, food rationing started. It became obvious to Ben that war with rationing and sudden shortages offered new ways of earning money, and he wasn't alone in wanting to exploit the situation. He had a group of trusted friends amongst the fairground workers who thought in the same way. He'd known them all his life and mostly they'd been friendly with his father before him.

One of his best friends was Steve Docherty, who ran his shooting gallery. He knew Steve had been a protégé of his father's and had been a wild rebellious youth who had served a sentence behind bars. He'd come out of prison in the depths of the depression in the early thirties and been unable to support himself. His wife and family had abandoned him and he'd lost his home.

Steve had been hanging about the fairground leading a

chaotic life existing on odd jobs and handouts until his father had taken him in hand. He'd persuaded Mrs Philpin to take him into her boarding house and given him the means to pay her by allowing him to run his rifle range.

Steve had given the McCluskeys unswerving loyalty ever since. He knew more about guns than anybody else, not that the rifles they used were real guns, they would never have been allowed in the arcade. These were specially made; they had a mechanism that compressed air, and when the trigger was released they fired a harmless pellet at the target. Steve had taught Ben to aim with them when he was young. He'd always liked him and couldn't remember a time when he hadn't worked for them.

Lennie O'Dowd had been a friend of his father's. He was a family man and the elder statesman of the group. He owned the Rose Garden Tea Rooms and Restaurant and Ben thought he was the one with the best brain and the best ideas. He was a competent businessman with his head screwed on straight.

Alec Hooper was nearer his own age and was a friend he'd made more recently. He owned the boats on the lake and rented them out by the hour. Then there was Jimmy Cox, who worked for Alec and who was ready to do anything for a bit of extra cash.

They and all the fairground staff had been up in arms against the government for closing down all entertainment on the day war had broken out, and they'd rejoiced since to find that up-to-the-minute Hollywood films were being imported to keep the public quietly contented and going about their war work.

They denounced the government as fools and met often in

the bar of the Anchor Inn to do so. Ben knew they had already tried a few deals. Lennie O'Dowd had been the most active, and they'd all helped him one way or the other.

He owned both a car and a van and received a ration card for petrol to enable him to continue running his business. 'A totally inadequate amount,' he said. 'The ration for pleasure motoring is really mean and I'm told they're thinking of stopping it altogether.' So they'd helped him lift petrol coupons from one garage and use them in another.

There were growing food shortages and he was dealing in the black market, both buying and selling to augment his supplies. Jimmy and Alec had even broken into the Co-op supply depot one night and taken a generous amount of their stock, but it didn't result in much profit when shared between them all.

'It might be great for you,' Ben said over a pint in the Anchor Inn, 'but we are fiddling around on a small scale. If we're caught the resulting punishment will be exactly the same as if we're dealing in large amounts. We need to put our heads together and think big.'

'Agreed,' Steve said. 'This way doubles the risks. We need one big job that will give us a good return, and then we can live blameless lives afterwards to enjoy our spoils.'

Milly was crossing the hall one Saturday morning when her father, who was talking to somebody at the front door, called, 'Emilia, come and see who is here.'

She didn't immediately recognise the handsome young man who put out his hand to shake hers. 'Harry Barr,' he said. She remembered then that he was one of Lizzie's ex-boyfriends, and Dadda knew his father, who was in charge of the Wallasey police force.

He said, 'My goodness, Milly, suddenly you're grown up.'

That was music to Milly's ears. Why couldn't Laurie see that? 'So what are you doing here?' she asked.

'I volunteered to help the police deliver yet another regional message.' He pointed to the pile on the carrier of his bike, propped up at the gate.

'Warnings and instructions on what to do in an emergency,' Dadda said. He played chess with his father.

'Actually, my dad asked me to help. Since the war started the police have been given more and more to do.'

'Certainly we're getting plenty of leaflets from them,' Dadda said. 'Didn't Lizzie tell us you'd joined the Merchant Navy?'

'Yes, sir, I'm on Atlantic Convoys, but I've got a bit of shore leave because my ship is in need of repairs. Nothing major, so just until Tuesday.'

'Enjoy your leave, Harry, you deserve it. From what we hear on the news the enemy U-boats are giving our shipping a hard time.'

'I'm afraid they are, sir. Is Lizzie at home?'

'She doesn't live here any more,' Milly told him. 'Lizzie's married now.'

'Oh dear, I hadn't heard. Everybody I know has left home; joined up or goodness knows what. May I have your permission, sir, to invite Milly to come to the cinema with me? That's if she'd like to.'

'Oh yes,' Milly breathed, 'I'd love to.'

Harry smiled at her. 'The thing is, I've been given two free tickets to see *Gone with the Wind* this afternoon.'

'*Gone with the Wind*? I've been dying to see it, Dadda, do say yes. It's said to be a marvellous film and everybody's talking about it. I can't wait to see it. Thank you for asking me.'

Milly held her breath, afraid Dadda was about to say she was still at school, and make Harry sorry he'd asked her, but he was all smiles too.

'Well, I can hardly say no after that. Emilia's still very young but provided you promise to see her safely home afterwards, you have my permission.'

'Thank you, sir. It's showing at the Savoy in Liverpool and the film lasts for over four hours, so there are special showing times. I'll need to collect you, Milly, at two o'clock. Can you be ready by then? And it may be late when I bring her back, but I promise I'll take good care of her. Till two o'clock then, Milly.'

Milly was thrilled; she was going to be the first in her class to see *Gone with the Wind*. It was her first real date too, and what a handsome man he was. She felt proud to be asked out by Harry Barr, and hoped they'd meet somebody from her class at school to witness this, even though Lizzie had been his first choice.

What should she wear? Once he'd gone Milly was in a dream. Harry Barr was taking her out and he thought she was grown up. Why couldn't Laurie see that? She went to Lizzie's wardrobe to see if there was anything she could borrow, but she'd taken all her best things, and Lizzie's clothes didn't fit her anyway; she was too tall and stringy.

It was a decent coat she really needed. Lizzie did take her to her shop every year and let her choose a new dress as her birthday present, but the only coats she had were her navy school coat, her gabardine and her Sunday coat for church, and that was years old and styled for a child of ten. Mum had agreed she needed a new one and now it was too late.

Harry came to collect her by taxi and looked very smart in his Harris tweed jacket with leather patches on his elbows. She felt effervescent with anticipation and couldn't stop chattering; he seemed to laugh a lot.

The Savoy was a grand new cinema and they had seats on the front row of the balcony. The film was in full colour and, apart from *Snow White and the Seven Dwarfs*, most of the films she'd seen were in black and white. From the first scenes the story gripped her. Harry was an attentive host and bought chocolates in the first interval and an ice cream for her in the second. Milly found the whole experience enthralling and came out into the blackout feeling dazed.

'That was marvellous,' she told him. 'Scarlett O'Hara was not a good girl, and did some very bad things, but I couldn't help liking her.'

He laughed. 'I thought I didn't like love stories but I did enjoy that. And those pictures of Atlanta being set on fire in the Civil War were impressive.' They were going down the front steps with the crowd. 'I'm quite hungry after all that,' Harry said. 'Do you fancy a bit of supper?'

Milly had expected to be taken home and was thrilled all over again to be asked. 'I'd absolutely love that. I'm hungry too.' This was as good as two dates, a trip to the cinema and then out for a meal. He took her to the Chinese quarter where he ordered her first Chinese meal. She warmed towards Harry; he was a real adult, and in the fighting services. Almost everyone was in uniform these days and she would have liked him to come in his. 'Why didn't you?' she asked.

'I thought it would be a pleasant change to get away from all that while I'm on leave.'

The meal amazed her, though she found it tasty. Could this be lettuce? She'd never heard of lettuce being cooked before and where would they get it at this time of the year?

Harry wanted to talk about Lizzie and asked all sorts of questions about the man she'd married. 'She always had lots of boyfriends,' he said. 'She was very popular.'

'She's very beautiful,' Milly said, 'far better-looking than me.'

Harry had a lovely way of smiling into her eyes across the table. 'You are two very different people,' he said. 'You're pretty too, and perhaps you have qualities she doesn't have.'

'Lizzie and I were close until she got married. I miss her now she's left home. Lizzie is lovely in every way.'

'All I'm saying is don't compare yourself with her. You do your own thing.'

Milly held on to his arm as they walked down to the Pierhead to catch the ferry to New Brighton. There was a real chill in the wind now but the moon was up and they stayed on deck leaning against the rail.

'It's been a good day,' Harry said, 'and it's lovely to be in home waters.'

'We know exactly what's all round us,' Milly said, 'even though we can't see much because of the blackout.'

'We can see the moonlight glinting on the water,' Harry said, 'and the shape of the ships and docks. It feels quite romantic until I remember that an enemy plane would be able to see this too, if it was above us.'

That made her shiver, but he started to tell her about his job. The *North Star* was a tanker bringing much needed crude oil from Galveston into the Mersey. 'We have to wait for other ships loading food in other American ports before we form up into a convoy to come back across the Atlantic. It's considered more dangerous to cross alone these days without an escort from the Royal Navy.'

They caught a bus on New Brighton promenade to the end of her lane and he was still talking about his job. 'On this last trip we were twice intercepted by U-boats.'

Milly felt locked in horror as he told of the shock of seeing one of the ships in the convoy on fire and men in the water all round them. In the last bend of the lane before the farm came in view he pulled her back to lean against the grassy bank while he finished his tale. She was about to ask him if he'd been scared, but clearly he had; and yet he would have to go on another trip on Tuesday. That took real courage.

'Will you come out with me again?'

'I'd like that.'

'I haven't much time left – I have to go back to my ship on Tuesday morning. Tomorrow? What is there to do in New Brighton on Sunday afternoons in wartime?'

'Plenty. Most of the fair is open and I love going there. All the cafés and snack bars are, and so is the boating lake.' Milly laughed. 'Perhaps the boating lake is too much like work for you?'

'I could handle that.'

Milly had a fit of the giggles. She told him how all entertainments had been ordered to close down on the day war was declared but the public became restive with nothing to amuse them, so the government imported films like *Gone with the Wind* to entertain and keep spirits up.

He laughed with her. 'You keep my spirits up.' He pulled her closer in a hug and then bent to kiss her on the lips. Milly was ecstatic; she had a real boyfriend and for the first time ever felt fully grown up.

CHAPTER TWENTY-THREE

WHEN MILLY GOT OFF the bus on the promenade the following afternoon, she could see Harry waiting for her. She'd told him yesterday she'd like him to wear his uniform as everybody else was doing that, and he looked very smart in it. 'You're an officer then,' she said.

'Second officer,' he said. 'It's years since I've been to the fairground. Does your father approve of you going there?'

'No, but I do because it's fun.'

'The fairground was forbidden when I was at school. Now he thinks I'm old enough to make up my own mind.'

'I wish my father thought like that.'

'Give him time and he will.'

'No, he's set in his ways. He forbade Lizzie to go near the place when she was nineteen, and he doesn't approve of her husband or where she lives or anything. I think Ben is lovely, I'll introduce you if you like; he'll give us free rides on his roundabout. He owns the caterpillar ride and the shooting gallery too.'

'A businessman – he's older than Lizzie then?'

'Yes, but younger than you.'

She found Ben at the controls of his roundabout in deep discussion with one of his employees. He was brandishing an oil can and had smears of black oil on his cheek and on his clothes. 'Hello, Milly,' he called. 'The engine is giving me a bit of trouble this afternoon but I think I've got it going again.'

He was taking a lot of interest in Harry so she introduced them, though she remembered he was an ex-boyfriend of Lizzie's and to mention that would only embarrass them both.

'Sorry I can't shake hands with you,' Ben said, showing his very oily hands, 'you've caught me at a bad moment. I knew our Milly would be snapped up by some young man before long . . .' his smile was pure Irish guile, 'she can be good company.'

Milly knew it was impossible for anyone to feel miserable with the hurdy-gurdy music beating out. Harry took her out on the boating lake in a skiff and showed great skill in manoeuvring it and they had tea and cakes in the Central Hotel before going for a walk along the prom.

There was fitful sun and a cold wind that made them step out briskly. The music from the fairground could still be heard in the distance; the Liverpool ferry was just leaving the end of the pier. Further out, a coastal vessel followed by a dredger were nosing into the river. 'A typical Sunday afternoon,' Harry said.

'The war seems miles away, doesn't it? Nothing much seems to be happening here.'

'War! There's plenty happening in the Atlantic. It's another world out there. A completely different world,' he said.

Milly had so much to tell the girls in her class on Monday morning, and she also had a date to go dancing at the Tower Ballroom with Harry that night.

A LUCKY SIXPENCE

* * *

Every day since he'd burned his call-up papers Ben had inspected the incoming mail, dreading to find he'd been sent another set, and it felt like a reprieve when no replacement papers came. Steve told him that his friend with a heart condition had found clients all over Merseyside, Chester and Manchester, and that he wanted no more business on Merseyside as he was afraid to return to the same recruitment centre twice in case he was recognised.

Ben had no further plans in place now, and his fear of the major was growing. This week at the Monday night supper he said, 'Your call-up papers are a long time coming; I'd have thought they'd have you in the forces before now.'

Ben could feel his suspicion like a black cloud and his whole manner seemed to question the truth when he told him yet again he hadn't received them. As an excuse that wasn't going to wash for much longer.

Milly knew her parents would be reluctant to let her go out again on Monday evening and she really wanted to go. 'It's the last night of Harry's leave,' she told them, 'and he's specially asked me to go dancing in the Tower Ballroom.'

'Harry Barr is a very trustworthy young man,' Elsie said.

Milly had arranged for Harry to call and collect her, as that way Dadda was less likely to stop her going.

Milly persuaded Mum to have dinner ready earlier than usual and in her excitement was reprimanded for gobbling her food. Harry arrived and Dadda said, 'It's good of you to come all the way out here to pick Milly up, especially as you'll have to bring her back again.'

'My father has generously allowed me to borrow his car tonight,' Harry said. 'A special treat for the last night of my leave.'

'Although petrol is rationed?' Dadda asked. Milly detected a censorious note in his voice.

'Yes, my mother is going to a WVS meeting later, but has agreed to go by bus. She says she may have to get used to doing that.'

'And you're not wearing your uniform,' Dadda said. 'Surely you're proud to be seen in that?' Harry was wearing the same Harris tweed jacket and slacks he'd worn on Saturday.

'Yes, sir, I am, but I want to forget the war for one more evening.' Milly could see that Harry could handle Dadda, though he seemed more subdued tonight. She was thrilled to be whisked down to the Tower Ballroom in such a magnificent car. Many of her school friends were from car-owning families, but Dadda said having only one arm made driving difficult. He hadn't tried since he'd lost it.

She could hear the music as soon as they reached the ballroom doors, and it started her feet tapping. Harry was waiting for her when she emerged from the cloakroom and swept her onto the floor in a quickstep. 'You're a good dancer.' They spoke the same words at the same moment and laughed.

'Lizzie taught me,' Milly said.

'I was about to say that too.' They both laughed again.

'Do you mean Lizzie taught you to dance?' Milly asked him.

'Yes, I used to bring her here. She improved my dancing, knocked the awkward corners off me. She loved this place.'

'This is my first time ever, but I love it too.'

216

They laughed again. 'It cheers me up.' Harry no longer looked subdued.

They agreed that the twenty-piece band was excellent and danced every dance until the interval. 'Let's go to the cafeteria,' Harry said. 'I could do with a drink after that. It'll have to be lemonade here, or tea, I'm afraid.'

Milly managed a cream cake as well as the lemonade. 'There were a lot of men in uniform but they've gone now.'

'They've just gone to the pub. You can collect a pass as you leave so you can come back without having to pay again.'

'You must have been here lots of times to know all this.'

'I have.'

That made Milly wonder why Lizzie had thrown him over. Later, they had to sit out some of the dances because they were tiring, but they were still on the floor for the last waltz. Milly felt Harry's arms tighten round her. Back in the car on the way home he said, 'I've had a good leave, Milly, thanks to you. You've been great.'

He was pulling up at her garden gate, and she said, 'D'you know, you're the first man I've ever been out with? Lots of girls in my class rave about their boyfriends and I now see what they're on about.' She could see Harry laughing at her in the light from the dashboard. 'I bet I won't be the last,' he said as he switched the engine off.

'Can we do this again next time you come on leave?' she asked. 'You've given me a very good time.'

'Yes, we must, but I don't know when that'll be. I've had shore leave this time while we're in port, but next time I'll probably have to stay on board.' He pulled her into a hug and kissed her with more passion than she'd expected. 'I'll phone you the next time I'm home.'

Milly reached up and kissed him on his lips. 'I'll look forward to that. Thank you for everything.'

'I wish I didn't have to go, but I do.' He shuddered.

She felt his fear. Dadda had told her it was often harder to cope with fear than doing what you were afraid of.

She thought about Harry as she got into bed that night; he'd kissed her, he'd shown some passion, but somehow he had not behaved in quite the way she'd expected after hearing the girls in her class talk about their boyfriends. When she'd told him he was the first man to ask her out, he'd implied he expected her to have other boyfriends. He wasn't suggesting that they spend their lives together.

The girls at school believed a boyfriend brought romance into their lives, that he would love them, thrill them, sweep them off their feet. Clark Gable had given her something of that feeling when she'd watched *Gone with the Wind*.

Basic instinct told Milly that Harry Barr was not seeing her as a thrilling and glamorous life partner, not at all. He was seeking something from her, but what? He wanted a companion for his leave, certainly, someone on the same wavelength he could talk to. Wasn't he treating her in much the same way that Laurie Coyne did?

All Harry wanted was a friend. That was not something she was going to tell the girls in her class. And she couldn't help wishing it had been Laurie who had taken her out.

Lizzie felt the rift between her and Ben was widening. These days she didn't talk to him about placing bets, not even when she'd had a win, because he didn't like her doing it. He no longer spoke of it either, though he must know, as his mate Alec Hooper would tell him or Jimmy Cox would let it drop. He had less and less time for her because Father was giving him jobs to do and Ben wanted to keep on the right side of him; also he was very involved with his friends at the fairground now.

This week she'd seen him with Lennie near his restaurant and suspected they were doing something with black-market food, but Ben certainly didn't want to talk to her about that. She wasn't being as open with him as she used to be and was afraid he was treating her in the same way.

It had been his idea that she should open a post office savings account to save for her own dress shop. He'd said she need not contribute towards the running of their home and Mum thought that very generous of him. It was true that her luck seemed to have gone but she didn't doubt it would return. It always had in the past, though this time it was taking longer. Some time ago, she'd begun to draw out money from her savings account to stake her bets; she had to if she wanted to carry on.

Now, several weeks later, she was in the post office to draw out more, and was shocked to find so little there. She'd been losing more than she realised, but she couldn't possibly stop now. The only way she could recoup what she'd lost was to carry on, and hope her luck would change.

Tomorrow was the first day of the race meeting at Doncaster and she went looking for Jimmy to put a bet on. She spent much of the next day thinking about the horses that would race on the following day and when the shop closed, giving Ben's roundabout a wide berth, she went to find Jimmy at the boating lake.

'Came in first.' Jimmy was grinning all over his face as he paid out her winnings. 'Lady Luck is smiling at you again, Mrs McCluskey,' he said. She gave all the money back to him to put on a horse called Honeybunch that would run in a race the next day.

That day at work she could think of nothing else. If she won again it meant her run of bad luck was over and her bank balance would be heading in the right direction. Everything was coming right: one big win now and she'd be able to put back all the money she'd lost.

Lizzie thought very carefully about which horse she'd bet on for the big race which would take place on the last day of the meeting. She meant to make sure she got it right. Mrs Field wasn't well and left Lizzie in charge of the shop. She left most of the work to the other girl and spent her time surreptitiously reading all the sporting news and tips she could find. By the time she was locking up for the night, Lizzie had made her decision. Teazle was the horse most likely to win or be placed.

Lizzie didn't go to the boating lake to find Jimmy because Milly came to the shop to see her. Later, Ben wanted to go to the Anchor for a drink and she went with him, knowing Jimmy would come there to pay out. As it happened, Ben had gone to the bar for another beer when Jimmy came to the lounge. 'You really have hit a winning streak.' Jimmy was grinning all over his face. 'Honeybunch was first past the post, and you've won a good payout this time. Because you picked him out I put a couple of bob on him too, so we're both in the money. I take it you'll have a flutter on the big race?'

'Yes,' Lizzie said, 'Teazle is my choice.' She handed him the slip of paper that she'd already made out, and gave all her winnings back to Jimmy.

'Phew,' he said. 'You're sure?'

'Certain.'

That gave her such a lift; it was almost like old times, and she felt like singing. She laughed and joked all evening with Ben and his friends in a high old mood. In bed that night Lizzie relived the lure of the race track, the tense excitement before the race, the jockeys in their colourful jackets and, most of all, the huge thrill of winning money. The next day she went to work as usual and danced round the shop with a smiling face, serving customers at twice her usual speed. She spent any quiet interval trying to work out how much she would win, and dreaming of what it would buy, and also of Ben's congratulations when she told him. She felt certain of her choice and fully expected Teazle to win.

She enjoyed it all. Mrs Field was in the shop again and praised her ability and enthusiasm for the business. She'd thought of asking to go home early, because she knew there would be a commentary of the race on the wireless, but Mrs Field left early and asked her to lock up so she couldn't.

She still felt amazingly optimistic as she made her way to the pay desk at the boating lake to find Jimmy. He wasn't there but his boss Alec Hooper was discussing the race with another man, while his wireless was still relaying results.

Lizzie was laughing. Her face ached with the enormous smile she'd worn all day, until she caught the name of another horse in the commentary. She asked, 'Did Teazle win?'

Alec looked sympathetic. 'No, no, it was Corrymander.'

She felt she'd been kicked in the stomach, though still not sure she'd heard right. 'No?'

'No, Teazle came in fifth. Sorry about the loss,' he said. 'Jimmy told me to tell you he'd buy you a drink in the Anchor tonight to cheer you up.'

Lizzie was afraid she was about to throw up. She knew Jimmy sometimes bought a drink for a big winner though he didn't drink himself, but it was the last thing she wanted and she couldn't get the words out to say anything. Tears stung her eyes, as she turned away and stumbled home. Oh my God, this was a hell of a blow.

Ben was home before her and busy getting their evening meal ready. He told her, 'I have to go out again when I've eaten, the owners are having a business meeting at the arcade.'

Once it would have upset her to find him going out without her but tonight she was glad. She couldn't think of anything but this shattering loss. She couldn't tell him; he'd be furious. Lizzie wept once it was safe to do so. She'd really believed she would win and with good reason: betting for her had turned to gold so many times.

She went to bed before Ben returned but tossed and turned for what seemed hours, worrying about how she could tell him she'd spent all her savings. She slept only lightly and heard him come home in the early hours but pretended she was asleep.

They were late getting up the next morning and Lizzie had to rush to get ready for work. Ben was less concerned about time-keeping and still eating toast at the table. She ran down from the bedroom, threw her handbag down on the armchair to put on her coat, and her bank book slid out.

Ben got up from the table, saw her bank book but made no

effort to pick it up. He said, 'How much have you saved towards your shop now?'

Full of guilt she hurriedly stuffed it back inside her bag. 'Not so much as I'd like.'

'I hear you've been betting regularly over the last weeks and you had a loss.'

'What if I have? Who is spying on me?'

Ben was frowning. 'Lizzie, nobody's spying. Everybody knows you in the fairground and they see you heading towards the boating lake and know what goes on there. Alec was concerned about you.'

'It's none of his business and it's none of yours.'

'I'm afraid you're going way too far, Lizzie.' He looked grim. 'You're keeping things from me. I happened to see Jimmy Cox last night. You didn't tell me you were betting regularly. I had to hear from him that you'd put an enormous bet on and lost. I don't like you keeping this sort of thing from me.'

Lizzie felt threatened by tears and growing despair. Everything was going wrong for her. 'I wanted it to be a surprise for you. If I won I knew you'd approve, because it would give me a tidy sum to add to my dress shop money.'

Ben wasn't smiling. 'Lizzie, this really worries me,' he said.
'What does?'

'That you want to bet all the time. You're becoming obsessed with it.'

She glowered at him. 'You and your family showed me how. You approved then.'

'Yes, but what you're doing is quite different. I took you to watch the races and we bet small amounts to make it more fun.'

'I could kick myself,' Lizzie said. 'Corrymander won at Doncaster and Ascot last year. I should have backed him.'

'Lizzie, why can't you see betting is all right once in a while, but not regularly like this? You're becoming obsessed with gambling.'

'You're obsessed with your plans for the future and saving up for more sideshows.'

'Betting can get out of hand. Some people get addicted to it.'

'Addicted?' Lizzie was indignant; she'd never thought of it like that. 'Not me. Don't be silly.'

'Well, it does happen to some. You'd be much better giving it up and saving sensibly for your clothes shop. No good pinning your faith on the horses, Lizzie. You have no control over what they do.'

She went, slamming the front door behind her, but she felt terrible as she jogged along the street. She'd lost everything and she was losing Ben. She felt bereft.

CHAPTER TWENTY-FOUR

BEN WAS UNDER STRESS between the worry of his own difficulties, the war, and Lizzie's problems. He knew there was nothing he could do about the war, and he'd done his best for Lizzie and failed, but he really had to do something soon to divert the major's attention from his call-up papers.

He spent days pondering over it and the best plan he could come up with was to announce that his call-up papers had arrived at last. He'd wait for ten days to allow time for his medical exam to take place, and then say he'd been turned down as medically unfit, that he had a heart problem. Just to tell people should be enough.

He thought about it long and hard and hoped that it would ring true to the major. He couldn't see any way he could check the truth of that, but convincing Lizzie was another matter.

He didn't want to tell her any more lies; he wasn't proud of what he'd done, and he wasn't sure Lizzie would believe him as he'd have no papers to show her. If she found out he was no saint and her father had been right about him from the start, how would she take that?

But unless he could think of some other ruse, he'd have to do it sooner or later.

Ben knew the major wasn't one to give up, and two weeks

later he brought up the subject again. This time he also asked how old he was and Lizzie, in her innocence, told him to the day. He wouldn't put it past Esmond Travis to walk into the recruiting office and ask why his son-in-law had not been conscripted. He had to get the major off his back but he needed to be careful about what he told Lizzie.

Mrs Field had a second shop in Wallasey and when Lizzie was asked to work there for a few days because one girl was on holiday and another had gone off sick, Ben decided this was the opportunity he needed. This shop gave Lizzie a longer journey to work, and she'd have to catch buses. It meant she wouldn't come home in her lunch hour and therefore wouldn't know what the postman brought. She'd be home later in the evenings and this would give him time.

Ben bought a bottle of beer which he drank just before she was due home, and he deliberately spilled some on his pullover so he'd smell of beer. He wanted to appear fraught, but when he came to do it he didn't have to act, he was very nervous of telling Lizzie such a porky.

To set the scene and make himself look a distracted mess, he ruffled his hair and stretched out in the armchair. 'I got my call-up papers today,' he announced before she had her coat off.

'Oh, Ben!' She rushed over to him and threw her arms round him. 'How awful! How soon . . . ?'

He had that all worked out and said, 'A week on Wednesday. Ten fifteen.'

'Have you been drinking? You smell of beer.'

'At lunchtime I went to the Anchor and Jimmy Cox bought me a beer, he said it would give me strength.'

'You mean Dutch courage. You've had more than one.'

'Yes, several of the boys were there and showed their sympathy, and d'you know what I've done? I've gone and lost the damn letter.'

She laughed. 'Nobody will want it. It's probably behind the bar waiting for you.'

'No, Lizzie, I missed it while I was there and I had everybody looking for it. I don't know where I lost it.' He made that a cry of pain.

'Well, you know the time that you have to present yourself. Is it here in Wallasey?'

'Yes, the army recruiting place. I do feel a bit of a fool.'

'I don't suppose it matters whether you have the letter as long as you go.' She went to the kitchen. 'Ben, you said you were going to buy chops for dinner.'

'Oh, gosh, Lizzie, I forgot.' That was supposed to show he was upset. 'Let's go and get fish and chips. No, I'll go, you have a rest.' He picked up the matchbox and lit the fire. 'I don't know what I'm doing today. What's going to happen to my business now? I'm worried stiff about that.'

Lizzie was worried about Ben's business too. Its healthy profit kept them comfortable; without it, and wholly dependent on her wages, life would be much harder. Of course, Steve would still be looking after the rifle range, but she regretted now that she hadn't agreed to learn how to run the roundabout and the caterpillar ride while there had been time.

She was passing the local newsagent's on the way to work the next morning when Jimmy Cox came out already opening the pages of the *Sporting Life*. 'Hello,' she said, 'has Ben asked

227

you to work overtime?' Jimmy was always the first person he asked to do extra work for him.

'No, what job does he need doing now?'

'He's worried about running his business while he's away, and can talk of nothing else. And he hasn't found his call-up papers.'

'He's had his call-up papers?'

Lizzie was surprised at that, but Jimmy's face showed equal surprise. 'And he's lost them?' He laughed. 'Well nobody else is going to want them.'

Lizzie had recovered somewhat. 'Didn't you see him yesterday lunchtime in the Anchor? Buy him a drink to drown his sorrows?'

'I was there but I didn't see him. Poor old Ben, so he's on his way? Sorry, poor you as well, you'll be lonely without him.'

Lizzie walked on, feeling confused. The last thing Ben wanted was to get his call-up papers, so why would he say he'd received them if he hadn't? It didn't make sense.

She couldn't get it out of her mind all day, and returned home that evening to find the fire lit, chops bought, potatoes peeled and cabbage chopped. Ben was his relaxed and smiling self again.

That made her bristle. 'What's going on?' she asked. 'I met Jimmy Cox on the way to work this morning, and he didn't know you'd lost your call-up papers.'

His smile disappeared and he looked shocked. 'There were a lot of people there showing sympathy, buying me drinks, and as I told you, I was very fraught.'

It took Lizzie a moment to take that in. Was he making all this up? She felt a spurt of anger. 'Jimmy Cox said you were not in the Anchor yesterday afternoon when he went there. Why are you telling me lies? That is what you're doing, isn't it? Telling me lies?'

Ben seemed to collapse. 'Lizzie, I'm sorry. Terribly sorry, I don't know whether I'm coming or going.'

'You do, you know exactly what you're doing. Nobody is better organised than you. I know you well enough to know you'll have good reason for doing this.'

His face was twisting; she knew she was right. 'I hardly know where to start. I've been worried sick . . .'

'It's no good looking for sympathy from me.' She felt another rush of anger. 'You've been telling me lies, and I want to know why.' She could see tears gathering in his eyes. 'I thought we shared everything, that we had no secrets from each other?'

'I hated keeping this from you, but I knew you'd be shocked.'

'I am, so what have you done?'

'I put my call-up papers behind the fire. Burned them and I've been telling everybody that I haven't received them.'

'Oh my God!'

'I don't think your father believes me.'

'Do you blame him?'

'He doesn't like me. I can't do anything right. I'm afraid he'll start chasing things up. You know what he's like.'

'Oh, Ben, when did you . . . ?'

'Months ago. I did it on the spur of the moment. I can't go away and leave my business, can I?'

'Ben, the country is at war. National Service is compulsory. What you did is now a criminal act. Everybody will think you're a coward. Too frightened to fight for your country.'

'I am frightened, lots of us are.'

'I'm horrified. You've been lying to me for weeks. And you're planning to tell my family this cock-and-bull story?'

'I have to. Your father keeps on at me, pondering why I haven't been called up. I'm afraid he'll go to the recruitment centre and start them probing. He's just that sort.'

'Oh, heavens, and I'm expected to sit beside you, listening to your lies?'

'I'm in a cleft stick, Lizzie,' he wailed. 'I want you to support me. I need this. Please don't let me down. I do love you, you know.'

Lizzie wasn't sure she believed that either and she couldn't sleep that night. She wasn't sure how she felt about Ben and she couldn't make up her mind what she should do. This was a side of his personality she hadn't suspected until recently.

A few days later, when they went to have supper with her family, she sat silent while Ben led up to his lie in a skilful manner. He told the cock-and-bull story he'd outlined to her with what seemed genuine sincerity. He showed he was anxious about everything: the war, his business, his health, and leaving Lizzie to live alone.

When the following week he came up with the story about failing his medical because he'd been found to have an enlarged heart, she could see her family believed him. Mum was very upset and so was Milly. 'Did you not know? What a terrible way to find out. It must make you feel ill.'

'I don't have much energy these days,' he agreed, 'and I do get out of breath. He gave me a note to take to my doctor.'

'He'll be able to help,' Elsie said. 'I'd see him without delay.'

Father was quite sympathetic. 'It must have come as a

shock,' he said. 'I know what it's like not to be able to do all you want towards the war effort, but I can help you sign up as an air-raid warden and for fire-watching duties. We have to accept our infirmities and do what we can.'

Lizzie sat silently, trying not to shiver. She'd learned one new fact: Ben was a practised liar.

Lizzie was feeling out of sorts. Things had gone a little sour and nothing was fun any more; she had no energy at all and was getting headaches and feeling sick. She didn't trust Ben, not now she'd heard him tell real whoppers, and he seemed to have so many things to do that she didn't understand and he wouldn't explain. But could he be right about her being obsessed with betting?

She wanted to deny that. She'd tried to talk to him about it again but it had ended up in another argument. He'd been angry and said, 'The way you're gambling is a mug's game, Lizzie. Think of the line of bookies you saw on the course at Belle Vue, all making a living from the losses of punters. Not only those who get things wrong but those who don't know when to stop. You'll never have your own dress shop if you carry on like this.'

Since the big loss, she'd had this niggle at the back of her mind that Ben could be right. She'd truly believed Teazle would win. That he had not had come as a nasty shock. Lizzie knew Ben hated to see money wasted and she had wasted a good deal on that wretched horse, more than she'd lost on any other. But the racing scene was what interested her – if she wasn't betting it still filled her mind. She couldn't resist reading the racing papers, listening to racing commentaries on the wireless, and talking about it to Jimmy Cox and anybody else who was interested.

But now things had turned really bad and she didn't feel at all well. Ben had disappointed her; this wasn't at all what she'd expected from him. He was a coward and he certainly wasn't being fair. He'd told massive lies to her and her family and involved her in keeping his secrets, but he complained because she'd lost her own money on a bet, that she'd placed it behind his back.

She felt horribly estranged from him and though he said he still loved her, she was afraid that was another of his lies. She had nobody else and she was missing his love and support. Nothing was going right; what she really wanted was to get things back with Ben to the way they'd been when they were first married. Lizzie spent a thoroughly miserable day.

In bed that night Ben said, 'Lizzie, I can't stand this, come here.' He tried to pull her closer. 'We mustn't fall out over this. I want to help you.'

She relaxed and snuggled against him; he put an arm round her and pulled her closer. She felt comforted and for once let her anguish pour out to him, and finally whispered, 'I'll give up betting altogether, if that's what you want.'

'It is until you can see the difference between a harmless two-bob flutter and staking a month's wages on a horse,' he murmured. 'Don't worry, Lizzie, we're both hectically busy and tired out. We'll get over this. You put all this betting behind you, and we'll both forget about it.' Within moments he was deeply asleep.

The next day she went to see Jimmy Cox and told him she was not going to place any more bets with him, but for her it rankled. She was bored and was missing the thrills and social scene of her early married life. The war and what Ben was doing terrified her.

April came and the days were getting warmer and the nights were shorter. Dadda predicted that the Luftwaffe would not come so often. 'They like the dark,' he said. 'We can't see them to shoot them down.' But Dadda, for once, was wrong. They hadn't bombed Liverpool yet but elsewhere they were coming more often and the raids were getting heavier. Milly knew the war news was frightening everybody; even Dadda admitted he was scared. He said, 'The Nazis invaded Norway and Denmark and have spread across France, Belgium and the Netherlands. The British Expeditionary Force has been retreating and retreating and it looks as though they are going to be trapped. It doesn't bear thinking about that we shall lose them all.'

Nowadays they tried to snatch what sleep they could between the air-raid warnings. Milly would rush to the kitchen each morning to switch on the wireless to find out what was happening.

That was how she heard about Dunkirk, and how the remnants of the Expeditionary Force had to be rescued over several days by the many civilians living on the south coast who owned small boats.

'The Nazis are only twenty-two miles away from the English coast,' Esmond said when he came home from his warden duties. 'We've never been closer to being invaded. It could come at any time.'

CHAPTER TWENTY-FIVE

MILLY COULD SEE THE war was bringing huge changes to everybody's life except hers. She still had to go to school and if they had a daylight raid they all had to run across the playing fields to the shelters. At home she helped Mum with the chores in the evenings, looked after the chickens and started growing vegetables. She'd turned sixteen in May but she wished she was grown up and had more of a life.

What she liked doing best was walking the dogs with Laurie. One of the girls in her class had seen them together and said, 'You get all the best boyfriends. Isn't his father the vet? I like his dark wavy hair, he's really handsome. You are lucky.'

But Milly knew Laurie Coyne wasn't worshipping at her feet, and hoping to rush her to the altar. The girls at school thought every boyfriend should be like that and nothing would please Milly more if he was. But although Laurie was still engaged to Gina Flowers, all his talk was about the animals he was looking after – he rarely spoke of Gina, and she couldn't ask him about her.

She saw them together from time to time in the lane. They'd stopped to talk to her and Lizzie last month. 'I come from Morecambe,' Gina had said, 'and they want me to go home.

234

They think I'll be safer there than in Liverpool.' She was always beautifully dressed and made-up. Even Lizzie admired her clothes.

Milly couldn't take her eyes off her emerald engagement ring. She could feel Gina between her and Laurie all the time.

Laurie continued to walk Mutt up and down the lane and if Milly happened to be in the kitchen she would often see him through the kitchen window. Often he would knock to see if she wanted to walk Dido. He was just as friendly and listened with interest to all her news, but for Milly his engagement to Gina had changed everything. She found it hard to believe it had not had that effect on him, but nothing in his manner had changed.

A week later, on a gorgeously sunny Sunday morning, she was in the lane walking Dido when she saw Laurie coming down with Mutt. 'I've changed my mind about going to Leahurst,' he said. 'I've cancelled that and I joined the army on Friday, so it'll be all change for me now.'

'What?' Milly was shocked. 'You've volunteered, but why?'

'I can't hang around a classroom now we're at war. I want to get on with things, help the war effort.'

'I feel exactly the same way, but Dadda won't let me.'

'Quite right, you're too young.'

'But your dad said you needed more experience and—'

'I'm qualified. I can do a course at Leahurst when this war is over.'

Milly was silent for a moment. 'That means you'll have to go away?'

'Yes, like every man of my age,' he said. 'This is where you girls gain. Gina hasn't been called up. She can work where she likes and she's found a job in Morecambe.'

'Dadda says we girls will be directed into war work before much longer,' Milly said. 'I think he's worried that it might happen to me.'

Knowing Laurie would soon be gone, the days began to pass even more quickly for Milly. Yesterday he'd said, 'I've had my medical and been passed as fit. In fact, I'm told I'm classed as A1. I've also had an interview. I'm to be posted down south for a few weeks of army training.'

'When will you be going?'

'Tomorrow,' he said. 'I'd better come in now and say goodbye to your family.' He was tying Mutt to the front gate when Ben and Lizzie came home. Milly let them all in. Her mother came to the kitchen door to see who it was, but immediately led them to the sitting room where Dadda was reading the paper by the fire.

Milly said, 'Laurie has come to say goodbye to us. He's leaving to join the army.'

'There was a lot on the news at breakfast time about the British Army fighting in France,' Lizzie said. 'Awful to think you will soon be in the thick of it.'

'I'll not be in too much danger, Lizzie. I'm to have a few months of military training down south, and then I'm to join the Veterinary Corps and possibly I'll be working with homing pigeons.'

That made Lizzie laugh. 'Don't tell me the army is still using homing pigeons? I thought all that went when they gave up fighting with swords and shields.'

'Apparently not.' Laurie grinned. 'A homing pigeon can fly

across the German lines with a message and it isn't easy to shoot down. I shall have to read up about them though. I was expecting it to be horses.'

'I'm glad it doesn't sound like dangerous war work,' Milly said.

'I have a favour to ask of you, Mr Travis,' Laurie said. 'I'm wondering if I might ask Milly to look after our little flock of chickens now I'm going away.'

'Yes, of course,' Milly said.

'Don't your parents want to keep them for their eggs?' Esmond asked.

'No, my mother has taken a part-time job lecturing at the university, and she's in the WVS and has the house to look after. She and Dad don't have the time or energy to look after hens. The thing is, our hen house is on wheels and it would be easier for Milly if I could roll it down into one of your fields.'

'Yes, Laurie, you're welcome to do that.'

'I'll site it well away from yours, and I know each flock will stay in its own quarters.'

'I'll come and help you bring it down,' Milly said. 'You said you have twelve now?'

'Twelve hens and three new pullets that have just started to lay, as well as a cockerel. They keep us in eggs.'

'I'll give you a hand too,' Ben offered.

'Hang on,' Mum said. 'What about getting hen food? We had to give up our weekly egg ration to buy food for the hens, and we can't stretch it to feed sixteen more.'

'Oh goodness, I'd forgotten that,' Laurie said. 'We had to do the same. But they lay many more eggs than our ration which is why I decided to get them in the first place.'

Ben said, 'There's a little business for you, Milly, and it's almost risk-free. Milly needs to negotiate with your mother, Laurie. She will promise to sell them two eggs weekly to replace their ration, and in exchange she gets the coupons to buy hen food. It sounds as though you'll have many more eggs to sell, so, Milly, you can't lose on that.'

'What a good idea.' She laughed. 'I can give your mum more than two eggs each week.'

'Sell, Milly, not give, make yourself a bit of pocket money,' Ben advised.

'Yes, I've got surplus vegetables much of the time too. I'm doing really well in the kitchen garden at the moment.'

'You're a real businessman, Ben,' Dadda said in a tone that sounded as though he didn't approve of it, 'but you're forgetting hens don't lay so many eggs in the winter. Milly may not be able to provide their ration all the year round. We eat a lot of eggs now because there is so little meat.'

'We can negotiate that now you've reminded us, Mr Travis,' Laurie said. 'Why don't I take you straight up, Milly, and we'll talk to Mum about it?'

'Yes,' Mrs Coyne told her when they put the question to her. 'Only fair you get some reward for your work. I'll be more than happy to buy all the eggs you can provide, as well as any surplus produce from your garden.' Milly was pleased with the arrangement. She ran home to get Ben, and the three of them brought Laurie's hen house down to their field.

He shook Laurie's hand. 'All the best,' he said. 'Look after yourself, we all wish you a safe return,' and went indoors. Milly leaned on their front gate, not wanting to say goodbye to Laurie.

'Don't look so woebegone, Milly,' he said. 'I'll be back. It's not the end of the world.'

She tried to smile. He pulled her into a hug and dropped a brotherly kiss on her forehead, but it left her feeling empty.

Laurie walked home slowly; he was worried about Gina. He hadn't seen her since she'd gone up to Morecambe and she wasn't a keen letter-writer. He'd suggested going up for the weekend once, but she'd said she would have to work then and asked him to put it off.

Last week he'd written asking her to come down for a few days before he left, enclosing a note from his mother offering her their spare room. Gina had agreed and he'd thought the visit was on until yesterday. Then he'd had a brief note from her apologising and saying she was terribly busy and she couldn't get the time off work. Now it was too late. They really needed to talk. He was beginning to wonder if he'd made a mistake.

For years, Gina had sat beside him in class and then wanted to go out partying almost every night. Often he'd gone with her and she'd been the life and soul of the occasion; she was a real party person. Laurie had not been able to keep up with her.

But when the exams came near she'd lost her sparkle and her confidence. She'd panicked and begged him for help. Gina had a perfectly good brain but rarely stopped to think anything through. She'd been very needy before her finals and pleaded with him to go over most of what she should have known backwards by then.

She'd been ecstatic when she passed and had thrown herself in his arms. He'd been very pleased with himself too, and somehow he'd come to believe he wanted to spend the rest of his life with her. Now that he hadn't seen her for some time, he wasn't sure that had been a good move, especially as it seemed Gina was having second thoughts too.

CHAPTER TWENTY-SIX

ONE AUGUST MORNING, MILLY was eating breakfast with her parents while they listened to the news on wireless, when she heard, 'Last night, the Luftwaffe made its first air raid on the Liverpool area. Many of the bombs fell harmlessly in agricultural land but some damage was caused in Prenton, a suburb of Birkenhead, and there was one fatality.'

Milly was left gasping, and she could see her parents were struggling too. 'The Luftwaffe is bombing Prenton? That's no more than five miles or so from here.'

'If that,' Dadda said.

It brought the war unbelievably close. Milly felt her stomach muscles tighten with horror as her mother's frightened eyes met hers.

'They'll be aiming for the docks or Cammell Laird,' Dadda said in derogatory tones. 'They're not very accurate.'

'There was an air-raid warning last night when we were going to bed,' Mum whispered, her face white, 'but we ignored it.'

'Because we've been having the warnings from time to time but nothing has been dropped before.'

'At school we always go to the shelters when there's a warning,' Milly said. 'They're horrible, full of spiders and they smell of damp.'

'We will be going to the shelter in future,' Dadda said, 'whenever we hear that wailing sound. We need to stay safe. Get Gladys to clean ours out, Elsie. Do we have some spray we can use against spiders?'

'I must bring out the bedding and air it,' Elsie said.

When Milly went to school that morning she heard that the first bomb had damaged the home of Mr Bunney, who owned the famous Liverpool department store of that name, and the first casualty was his housemaid. Everybody in her class said they were terrified.

Lizzie and Ben also heard that item of news at breakfast and the response was the same. 'In future,' Ben said, 'we must go to the shelter when there are warnings.'

'But sometimes they come in the middle of the night,' Lizzie protested, 'and you're out doing your fire-watching or whatever. I can't go out to a public shelter in my nightie, can I?'

'You'll have to get dressed first, Lizzie. Put on something warm. Or you could volunteer for fire-watching duties too and spend half the night outside.'

'No thanks,' Lizzie said disdainfully.

'It was your father's idea that I should do it,' Ben complained. 'I can't see why you girls can't do your share.'

'Ben, will you come with me to look at the public shelters? There isn't one in Alvaston Terrace, but there are several around here.'

'I've looked at the map in the ARP post,' he yawned. 'The one in Gladstone Street is the nearest; take a look inside on your way to work this morning and see what you think.'

Lizzie fumed; as if she hadn't already done that.

As summer drew to a close the bombers continued to come, though at first not very often. The trouble was nobody knew whether they'd be allowed to sleep, or whether the wailing siren would wake them in the middle of the night. Lizzie resisted going to the Gladstone Street shelter at first, but when the bombs began to fall she'd rush there with her bag of essentials and a warm blanket.

She loathed the place and her neighbours who used it; it stank of sweat and fear. Siren suits were suddenly fashionable: one-piece garments that could be pulled on over other clothes; it was what everybody needed. Lizzie bought herself a warm one as soon as they began stocking them in the shop.

All the public shelters had uncomfortable slatted wooden seating, and she hated going alone to sit amongst the rough workmen and their families. Ben was no longer any help and certainly no fun; in fact, he was taking no interest at all in what she did.

She'd said exactly that to him only yesterday. 'There's so much I have to fit in now, Lizzie, forgive me. I feel as though I'm chasing my tail. I have no time for anything. It's the war.'

Well, it seemed she'd just have to forget him and find something she could do on her own. She had to admit it wasn't so easy to find pleasures in wartime. She used to love the pictures and still took Milly occasionally, or went with the girls from the shop, but it wasn't enough, though the girls raved over Errol Flynn and Milly was very enthusiastic about Bette Davis in *Jezebel*.

Having a bet and winning a little extra money had always

given Lizzie pleasure, and now deprived of it she couldn't stop thinking about it. It was a torment in the back of her mind all the time she was at work.

If Ben switched the wireless on and there was some racing commentary, she made it a habit to go to the kitchen and start some chore. This morning, one of the girls brought a newspaper to the shop and left it in the cloakroom. Lizzie picked it up and automatically turned to the back pages and then, tantalised by the picture of the winning horse in some race at Sandown Park, she threw it down. She must not do that; it only increased the temptation. Between one thing and another, Lizzie felt a nervous wreck. She was finding it harder than ever to resist the urge to have a flutter.

She often saw Jimmy Cox on her way home from work, and whenever she did he'd talk of racing and suggest a likely winner. Today he said, 'You've got the luck of the angels, Mrs McCluskey. A shame to stop when you have such a gift for spotting a winner.'

Lizzie hesitated, sorely tempted, but no, she'd stand firm. 'Not any more, Jimmy,' she said. 'This war has driven all my luck away. It's all work and no play now.' She didn't entirely trust Jimmy Cox.

He was too close to her and her family for comfort.

To please Ben, she hadn't placed a bet since the beginning of May, but she had spent a lot of time reliving the success she'd had on her honeymoon in Cheltenham last year. And every night she dreamed of having another big win that would make her rich. Make both of them rich. That would solve everything.

* * *

The weeks were rolling on. There were more air raids and like everybody else Lizzie had to go to the public shelter and was growing more frightened. To go with Ben was bad enough but she hated having to go alone.

It was one of those rare autumn days that could almost be August; the sun had been shining all morning, tantalising Lizzie, who had been put to work in the little office behind the shop checking bills and invoices for Mrs Field. The lunch hour was a long time coming.

At breakfast Ben had said he'd not be home at lunchtime: 'I have to go into Wallasey to fix a business deal with a friend.'

'What friend is this?' she'd asked, resentful that he kept a part of his life hidden from her. He'd explained in vague terms that black-market jobs kept him busy and that he thought it safer if she knew nothing about them.

As the morning went on she was getting hungry and imagined Ben sitting down in a restaurant to a hot roast dinner, while she'd have to make herself a sandwich and a cup of tea. She had nothing to put in a sandwich but the wartime bloater paste.

When they closed the shop, Freda, the other assistant said, 'It's such a lovely day, I'm going to walk along the prom and buy chips and ice cream for my lunch.'

Lizzie said, 'Good idea, I'll come with you.' They bought chips in the fairground and took them out to a seat on the prom to eat. With the sun on her face she thought it was lovely after being cooped up in that tiny dark office all morning. Life seemed normal.

Freda was chatting about her boyfriend. 'My mum wants us

to be engaged for two years so we really get to know each other before we get married.'

Half Lizzie's mind was on Ben. 'As a married woman,' she said, 'I can tell you that marriage is a lottery. You never truly know what a man is like until you live with him.'

She felt relaxed and turned to admire the distant Welsh hills, blue and beautiful in the sunshine. She did a double take; surely that was Ben a hundred yards further along the prom? Yes, it was. A bus drove past her; had he got off that? What was he doing here talking to that young girl in a red dress? Instantly, she was suspicious.

'Shall we go for our ice cream?' Freda asked.

Lizzie stood up. 'Count me out. I think I can see my husband. I'll see you back at the shop.'

She ran down the prom after him. He was wearing the new pullover she'd bought for him. He had a carrier bag and she saw him give the girl something from it. The girl was a pretty blonde but her red dress was terrible. Now they were waiting to cross in front of the traffic to the other side of the prom.

'Ben,' she called, 'Ben.' Lizzie saw him turn and look straight at her; she could see he'd recognised her. Deliberately he turned the girl away and behind her back he was waving her away, signalling that he didn't want her to come any nearer. Taken by surprise, she gasped and stopped running. Ben didn't want her to speak to him!

Yes, there it was again, he was waving her away. Then he took the girl's arm and led her across the road. A moment later they were lost amongst other pedestrians.

Lizzie was so shocked she couldn't get her breath. She knew only too well that Ben was a fraudster and a practised liar, but was he a womaniser too? All afternoon she mulled over that incident as she served in the shop. By closing time she was bristling with fury.

She hurried home to find Ben was there before her, wearing his old fairground clothes and preparing an evening meal of lamb chops. 'So who was that girl I saw you with?' she demanded. 'You lied to me. You said you were going into Wallasey.'

'I did go to Wallasey, I was coming back when you saw me.' His air of calmness infuriated her further. 'That's the truth.'

'Well go on, who was the girl?'

'Lizzie,' he took a deep breath, 'she means nothing to me. You mustn't worry about things like that.'

'Come off it, I want to know who she is.'

He looked at her, exasperated. 'That was Lennie O'Dowd's daughter. It was him I went to meet and she happened to be with him.'

'Oh, your friend Lennie O'Dowd of the restaurants and the nefarious money-making schemes? I suppose we can thank him for the lamb chops?'

'And he gave me some decent rump steak for tomorrow. We'd be eating pap if it weren't for Lennie, but he involves his family while I try to keep you away from all that.'

'You don't try hard enough.'

'Lizzie, you know I dabble a bit in the black market, but as far as I'm concerned the less you know about it the better, and the safer you are from being questioned by the police.'

'Thanks a million but you shouldn't be doing anything like that. It's against the law and when you lead a double life of lies and theft, you force it on me. I can't avoid knowing what you're up to.'

'There's a war on, Lizzie, and it throws up opportunities. It won't last for ever. Right now I'm building up our fortunes. I want us to have enough money so neither of us ever needs to work again.'

'Pull the other leg.'

'I mean it, once this war's over I'll turn over a new leaf, live a blameless life immersed in good deeds. We'll go round the world, have a good time again.'

'How can I believe a word of that? No, not when I've heard you spin real whoppers to my family.' Lizzie shuddered; she felt full of foreboding. 'Lying comes naturally to you and you're very convincing. You're a thief and a fraudster too and you're proud that you can get away with all these schemes. It keeps me on a knife edge and I'm sorry I ever married you.'

'Lizzie, don't say such things. I love you.'

'I could have had anybody but I fell for your Irish blarney. Sooner or later you'll end up in prison.' Lizzie knew she was getting worked up, and letting all her resentment out. For too long she'd tried to go along with him but he'd hardly noticed that. 'I made a mistake. I should have listened to my parents. They took against you. I think they could see through your lies. They knew what you were like.'

'Your father is prejudiced because I work in the fairground, and your mother thinks I can't provide a good life for you. They both think I'm from a lower class than they are. I am not the man they'd have chosen for you, but, Lizzie, we are married, happily married.'

'No. I wish I'd listened to them, I wish I hadn't fought them for permission to marry you. I must have been mad. Oh God, I wish I never had married you.'

'You don't mean that.' She felt his arms come round her in a hug. 'I do love you, Lizzie. Honest I do, and I'm sorry I've upset you, but dinner is ready. Do come and eat now. We can't waste these chops and they're overcooked already.'

Lizzie fought him off. 'You eat them. I hope they choke you.' She rushed to the bedroom and slammed the door.

CHAPTER TWENTY-SEVEN

O NE EVENING, WHEN LIZZIE had gone to the pictures with the girls from the shop, Ben went to the Anchor to have a beer with Steve Docherty from his rifle range.

Once inside, they met up with Lennie O'Dowd, who was complaining bitterly that the supplies of food he needed to run his business had been cut. 'I'm allowed nothing like enough. When people come out for a meal they want generous helpings of good quality food. This trade is impossible in wartime.'

When his father had retired to Ireland, Ben knew he'd asked Lennie to keep an eye on him. Ben admired the efficient way he ran his successful business, and was currently helping him obtain supplies on the black market.

'You've no shortage of customers though,' Ben reminded him. 'I see them flocking to your restaurant.'

Lennie grumbled on. 'There's very little profit in it these days. I'd just about sorted out my menus after basic rationing started in January but it's getting worse, and rationing brings so much extra work.'

Jimmy Cox was here with his boss Alec Hooper. 'You should hear my mother complain about the extra work.' Jimmy lived with his mother who was a widow and worked as chief clerk in the Wallasey Food Office. 'She reckons they've been desperately busy since those incendiaries fell on the Birkenhead Food Office and burned their stock of ration books. She's had to keep them going on what she has in her stock room and now she's running out too.'

Lennie O'Dowd took a gulp of his beer and said, 'She needn't worry, she can order all she needs.'

'More work for her,' Jimmy went on. 'There are only three of them working there now and she says you wouldn't believe how many people lose their ration books and petrol coupons, not to mention those bombed out who have to apply for coupons to replace almost everything. Mum has to go into all the reasons why and make sure they're not just trying it on to get extra.'

'That's a thought,' Lennie said. 'How does she get more stock?'

'She gets a delivery of documents every month, and this month she's expecting a bigger delivery than usual. More work again.'

'So what day does this delivery take place?' his boss asked. He sometimes teased Jimmy.

'Friday, I think.'

'What about raiding the Food Office and getting a good supply of the new ration books?' Lennie suggested jokingly. 'Jimmy, what is the best way to get into the Food Office?'

'Not a hope,' Jimmy laughed. 'My mother reckons it's like Fort Knox once she's locked up. There are locks on the windows and locks and bolts on the doors.'

'So all the clerks have keys?'

'No, my mum is the manager now.' There was a hint of

pride in his voice. 'The other girls have to wait on the doorstep in the mornings until she arrives.'

That started Ben thinking. Could this be their big chance? Several times they'd discussed ways and means of profiting from the current shortages and how to find bigger, more profitable ways of doing it.

'If we could get our hands on a large number of ration books, they'd sell like hot cakes,' Lennie said, half joking with Jimmy, 'and it would make life easier for me.'

'Documents are easier to keep hidden than food.' Ben grinned at Jimmy; they all treated him like the eager teenager he was.

'Can you get her to lend us the key?' said Alec.

'Hang on,' Jimmy said, 'I don't want you to land my mum in trouble.'

'We'd be very careful not to do that,' Alec said. 'You can trust me, can't you?'

'Hell, you're not serious?'

'Perhaps I am. We have to talk about it to see if it's practical before we decide.'

'Oh, I don't like it,' Jimmy said. 'Not a good idea at all. Not for me.'

'We can't talk about it here in the pub . . .' Lennie dropped his voice, 'too many ears.'

'Where are we going?' Jimmy was full of suspicion now.

'Down to the prom,' Alec said. Now it was dark there was a stiff breeze blowing but they found shelter behind a stone wall where steps led down to the beach. There was just room for the five of them to huddle together in the alcove. 'Come on, Jimmy, would it be possible for you to borrow your mother's keys and put them back again without her knowing?'

'Oh my God.'

'We're only talking about the possibility. Where does she keep her keys?'

'In her shoulder bag.'

'What time does she get home? And what does she do with her bag then?'

'She's home by about half five and hangs her bag on the row of coat hangers that we have up in our hall, then she goes into the kitchen to cook our dinner.'

'She covers it with her coat and she leaves it there until the next morning?'

'I suppose so,' he shrugged, 'unless she goes out again to the pictures.'

'She doesn't take it up to her room when she goes to bed?'

'Sometimes, I suppose.'

'Would it be practical for you to take her keys and put them back later?'

'I'm having nothing to do with that.'

'Come on, Jimmy, you always say yes to making a bit more cash. Yes or no?'

'I don't like that. Mam would kill me if she knew.'

'Jimmy, I've always looked after you, haven't I?' Alec said. 'We've done a few wild things but nothing has ever gone wrong. If things are planned carefully, it doesn't.'

'But nothing as big as this.'

'If we can use a key, it would be quicker and quieter than breaking in.'

'No, no.' Jimmy shivered. 'That sounds fine in theory, but

not at my mam's place.' He was an underweight, rather puny youngster. 'I'm afraid you're going to land her in a load of trouble.'

'We won't expect you to help in any other way,' Lennie said. 'And if it's Friday you'll both have cast-iron alibis. You've got your invitations to our party, haven't you?'

The frightening sound of the air-raid siren began to wail over the town and Jimmy shivered again. 'It might work provided I can put the keys back without her knowing but no, I don't like this. My mother would be horrified if she knew I was involved in a theft like that. She has to be honest in her job. I'm not doing it. I've had enough. I'm going home.'

Everybody was becoming more blasé about air-raid warnings because on so many occasions nothing more happened until the all-clear siren sounded an hour or so later. The others watched Jimmy disappear into the blackout of the promenade. They were all much older and Jimmy did the jobs they found for him. They agreed he was the least trustworthy in the team.

'You're his boss, Alec,' Ben said. 'Can you persuade him?'

'I've talked him round many times, and I think it's something of a good omen that Friday is my wedding anniversary and my daughter's twenty-first birthday. Our Dolly wanted a dance so I've booked the church hall and I've got a three-piece band to play for us. If Jimmy gets the keys for us I don't want him to go anywhere near the Food Office. He and his mother can come to our dance and they'll be seen by lots of people.'

'Is this job feasible?'

'It could certainly be profitable – the big one we're looking for – but the police will be on it like mustard as soon as a theft like that is reported.'

'Could we do it?' They deliberated and argued for half an hour.

'Lennie, you'd have to remind Jimmy that when his mother wants to leave your dance, he must go home with her and be sure to get his key out to open the front door,' Ben said.

Alec said, 'Oh yes, we can't let her find out she doesn't have the shop keys.' He shivered. 'She's good-hearted but frilly. You know, not the sort to stand up to police questioning.'

'She'd collapse,' Steve agreed.

'Then for this to work, we'd need to keep them both out of it,' Ben said.

'And we'd need to work out exactly how we pick up the keys, and how and when we take them back,' Steve said.

'But it might just work out,' Alec pondered. 'Let's mull it over.'

Friday was on them before Ben felt ready. His friends had decided that as a bigger than usual delivery of ration documents to the Food Office was expected today, and Lennie's long since arranged dance would give them all alibis for tonight, that would be a good time to do the job.

He was waiting for Alec, who had promised to walk round the fairground at lunchtime to keep the members of the team in contact and let them know any last-minute arrangements. If all went well it should put them all on easy street and be well worth the risks they'd have to take.

These days it wasn't just money that was needed to buy essential goods and food stuffs. Ration books were now essential; everything depended on having the correct coupons too. They were like gold dust: everybody wanted them.

Alec came at last and said, 'Jimmy confirms that the big consignment of ration documents is expected this afternoon, so it's on.'

'How is he?'

'He's a bag of nerves but he's agreed to bring me the key at around six thirty, and I'll return it under a stone that he's placed outside his front door when we've completed the job. He says while his mother gets their breakfast, he usually brings in the fresh milk from the doorstep, so he'll be able to put it in her bag then.'

'Great. Steve and I will get to the Food Office early. What about Lennie?'

'He's had a scout round and says the best place to park his van for loading up is in the street behind,' Alec said. 'I'll be there at the front with the keys and hope to see you and Steve. We'll all be ready to start at ten o'clock, OK?'

Ben took the bus into Wallasey feeling wired up. This was the biggest job he'd ever done and he could think of little else; it was giving him butterflies in his stomach. He felt hot in his ARP uniform. When the air-raid warning sounded, all ARP wardens were expected to get out on the streets and provide help to the general public, and Ben had undergone training in the sort of help he should be ready to give.

According to the rota, Ben was supposed to be on duty tonight, but not in the area of the Food Office. It added to his anxiety that his absence in his allotted area might be noticed and reported to the major who arranged these things. Steve Docherty had been roped into being an air-raid warden too and this was his area so thankfully he was in the right place.

However, he had a partner who Ben was hoping to avoid as he would know he should not be here. They'd come to make sure the coast was clear near the Food Office, and be on hand to load Lennie's van.

Just before the war had started Lennie O'Dowd had ordered a new van and had colourful adverts for his restaurant and tea rooms painted on both sides. Petrol rationing was on the cards by then and nobody had rushed to buy his old one, although he'd had all the writing removed. Now it was just a plain black van, ideal for jobs like this.

Steve was waiting outside Woolworths as they'd arranged. 'I feel a bit jumpy,' he said. 'Everywhere is so quiet. I hate the waiting and it isn't yet nine o'clock. I wish we hadn't got here so early.'

'Terrible thing to say but we need an air raid.' Ben wasn't feeling too calm either. 'To do the job under the cover of a raid would be a good thing. Nobody will be worrying about theft.'

'We haven't had a warning today, but we'll probably get one any time now.' The Luftwaffe came on fine nights such as this when the moon was full, and they could see their targets, the docks, rail installations and factories.

Ben had taken a look round yesterday in daylight. The Wallasey Food Office was at the end of a row of old-fashioned shops, once owner-occupied with living accommodation above. It had had its big front window half boarded up, leaving just enough glass to let daylight in. Next door had once belonged to an estate agent but had now closed as nobody wanted to buy property, and with the air-raid damage there was nothing to rent.

As they rounded the corner the Food Office came in view. 'Oh hell,' Steve said, 'they're showing light.'

'A lot of light,' Ben gasped, his heart pumping with shock. It was coming from a small window on the side of the building. 'There shouldn't be anybody there, the place is supposed to close at five. Perhaps it's lucky they are; we can go to tell them to put it off and find out what's going on.'

Steve snatched at his arm. 'What about Jimmy's mother? She'll recognise me, I spoke to her and Jimmy only the other night. What about you?'

'I know her, of course. Oh my God, but we've got to do it.'

'Will she recognise you?' He could hear panic in Steve's voice.

'I don't know her all that well, enough to say hello.' He'd seen her at the fair. He pulled his uniform cap more over his face. 'We have to know why they're still here, and we mustn't dither about in case someone is watching us.'

'This is up to you.' Steve's hand pushed him forward. 'I'll stay near and keep my eyes peeled.'

Ben tried the shop door; it was locked. 'Put that light out,' he bellowed and rapped loudly on the glass.

The door half opened, letting out another broad shaft of light, and a flustered girl said, 'What is it?'

'ARP warden, put that damned light out,' Ben said loudly and stepped inside. The original shop was now an office furnished with three desks. He crossed it to the passage behind where he could see a lot of large cardboard cartons. The light went out, but not before Ben had another shock that pulled him up abruptly.

'Sorry.' It was Jimmy Cox who'd switched off a light in an adjoining room. He was staring blankly at him.

He should be at Lennie's dance by now. Oh lord. Ben shook his head slowly and put a finger across his lips. What on earth had gone wrong? He'd have to keep his wits about him.

'Sorry.' Ben turned to the other voice behind him and recognised Jimmy's mother. She looked distraught. 'We've accidentally knocked down the blackout covering the storeroom window and we're trying to put new stock away. A very late delivery. It's been one thing after another today.'

Ben was fighting to keep calm. 'Can't you leave it until tomorrow?'

'No, not all up the corridor. I'm supposed to keep these in the safe but it won't hold any more. We've got to get them locked in the storeroom for the night.'

The air-raid warning blared out at that moment, rising and falling and making the two younger girls cling together for comfort. Ben saw that as a blessing. 'But it isn't safe for you to stay here now. You should lock up as much as you can and go.'

'No,' Mrs Cox protested, 'my instructions are all ration documents must be locked in the storeroom overnight.'

Ben stood his ground. 'And the government rules everybody must go to a shelter when there is a warning. As warden, it's my duty to make sure you do. It's for your own safety.'

'I want to go home,' one of the girls cried. 'I'm shattered.'

'You can't go home,' Ben ordered. 'You must go to that shelter at the end of the street. Get your things together and I'll see you safely down there.'

'I must lock up at the back,' Mrs Cox said, running back to

her desk in the shop. Ben watched her take the keys from her desk drawer. She was at the end of her tether too.

'You told me to lock up as soon as the delivery van left,' one of the assistants said.

'Did I?'

Ben was on a knife edge – what should he do now?

But Jimmy came forward. 'I've left my bike in the yard, Mum,' he said, taking the keys from her. 'I'm going to get it. It'll be quicker for me to wheel it through the shop.'

Ben saw his chance. 'I'll walk round with him and we'll check that everything is safely locked up,' he said. 'The rest of you get your coats on.'

Jimmy led the way to the back of the premises. In what was the kitchen he slid off the bolts and unlocked the back door. Ben snatched the keys from him and ran down the yard to the back gate, slid back the bolts there and turned the key in the lock. When he returned to the kitchen he found Jimmy had wheeled his bike inside and was standing over it looking shocked and frightened.

Ben made a great show of locking and bolting the back door while keeping it slightly ajar. 'No need for the keys now,' he hissed. His heart was thudding and his knees felt weak as he remembered that they'd intended to wear gloves before they came in here. He must not leave evidence.

He tried to rub the keys on his trouser leg before pushing them back into Jimmy's hand. 'What about locking up after-wards?' Jimmy hissed.

Mrs Cox had followed them in a state of agitation. 'We're ready.'

Ben swallowed hard in desperation. 'All safely locked up at

the back,' he said, trying to sound calmer than he felt.

'Lock the storeroom door,' she said to Jimmy and Ben saw him turn the key in that before turning the shop light out and pushing everybody out into the street. Mrs Cox carefully locked the front door behind them, using both Yale and ordinary keys, and Ben escorted them down the road. His mind was running wild; he'd forgotten all about the need to lock up again when they were leaving.

It was no longer peaceful; bombs were dropping. Ben heard an explosion upriver, followed by another and another. The two young girls were running ahead with their hands over their ears. Jimmy was holding on to his mother's arm, hurrying her along and pushing his bike with the other hand. Ben could see fire lighting up the sky somewhere over New Brighton. The ack-ack guns were firing from the site in Harrison Park and searchlights were criss-crossing the sky, searching for enemy planes.

Mrs Cox shot inside the public shelter. Ben held on to Jimmy's arm to whisper, 'Get yourself and your mother to Lennie's dance. Be sure to show your faces there.'

'She won't want to go after this. Anyway, he'll probably call it off.'

'You've done very well tonight, but you've got to do Lennie's dance.'

Jimmy leaned forward to whisper, 'My mother keeps the key to the storeroom in the top drawer of her desk.'

'Marvellous, we'll do everything else. Just keep your mouth shut.' Ben was sweating in both panic and relief when he turned round to find Steve and Alec had followed at a distance. 'What's happened?' Alec whispered. He had to repeat himself as Ben couldn't hear him; screaming fire engines and ambulance bells were filling the night.

'The back door is wide open,' he gasped. 'The sooner we go in and take what we want the better.' All was quiet as they passed the front of the Food Office and they found Lennie O'Dowd's van parked in the street behind. 'OK. We're all here now, so let's get on with it.'

CHAPTER TWENTY-EIGHT

LIZZIE WAS TERRIFIED OF air raids. If there was one thing she loathed more than anything else, it was getting up in the middle of the night and going alone to a public shelter. She accepted now that she had to go; even having strangers around her was better than being alone. She resented Ben leaving her to look after other people, though she knew he'd only signed up as an air-raid warden to placate her father. These days he seemed to have so many things to do that she didn't understand and he didn't explain. Without Ben's companionship she felt isolated and very much alone, and that the gulf between them was widening.

Tonight he'd put on his uniform and said, 'I'll be late back tonight, go to bed and don't worry about me.'

That was unusual. Normally he seemed to give her little thought. 'Let's hope there are no air raids then,' she said. She took off her dress to keep it fit for work tomorrow and put her siren suit on over the rest of her clothes.

Tonight the siren sounded its warning early and she was up and out right away. More people were using the shelter now and though she had room to sit on the wooden bench, after an hour or so she found it very uncomfortable. A fat man in dirty overalls was snoring next to her and hardly gave her space to move.

She could feel the tension rising in those around her when the explosions were nearer. They could all hear the horrifying crump crump and the wailing sirens of ambulances and fire engines outside. The children screamed louder and some of the women did too. Lizzie was terrified.

But eventually it quietened down and she was able to relax a little. The children went to sleep but she fell into a stupor that was neither sleep nor wakefulness. At midnight the all-clear sounded and her fellow occupants began to leave in pairs and groups. She longed to lie down and stretch her legs out in bed. Sleepily, she got to her feet and set out slowly for home.

She sensed something was terribly wrong. Within moments she was fully awake and choking on the smoke and stench of burning. Her face stung from the bits of ash and burnt material flying in the air. In no time her eyes were streaming with tears and she could make out a fire engine and a small crowd collecting in Alvaston Terrace.

'Oh my God!' The roof looked completely different. What had happened to it? Smoke was billowing from the first cottage, all the doors and windows were open and she could see men working inside.

Dread gripped her. 'Ben?' she called, but none gave any sign they heard. They looked like wardens but were so covered in dust it was impossible to see who they were. She staggered nearer and tugged at the sleeve of the first person she came to. 'For God's sake, what's happened?'

He coughed, and said, 'Incendiary bombs started a fire in the roof space, and it spread along the terrace.'

Lizzie could see an ambulance was standing by. This was a nightmare. Now in a rising panic she pushed her way through

264

the people down the terrace to her home, which was second from the other end. It wasn't that easy to make out in the drifting smoke, but she could see some of the roof timbers sticking up, bare of slates. She got out her key and pushed towards the front door. She must see what the place was like inside.

'No,' the arm of a policeman restrained her, 'you can't go in.'

'It's my house. I live here,' she sobbed.

'Sorry, no, it isn't safe.'

Lizzie hammered on his chest with both fists. 'Everything I own is in there,' she cried. 'I have to go in.'

'It isn't safe for anybody. They're still damping down the fire. The roof could come in on you. Do you have family or a friend you could spend the night with?'

'No, all my things are inside, I want to save what I can.' Lizzie's face was streaming with tears.

He caught at the hand she was waving and saw her wedding ring. 'You're married. Where's your husband?'

'He's a warden, looking after everybody else.'

A woman came and pushed a cup of tea into her hands. Lizzie gulped at it. 'Would you like a sandwich?' she asked. 'The WVS van is on the next corner.'

'Can I leave her with you?' the policeman said. 'She's shocked. See her somewhere safe for the rest of the night, will you?'

Nothing could calm Lizzie. She hardly knew what was going on. Eventually she found herself in a car, being driven out to Oakdene Farm. When the door was opened by Milly, she fell into her arms, sobbing out her story.

Mum and Father ushered her to the kitchen offering sympathy. 'Make some tea, Emilia,' Dadda said. 'We all need it.'

Mum was wringing her hands. 'I'm afraid your bed isn't made up,' she said, 'and it will need airing after all this time.'

Milly said, 'Don't worry, Lizzie can share mine.' Lizzie spent what remained of the night still cramped for space, but clinging to her sister and gaining some comfort from her warmth.

Ben and his friends were loading up Lennie's van as quickly and quietly as they could. The all-clear had sounded and all was quiet now outside. 'More here than I ever envisaged,' Lennie said. 'New ration books and ration coupons of every sort.'

'I don't know what some of them are for.' Alec pushed in another carton.

'Ministry of Food probably hasn't decided yet,' Steve said. 'Are we all ready to go?'

'Yes, but I think we should we break the kitchen window to make it look as though we came in that way,' Alec said. 'This place is bound to be crawling with police in a few hours. We want to put them off the scent of Jimmy and his mother if we can.'

'Good thinking,' Lennie agreed, 'but it will make a noise. We should have done it during the raid; it's all gone quiet now.'

'That window is quite high on the outside. We'd have to stand on something to get onto the sill.' Alec tipped the dustbin upside down and placed it under the window so he could stand on it. 'Are we ready to go? The breaking glass might attract attention. We need to get away quickly afterwards.'

Ben said, 'Hang on a minute.' It was only when he went to lock up the empty storeroom and put the key back in Mrs Cox's desk that he remembered Jimmy still had the keys to the yard and back doors. He rushed back. 'We can't lock up behind us,' he gasped. He was deafened by the almighty smash as Alec shattered the window. The noise of tinkling glass seemed loud enough to wake the dead. They hadn't heard him. Ben felt rising panic as a terracotta flower pot containing dried-out soil and withered stems rolled down the yard. Alec was reaching inside to lift the catch and the sash window slid up.

'Climb through, make it look authentic,' Lennie urged. Alec did and was out beside them again through the back door.

Ben pulled it shut behind them and ran to the van. There was nothing else he could do. Lennie started the engine while he climbed over the front seat into the back of the van so Alec could use the passenger seat. Steve was already squashed into the space they'd left for passengers when they were loading. 'Thank goodness that's over,' Steve said, sounding euphoric.

'Everything went according to plan there,' Lennie said, 'even though you arrived to find the staff still there. Jimmy did all right, didn't he?'

Ben was sweating. He'd slipped up; he'd never got round to telling them the whole story. 'No,' he said, 'no.' He was struggling to get the words out; his mind was addled; he could no longer think straight. 'Should we have broken that window when we've had to leave the back doors unlocked? Where's the sense of that?'

That sobered them all up. 'Plenty of time to think of that later,' Lennie said. 'We need to keep our minds on what we still have to do.' While driving through Wallasey, Lennie said, 'Just look at the damage! We've had a very heavy raid tonight.'

They were back in New Brighton when Steve said, 'Goring Street got it too. They're still digging people out, by the look of it.'

'That's where I should have been this evening,' Ben said. He had a restricted view of the outside, but he knew his friends were shocked and felt a moment of complete panic. He should have been there to help. He'd have been missed. He must ask around tomorrow to find out exactly what had happened, so that if he was asked about it, he wouldn't make it obvious that he hadn't been there.

When they were further on, Steve said, 'Oh hell, Ben, there's been a fire in Alvaston Terrace. The fire engine is still there.'

'What?' That gave him a real jolt. 'A bad fire? Is my house all right?'

'I can't see that far along.'

'Oh my word, I hope Lizzie is all right. Everything's going wrong tonight.'

Lennie drove them back to his restaurant in the fairground. 'Let's get the van unloaded and everything safely stowed away as soon as we can. That's the important thing now. '

Ben stayed to help but he felt in a flat spin about Lizzie and their home. 'What if she's been hurt?' he moaned.

'Don't forget Lennie's giving a birthday bash,' Alec said. 'Steve and I are going to show our faces at the church hall.'

'Count me out of that.' Ben ached in every limb; he was exhausted and felt in a state of mortal terror. 'I have to go home and see what's happened there.'

'That's a good enough alibi for you,' Steve said. 'Hope all is well with your place.'

'We've done marvellously well tonight.' Lennie clapped him on the shoulder. 'We'll make a small fortune from this lot.'

Ben closed his eyes and shuddered – had Mrs Cox recognised him? And what would the police make of the story she and Jimmy would tell? The shattered window indicated they must have found another key inside and not bothered to lock up as they'd left. But they'd have had to climb the yard wall to get as far as the window. It was over six feet high and they'd planted no false evidence of that. And also, should they have forced their way into the storeroom instead of using Mrs Cox's key?

In every way they'd made it look like an inside job, which was the last thing they'd intended to do.

CHAPTER TWENTY-NINE

WHEN BEN REACHED ALVASTON Terrace he spoke to the wardens who were just finishing off and preparing to leave, and learned that the old couple living at number ten had been killed and that three more people injured in numbers eight and seven had been taken to hospital. He was careful to tell them he'd been working in the Goring Street area and had had a bad night there too. 'Have you sent anybody to hospital from my house, number two?' he asked.

Everybody he asked shook their heads; nobody had seen Lizzie. He felt scared out of his wits and was growing more agitated by the moment. He walked to the shelter where she should have gone. It was undamaged but deserted now. But sometimes she just turned over in bed and stayed where she was.

He leaned against a wall and tried to calm himself. Logically, the most likely thing was that Lizzie had been in the shelter and after the all-clear had gone home. She would not have been allowed in and when she'd seen the damage, she'd go to spend the rest of the night with her parents. There was nowhere else she could go. He took a grip on himself and went back to Alvaston Terrace.

A fire engine was still standing by and he was told the fire had flared up again in number nine. The bare spars jutting up from his roof meant there would be a lot of damage inside. The police had taped the whole terrace off and left notices at intervals forbidding entry, and saying looters would be prosecuted.

Ben stepped through them and unlocked the door to his own house. The stench of burning made him gasp. Water was dripping down the stairs. Part of the upstairs ceiling had burned away and their bed was soaked. Downstairs it wasn't too bad. He locked up again and decided he could salvage quite a lot of his things if they weren't stolen first.

He could see by the clock on the mantelpiece that it was after two o'clock. He was so tired he felt dizzy and could hardly stand up straight. He had to get some sleep.

He knew a nearby primary school had been opened as a shelter for those temporarily homeless. The WVS trolley was at the entrance; he was given a cup of tea and a sandwich and then he curled up with a blanket on the floor of the school hall and fell instantly asleep. The activity all round him woke him when daylight came. He was stiff and cold and longed to turn over and try to go back to sleep, but he had to get up to Oakdene Farm to find out if Lizzie was all right.

Milly had trouble getting back to sleep with a restless Lizzie taking half of her bed. 'I haven't seen Ben,' she told her half a dozen times. 'I do hope he's all right.' She was very distressed. Milly did her best to comfort her. There was another air-raid warning at three o'clock which they ignored because all was quiet and by four o'clock both were deeply asleep. Breakfast the next morning was very late. After a bad night like that, Gladys was late coming to work and the family late getting up.

Lizzie was white-faced and subdued. 'I must go and look for Ben,' she said, pushing her scrambled egg round her plate. 'And now it's daylight I want to go back home to see just how badly damaged it is.'

'You'll need to go to work, won't you?' Esmond asked.

'No,' her mother said, 'surely she can't be expected to do that after the night she's had, not today. Ring your boss and tell her you haven't seen your husband since yesterday and your home has been damaged.'

Lizzie lifted the phone dutifully but the operator said, 'Sorry, please try again later. The lines are down after last night's raid and we can't connect you.'

'If you like, I'll come with you to see your cottage,' Milly offered. All her life Lizzie had been her big sister and charged with taking care of her, but last night she'd felt that Lizzie had changed and was seeking support from her.

'Yes,' she said, 'I'd be glad if you would.'

'You should go to school,' Dadda said. 'No reason why you should not.'

'I'm already too late for assembly, Dadda. I'll go this afternoon and hope the buses are running by then.'

'Elizabeth, if your cottage is too badly damaged to live in,' Dadda went on, 'you and Ben can move into the old servants' quarters upstairs.'

'Thank you, Father, but I hope that won't be necessary.'

'We all hope that, Lizzie,' her mother said. 'But just in case we'll air the bed in your old room and also start to clean the upstairs rooms. So many people are being bombed out it will be impossible for you to find any alternative.'

The letter box on the front door rattled, and a voice came,

'Hello?' Milly went to see who it was. A very tired and dishevelled Ben said, 'Is Lizzie here?'

'Thank goodness. Come on in, Lizzie's worried sick about you.' Milly ushered him to the dining room. 'We were all wondering about you.'

Lizzie had followed her and now threw herself into his arms. 'What happened to you?'

He kissed her. 'You're all right? You haven't been hurt? Such a relief, thank goodness, I looked everywhere for you but I couldn't find you,' he said and slumped into a chair at the table. 'Morning, Major. Goring Road caught a basinful last night. Four people killed and I don't know how many injured.' He'd heard that this morning.

'That's where you were on duty?' Elsie asked.

'Yes, I spent half the night digging out. Then I heard there'd been a fire in Alvaston Terrace so I went to see what our place was like.'

'Is it bad? Can it be repaired?'

'Quite bad, I'm sorry to say. I think it can be repaired. The war damage people will put the roof back on and make the houses fit to live in, but it won't be happening any time soon. We'll have to find somewhere else to live.'

Esmond was shaking his head. 'Ben, you've done a good night's work,' he told him. 'The air raids are making people homeless at a terrible rate, your best plan would be to move into the old servants' quarters upstairs. At least I can do that for you.'

Gladys asked if he wanted scrambled egg on toast for his breakfast. 'Just tea, please,' he said, 'I've had a sandwich already from the WVS trolley.'

273

Milly was despatched to find Clover and ask her to come and help clean out the attic rooms while Lizzie's old bedroom was hastily made fit. She took Ben up to share her single bed and have another few hours' sleep.

Lizzie dozed off quite quickly, but although Ben felt shattered he was too worried to sleep. He didn't know whether he and his friends had got away with that robbery, or whether they'd left evidence that would lead promptly to their conviction. He tried to doze, but felt restless and decided he'd go down to the fairground to see how the rest of the team had fared. He slid gently off the bed; Lizzie hardly stirred as he pulled the eiderdown over her and tiptoed out of the room.

Elsie was in the kitchen. 'Esmond has gone out to see if there's any further help he can give those made homeless.' Ben was afraid he'd find out that he'd not been working in Goring Street last night, and worried that Mrs Cox had recognised him. Last but not least, he was not looking forward to living so much closer to the major. He could wind him up just by looking at him with those pale searching eyes.

He borrowed Milly's bike. If he was going to live at Oakdene Farm he'd need one of his own to get about; it wasn't going to be as convenient as Alvaston Terrace.

It seemed strange to see normal life going on in the fairground after such momentous changes in his own circumstances. He headed straight for the boating lake – it was Jimmy Cox and his mother he was most concerned about. Alec Hooper was in the boathouse selling tickets for hourly hire of his boats. Ben asked, 'Have you any news? How's Jimmy?'

'I gather the police were round at the Food Office shortly after nine this morning, as soon as his mother reported the loss.

They came here to collect Jimmy about noon and they've taken him to the police station. To tell the truth, I've got the willies. Jimmy was a nervous wreck all morning.'

Ben shivered; he must not lose his nerve now. 'We knew it would happen like this. Did they go to Lennie's dance?'

'We all did. After that air raid not all that many were there, so there was plenty to eat. The Coxes didn't stay much more than half an hour.'

'That's long enough for them to be noticed.'

'Yes, the dance hall wasn't damaged and Lennie and his daughter were in great form.'

'What do we do now?'

'What can we do but wait? We must expect the police to contact Lennie to confirm their alibis. He's going to tell them Jimmy and his mother were at the dance while the raid was on and when it got bad he took them to the shelter under his restaurant.'

'But wouldn't there be others there who might say otherwise?' Ben sighed. 'There are so many ways we could open up a load of trouble.'

'I thought of that too,' Alec said. 'But according to Lennie there were not many eating in his place last night, and he locked up before bringing the van out to meet us. I'm hoping Jimmy will come back here soon and can tell us more.'

It was four in the afternoon when Jimmy returned, looking really ill. 'The police grilled us one at a time about exactly what had happened last night, about who had handled the keys and who had locked up. They kept on about whether extra keys were kept on the premises, but I said as little as possible. We were asked more than once if we knew the ARP warden who came, and we both said no to that.'

'Does she honestly not know?' Ben asked.

'I don't think she does. Mum was flustered last night because they'd been waiting all afternoon for the ration books to be delivered and they were working very late. Then when they were trying to lock the stuff safely away she lost her temper with Edna because she knocked down the blackout in the storeroom and they couldn't fix it back.'

'Good. How is your mother today?'

'A total wreck, a complete bag of nerves. She's worried they'll think she left the place unlocked, that she was careless. She's never that and I told them so.'

Ben was relieved she hadn't recognised him, but he had yet to find out if he'd been missed in Goring Street. If he had, he'd have to say he went to Alvaston Terrace to look for his wife. He still felt exhausted and absolutely drained. He was still worried too, but he could do little more today.

On the way back to the farm, Ben called in at Alvaston Terrace. He found their clothes in the wardrobe and drawers were still clean, and pushed as many as he could into a suitcase and strapped it onto the carrier on the back of the bike. Lizzie had nothing to wear but her siren suit, and he hadn't taken his warden's uniform off since he'd put it on.

When she got up, Lizzie went to inspect the Anderson shelter out in the garden. 'Of course there'll be room for you,' Mum had said, 'it has four bunk beds. Dadda and Ben are often on duty when there's a raid, but there's a chair and a stool between the bunks if we are all at home.'

Lizzie knew that would be much better than sitting with

strangers in a public shelter; she could at least stretch out and try to sleep. She went to work the next day and was shocked to see how much other damage had occurred around the town during that raid. All the windows had been blown out of the shop where she worked, as they had all along the shopping parade.

Quite a lot of their stock had been damaged and she had to help wash and iron that. Mrs Field had to reduce the prices and she was worried about her business. 'I think it's hardly worth keeping two shops open now. Everything's in short supply and the only stockings I can get are thick and serviceable. Nobody wants them. There's no fashion any more, everything is the same and of utility quality, and there's talk of rationing even that.'

That news depressed Lizzie. 'What about my job?'

'Don't worry about that,' Mrs Field said. 'Three of my girls have given notice; two are going in the Wrens and one is getting married and going to live in Blackpool. I'll need the rest of you to run my Wallasey shop. You'll be happy to move there, will you?'

'Yes,' Lizzie said, but she didn't like the idea because she'd have to catch two buses to get to work, one into New Brighton and another from there to Wallasey.

Over dinner that evening, she said to the family, 'Gladys tells me that Clover is thinking of going to work at the munitions factory on the prom when it opens. She says she'll earn much more than any shop assistant so I'm thinking of doing the same.'

'I wouldn't if I were you,' her mother said. 'It must be dangerous work. You'd be dealing with high explosives.'

'Stay well away from that,' Father advised. 'You won't like it.'

'I think I might.' Lizzie explained about Mrs Field's shop. 'It's handy down there on the prom and I'd be helping the war effort.'

'Won't it be monotonous work in a factory? You'll soon get bored with it,' Milly said.

'I won't,' Lizzie insisted. 'I think we should all help the war effort if we can. We all want to get it over.'

Milly thought for a moment. 'You're right about that,' she said. 'I'm doing nothing to help the war, and it's on my conscience. Here I am at sixteen still studying. I could do factory work as well as you, Lizzie.'

Dadda looked up. 'No.'

'I could put off training to be a journalist until we've won the war.'

'Absolutely not, I forbid you to do any such thing.' Dadda was cross. 'You said you wanted to be a journalist, that it was your ambition. You'll need to learn shorthand and typing before you can start that, and you must not change your mind now.'

'Heaven knows why you want to be a journalist,' Lizzie scoffed. 'You'll find it's like writing school essays all day. And I absolutely hated Skerry's College. You'll have to spend a whole year battling with a typewriter, and learning shorthand is worse.'

'Emilia may find it easier at the New Brighton College.'

'You told me Skerry's was the best commercial college in Liverpool,' Lizzie said. 'Will the New Brighton place be any good?'

'Elizabeth, sometimes plans have to be changed. Public transport cannot run to its timetable now roads and railways are being repeatedly damaged. I'm sure Emilia will do very well and learn all she needs to know nearer to home. I do not want her to jeopardise her future by working in a factory now. I'm afraid we'll all have to leave it to you to help the war effort.'

CHAPTER THIRTY

IT TOOK A COUPLE of weeks before Mrs Field was ready to close the New Brighton branch of her shop, and Lizzie worked there until the last day. After that she had to take two buses in the morning. Public transport was unreliable: routes were frequently altered because of holes in the tarmac or rubble blocking the way. If there was an air-raid warning while she was on a bus, the driver was ordered to take passengers to the nearest shelter and they were all supposed to stay in that until the all-clear sounded.

After a time, Lizzie said, 'The bus didn't come again tonight and I've had to walk part of the way home. I'm sick of waiting around for them. I'm going to apply for the munitions factory job.'

Milly told her, 'Clover has heard it's due to open at the end of the month – she's looking forward to working there.'

'I thought she had a new job,' Lizzie said.

'She has but she hates it. She's working for a cleaning firm and has to get up early to clean shops before they open and they don't pay very much.'

'I never see Gladys these days,' Lizzie complained. 'I have to leave before she gets here. Ask her to let you know when Clover starts and perhaps I'll go there too.'

'It's dangerous work,' Mum worried, 'and you'll be permanently underground.' Milly heard Dadda give the same advice as before but she knew Lizzie would take no heed of it.

It was another week or two before Gladys told them that Clover had got the job at the munitions factory. 'She's been told to start at eight o'clock on Monday morning.'

'Then I'll apply too,' Lizzie said. She went to the labour exchange in her lunch hour and was given a form to fill up. She had to give Mrs Field a week's notice.

'I'll be sorry to lose you, Lizzie,' she told her. 'You seemed to take more interest in the shop than the others.' On Lizzie's last day, Mrs Field wrote out a good reference for her, gave her a leaving bonus, and provided cake for the tea break so they could have a little party to wish her well in her war work.

On her first day at the factory, Lizzie found the general noise level, the spinning machinery and the speed at which she was supposed to work a bit of a shock. She was glad to find Clover had learned her way round and was willing to show her. It was repetitive work and she found she was just a cog in the workplace instead of being a valued member of the team. She wished heartily that she'd stayed where she was, but they all knew this was essential work and they'd have to have a good reason to leave. After a week or so, Lizzie was able to tell her family, 'I don't much like being underground all day. It makes me feel like a coal miner, but it's never going to be cold in there and the other girls are jolly.'

Elsie frowned. 'It can't be good for you, having no daylight, fresh air or sun all day and every day. I couldn't stand that.'

'It's not too bad; we get music while we work and the money is excellent. I'm making machine gun bullets, but others are making shells and press button switches for aircraft radios. And it's said to be safe from air raids. We don't even hear the warning siren down there.'

'At least you have the satisfaction of doing essential work,' Esmond said.

Lizzie had thought her new home and new job would take her mind off gambling, but it hadn't. She stared hard at her reflection in her dressing table mirror and could see no change. She was a bit pale and she'd lost a bit of weight but she was working underground and everybody put it down to that, and the air raids and this miserable war.

But it was much more than that. There were lots of men interested in racing working in the factory, and she couldn't help hearing them talking about possible winners when there was a race meeting on somewhere. Working with them made it twice as difficult.

When she'd had that shattering loss on the horse called Teazle she'd been scared that Ben could be right, and she might have become, well, not addicted but perhaps obsessed with gambling. But it was just Ben's idea; really, he was impossible. He'd kept on about her being addicted and to please him she'd cut gambling out of her life.

He was definitely wrong about being addicted because she'd made up her mind to stop and she had, for over five months. It was a matter of self-discipline, though by then she'd had no money anyway because her nest egg was gone.

It was the lack of joy in her life that was eating into her.

What she craved was more fun. Yes, she really had missed gambling. She'd tried to tell Ben, expecting sympathy, but he'd said briskly, 'Could it be withdrawal symptoms?'

'Nonsense,' she'd said, and here she was, crumbling to pieces and he hardly noticed. She decided she'd feel better if she stopped thinking about betting, and the way to do that would be to have just a little flutter now and again.

Why not? After all, she was accumulating money in her account now and there really was very little to spend it on in the shops. She intended to be very careful, very cautious, and bet only small amounts. She went to buy a *Sporting Life* and then to see Jimmy Cox again.

It brought utter relief. She felt so much better and it gave her the energy to get through the grinding boredom and hard work at the factory.

After only a few days, Mum smiled at her and said, 'You're feeling better, thank goodness. I never liked the idea of you spending all day and every day working underground, but it seems you can stand up to it.'

The next morning, Ben was working his roundabout when he saw Alec with Jimmy Cox, waving to attract his attention. He hopped off to join them. 'Has something happened?'

'Yes.' Jimmy looked agitated. 'Two police officers came round last night; one took me out to the car and we were grilled again separately.'

'What about?' Ben asked.

'Exactly the same things over again. Who had handled her keys the other night, who had locked up, who else had keys and was another key kept in the office? They thought Mum had lent her keys to someone else but she swore the keys were in her possession all the time.'

'Which they were,' Alec said. 'Good.'

'They rained questions at me. I told them half a dozen times I didn't know the air-raid warden who came. I felt half dead by the time they left.'

'You didn't say anything to make them suspect? Steve and I told you how to handle them.'

'I did exactly what you told me, Alec. I answered every question and tried to sound truthful. I volunteered nothing and said as little as possible.'

Ben said, 'We all told you to expect plenty of police attention as you were close to those keys, but as things turned out you were the one person in the Wallasey Food Office on the evening of the robbery who didn't work there. That guaranteed they'd pick you out first.'

'They did; they seem to think I helped somebody else to do it. They wanted to know why I was there. I'm scared stiff.'

'What explanation did you give?' Ben was feeling jittery.

'The same again: that I knew Mum was expecting a big delivery that day and when she didn't come home at teatime I went out on my bike to buy a loaf from the corner shop before it closed. It's what I always do if she isn't home. I was worried because she's never that late and the buses are often full at that time, but when I got to the Food Office the stuff she was expecting was just being delivered. I helped carry it in so Mum could come home.'

'They accepted that?' Alec asked.

'How do I know? They leaned on me, wanting to know if I'd gone there before, all that sort of thing. Over and over.'

'Did they ask your mother the same thing?' Alec was nerve-wracked too.

'Yes, she said they did ask her that and she told them the same thing, that I'd done it once or twice before. That's the truth. They kept on at me as though they hoped to wear me down, but I didn't change anything, however many times they asked. Honest.'

That did nothing to ease Ben's worries. 'How's your mother taking this?'

'Badly. It's driving her round the bend. She can't sleep for thinking about it and she's afraid she might lose her job.'

'No, Jimmy,' Alec soothed. 'This is the way the police go about investigating things. It doesn't mean they suspect you. They were trying to get you to talk. They want to know what really happened. Information is what they were seeking from you.'

'You did well not to fall into that trap,' Ben said.

'I didn't, but they kept on at Mum too about the keys, and was she sure the place had been locked up when she left that night, and did she know the air-raid warden who came. And on and on about what instructions she had about locking up, all that sort of thing. She's supposed to keep new ration documents in the safe, but there was never the slightest hope of getting it all in there, it was packed tight anyway. She said her head was whirling after that.'

The team of friends spent the rest of that day going back and forth across the fairground assuring each other they had no reason to worry and should calm down, but Ben knew he was not the only one to find that impossible.

The next day Lennie reported that the police had contacted

him asking him to confirm that Jimmy and his mother had been at his dance that evening. 'Everything's all right, it's what we expected, isn't it?' Ben thought that should have helped but it didn't.

A day or two later Steve brought a copy of the Wallasey *Gazette* to Ben's roundabout at mid-morning. 'Read this,' he said. It carried a report of the theft from the Food Office.

It made Ben's hair stand on end. 'Oh my goodness, but we should have expected it.' He read on. 'I think we took much more than it implies here. Do you think the amount of stuff we got has been played down? Does it seem like that to you?'

'Possibly, but everybody's talking about it.'

Ben heard that copies of the newspaper were being passed round the customers in the Anchor that lunchtime, and when he went back to Oakdene Farm and was eating his dinner, it seemed his in-laws had read it too and were equally horrified by the theft. Worse, last night the major had attended some function with Harry Barr's father, who was in charge of the Wallasey police and had spoken with him. Ben was eating his dinner with his in-laws every evening now he had to live here. Lizzie said it meant they had a lot less work but Ben would much prefer them to be on their own. Tonight, as Ben expected, the major had something to say about the robbery and was aghast. 'I feel very strongly,' he said, 'that these thieves must be caught as soon as possible. We have to stop this sort of thing.'

That made Ben quake inwardly. While Milly and Lizzie cleared the plates and Elsie brought in the pudding, the major got up to find the newspaper and read it out to him, his voice full of disdain. 'We have Harry Barr risking his life to bring fuel to Liverpool and in Wallasey we have petrol coupons stolen.

The villains make a fortune from selling them and the rogues who buy them use it to go on picnics. A despicable thing to do in wartime; they are helping the enemy.'

It was all Ben could do not to wince. He didn't know where to look; he was afraid Esmond had guessed. Worse, he felt a guilty flush run up his cheeks and hoped he wouldn't notice.

He could hardly sit still as the major ranted on. 'Petrol should be used only by doctors and other essential users.'

Ben knew he must not betray by so much as a muscle anything that might convey guilt. His heart was pumping and he was afraid that would be noticed by the family. Nobody mentioned that Harry Barr had used petrol to drive Milly round. Presumably, for heroes like him, that was allowed.

Even more frightening was the fact that the family were on good terms with Harry Barr, and his father was in charge of the Wallasey police. Just to think of that gave him the jitters. His hand trembled and made his spoon tap against his plate. He could hardly swallow the rice pudding in his mouth.

He and his friends were now very much involved in selling the new ration books and petrol coupons, and yes, they were getting richer too; it was proving as profitable as they'd hoped. He wouldn't be able to stop now even if he wanted to, because his friends were keen to carry on and he was part of the team.

Besides, they had done what they'd set out to do: a really big job that would keep them in comfort for a long time. They could give up smaller less profitable jobs now, except for Lennie, of course, who had to continue dabbling in black market foods to run his business.

Ben didn't stay to have a cup of tea after supper, though Lizzie did. He went back upstairs feeling ashamed of what he was doing. He could have got them the coffee they said they craved, but he couldn't offer such a service; he wouldn't dare. He disliked living at Oakdene Farm because it put him too close to the major, and at this moment he was using the attic flat as a refuge.

They hadn't fully moved in yet. Gladys had put up a camp bed in Lizzie's old room and they were sleeping there because the attic rooms, although clean now, still needed clearing out. Elsie had helped him reregister for their rations in the shops she used, because they were nearer. They were relying on her to buy their entitlement. Ben meant to put more distance between him and the major just as soon as he could.

CHAPTER THIRTY-ONE

BEN LOOKED CAREFULLY ROUND the attic. He knew Elsie had brought her daughters to live here while she was employed as Esmond's housekeeper. She'd used only two bedrooms, though there were three, as it was originally intended for live-in servants.

The rooms were fully furnished but with shabby stuff compared with what they'd had at Alvaston Terrace, and every wardrobe and cupboard seemed stuffed with unwanted possessions, leaving no room for their things. There were no double beds that he and Lizzie might use.

Lizzie's room, with two single beds jammed in, was pokily small and chaotic with clothes and unwanted belongings that had been dumped there. He and Lizzie needed order.

Ben looked again at the shambles in the main bedroom, really the only one of decent size; it was furnished with Elsie's single bed and one bedside table. He dragged them to the third bedroom to get them out of the way, and was intrigued to find the top drawer of the bedside table was locked.

He positioned the Georgian mahogany bedstead he'd bought at auction and placed his own bedside cabinets on each side. They were waiting for a new mattress as the one they'd used was a write-off – dirty and sodden after the fire in the roof.

He'd had to get Lizzie to go to the Wallasey Food Office and apply for the dockets and coupons to replace the furniture and bedding they'd lost, as he couldn't risk facing Mrs Cox. There was a large wardrobe and a chest of drawers he and Lizzie would need to use, but they still contained Elsie's old clothes and possessions.

He went downstairs to look for her. Lizzie and Milly were washing up in the kitchen. 'She's in the sitting room,' Milly told him, and he knew he'd find her with the major, relaxing with a cup of tea. That meant he had to face the major again to explain the situation to Elsie.

'I'll get rid of them if that's what you want,' he told her, 'but I'd like you to come up with me and see if there is anything you want to keep.'

'She'll come when she's finished her tea,' the major answered for her.

'Also,' Ben went on, 'there's an old cabinet up there that I could keep my tools in but the top drawer is locked. Do you know where the key is?'

Elsie paused to think for a moment. 'I brought that with us when we moved here. The key used to be kept in the lock but it's been missing for a long time. I don't know where it went. My mother used to keep her shop accounts in there. Couldn't you force it open?'

He went back and waited until he heard her coming upstairs. On the landing she looked round with wary distaste. 'I know this was once my home, but that now seems another life. I don't think I want anything from here.'

He led her to the main bedroom. 'The wardrobe is full of clothes and Lizzie will want to use it.'

'Yes, get rid of the lot, Ben.'

He pulled down a battered suitcase from the top of the wardrobe and opened it. 'Oh,' she said. 'Those are Lizzie's first school books.' She picked them up and flicked through the top one, then put them under her arm. 'She'll laugh at these now. I don't want anything else.'

'Hadn't you better look through these handbags? This one is lizard skin and looks in good condition. Nice bag, don't you want it?'

'No, Jasper gave me that. I did use it for a while. Did Lizzie tell you about her father?'

'Yes.' She was staring at him. He wouldn't have dared say this in front of the major. 'She said he was a bit of a rogue.'

'He was. I think he probably stole that from the woman he worked for, that's why I don't want it. He was her gardener.'

'Everything is so scarce now,' Ben said. 'I reckon I could sell most of this to a second-hand shop.'

'Then please do it for me.'

'This is a warm coat, wouldn't this be useful now?'

Elsie pulled a face and shuddered. 'No, I was not the first owner of that. I'll send Gladys up tomorrow morning to see if there's anything she could use. Please sell what you can of what's left. Lizzie's father was a very difficult man. I want nothing to remind me of those days.'

When she'd gone, Ben carted armfuls of clothes from the wardrobe and made a pile of them at the top of the stairs. The lizard handbag caught his eye when he went to move it to the pile. He pressed the catch and it opened to reveal a suede lining – it had hardly been used. There was a sheet of notepaper at the bottom which he fished it out and found it was folded round something small – a key.

His first thought was that Elsie should really have gone through all this stuff in case there was something private she'd prefer others not to see. But then he smoothed out the sheet of paper. It was a letter, undated and written in pencil.

Dear Elsie,

Not many people write two suicide notes so you'll be surprised, but when you read it you'll understand. I never did the right thing for you and Lizzie and I feel guilty about that. You deserved better. I'm sorry.

I've felt at the end of my tether since you persuaded me to see the doctor. You knew I'd been feeling short of breath for months but I never dreamt it could be anything so deadly as a tumour in my lung. They want me to go to the hospital for more tests which is why I did this last job to get money to pay for it. But as I've torn my leg climbing a fence I can't go. I'm afraid the police will have seen my blood and will have alerted all hospitals.

I thought we had troubles before, but this means I'm most likely finished. I've always been a burden for you and a dead loss to everybody. Nothing I ever do is right.

I got a good haul and I'd rather you had it than the police find it; that leads to trouble all round. Let the frenzy die down before you do anything. You know which of my contacts can help you. I can feel the police noose tightening round my neck and between one thing and another I'll be better out of it.

In my own way, I've always loved you Elsie, but you'll be better off without me.

Jasper

'Wow.' Ben sank back on the bare bed frame with his brain racing and his heart thudding. This was a voice from the dead. A second suicide note nobody else had found! Jasper had been quite a lad.

Ben counted himself tremendously lucky to have come across it like this. He had to read it through again to take in what it was telling Elsie. He heard Lizzie coming upstairs and hastily rammed the letter and key into his pocket.

Lizzie began sorting through the mound on the landing and he had to listen to her chatter while his head whirled, trying to make sense of what he'd found.

Before he'd killed himself, Jasper had written one letter to guarantee a suicide verdict, and one for Elsie's eyes only. Ben understood now why he'd killed himself. He'd realised at once that Jasper meant Elsie to benefit from what he'd stolen, and guessed the key he'd found would fit the drawer in that bedside cabinet.

He could feel it in his pocket and he burned with impatience to find out if he was right, but he must keep this to himself. The major's first thought would be to take everything to the police, and so would Lizzie's. He wasn't so sure about Elsie, but probably she'd agree with them.

He couldn't stop thinking about it and would have liked to take Lizzie out for a drink to get away from temptation, but here they were, some distance from any pub or hotel, and neither of them had the energy to pop out for an hour after dinner.

Ben felt things were moving too fast for him, and he was scared of Esmond, who seemed suspicious of everything he did.

* * *

That night Ben tossed and turned in bed, anticipating what he might find, but he was determined to wait until Lizzie had gone to work and he had the flat to himself. He struggled to hide his impatience while he made the breakfast tea and ate a bowl of cornflakes with Lizzie, but at last she was clattering downstairs and he felt it was safe to return to that dusty spare room.

The key turned easily in the lock and the drawer was packed tight; the account books Elsie had mentioned were there, together with paper packages and cloth drawstring bags. He sat on the sagging bed and started to open them up. His hands shook.

The contents made him gasp with amazement; some contained bank notes but in most jewellery sparkled up at him. Jasper's last theft had clearly been from a jewellery shop. He'd left quite a cache for Elsie. Ben liked her well enough and they got on fine, but she was not in need now she was the major's wife. He intended to cash this haul in for himself.

Steve would know how to find a good fence and would help him. He locked the drawer again and went to pour himself a second cup of tea. He needed to think about this. If Lizzie had been six when her father killed himself and she was now twenty-two, that meant the theft had taken place fifteen years ago. He need not delay selling it; the police had wartime duties to occupy them, and the last thing on their minds would be an historic robbery. He'd have a word with Steve today.

He'd need to have another look at those banknotes to check they were still legal tender and if so, he'd pay them into his bank accounts with his income from the fair. He rinsed his cup and saucer and went back to the bedside cabinet to push one of the packages into his pocket to show to Steve. He unwrapped one bundle of banknotes and as they looked all right he decided to pay that into his bank today.

He hesitated over Elsie's mother's old account books and decided to leave them where they were for the time being. When he'd cleared everything of value he could let her have them so she could peruse them if she wanted to.

Before locking up carefully and leaving that room, he put a match to Jasper's letter in the empty living room grate; nobody must ever see that.

Lennie had given him an old bike and he rode down to the fairground feeling reasonably confident that he had it all in hand. The one thing that did give him some concern was the amount of money he was handling. Now they were selling off the ration books and coupons he was paying a much increased amount into his bank, which might be noticed. It would be safer to spread it out a bit. Today he'd open an account in Lizzie's name without telling her and pay this money into that.

When he got home that evening, Elsie told him that Gladys had rummaged through the collection of clothes at the top of the stairs and taken quite a lot. 'She wants to bring Clover up this evening as there are things there that she might like to have.'

They came and he and Lizzie watched through the open doorway of their living room as they went through everything again with a fine-tooth comb. He couldn't help but notice Clover's delight when she came across the lizard handbag.

He suggested that Lizzie take them into the bedroom they were using temporarily, and show them the clothes she and Milly had worn as children. Gladys said, 'I have a friend with a large family, she would be delighted with these. I know she's finding it hard to fit them all out.' Ben and Milly helped to carry great armfuls down to Gladys's house when they took Dido for her walk.

The next day, Ben borrowed a handcart and took what they had left to a second-hand shop, then gave Elsie the money he received. She was delighted with it.

The following night Ben was late leaving the fair and cycled hard all the way up to the farm to be there in time for dinner. Nothing annoyed the major more than being kept waiting for his meals, and if Ben was late good manners prevented the family starting without him.

He was hot and tired when he arrived and found the major was not yet home. 'He shouldn't be much longer,' Elsie said, 'he had a call from the police station asking him to take in his registers showing the rotas for wardens and fire-watchers for their inspection.'

'I didn't know they took an interest in warden rotas,' Lizzie said. 'I thought they pushed all that on volunteers like Father.'

Ben could hardly breathe; he felt paralysed. What else could this mean but the police were trying to find out which warden had been in the Food Office on the night of the theft? He'd done his preparation about that and he was all prepared, but he was scared stiff this was going to land them all in prison. He felt sick with dread and could hardly eat when he was sitting at the dinner table hearing all Esmond had to say about that.

For Ben, that evening was free of duties but he couldn't sleep; he tossed and turned all night. He heard the air-raid siren, and the family, with Lizzie, went down to the shelter but he stayed behind. He was glad to be alone; this was not a worry he could share with her. He stood at the window watching the searchlights cut across the sky. He knew bombs were being dropped across the river on the Liverpool side, but though there were a few explosions on the Wirral side, none came too near. In the early morning hours he fell asleep; and woke up feeling worse than ever as he cycled back to the fair.

At lunchtime he went to the Anchor Inn hoping to find Fred Smith, his usual partner for warden duty in the Goring Street area. He was afraid he could be blurting out to all and sundry that he hadn't seen Ben McCluskey on that night.

Fred Smith was older than his father and worked for the corporation in their parks and gardens department. Ben had found him little help in a raid and thought him a useless layabout who drank too much and was often the worse for wear. He thought the corporation must continue to employ him out of kindness because nobody else would.

Fred had his pint of beer and his chaser in front of him and was immediately defensive. 'Sorry, Ben,' he said when he saw him. 'I was so tired when I got home that day that I went to sleep and didn't hear the siren. I gather you had a bad night, two killed?'

'We did.' Ben clapped him on his shoulder and smiled with relief; he was in luck. 'We could have done with your help,' he said. 'Don't leave it all to me, Fred.' Ben didn't usually drink at lunchtime but he bought himself half a pint to celebrate.

The Anchor was the best place to hear the local news and at the bar they were all agog that the Wallasey police station had been set on fire by incendiaries during the night and was quite badly damaged. It seemed they'd lost most of their paperwork. Ben couldn't stop smiling; he counted that as extraordinary

297

good luck. It gave him renewed vigour and he ordered the other half.

Such a weight off his mind; he could now reasonably suppose that the major's register of rotas had been reduced to ash. An angel up above must have taken pity on him. He returned to the fair and was delighted to pass the news on to his friends. That night he slept well for the first time since the robbery.

CHAPTER THIRTY-TWO

ONE MORNING, HARRY BARR rang Milly up and said he was home on leave again but only for a day or two this time. 'Will you come out with me?' he asked.

'Thank you, I'd like to,' she told him. 'Where are you planning to go?'

'Anywhere you like. I feel almost a stranger here after all the time at sea. The thing is, I got home yesterday lunchtime and had to spend the first day with my parents to catch up. That only leaves me one night free to go out so I'd like to make the most of it: a meal, and perhaps a show as well. My father has promised to lend me his car so how early can I pick you up?'

'Oh, come as early as you like, I'll be ready about half five to six o'clock, but Dadda likes to talk to you. Lizzie has moved in with us, she's been bombed out so you'll see her too.'

Milly was excited at the prospect; for her this was a big occasion.

Had she been wrong about Harry? Did he really like her? But by any standards this counted as a real date. She told the family Harry would be coming to pick her up and take her out to dinner.

Like all the girls in the factory, Lizzie wore overalls and a turban at work to keep the dust out of her hair, but she rushed home to comb it out and change into her best blouse and pullover before Harry arrived. She looked dazzlingly beautiful.

'I hope you aren't planning to come with us?' Milly said, feeling a prickle of jealousy.

Harry arrived and Milly took him to the sitting room. He looked older and a little drawn, but he seemed pleased to chat to her family for a few moments. Lizzie followed them in and was all smiles. She'd certainly livened up.

Harry's manners were formal and once outside, after he'd opened the car door and handed her in, he still seemed unable to relax. He took her to the restaurant in the fairground belonging to Ben's friend and Milly thought the meal was luxurious. They had tender succulent steak, the like of which they didn't have at home.

Afterwards she said, 'Let's go dancing at the Tower, that'll take you out of yourself,' and it did. He twirled her round the immense floor in a rapid quickstep.

Harry wanted to talk, so she sat with him drinking lemonade. He apologised for being edgy and told her she relaxed him, but that it would take at least a week to make him feel normal. He put it down to the tension of crossing the Atlantic, of being attacked by U-boats and sometimes seeing one of the ships in the convoy holed and suddenly sinking with the crew in the icy waters.

'We are forbidden to stop and pick them up,' he told her, 'because it would slow the convoy down and put other ships in danger. To press on full steam ahead, while they're all waving to attract attention, and knowing they will all perish if we don't stop, is heartbreaking.'

Milly shuddered; she was horrified. No wonder Harry was tense.

'We were south of Ireland, almost home this time, when the *Atlantic Voyager* went down. I sailed on her for two years and of course knew some of the present crew. That made it ten times worse.'

'You had to sail on? Leave them . . . ?'

'We have to obey orders.'

Milly had a lump in her throat.

They stayed till late and then he drove her to her gate and said, 'My parents say I can invite you to supper tomorrow evening. Would you like to come?'

'Won't they want you to themselves on your last night?'

'They said they'd like to meet you,' he said. 'I think they're curious about a girl who is willing to put up with me in my present bad mood.'

'That's kind, thank you, I'd like to come,' Milly said.

'I'll come and collect you tomorrow then, about the same time?' His kiss was quite passionate and though Milly liked it, it didn't excite her. Harry was good-looking in a middle-aged sort of way, and he could borrow a very nice car to drive her round, but she didn't see him as a boyfriend. He didn't send little shivers up and down her spine and she didn't dream of him when he was away.

Laurie was much more her type, always relaxed, but since she couldn't have him, she'd prefer someone more like him. She could see Harry only as a person in need of comfort and support.

One morning Lennie came to see Ben at his roundabout. 'I'm worried,' he said. 'Jimmy says the police have inspected the Food Office again. They went round checking all the locks. He's asking for a greater share of the proceeds; he reckons he deserves it because he and his mum made it possible, and they're having all the trouble.'

'More trouble.' Ben felt sick again; he'd never get used to the pressure of worry on top of worry. 'I suppose Jimmy's right in a way: we couldn't have done the job if he hadn't told us about the big delivery. We always knew he'd be the weakest link; we'd better try to soothe him.'

'Right,' Lennie said. 'Let those of us who can meet in my office when the lunchtime rush is dying down, say two o'clock. We'll talk to him.' The difficulty was the sideshows had to be kept running.

'I'll be there,' Ben said, and apart from Steve, they each managed to find somebody to stand in for them. Jimmy's cheeks were fiery when he came; he was in a rebellious mood.

'It's no good getting impatient, Jimmy,' Lennie told him. 'It's important that you, in particular, show no sign of having extra money.'

'I haven't,' he said, 'you know I haven't. I could have had that motorbike I wanted but Alec wouldn't let me.'

'No, we all have to lie low until this dies down. If you'd started riding round on a motorbike instead of that old pushbike, you'd have brought the police force down on your head. They'd have knocked it out of you and we'd all have landed in court.'

'But I told you where my mother kept her keys, made it easier for you, and I don't think I'm getting my fair share anyway.'

'You are, Jimmy,' Lennie said. 'I'm paying us all in equal shares.'

'It doesn't seem like it, I'm only getting five shillings a week more,' he wailed at Alec.

He sighed. 'Haven't I always been fair with you? Your wages are one thing, cash from this is another. We've opened a post office savings account for you, and an account at the Midland Bank, and we are paying your share there.'

'But you're keeping the bank books, and I can't see how much it is.'

'Look at them now.' Alec brought them from his pocket. 'It is all there in your name, but we don't want your mother to come across them, do we? There's too much here.' Alec was explaining patiently. 'If your mother saw these she'd know you'd taken part in the robbery.'

'Everybody knows you'd never be paid this sort of money for working,' Lennie told him.

'Yes, I've always had to work for peanuts,' he said. 'I've never had a chance like this before. I want my fair share.'

'I keep telling you, you're getting it. I've given each of us the same amount,' Lennie's patience was wearing thin, 'and there'll be more to come. It might be a good idea if you went to the Midland Bank and asked for a safe deposit box. Tell them you want to keep important papers safe from the bombs. I think they store them deep underground in lead-lined boxes.'

'I haven't any important papers. You'll put some of my money in there?'

'Yes, but you must not spend it yet. Might be a good idea if we all had a deed box,' Lennie said. 'Too much money suddenly going into an account can attract suspicion from bank staff.'

'We'll do that.'

Ben was thinking. 'How old are you, Jimmy? You must be nearly eighteen by now.'

'Yes, next month.'

Ben felt the weight lift from his shoulders and saw Lennie and Alec visibly relax. 'You'll get your call-up papers soon,' he said.

'We'll look after everything here until you come back,' Alec said, smiling.

'But that could be years, and anyway once I'm away from here I'll be able to spend a bit.'

'Yes, we'll give you something to take with you,' Lennie agreed.

'How do I know you'll still be here when I come back?' Jimmy was belligerent. 'Nobody will be watching me once I'm in the army. I'll be miles away from here and nobody will have heard about that robbery. I want to take everything of mine with me. I'll be able to have a motorbike there.'

'It would be safer,' Ben was beginning, 'if you—'

'If you don't agree to that, I'll tell my mother everything,' he said. 'You know Mum's very much into the church, and anything like that'll send her over the top.'

'Jimmy, that's blackmail.' Alec was severe. 'You can't do that.'

'I can and I will,' he said, and stormed out banging doors.

Ben closed his eyes. 'The sooner he's being chased across the Sahara desert by Rommel's crack marksmen the better.'

'Ungrateful little bugger,' Alec said through clenched teeth.

CHAPTER THIRTY-THREE

B EN WAS EXHAUSTED BUT he felt he was holding up quite well. Lizzie had told him her new job was giving her a new life and she'd even agreed it had taken her mind off gambling. She seemed more cheerful and he hoped she'd got over her addiction. Perhaps he'd worried unnecessarily over that.

It was so long now since they'd done the job at the Food Office that people no longer talked about it. The police had not been in contact with any of them again and Ben was hoping they never would. Even Lennie said he was feeling less stressed about it. The sale of the ration documents had gone particularly well, and the number of stolen cartons he'd had to take to his premises had now mostly gone. He was able to hide the few he had left more securely.

For Ben, things were also going well with the disposal of Jasper's cache of jewellery. Steve had introduced him to an efficient fence but, of course, he wasn't getting anything like its value. However, he'd paid all the money into his bank accounts, and felt a success. In fact, for the first time in his life he had too much cash but he was dealing with that too. He had a new ambition: after the war he'd retire from all this grafting, including the funfair. He'd take Lizzie on a world tour and they'd enjoy themselves again.

He'd finally persuaded Lizzie to move fully upstairs and give up eating meals with her family entirely.

Lizzie had not been exactly keen: 'It's a lot more work to cook for ourselves,' she said. Elsie was still buying their rations and doing other shopping for them.

'We shouldn't leave it all to your mother,' he protested. 'That isn't fair, and the war has given her lots of other things to do.' Elsie had been persuaded by Laurie's mother to join the WVS and she was proud to have a uniform. She was now knitting comforts for the troops, and making cakes to sell at bring and buy sales to earn funds to buy more wool and ingredients to carry on. She was trying to do her bit for the war effort.

Ben found Lizzie was leaving most of the cooking to him. One evening, they were eating the corned beef hash he'd made for supper when he heard the major coming up the stairs, calling, 'Ben, are you there?'

He put down his knife and fork and went out to the top of the stairs to meet him. 'Yes, hello.'

'I have a problem,' Esmond said. 'The team is two short tonight and I need reinforcements. Would you be willing to change your fire-watching duty? I'll probably be able to get somebody to take your turn on Tuesday night.'

The major was now arranging the New Brighton rotas that made sure there were fire-watchers and wardens in every position around the area. Ben's spirits sank. 'Where do you want me to go?'

'Up to Liscard electricity station, have you been there before?'

'No. I usually watch in the fairground area.'

'I give you that because it's an area you know well and it's handy for you. The thing is, the electricity station has a weather station on the roof and they like you to take readings while you're there.'

'What sort of readings?'

'Wind speed and rainfall, that sort of thing. I'll come up with you and show you how to fill in the record books. Can you be ready to leave in fifteen minutes?'

Ben had counted himself lucky not to be partnered with him so far; it was the last thing he wanted to do. He'd been looking forward to a good sleep tonight. Recently he'd been staying in bed even if there was a raid, though he sent Lizzie down to the shelter. But he dared not refuse; he was already in the major's bad books and didn't want to sink further.

Esmond Travis might have only one arm and appear to be an invalid but he had an alert mind and strong legs. He set off at a fast pace and Ben struggled to keep up. 'Hang on, Major,' he said, no harm in reminding him of his workload. 'I've been working all day and I was on duty last night.'

'That was a quiet night,' Esmond said. 'The weather was bad and we didn't have a raid. Tonight could be different.' It was a clear moonlit night, just what the enemy needed, and sure enough the warning screamed over the town five minutes after they set out.

The electricity station was a single-storey concrete block construction isolated in a field belonging to a farm. It had a wooden staircase going up to the roof that had a wooden balustrade round it. Ben doubted he'd have found it on his own. There was no high ground surrounding New Brighton, just a gentle slope away from the coast, but he had an excellent view in all directions from the roof.

The weather-recording equipment was installed along one side with an open wooden shelter over part of it. 'I know nothing about recording readings from weather stations,' he said. 'Never done it before.'

'Don't worry, I'll do them now and show you how. You can really feel the force of the breeze here, can't you?'

Esmond was pointing out figures on the dials and writing them in a book attached by a string to a shelf when they heard the unmistakable sound of enemy planes in the sky. 'Their engines sound completely different to those of Spitfires,' he said, looking calm and ready for anything.

'They're here early tonight.' Ben was scared stiff and his stomach was churning, but he must hide all that or be labelled a coward.

Immediately, the searchlights were switched on and were criss-crossing the sky so that the ack-ack battery in the park could pinpoint a target. Then came the sound they dreaded, the crump crump of high explosives over Wallasey. Ben could see the bursts of flames.

'I think that one fell in the cemetery,' the major said, 'and it looks like incendiaries have fallen in the Derwent Drive area. Yes, the blaze is growing.'

Ben rushed to the field telephone to relay the position of the fire to the fire station. It needed a vigorous wind to make the connection. His heart was pounding and his legs were suddenly weak. 'Another towards the pumping station,' the major went on. 'I hope they miss the waterworks or we'll have no water tomorrow.' The sky seemed full of aircraft and there were more and more fires for Ben to report. 'I should be down in the wardens' post,' Esmond groaned.

Suddenly there was a stream of missiles landing around them. 'Incendiaries here,' screamed the major. He elbowed Ben aside, taking the phone from him. 'Look, there's a fire starting on the stairs and another over there. Get the stirrup pump. Put them out.'

But Ben had already leapt over the railings onto the stairs. He could see three of the missiles bursting into flames, but he'd had to deal with small incendiary bombs before and knew what he must do. He grabbed them one at a time and flung them as far as he could into the field below. Then he rushed back to the roof to throw off the others.

The major had grabbed the stirrup pump but couldn't make it work with only one hand. The noise was terrible as another bomb tore away part of the weather station and set fire to its shelter. Ben raced to pitch everything alight over the side, but found the balustrade was firmly fixed. He stripped off his coat and batted at the flames until he'd choked them out. A fire in the electricity substation meant no lights for New Brighton.

'Are there any more?' he panted, looking wildly round. Down below, some of the incendiaries were still burning in the field.

'That's it for the moment,' Esmond said. 'You've got rid of them from here.'

Ben was spent. He'd burned his right hand and it hurt, but the sky was empty of planes and all was quiet again. He was beginning to relax.

'You need to go to a first-aid post with those burns,' Esmond was saying, when suddenly he screamed into action again. 'Look, look. Behind you. This breeze is rekindling the fire on the stairs.'

Ben jumped down to stamp it out. The major was on the phone again.

There was another raid that night and it was late when Milly woke up. She realised she was the only one still in her bunk in the Anderson shelter, and got up still feeling half asleep to streak across the grass in her siren suit, then went to her bedroom to get ready for college. When she went down she found Mum alone in the kitchen. 'Just us two for breakfast this morning,' she said. 'We might as well eat it in here, it'll be less trouble.' Usually they ate in the dining room.

'Where's Dadda?' Milly had never known him miss breakfast before.

'He and Ben have only just come home; he's exhausted and needs sleep more than anything else,' Mum told her. 'It was a terrible night, one air raid after another. Ben has burned his hands; Dadda says he was very brave. You are lucky, to be able to sleep through that. Lizzie and I were up and down all night.'

'I did wake up once. It was very noisy with explosions quite close.'

'Yes, they say one of the ferryboats has been sunk on its moorings at Seacombe landing stage, and it's blocking everything up. I'm sorry for people who have to get to Liverpool to work.'

They heard Lizzie running downstairs; she came to the kitchen door. 'I'm going to be late for work this morning,' she said. 'I do hope there'll be a bus.'

'How is Ben?'

'He's asleep. I gave him breakfast and some aspirins. He said he needed a couple of hours' sleep before he went to work.'

310

'Esmond said he'd burned his hands?'

'His left hand isn't too bad. First and second degree, he was told, but his right hand is still bandaged.'

At the dinner table that evening, Milly listened open-mouthed as Dadda praised Ben. 'We've had no phone since last night and we'd have no electricity either if it hadn't been for him. A whole line of incendiary bombs fell on the roof and were setting fire to the place. Ben tossed them off one by one before they could. I've never seen anyone move so fast, he even leapt over the balustrade onto the stairs because a fire was starting there. He did well, marvellously well. Yes, Ben was quite a hero last night.'

Milly was intrigued; this sounded like the sort of story Mr Thornley would want to put in the *Gazette*. The next day, she rode down to the college on her bike, because the buses were always a problem after a bad night. Only half the class turned up.

Mum had their evening meal ready early that evening because she wanted an early night. Milly went upstairs to talk to Ben as soon as she'd washed up, and found he was trying to fry fish with his right hand bound up in a bandage. Lizzie was lying on the sofa. Both were white-faced and looked exhausted.

'Heavens, Ben,' she said, 'you don't have to carry on being a hero now you're home. Here, let me do that, you're going to get that bandage splashed with fat.'

'I'm told it'll have to be redressed tomorrow,' he said, 'and that burns heal better if they're left open to the air so I may not need bandages. Well, not like this anyway.'

311

'What's the matter with you, Lizzie?' Milly asked. 'Shouldn't you be doing this?'

Lizzie sat up, her face grimacing. 'What a bossy little madam you've become.'

'Lizzie isn't feeling well,' Ben said. 'We just need to eat and then we're both going straight to bed.'

'Dadda told us what you did the other night. I came up to hear what you had to say about it. I want to write a piece about it and see if I can get it published in the Wallasey *Gazette*.'

'Our budding journalist,' Lizzie said in derisory tones.

Milly was dishing up their fish. 'Just fish and bread and butter?' she asked, putting it on their table together with knives and forks.

'I intended to make fish and chips,' he yawned, 'but I just couldn't be bothered. Too tired.'

'Let's hope those bombers don't come back again tonight,' Milly said, heading downstairs to write up her piece. She finished it before bedtime and showed it to Dadda.

He praised it though he corrected her punctuation. 'I'd like to type it up,' she told him. 'I'm not all that good at typing yet, but I think I could cope, though it'll have to wait until I get to college tomorrow as I don't have a typewriter.'

Dadda got to his feet. 'I'll check to see if the phone is working yet. John Thornley might have a deadline for something like that. I could tell him it was coming.'

The phone lines were still down and they had another air-raid warning before ten o'clock. Neither Lizzie nor Ben came down to the shelter; Milly wished Lizzie would come because Mum was worrying about her safety.

'It sounds more distant tonight,' Milly comforted her. 'Somebody else is getting it.'

'Must be Birkenhead,' Dadda murmured from his bunk, 'or perhaps across the river in Bootle.'

The following afternoon, Milly took the piece she'd written straight to the *Gazette* office and spoke to Mr Thornley before going home. 'This isn't bad, Milly,' he told her, and questioned her about the episode. 'Leave it with me.'

When she got home, Dadda told her that John Thornley had rung him to ask about his version of what had happened. Milly spent the evening in hopeful anticipation that it would get into next week's *Gazette*.

On Thursday, the *Gazette* was pushed through the letter box with Dadda's *Times*. She was absolutely thrilled to see her article published and took it to college to show to her friends. They were impressed both with her and with Ben's heroism. Many knew who he was, having seen him at the fair.

I'm a journalist, Milly thought proudly, a working journalist, though there was no mention of her name in the paper. She felt even better when she reached home that evening and found an envelope waiting for her on the hall table. The *Gazette* had paid her seven shillings and sixpence.

CHAPTER THIRTY-FOUR

THE AIR RAIDS WERE happening more often now and were wearing Lizzie down. She knew it wasn't just the raids. Everything was getting on top of her. She couldn't sleep and was having headaches; sometimes she felt sick, and really she was feeling quite ill. She was making mistakes in the routine work she was expected to do at the munitions factory, and her boss had spoken to her more than once to remind her she was working with high explosives and forgetting safety rules was dangerous. She could see he didn't trust her.

She'd changed, she knew she had, and she was going down the drain. Mum had given her two slices of apple pie last night for their pudding and because Ben kept saying she did nothing to help with their dinner she'd tried to please him by making custard to go with it. But she'd turned away at the wrong moment and let the milk boil over onto the grill beneath and it had taken her ages to clean up the mess. Ben had gritted his teeth and told her to concentrate.

Her way of coping recently had been to carry on placing small bets with Jimmy Cox. It gave her something to think about. The stakes had to be small because she'd used up most of her savings, and that meant the amounts she won were too small to change the situation.

She knew she hadn't been winning as much, barely an average number of her bets, but Jimmy jollied her along, saying her luck would change. Lizzie went doggedly on placing her small bets, but all she ever seemed to do was work, gamble, and shelter from the bombs. She had neither time nor interest in anything else. Somehow, over the months, betting on the horses had become the most important part of her life, and she was losing more money than she won.

Today, she'd gone to draw out another five pounds and realised suddenly that, once more, all she'd saved towards her own dress shop was gone. It came as a shock, though perhaps it should not have done. It felt as though the tide had turned against her.

She really had to stop gambling away every penny she earned. She knew she could; she'd done it before. She just needed time. She was both bored and scared of working in that factory. Ben was neglecting her, and they both really missed not having a house of their own.

She didn't have to buy the sporting newspapers now she worked in the factory; the men working there bought them and left them lying around. It had become a habit to pick them up and scan them for a winner.

Today she took the paper to the ladies' cloakroom, where she could get a few minutes alone. Suddenly, a name jumped out of the list of runners. She could see an absolute cast-iron winner! She'd won on Hurricane Henry before, quite a big win, and she had that gut feeling that he would win again.

She needed a lot more than one win to regain what she'd lost, but to have even a moderate win would make her feel better, and indicate her luck was returning. But she had no more money until payday and that would be too late.

At home that evening Lizzie looked for Ben's bank book; he always had plenty of money. She looked in every cupboard and drawer in their flat, and then she went through the pockets in his best suits but she couldn't find more than a little loose change. She was frustrated and angry. Her guess was that he'd hidden it from her.

She went to see Jimmy Cox and, though embarrassed at having to do it, she asked him to pay her stake for once and let her pay later. 'No,' he said. 'If you lose you won't pay me.'

'I will, I promise.'

'Or you'll put off paying me. Sorry, Mrs McCluskey, I'm likely to lose out on that.'

Lizzie couldn't give up; everything depended on backing Hurricane Henry at Sandown Park. She knew only one other place where she'd find money. Father was totally habit-bound; he used to give her mother an allowance to pay the household bills when she was his housekeeper and he'd continued to do this after they were married, although now he added what he called her dress allowance to it.

Mum had continued to keep the housekeeping money in the same old purse in a drawer in the kitchen table. Gladys paid the milkman and coal merchant from it, and she used to pay the butcher and grocer before the war when they made deliveries. Lizzie knew there would be money there.

She ran down to the kitchen to see, but Gladys was mopping the floor; she would have to come back later when there was nobody about. She wouldn't take much, just three pounds for one bet. It was not what Ben would call a small bet, though — he thought more in shillings when he had a flutter.

She could pay Mum back from her winnings, though she probably wouldn't even miss it. She had to bet. Lizzie knew it was wrong, but at the same time she felt excited at the risk she was taking. Hurricane Henry sailed home first, just as she'd known he would, and that made her feel on top of the world. Her luck had changed; she'd found her winning streak again.

By the time Jimmy Cox paid over her prize money she'd chosen another winner from those running the next day. Gorgeous Jess was guaranteed to win. In a mood to chance everything, she gave Jimmy every penny she had, including the contents of her last pay packet.

Lizzie spent the next day on tenterhooks. She was fizzing with optimism as she left the factory and walked through the fairground to the boating lake. As she walked towards it she could see Alec Hooper in the sales booth; he looked up and caught her eye. His smile disappeared and he was shaking his head. A cold shiver ran down her spine. Surely not? No, that couldn't be right; she had to hear it in words.

'Sorry, love,' he said, looking sympathetic. 'Gorgeous Jess was next to last.' Lizzie felt the icy weight of disaster on her shoulders. Her feet could hardly step one in front of the other as she went to her bus stop.

What had she done? She was in debt and couldn't put the housekeeping money back in the purse. She knew she wouldn't be paid another penny until Friday. On the bus tears were scalding her eyes and it took all her self-control not to let them fall in public.

Oakdene Farm was quiet when she let herself in. She was speeding upstairs to her attic but found Mum adjusting the blackout on the landing window. 'Hello, Mum.' She pulled up abruptly.

'Are you all right, Lizzie? You look really washed out.'

'I'm fine,' she mumbled.

'You haven't looked yourself since you started working in that factory. I think you should see the doctor, he'll give you a tonic that will help you pick up.'

Lizzie could feel herself shaking; the doctor would expect her to pay three shillings and sixpence for a consultation and there'd be more to pay for a tonic. She ought to tell Mum now, admit she'd stolen from her purse, and make a clean breast of it. She paused with the words hovering on her tongue, but Mum believed her to be honest and upright. She couldn't bring herself to do it.

'I'm perfectly all right, Mum. Really I am, don't you worry.' She went on as quickly as she could. 'I'm tired with the raids and the long hours at work. It's just the war.' She fled.

The flat was quiet, thank God, Ben wasn't yet home. She threw herself on her bed and let the tears flow. She'd lied to keep this a secret and she'd just made matters worse. How was she going to look Mum in the face now? She'd never ever mentioned a word about gambling or betting to her family, and her secret had been safe with Ben.

But she was going to pieces and was afraid she wouldn't be able to hide it any longer. They were all going to find out and she'd be shamed. Lizzie felt she was touching bottom and knew she'd lost control and needed help. It was no good denying she had a problem; she was addicted. She couldn't fight this on her own any longer.

She dried her eyes and washed her face. Ben would be back

and expect to find she'd made some preparations for dinner. There were four small lamb chops in the kitchen with potatoes to peel and cabbage to chop.

Milly came home from college in a buoyant mood. The Christmas holidays were almost on them and in the end of term exams she'd come top in shorthand, and Lizzie had agreed to go to the pictures with her tonight to see *Pinocchio*, the first full-length cartoon from Walt Disney since *Snow White*. The girls in her class were full of praise for it.

She found Mum in the kitchen and asked, 'Is Lizzie home yet?'

'Yes, she doesn't look at all well.'

'We're going to the pictures tonight. I'd like to eat early.'

'I haven't forgotten. Dadda and I had our main meal at lunchtime today because he's gone to play in a chess tournament. What did they give you for dinner?'

'Spam with mash and cabbage, followed by rice pudding and four prunes.'

'Well, scrambled egg on toast should be all right for you. We might as well have it straight away.'

Afterwards, Milly said, 'I'm going up to see if Lizzie's ready.' As she went upstairs she could see the kitchen door was open and her sister was staring silently out of the window. 'Lizzie,' she said, 'why aren't you getting ready to come to the pictures?'

She spun round. 'Oh goodness, Milly! I'd forgotten about that.'

'Forgotten? What's the matter with you? You forget everything these days, but there's still plenty of time to go.' Milly took in Lizzie's ravaged face and the raw state of the chops and

319

cabbage. 'You'll have to forget dinner though; I'll make you a sandwich while you get ready. Where's Ben tonight?'

Lizzie gulped. 'I don't feel like going out, Milly.'

'What? I was looking forward to it.'

'It's just a cartoon.' Lizzie burst into tears.

Milly was shocked and threw her arms round her in a hug. 'What's the matter?' Lizzie's head went down on her shoulder; she was clinging to her. 'Come on, it can't be that bad.'

'It is. It's terrible. I don't know what to do.'

Milly could feel her distress. 'Where's Ben?'

'I don't know. I don't care. You've got to help me, Milly.'

'Of course I will, but I don't understand. What's happened?'

'I've been betting on horses. I thought I'd continue to win, but I'm not any more and I can't stop.' Milly seemed as confused as she was. 'It's out of hand. Something drives me on and on.'

'Horses?' The only gambling Milly had experienced was a flutter on the dogs.

'Yes, I can't get betting out of my mind. I'm thinking about it all the time.'

'You can't stop thinking about betting on horses?' Milly felt this was beyond her. 'But we did it on dogs and that was years ago.'

'I've been doing it on horses. It's a torment. I can't stop.'

'But you've never mentioned it before.'

'I've been hiding this from everybody for years.'

'But why?'

'I'm ashamed to say I've been spending all my money on gambling. I'm addicted.'

'Addicted? No, you're imagining that, but you've told Ben? He knows about this?'

'Ben doesn't know the half of it. I haven't told anybody before. I've been pretending everything is fine, hiding it, lying about it.'

'Ben will help you. You know he will.'

'No, he's been telling me to stop for ages. He's lost patience with me. He's always out. He hardly wants anything to do with me any more.'

'That's not true, Lizzie.' Milly gave her another hug. 'Ben has to go to work like everybody else, and he has fire-watching and warden duties on four nights each week. He has to do those.'

'He does much more than that.' Lizzie's laugh was hollow. 'I want to stop and I've tried so many times. I stopped for five months once but I always go back to it. I feel trapped in a bubble going round and round. I'm horrible to everybody and I hate myself. I'm addicted.'

Milly had her doubts. 'It can't be that bad. You don't go near any horses, how can you bet?'

'Jimmy Cox puts bets on for me. He does it for lots of people.'

'Dadda would know what to do, he knows everything. You should tell him.'

'For God's sake, no! He wouldn't understand.' Lizzie burst into another storm of tears. 'Milly, I've done a terrible thing. I've taken money from Mum's housekeeping purse in the kitchen. I used it to back a horse and it lost. I can't put it back.'

'Oh goodness! That's stealing, Lizzie. Heavens! How could you? Mum trusts you. How could you steal from her?'

'I must have been mad. I don't know what came over me.'

'When she find out she'll think . . . ? Don't you care?'

'Of course I care. I want to put it back but I won't be paid again until next Friday.'

'How much did you take?'

'Three pounds. Once Mum knows I've stolen money from her, she's going to despise me.'

'No, Lizzie, she loves you, she loves us both.'

'The money had built up in that purse; do you think she'll notice?'

'An amount like that, she's bound to. She still fills in that account book that's in the same drawer. We've both seen her do it, so much spent on rations and so much on milk. She'll miss an amount of that size.'

'I want you to help me be normal again. I can't ask anyone else. Please, Milly.'

Milly's heart turned over. 'I would if I could but I don't know how.'

'Can you lend me three pounds?'

'No, I don't have that much but I'll lend you what I have if it will help. I was paid seven and six for that article I wrote for the *Gazette* and I've been saving up to buy a typewriter, but I have only two pounds and tuppence.'

Lizzie groaned. 'I do hope Mum doesn't think Gladys has stolen it. Or Clover, she's often about the place.'

'Heaven forbid, but she won't. Gladys has worked here for years and she pays for things from that purse. Mum trusts her. We all know she's honest.'

Milly thought for a moment. 'Wouldn't it be better to tell

Mum, apologise and make a clean breast of it? She'll want to help you.'

'No, she's just asked me if I was all right. She wanted me to see the doctor and I've told her I'm fine. I couldn't bring myself to say anything about this.'

'Then what do you want to do?'

'Lend me your savings, Milly. I still have one shilling and sixpence, I'll put that in the purse. She'll be less likely to notice if the amount missing is smaller. She'll probably think she's paid for something and forgotten to write it in.'

'I'm not sure about that, but if it's what you want, I'll go and get it for you now.'

'Thank you, Milly, thank you, that's very good of you.'

Milly went down one flight to her bedroom, and returned with her savings. She felt Lizzie's arms go round her in a grateful hug. Her cheeks were wet with her tears. 'I'll pay you back on Friday night. Stay here, I'll go and put this in the purse straight away.'

She came back to report. 'Thank you, I feel better now. There are bills just stuffed in the purse, for electricity and all that, so I don't think Mum's done her accounts recently. She writes "paid" across those when she does.'

Milly believed their mother to be efficient in her accounting and was afraid that by trying to cover up what she'd done, Lizzie was making matters worse still.

'I knew I could rely on you,' Lizzie said. 'I desperately want to fight this thing and be normal again. You will help me, won't you?'

Milly was scared as well as worried now. She couldn't believe such a thing could happen to Lizzie and didn't really understand it even now. She'd sworn to help her sister but she had no idea how to go about it. 'What is it I can do to help you?'

But Lizzie didn't know either. Now Milly thought about it, Lizzie had seemed different recently; she was spending a lot of time alone in that flat, withdrawing into herself, and she was right about Ben being out much more, but he'd surely want to help her? Ben was a kind and considerate person. Of course he'd want to help her.

She didn't like being the only one who knew how distressed Lizzie was, and wished her sister had agreed she could tell somebody else.

CHAPTER THIRTY-FIVE

MILLY TOOK DIDO OUT for a long walk and tried to work out some way to help Lizzie. On the way back she was no nearer an answer but Ben was just pedalling up as she reached their gate. 'I read your piece in the paper, Milly,' he said. 'You made me out to be a real hero.'

'Dadda says you are.'

He laughed. 'I only did what anyone would have done, but it's made my reputation, not only with your dad but also down in the fair.'

'Dadda knows the editor so it wasn't that hard for me.'

'You still had to write it up and deliver it to him. I'd say you're on your way to being a reporter.'

'I was afraid I'd not be quick enough. These things need to be typed up but I have no typewriter. I was . . . I'm saving up for one.'

'Really? I'll let you into a little secret, if you promise to keep quiet about it.'

She giggled. 'I promise.' She liked Ben; he was always friendly and she could see he was in a jolly mood.

He lowered his voice to a whisper. 'Forget the saving up, your father has asked me to find a good second-hand typewriter for you as a Christmas present.'

'Oh goodness, has he?' Milly's spirits soared.

'And I've found one.'

'That's marvellous. What sort?'

He laughed. 'I'd better keep you waiting to find that out.' He was wheeling the bike towards one of the buildings so she pulled Dido and went along with him. Lizzie had forbidden her to speak to him about her secret, but he always had money and he'd want to help Lizzie. 'Ben,' she said, 'would you do me an enormous favour?'

'That depends.' She knew he was teasing.

'Will you lend me a pound? I can't tell you what I want it for, but I need it urgently.'

Once the bike had been shut in the building he took out his wallet and peeled off a pound note. 'Of course I will.' He was grinning at her. 'It wouldn't be to buy Christmas presents, would it?'

Milly noticed his wallet was stuffed with notes. 'No, not Christmas presents,' she said. 'Thank you, thank you, Ben. I'll pay you back on Friday night.'

'No, you needn't. Count that as a present for you.'

Milly ate her dinner with Ben's pound note burning a hole in her pocket. She couldn't rush upstairs and give it to Lizzie now Ben was with her. Afterwards, when the washing up was almost done, she could encourage Mum to join Dadda in the sitting room and put it in the purse herself.

Finally alone in the kitchen, she took the purse from the drawer and pushed the pound note inside. The week's bills and receipts were still stuffed in it, Mum had not yet done her weekly accounts, and when she did, she would expect them to balance. Any discrepancy and she'd try to work out why. Milly remembered that Lizzie had put in one shilling and sixpence of her own money. She fumbled through the coins and slid one shilling and eightpence into her own pocket before slamming the drawer shut.

She didn't see Lizzie until the next day, and she wept with relief when she told her. 'Thank you, Milly, I don't know how to thank you enough.'

'You should have told Ben,' she said fiercely. 'He'd have given you the money.'

The next morning, Milly was in the kitchen when her mother took out her account book and bills, laid them out on the kitchen table and asked her, 'Will you go into town and pay the paper bill for me?'

'Yes, Mum.' Her mother took a ten shilling note from the purse and pushed it towards her. This was proof she didn't know Lizzie had taken money from her purse and now she need never know.

Milly knew it would have upset her, but wished she could tell her how troubled Lizzie was.

Milly was pleased she'd been able to help Lizzie put the money back, but that was the easy part. She had to find out more about addictions and how they could be cured. Dadda was the only person she knew who was likely to know, but Lizzie had panicked when she'd mentioned his name.

She went into the Wallasey library and looked for a book on addictions. The only one she could find was on alcohol addiction, but she took it out to read about the AA meetings and that those addicted must never touch another drop. Even

Lizzie knew she'd have to stop for good and never do it again. There was no further help on gambling addiction.

On Saturday morning Milly took six eggs and some vegetables up to Mrs Coyne. 'I'm so grateful,' she said. 'I feel our arrangement gives me all the advantages.'

'No,' Milly said. 'It helps us both. By the way, I wrote to Laurie for his birthday and he replied, but that was some time ago. Is he coming home for Christmas?' she asked.

'No, unfortunately, it's his boss's turn, but we expect him later. He's due for ten days' leave and he hopes to be here between Christmas and New Year.'

Milly was instantly cheered. She'd really missed Laurie since he'd gone. 'That's marvellous. I mean, if he can't be here for Christmas it's the next best thing. I'll come up and see him. When will he get here?'

'He wasn't sure when he wrote. I'll let you know, Milly, when I hear more. He'll want to see all his old friends.'

Milly saw that as a ray of sunshine across an otherwise black sky. She could talk to Laurie when he came home. But would he be likely to know how she could help Lizzie? He just might.

One Sunday afternoon shortly before Christmas, Elsie took the family round the fields they owned to collect firewood from the hedges that were no longer being cut. Dadda came with them and Dido was flitting everywhere because she was allowed off the lead in their own land where it was fenced. It was a grey, damp day. 'It doesn't seem like Christmas,' Lizzie complained.

'It doesn't,' Elsie agreed. 'This is the second of the war and there's nothing seasonal in the shops at all, though I've managed to buy a few sultanas and a tin of treacle with my points ration.'

'We've been growing plenty of carrots all the year,' Milly said, 'and you know now they aren't too bad in puddings and cakes.'

'Sultanas and treacle are more authentic but I've had plenty of practice with carrots too,' Elsie said.

'That branch you've pulled out has been dead for too long,' Dadda interrupted. 'It's decayed and it'll burn up in five minutes.'

'It'll be good for lighting fires,' Elsie said testily. She turned back to Milly. 'We've been warned there'll be no more icing sugar until the war is over, and that goes for marzipan too.'

Milly was afraid the war was making them all tired and short-tempered.

The following Saturday she was up early and out in the garden straight after breakfast to collect the weekend vegetables for Mum, and to put together any surplus for her other customers. She'd been going to see Laurie's mother every week and so far she'd always managed to take her more eggs than the ration allowed. All summer she'd had plenty of vegetables to sell and she'd taken apples from their trees when they'd ripened, but now she had much less choice.

It was a bitterly cold morning and pulling up two swedes was hard on the hands. She had plenty of carrots, so she pulled enough for both households, and two cabbages as well. She'd picked too many sprouts last week, and those that were left needed time to grow a bit if they were to have plenty for Christmas Day. She added two leeks for Laurie's mother.

When Milly took them up an hour later, Mrs Coyne took her straight to their kitchen and unpacked what she'd brought onto the kitchen table. 'I've only brought you six eggs,' Milly said. 'The hens are not laying as well now the cold weather has come.'

'You can spare them, Milly? Six is still generous. You're not leaving your own family short?'

'I wouldn't dare.' She smiled. 'Dadda likes them for breakfast.'

'That's excellent then. I've just made a pot of tea. Will you join me in a cup?'

Milly sat down and relaxed in the warmth. The Coynes had a better heating system than they had. 'Have you heard yet when Laurie will be coming home?'

'No, he says everybody is clamouring for leave at this time of the year and army rules say there must always be a trained vet on duty. We had a letter from him this morning. Here, read it if you want to, there's nothing very personal, just news of him.'

Helen Coyne had done this before and for Milly it had opened a window into his life. 'Thank you.' She read eagerly; it was mostly about the carrier pigeons, and a little about the pleasure of living with a group of young men instead of his family. She felt she was getting to know Laurie better.

Back at home, Milly hung up the decorations they'd kept from previous years. Clover always used to come and help her and they'd thought it fun, but now she said she was too tired, that she had to work long hours. Milly still found time to cut fresh holly from their hedges, but it was a bad year for berries and there were few to be found.

It seemed this year nobody was looking forward to Christmas. All they craved was a rest from the air raids to let them catch up with their sleep.

A LUCKY SIXPENCE

* * *

Ben was downstairs with the family when Elsie invited Lizzie and him to share their Christmas dinner. 'I'll provide a turkey if I can get one,' he said. 'I should, otherwise we'll be eating your rations.' He smiled round the family, half afraid the major might accuse him of buying it on the black market. 'Poultry isn't rationed,' he explained, 'as there isn't enough produced to make that possible.'

'Rationed by price,' Esmond said. 'At this time of the year everybody wants it. Thank you. I'm sure it will be very expensive but it'll be a great treat.'

On Christmas Eve, when Ben went to collect his bird from Lennie he was told, 'Sorry, the turkeys have all gone but I've saved two decent-sized ducks for you.'

Elsie seemed pleased with them. 'That'll give us all a good dinner,' she said. 'I'll make apple sauce with them. Esmond loves duck.'

Esmond said Christmas wouldn't be Christmas if they didn't go to church for the midnight service on Christmas Eve. To please him Lizzie went with them. Ben asked her if he should go too, but she'd said no, he hardly ever joined the family so they didn't need him. He'd be better off staying at home and going to bed.

Milly got up on Christmas morning to find an office model Underwood typewriter on the breakfast table. It had a gift tag tied to it and a big bow of ribbon. 'Is that for me?' she whooped in delight.

'Sorry we couldn't wrap it up,' Mum said.

Dadda beamed at her. 'It's in good condition and should last you for years.'

331

'We have some like this at college.' Milly smiled. 'We have all the makes, of course, but this is the most popular. I'm thrilled, thank you both.' She hurled herself at each of them in turn to kiss and hug them, and wanted to take it up to her room to try it out.

'After you've eaten your breakfast,' Dadda said. 'Do sit down, it's all ready.'

Later, Lizzie and Ben came down in their best clothes to share a glass of sherry with them. They gave Milly two corn dollies. 'I hope you like them,' Lizzie said. 'I didn't know what to get for you.'

'They're lovely,' Milly said.

'I don't think there is much you can do with them except look at them,' Ben said. 'One of the fairground wives made a lot in the autumn to sell.'

'I shall keep them on my dressing table, they're pretty. I've had excellent presents this year, a typewriter of exactly the sort I like best.' She smiled knowingly at Ben but he didn't respond.

She thoroughly enjoyed the roast duck but Lizzie looked sad and hardly spoke, which drove home to Milly how much she was in need of help.

She thought Ben seemed tense and ill at ease, and in the kitchen afterwards as they washed up Lizzie whispered that Father hadn't relaxed either. 'It takes the gloss off Christmas. We're all supposed to be happy and enjoy ourselves at this time of the year,' she said.

Mrs Coyne was as good as her word and rang her on Christmas Eve to say that Laurie would be home quite late on Saturday. Milly could hear joy and excitement in her voice.

'Excellent, he'll be here for the new year. He has ten days in all?'

'Well, eight really, he has to spend the first day coming home, and most of the last one travelling back. He asked after you. Why don't you come up on Sunday morning around eleven and have a mince pie and cup of tea with us?'

That made Milly feel better, and by ten o'clock on that day, she was dressed in her Sunday best and ready to go. Mum advised her to wait half an hour to give Mrs Coyne time to clear away after breakfast, but she could hardly curb her impatience.

Laurie had a beaming smile when he opened the front door to her. 'Great to see you again, Milly.' He swept her into a bear hug and swung her round, then he held her at arm's length and his eyes met hers. 'You're growing up and getting prettier, blossoming in fact.'

'I am grown up,' she retorted. 'I've left school now.'

'So I've been hearing.' The smile didn't leave his face.

Laurie looked older, though he was wearing a red pullover she found familiar. She asked, 'How are you getting on with your homing pigeons?'

'I've learned to love them,' he said, 'but it took me time and I've had a lot to learn. Given a choice I'd have gone for horses, but I'm glad now to have the pigeons.'

He sat back in his armchair and told Milly a lot more about them. How some flew back many miles though injured by gunfire; and how an electric bell had been fixed to the wire so the pigeon rang it when it reached home and the message could be dealt with straight away.

His mother was in and out of the room, as fascinated as

Milly was. She wanted to ask about Gina, but dreaded to hear he was going away to spend half his leave with her. Mutt was asleep on the hearth rug in front of the fire. Within an hour Milly'd put Gina out of her mind and it felt as though he'd never been away. It was always like this. Milly enjoyed the remains of their Christmas cake as well as a mince pie.

Laurie had brought her a gift of chocolate and he loaned her a book about homing pigeons as she was showing such interest. His mother went to the kitchen to start cooking their lunch and once they were alone Laurie asked, 'How is Lizzie?'

That sobered Milly up. There was nothing good she could tell him about Lizzie. She had to make an effort not to grimace.

'What's the matter with her? Is she ill?'

'No.'

'What then? You're all worried about her?'

'Actually, it's just me. She has a big problem that is really getting her down. I wish she'd tell Mum, but she wants it to stay a secret.'

'She's married now, isn't she? Her husband's away in the forces?'

'No, he was found medically unfit.'

'I remember now, their home lost part of its roof in a raid and they had to come and live in your attic flat. Poor Lizzie.' He sat for a moment deep in thought. 'Well, Milly, I think it's a bit unfair of her to burden you with her problems. She should tell either your mother or her husband.'

'I told her that but she doesn't want anybody else to know, and she's relying on me to help her. I want to, of course, but I have no idea how to go about finding out what would help.'

'You can't take on the problems of the world.'

'This isn't a problem of the world, Laurie, it's my sister's problem and I don't understand much about it. What I can do? Lizzie's really upset and desperately needs help. My difficulty is that she's asked me not to tell anybody.'

'How can you help her unless you do? She's asked the wrong person.'

'Oh, gosh! That puts me in my place.'

He smiled. 'Milly, would it take the weight off your mind if you told me? You might as well now you've gone this far. I promise to keep my mouth shut and I'll be back down south with my carrier pigeons in ten days anyway.'

She sighed. 'You're right, of course, I have to talk to somebody about this or I'll never get any nearer. Let's take Mutt out for a walk.'

'It's drizzling now and cold out there.'

'Come on, nobody else must know.'

No sooner had their garden gate clicked shut behind them than Milly said, 'Lizzie is afraid she's addicted to gambling.'

'Addicted to gambling?' He pulled her arm through his. 'Oh dear, I know nothing about that sort of thing. Do you think she's right?'

'Yes. She's desperate about it. What can I do for her that would help?'

'You've asked the wrong person too, but my mother will probably know, that's her line of business. I could ask her for you.'

'Lizzie would have a fit if she thought the neighbours knew.'

'I won't mention her name, but you're the only person I've spoken to since I came home, so it shouldn't be difficult for her to guess.'

'I have to find out about this, Laurie. Ask anyone, but nobody must say anything to Lizzie. Swear them to secrecy.'

'I'll talk to Mum this afternoon, while Dad is at work, though she'll probably tell him.'

CHAPTER THIRTY-SIX

MILLY WAS EAGER TO know what Laurie had found out, and lingered over washing up the lunch dishes, so she could watch for him through the kitchen window, though her mother saw him first. 'Laurie's taking Mutt for another walk,' she said.

'I'll take Dido out and go with him.' Milly reached for her coat and harness.

'It's quite raw out there. Wrap up well.'

Dido was fast asleep by the Rayburn. Milly was rattling her harness to wake her when the front doorbell rang. 'That'll be him.' She said nothing about Lizzie until they were safely away in the lane. 'Did you find out anything that might help me?'

'I did my best,' he said. 'My mother says addiction of any sort isn't easy to cure. I didn't mention Lizzie's name and she and Dad promised not to say a word about it to anyone. They think you're taking on a difficult task.'

'I've got to try. What can I do?'

'It's largely up to Lizzie. She has to make up her mind to stop completely. Has she?'

'She wants to.'

'That's not enough, she has to be determined to give it up, and you can't do that for her. All you can do is help and support her. She mustn't even think about gambling because if she once places another small bet, she'll go on doing it.'

'Lizzie said that has already happened to her, so she knows it's true.'

'Would she trust you to look after her wages?'

'She might. I know she isn't all that careful with her money, she lets it run through her fingers.'

'The idea is to block her from using it to gamble. You'd have to take charge of her bank book.'

'Well, I could do that if she'll let me.'

'You said she was desperate.'

'She is that, and worried and nerve-wracked, and she works in an underground munitions factory all day. She's safe from bombing raids but Mum said in the last war there was often an explosion inside and she's worried that could happen here. They're handling high explosives, after all.'

'Not the best place for her.'

'No, but there's a war on, she has to stay. What else would I need to do?'

'Keep her busy in her spare time. What interests her?'

'Fashion, but that's all gone now. There's only utility clothes in the shops, all skimpy, military styles to save on cloth, and there's very little variety.'

'There must be something she enjoys, does she read books?'

'She was more for fashion magazines but there are none of those any more because of the paper shortage. She used to go out with boyfriends a lot.'

'Yes, I remember from when I took her out, but she thought me no fun at all. She was very popular, chatty, and easily the best-looking girl in town.'

Milly wanted to ask him if he'd been in love with Lizzie, and about the sort of relationship he'd had with her. She had another hundred questions she wanted to ask about Gina but she didn't want him to think her nosy. 'Lizzie likes going to the pictures,' she said, 'and so do I. I suppose we go once a week or so, and she loves dancing.'

'Just keep her busy and her mind away from betting. Mum says if you can keep her away from it for four weeks the craving to do it should lessen.'

'No.' Milly shook her head. 'She's wrong there, Laurie. Lizzie told me that when she'd had a run of bad luck and spent all her savings she stopped for five months. She said it nagged like a hunger she couldn't satisfy, but she still thought it would be perfectly possible for her to have a big win and replace all she'd lost.'

'She started again after five months? Then it's harder than Mum thought. She must give up for good. Never ever have another bet of any sort. It sounds as though it's going to be very difficult for both of you.'

'Well, at least I have some idea of what might help. That makes me feel a bit better. Thank you.'

He squeezed her hand. 'I wish I could do more for both of you.'

'I'll put it to her tonight and let you know what she says tomorrow.'

'I wish you all the luck in the world over this, Milly.'

'It sounds as though we're going to need it,' she said.

'You said Harry Barr took you to the Tower Ballroom,' Laurie said. 'What about coming with me on New Year's Eve?'

'I'd love that.' Milly felt she was really getting somewhere with Laurie. 'There'll be a real party atmosphere that night, it'll be fun.'

He smiled. 'It will.' But when Milly took him indoors to say hello to her parents they found Mrs Coyne was there. She'd come to invite Milly and her parents to have dinner on New Year's Eve and see the new year in with them.

'We always used to welcome it in like this,' she said. 'We want to do the same this year because Laurie is with us.'

'We did indeed,' Mum said, remembering. 'We all missed you over Christmas, Laurie. Food is so scarce I can't leave everything to you, Helen. I'll make a pudding and bring it up.'

Milly worried about Lizzie and later that same evening she was helping her mother dish up their evening meal, when Lizzie came straight into the kitchen.

'You're late coming home,' Mum said, 'and you look tired.'

Milly thought she looked sorry for herself too.

'Ben came to meet me, to tell me he won't be home for dinner tonight,' she said. 'I had to walk home as by then I'd missed the bus.'

'Never mind,' Mum said, 'come and eat with us. I can stretch this stew for one more.'

Later, Lizzie whispered to Milly when they were alone for a moment, 'I had no money left for my bus fare, that's why I had to walk home. They passed a hat round at work to collect for one of our girls. She's been injured in a raid and is now in hospital. I feel mean because that was the only money I had and I'll have to walk down again tomorrow morning.'

'I can lend you your bus fare,' Milly said.

She noticed that Lizzie ate very little and once they left the table she was heading for the stairs to get away, but Milly said, 'Come on, you know the drill, you have to help clear away and wash up.'

'Sorry, I forgot.'

When that was done Milly went upstairs with her to the living room in her flat. Lizzie had always kept it neat and tidy but tonight it looked a mess; their breakfast dishes were still on the table. Milly sat down with her back to that. 'I've managed to find out the basics of how I might help you. Don't ask me how because I can't tell you.'

Lizzie straightened her lips and sat down on the sofa beside her. 'First of all,' Milly went on, 'I need to know how serious you are. Have you really made up your mind to stop betting?'

'I've told you, Milly, I'm desperate to stop. I can't go on like this. It's taking all my wages and making me feel terrible: I can't sleep, can't eat and I'm exhausted the whole time. I have no energy for work or anything else, I want to stay in bed in the mornings, not get up and go back to that factory.'

'There's a war on, you have to.'

'I know that.' Lizzie looked tearful.

'What makes you bet on horses? I didn't know you were interested in them.'

'On our honeymoon Ben took me to see the horse races, but it was the dogs that started it. I love everything about that, the tension before the race, the flashing lights, the smell, but it's winning money that really does it. Marvellous to have a lovely day out and come home with more money than you started with.'

'Money you didn't have to work for?'

'Yes, and the total thrill of winning, of guessing it right. You loved it too.'

'I did. Such excitement when the dogs burst out of the starting pens in their coloured jackets, but it was all over in seconds.'

'Yes, I believed I'd continue to win, that I was unstoppable. You used to call me Lucky Lizzie.'

'You won so many times. Yes, you were lucky, but really it's all down to chance. It was then and still is.'

'I know that in my saner moments, but the thrill of a big win . . . Of having plenty of money in my purse.'

'Lizzie, betting is designed so the odds are in favour of bookies.' Laurie had told her that. 'The odds are always stacked in their favour. You're very unlikely to win back what you've lost.'

'I've made up my mind to stop more than once and done it. I thought it was just a matter of being determined, but it gets harder as the days pass, especially if I know there's a race meeting on somewhere. I can't stop thinking about all the fun we once had and the urge comes to return to those happier times. I long to win back all I've lost.'

'It isn't possible and never will be. It's pure chance.'

'That's what Ben says.'

'You've got to break this habit, give it up for good. Never place another bet. Not of any sort. On anything.'

'I really must. I've got to pull myself together, be really firm, and not be persuaded otherwise. I've tried to do it on my own, but with you to help me, I think I could manage it. I must manage it. That's what I want, no more betting.'

'Right, this is what I want you to do. When you get paid you have to hand your wages over for me to look after. I'll give you back just enough to pay for bus fares and for lunch at the factory.'

'I've been taking a sandwich recently to save money, and I'll carry on doing that, but at work it's a penny for a mug of tea.'

'That's all right and if you want to buy shoes or clothes or anything else, I'll hand over what you need. This is to make it impossible for you to gamble. If you give me your post office savings book, I'll pay your wages in there, and give you just enough for bus fares and tea. You agree?'

'Yes, thank you, Milly, you're marvellous.' Lizzie's face was tear-stained. 'I do appreciate what you're doing for me, and I'll pay back what I owe you on Friday.'

The next morning Milly fastened on Dido's coat and harness; Laurie had told her he'd come down with Mutt at about ten and she couldn't wait to tell him that Lizzie had agreed to the plan he'd suggested. 'I feel so sorry for Lizzie,' she told him. 'She's always been my friend as well as my sister, and now she's fraught and unhappy and it's making her ill.'

'She doesn't look ill, no different really,' Laurie said. 'You say she's fraught but . . .'

'Nobody sees beyond her beautiful face,' Milly told him. 'She's kind and generous and warm-hearted. She used to be open about everything and full of fun, but now she's a bit miserable. Everybody puts it down to the war and working in that munitions factory, but it's gambling. I'm hoping this is going to work. Thank your mother for her help. I'm grateful.'

Laurie said, 'About my mother . . . I would have preferred to spend the evening with you, but our families are making such an effort for the festive season and I'm here for such a short time that I feel I have to fall in with Mum's plans.'

She managed to say, 'I know what you mean, I'd feel the same.'

'Sorry about the Tower Ballroom but we'll do that another night before I go back.'

That made her feel better and later that day she helped her mother whip up egg whites to make meringue for a pavlova. Mum opened her last tin of peaches and a tin of cream. Dadda provided a bottle of wine and Milly and Laurie carried them up to his home.

At dinner that evening Milly looked across the table set with the Coynes' best china and cut glasses, to admire the shine on Laurie's wavy brown hair. His wide smile seemed focused on her, and she wanted to lean across and touch him.

They all agreed that between them they produced a very decent three-course meal and Milly thought it a happy occasion, but it gave her no chance of being alone with Laurie and that was what she wanted.

Milly knew she was in love with him and had been for years. His parents had made her feel included in the family but they drank to Gina's health, and wasn't he continuing to treat her like a little sister?

'This year has been dire,' Esmond said, 'and the war news is depressing. At least there were no air raids over the holidays and we've had the rest we all needed.'

They stayed up late to see in the New Year but none of them were expecting 1941 to be any better. Milly walked home with her parents shortly after midnight feeling dissatisfied, while the ships in the Mersey really let their hooters rip through the night to welcome the New Year in.

New Year's Day was cold, wet and grey, with a cutting wind. Everybody was late getting up and felt somnolent. Only Ben went to work and Lizzie came to sit with her family round the sitting-room fire and talk. Milly found she had little to say and knowing why she looked sad, was sorry for her.

Coal was in short supply and Mum welcomed anything that would burn. Laurie came as usual and he and Milly walked the dogs round the fields of Oakdene, yet again looking for dead wood that might be burned in the grate. She was glad to get Laurie back indoors by the fire.

Lizzie looked up when they sat down. 'How is Gina? When are you going to get married?'

Milly noticed that he seemed somewhat lost for words but he eventually said, 'Don't know, no date set. The war makes things like that difficult.'

But not so difficult, Milly thought, that it couldn't be done. She'd seen cardboard cut-outs of magnificent wedding cakes on show in bakers' shop windows. If you had the rations they would bake a utility cake for you that would fit on a plate under the cardboard edifice and look lovely in a photograph.

She sensed Laurie wasn't as keen on Gina as he used to be. Or was that just wishful thinking on her part?

CHAPTER THIRTY-SEVEN

THE NEXT DAY MUM went out to a WVS meeting after lunch to help arrange the next bring and buy sale, and Dadda went to a friend's house to play chess. He decided that as they'd been late getting up and meant to spend much of the day out, the sitting-room fire should not be lit until evening. Milly was pleased they were going out; it meant she and Laurie would have the house to themselves.

'Use the parlour,' Mum said, knowing she preferred to do that. They now used an electric fire there though they frequently had electricity cuts. Today the power was on. Laurie had just arrived and they were in the kitchen making a cup of tea when the sound of the front doorbell rang through the house.

'Who can that be?' Milly was very surprised to find Harry Barr on the doorstep. 'Come on in, I didn't know you'd come home.'

'I didn't expect it. My ship was damaged before we'd gone very far and we had to turn back for repairs.'

Laurie came to the kitchen door and Milly started to introduce them. 'I remember you from school,' Laurie said. 'You were one year ahead of me.'

'So I was.'

Milly took a tea tray to the parlour and Harry started to talk about the war and the course it was taking. The men were getting on well.

Laurie said, 'We hear a lot about our Atlantic convoys being bombed; sailing with one must be frightening.'

'It is, the German U-boats are a menace that hangs over us. We lose a ship or two on almost every crossing. The worst part is seeing them torpedo a nearby ship and seeing it set on fire.'

'That sounds horrific, when you know it could have been your ship that was targeted.'

'Yes, and we are ordered not to stop and pick up survivors as it would endanger the rest of the convoy.'

Milly shuddered. 'Harry told me before that it has happened when he knows some of the men in the water because he's sailed with them on other ships. That would give anybody nightmares.'

'It makes me feel guilty,' Laurie said. 'I could be said to be doing my duty, but really I have a sinecure compared to you. I'm in the Veterinary Corps and look after hundreds of homing pigeons and enjoy doing it. I get the same uniform as those fighting on the front but that isn't what I do. And although I'm stationed near London and we've had a few air raids, my risk is no more than that of the civilian population.'

Milly was glad Laurie wasn't running the risks Harry was. 'It's all down to chance,' she said. 'Years before the war started you decided to follow your father's footsteps and become a vet.'

'And I decided I wanted to go to sea,' Harry sighed. 'Now I have to carry on doing it. The war has its consequences on our lives.' He stayed with them for two hours chatting, and when he got up to leave he said, 'I hope you don't mind my inter-

rupting you like this? I needed a change of scene and you've
cheered me up.'

'Of course not, we've had a good natter, haven't we?'

Harry paused again on the step. 'Milly, I have tickets for the
pantomime tomorrow night at the Floral Hall. It's *Ali Barber
and the Forty Thieves*, and I came to ask if you'd come with me? I
feel a bit old for it really, but there's not much else on at the
moment.'

Milly hesitated; really she wanted to spend the time with
Laurie, but Harry's eyes didn't leave her face. 'I'd like to,' she
managed. 'Thank you.'

'Oh good, it starts at six o'clock, they're doing three perform-
ances a night. Can I ask for more? What about a good walk
along the prom first and then tea and cakes somewhere? And
there'd still be time to have a bite of supper when the show's
over.'

When Milly turned round she saw that Laurie had followed
them and had heard everything. When the door clicked shut
behind Harry, he said, 'I feel quite shocked. You didn't tell me
you had a boyfriend. I've been monopolising your time.'

Milly smiled. 'No, it's not like that; Harry counts me a
friend, not a girlfriend. Like you, he comes on leave and finds
all his old friends are away fighting, and though he's delighted
to see his parents they have their own lives and it doesn't make
for an exciting leave. Taking me out is better than nothing.'

'You're a lot better than nothing, Milly. You've grown into
a very pretty girl. Of course Harry sees you as his girlfriend.'

'No, Harry's mind is not on romance.'

'What is it on?'

'He told you. He fears crossing the Atlantic and who

wouldn't? But he still does it; he's the bravest person I know.'

'He is, but . . . How about you, Milly? How do you see him?'

She thought for a moment. 'I like him and admire him. But very definitely, we don't see each other as the person we want to spend the rest of our lives with. Harry just wants a sympathetic companion for his leave.'

Laurie was staring at her. 'I'm losing touch. Milly, you've really grown up. You have a wise head.'

'Don't you treat me in the same way? A companion to walk the dogs.'

'No! Is that what you think? No, you've been my friend, my dog-walking friend for years, ever since you were a kid. How often have we put the world to rights?'

'Ever since the night Dido had her pups.' Milly tried to smile.

Laurie reached out and pulled her close in one of his bear hugs. 'Little Milly, you've surprised me.' He held her away so he could look into her face. 'What is the matter with me? Harry Barr has seen things in you that I had not. You're far more grown up than I realised.'

Slowly he bent over and he kissed her full on the lips. Milly's heart turned over and her arms tightened round him. She felt as though she was flying.

'You'll be out tonight with Harry, but tomorrow night we could go to the Tower and dance. How about it?'

'Lovely,' she said and could hardly get her breath.

The front door slammed. 'That'll be your mother,' he said. 'I'd better go. I'll be back with Mutt as usual in the morning.'

Milly watched him put on his coat. He must surely love her; that kiss had made her feel his love.

* * *

Laurie walked home in a daze. What a blind fool he'd been. Milly had been supporting Harry Barr for some time; she thought of other people and what she could do for them. It made him think of Gina. Milly was stronger and wiser, and altogether more adult than she was. Gina had always been calling on him for help in one way or another; she'd never been good at answering his letters, but suddenly all those months ago she'd stopped.

He knew she'd moved to her parents' house in Morecambe and found a job with a nearby practice. He'd tried to speak to her again but it was her mother who'd answered. 'Gina has moved to a flat of her own,' she said, 'and we haven't seen her for a few weeks. I'm afraid she has no phone there.'

Laurie had scribbled down her new address and had written to her again, but she didn't answer that either. When he'd joined up in the summer he'd expected her to come and stay with his family for a few days. She'd accepted his invitation but at the last moment she'd called it off and he'd heard no more since. It was now ten months since he'd seen her.

The only conclusion he could draw from that was she'd changed her mind and wanted no more to do with him, and with no contact he'd come to accept that. With hindsight he could see she was a social butterfly who wanted to go out every night, while he was more a work-orientated homebody. Their marriage would not have worked. Gina must have come to realise that too, but he'd have liked her to say so. He felt he'd been left hanging on and he wasn't sure whether he could consider himself free. When he'd proposed Gina had been very keen.

Milly was the most unselfish person he knew, but should he have kissed her like that? Her father would certainly believe that to be wrong before he'd freed himself from Gina Flowers.

He'd felt Milly respond and that had brought him to his senses. Milly was twice the woman Gina was; she could stand on her own feet. Why had he never thought of her as beautiful before?

The next morning brought him a letter that had been redirected from his billet in Kent. He ripped it open and it sent a shiver through him when he saw it was from Gina's mother. Did this spell trouble? He heard his parents laughing together in the kitchen and went hurriedly to his bedroom to read it on his own.

I'm very worried about Gina. I've been trying to ring you but I can't get through. Gina hasn't come home for several months and though I've been round to her address several times, she's never at home. I've been wondering if you've heard from her, or if she's gone down to stay near you?

Laurie was concerned; it reawakened the sense of responsibility he'd once felt for her. How strange that he'd been thinking of Gina yesterday before he'd had this. He went downstairs and asked his father, who was about to leave for work, if he might use the phone.

He went to his study; it was more private there, and he had no trouble getting through to Mrs Flowers. She sounded at the end of her tether. 'Gina's no longer going to work,' she said. 'She put in her notice and left at the end of November.'

'Oh heavens! Did you ask why?'

'They said they didn't know. I've tried ringing round her friends, but none have heard from her recently.'

Laurie tried to think. 'If she gave a month's notice before she left work it can't have been urgent, and she must have been all right at the end of last month.' He was trying to soothe her mother but to Laurie it sounded ominous. Something bad must have happened to her.

'Please help me,' Mrs Flowers pleaded. 'I think she must be living in her flat but she won't open the door to me. I can think of nowhere else she could be.'

'That is not like Gina,' he said. 'She's always sought the company of others; in fact she was a social butterfly, always going out to parties and dances. She knew lots of people.'

'More acquaintances than real friends.'

'Do you know her landlord? You could check to see if she's still paying rent.'

'I don't know anything about her flat. And now my husband has had to go back to sea so there's nobody else to help me. I'm afraid something's terribly wrong and I don't know what to do. Will you help me? Please.'

Laurie took a deep, shuddering breath. That was exactly the sort of thing Gina used to say. 'Yes, but I need time to think about what I can do. I'll get back in touch soon.'

Laurie thought hard and long about it, but the best he could come up with was that as he was home on leave and much nearer to Morecambe, he ought to go up and try to see her. He had to settle this once and for all, as much for his own sake as for Gina's mother. He'd go tomorrow.

He went downstairs to tea and toast and began telling his mother for the first time about Gina, that he thought they'd both changed their minds about getting married. He let it all pour out, including why he had to go and see her while he was here on leave.

'There are no refreshment cars on trains these days,' she said. 'I'll cut a sandwich for you to take.' After a little pause she added, 'At least you've seen the problems with Gina before you are married.'

Laurie rang Mrs Flowers again to let her know. 'I think you should go to Gina's flat by yourself,' she said and gave him directions to find it. 'It might be better if I don't come. I've called through her letter box and banged on her door several times. If she's there she must know I've been trying to see her. If you need to stay overnight, I can put you up in my spare room.' Laurie had stayed there before but hoped he wouldn't need to again.

He wanted to warn Gina of his visit but there was no time to write a letter; he'd have to compose a telegram. He needed to say he was very worried about her and that he was coming to see her tomorrow, and if she didn't open the door to him he'd get the police to come and open it for him. His mother said before she set out to work, 'I'll bring home a train timetable so you can work out the best way to get to Morecambe.'

Milly would be expecting him to walk down with Mutt about ten o'clock but he'd told her he'd take her dancing at the Tower tomorrow evening and now he had no idea when he'd be back. He'd not have much energy for that, even if he was home in time. He'd have to make his apologies, but he felt guilty because she'd asked him to take her and this would be the second time it was cancelled. He dressed Mutt up in his coat as it was a cold, dark morning.

* * *

For Milly that day started like every other of his leave. She waved to him from the kitchen window and already had Dido ready for her walk, but she sensed immediately that Laurie wasn't his usual self. He looked ill at ease and said stiffly, 'I have to go up to Morecambe tomorrow to see Gina.'

'Morecambe? You've only got three days of leave left.' Milly felt a flush creep up her cheeks and turned her face away so he wouldn't see it. Jealousy was an ugly trait.

'Yes,' he said. 'I told you Gina took a job in Morecambe.'

'To get away from the air raids.'

'Her parents live there.'

'Has something happened? Why go now? Why is this so sudden?' Blast Gina. She'd very much wanted to ask Laurie about her but she'd been too much of a coward. Gina's ghost had been between them ever since she'd set eyes on her. 'You won't be back in time to go dancing at the Tower tomorrow?'

'I may not be. I'm sorry I have to cancel that again.'

Milly swallowed hard. 'I hope you'll still have time to do that another evening.' But it was beginning to look as though it would never happen. 'No matter,' she said. 'Harry Barr is taking me out tonight.'

'To the theatre,' Laurie agreed.

'Yes. I don't know if he has another day's leave, but if he has I'll ask him if he'll take me to the Tower.'

CHAPTER THIRTY-EIGHT

MILLY HAD BEEN THINKING of Laurie and that kiss all night; she could think of nothing else. She'd thought that had shown his love for her but it seemed she'd been mistaken; he still thought of her as a friend. That afternoon, Milly went down on the bus to meet Harry on the promenade. The sky was heavy with cloud and it was another raw cold day, but at least it wasn't raining.

'I enjoy a good walk,' he said. 'It's something we can't do on a ship.'

He set a brisk pace and soon Milly could feel her cheeks glowing. They went passed Moreton Common but there was little to see of the Welsh hills because of the heavy cloud and mist. In Moreton they caught a bus back to New Brighton. 'Where's the best place to go for a cup of tea?' Harry asked.

'The Rose Garden Tea Rooms,' Milly said. 'You must know it, in the amusement centre and the Tower Gardens.'

'Yes, is it still open?'

'Yes, it's run by a friend of Lizzie's husband and the smartest tea rooms here. It's a lovely place.' Milly remembered eating chocolate cake with a cream filling there. It had been gorgeous.

When they arrived, though, when she looked round her, the decor was beginning to look a little tired, as it was everywhere else. When Harry ordered tea and cakes the waitress said, 'Sorry, there's no cake left, we have tea cakes and can toast them with jam, otherwise it's just marge.'

'Milly?'

'Yes please, toasted tea cakes then. What sort of jam do you have?'

'There's just apple and plum.' That was the only combination available everywhere and Milly, like everybody else, was tired of it.

A few moments later, she was surprised to see Ben and the owner of the tea rooms come out of a door marked Staff Only and come towards them. She caught Ben's eye; he smiled and they stopped at her table. She saw him look hard at Harry. 'You remember Harry Barr,' she said. 'I have introduced you before. You were having trouble with your roundabout and your hands were covered with oil.'

'Yes, I couldn't shake hands with you, so I'll do that now.' He smiled. 'Do me a favour, Milly, tell Lizzie I've had my warden duties changed again and I won't be home until late tonight? Tell her I'll get fish and chips down here. Oh, and you can tell her too that Jimmy Cox received his call-up papers this morning.'

'So has Tommy Long, my manager here,' Lennie O'Dowd said. 'All my staff is being called up.' Milly watched them walk on to the door together and stand chatting for a moment before Ben went. Mr O'Dowd smiled at her as he returned to what appeared to be his office.

When the waitress brought their order, she said, 'The boss says you're to have strawberry jam. He keeps it for his favourite customers, and I'm not to give you a bill. It's on him.'

'Wow,' Milly said, 'that's nice of him, isn't it? Thank him for us, will you?'

Later, Milly enjoyed *Ali Barber and the Forty Thieves* and in the dark thought thankfully of Jimmy Cox being called up. Lizzie would not find it so easy to lay her bets in future and that had to be a good thing.

Ben walked away, feeling uneasy at having seen Milly having tea with Harry Barr. He knew exactly who he was, that his father was in charge of the Wallasey police. Milly was an unlikely girlfriend for him; he must be about a decade older than her. Years ago, Lizzie had gone out with him and she'd said he was a very serious and self-righteous person, who believed in putting King and country first and that he was no fun at all.

It made him hot with suspicion; he was afraid Harry might be seeking information about him. Even if that had not been his intention, Milly was a chatterbox and likely to let drop things that would start him thinking. Anything might alert Harry to what he and his friends were doing.

Now Lizzie was spending too much time with her family; she and Milly always had their heads together. It was making him feel on edge.

When he went to his rifle range later to tell Steve that Jimmy Cox had received his call-up papers, he found Lennie O'Dowd already there on the same errand. 'Excellent news, that's Jimmy sorted, and another problem solved for us. Alec is upset because he'll have to look for another school leaver to take his place.'

'I'm delighted,' Steve said. 'We'll all feel safer now we know

Jimmy could be sent miles away to fight. Serve him right if it's the Afrika Korps in North Africa.'

'That his call-up papers have come can only be seen as a blessing,' Ben said, but he went on to mention his anxiety about Harry Barr.

'I didn't know who he was,' Lennie said, 'but yes . . .'

'You and I should not be seen together,' Ben said, 'and you shouldn't be giving them strawberry jam and a free snack. It's showing him we are connected.'

'Of course you're connected. Milly is your sister-in-law, for heaven's sake.'

'Even so, if Harry talks to his father they might get round to thinking we're involved in crimes together.'

'You're getting paranoid,' Lennie said.

It was a dark wet morning and the train journey was slow and tedious.

Laurie wasn't looking forward to facing Gina, but felt he had to settle this once and for all. He found her ground-floor flat in a shabby block close to the station. It was not the sort of place he'd have expected her to live in; her family home was a detached four bedroom house in a better neighbourhood.

Her curtains were drawn and her doorbell didn't work. He hammered on the door and flipped the letter box to make as much noise as he could. Full of trepidation he waited, afraid he was getting the same treatment as her mother. He was reaching for her letter box again when he heard her coming.

He was shocked when she opened the door. This wasn't the Gina he knew. She was agitated and embarrassed and looked really ill. It took him a moment to realise that it wasn't that she'd put on weight; she was heavily pregnant.

'Hello, Gina,' he said, knowing now why she hadn't replied to his letters. 'You've been hiding a secret from me.'

'What if I have?' She was defensive.

'Aren't you going to ask me in?'

'Come on then.' He followed her into a gloomy living room. The only sign of the festive season was a single Christmas card on the mantelpiece. 'Sit down.'

He drew back the curtains before he did so. 'Have you been by yourself over Christmas?'

She turned her face away.

'What is the point of hiding yourself away from everybody? I was worried about you.'

She turned on him aggressively. 'Oh, you still care? Then a quick wedding would solve a major problem for me.'

Laurie was shocked and said awkwardly, 'I assumed because you'd cut yourself off . . . That we'd both decided that it was all off.'

Gina reached for her handkerchief, blew her nose, mopped at her eyes but said nothing.

'Who is the father? Doesn't he want to marry you?'

Still she said nothing.

'I know it isn't me.'

'Oh, there was never any chance of it being you. You wouldn't make a mistake like this. You're far too cautious, too gentlemanly, too eager to keep all that sort of fun for our married life.'

'It might have been better for you to have done the same. Who is the father?'

'He's already married with two children.'

359

'Oh dear! Too much fun, Gina, one party too far.'

'Not that it makes any difference now, he's been killed.'

'Oh lord!' Gina was crying now, and he was filled with pity. 'I'm sorry.'

'You wanted to marry me once, would you still do that for me? Will you marry me? That would solve . . .' Her eyes were damp and pleading, her neediness never more obvious.

'No, Gina, it's too late for that. I don't think I could make you happy. You'd have far fewer parties with me.'

'I know that but we have a lot in common. Our work. I could help you in that practice you'll be running when this war is over.'

'No, we wouldn't suit each other. You must see that?'

'What am I going to do? I can't work now and I've no money.'

'Get your coat on, I'll take you home to your mother.'

'I can't go there, my mother will be furious with me and my father will throw me straight out. They'll disown me. I'll bring shame on the family.'

Laurie spent the next ten minutes persuading her otherwise. 'Your father has gone back to sea, and your mother is alone and worried stiff about you. She's been trying to get in touch, that's what she wants.'

'You'll stay with me for a day or two, won't you?'

'No, Gina, I've come to find you because your mother asked for my help. Your mother is the best person to look after you now. I'm going straight home.'

'I expect you want this back?' She was pulling the emerald ring he'd given her off her finger.

'No, you can keep it.'

'I ought to give it to you. I'm sorry I haven't treated you better, this is the least I can do.' She offered it in the palm of her hand.

'Your need is greater than mine,' he said. He wanted nothing to remind him of his big mistake.

Laurie was glad to get back on the train.

It was late afternoon when Laurie reached home. His mother wasn't in and he found it cold and dark. He was about to make himself a cup of tea and light the fire but changed his mind. He'd had a harrowing morning, but at least he knew where he stood with Gina. Marriage for them would never have worked. He should never have got himself involved with her. He went back down the lane to see if Milly was at home.

She opened the door to him and pulled him in quickly in the way everybody did these days to stop too much light showing. 'I didn't expect you back as soon as this,' she said, but she was smiling, pleased to see him.

'I haven't come to take you dancing, I'm afraid,' he said, 'I'm shattered.'

'Come into the kitchen and have a warm.'

The door was open, warmth and savoury scents spilled into the hall, but he could see her mother there. 'I want to talk to you,' he said, 'alone. Do you want to walk Dido?'

'I've done that, she's in for the night. Is Mutt out there?'

'No, he was fast asleep in his basket, so I left him.'

'Well, Dadda's in the sitting room.'

'Come for a walk then. Wrap up warm.'

Her mother came out. 'Hello, Laurie. Milly, you're not

going out now? Dinner will be ready soon and it's pitch black out there.'

'How soon, half an hour? I'll be back by then, Mum.'

'How did you get on with Harry last night?' he asked as they stepped out into the blackout.

'I had a lovely time, really enjoyed it,' she said. 'He's due back on his ship at midday today. You've something to tell me?'

Laurie began to spill out Gina's sad story.

'I thought you were in love with her,' Milly said.

'At one time, I thought I was too.'

'You did ask her to marry you, and you gave her an emerald ring. You've broken it off? You've ended your engagement?'

He sighed. 'I think you could say Gina did that. She took up with another man and didn't bother to tell me. I wasn't sure where I was, but our engagement is certainly off now.'

They covered a hundred yards in silence. 'Laurie,' she said, 'you've just complained that Gina kept quiet about what she was doing, but you've done exactly the same thing to me. You could have told me last summer.'

'I should. I thought I was a good judge of character but I got Gina completely wrong, and it took Harry Barr to show me you've grown up. Yet I've seen you almost daily and counted you a friend for years.'

'But just for walking the dogs.'

'No, Milly.' He put an arm round her waist and pulled her closer. 'I didn't appreciate what I had.' He bent and kissed her on the lips again. A lover's kiss, much the same as the one he'd given her before.

'I'm afraid it's Sunday tomorrow and the Tower will be

closed. I promised to take you dancing but I won't be able to on this leave. There isn't time.'

Milly's head whirled with delight. 'You'll have other leaves when we can do that,' she said.

Milly couldn't stop thinking about Laurie. She'd spent most of Sunday with him but knowing this was the last day of his leave weighed heavily on their spirits. 'Will you come and see me off tomorrow?' he asked. 'Both Mum and Dad have to go to work.'

'Of course I will.'

'It won't be exciting. I'll be getting an early train to Liverpool, as I need to catch the nine o'clock express to London.'

It was another cold wet morning with a blustery wind, but for Milly just being with Laurie was exciting. She travelled with him to Liverpool Lime Street and saw him to the London express. On the way he dropped butterfly kisses on her forehead, and that made her feel for his hand. 'I've wasted a lot of time on this leave,' he said. 'I'll make up for it on the next.'

When the time came for him to get on the train she whispered, 'Goodbye.' She felt his arms go round her in one of his bear hugs and his lips caressed hers in a real lover's kiss. He hung out of the window waving. Milly watched from the platform, trying to smile and wave until she could no longer see him.

She so rarely came into Liverpool that it had seemed an opportunity to go round the big Liverpool department stores, but she had no appetite for it. She walked round in the rain staring into shop windows, feeling that everything had suddenly gone flat. She didn't buy anything, although the sales were on.

* * *

363

Two weeks later, Ben was chatting to Steve at his rifle range when Alec joined them. 'I've just seen Edna Cox,' he said, 'and she was near to tears. Jimmy went for his medical and guess what? They sent him for a chest X-ray and now he's been told he has tuberculosis.'

'Oh dear lord, that's a turn up for the books.' Ben was shocked. Tuberculosis was a disease everybody dreaded and it was widespread in the population. If it wasn't diagnosed until it had reached an advanced state, it was considered almost a death sentence. Nowadays, some managed to recover and hopefully Jimmy would.

'He's being sent straight away to a sanatorium at Market Drayton,' Alec said. 'His mother says they think he'll have to stay there for two years.'

'Serve him right for being a pest and demanding more money,' Steve said.

'He can't have told his mother, can he?' Lennie worried. 'Perhaps that was just a threat.'

'But it kept us on edge, as if we don't have enough to worry about.'

'It's not such a bad thing for Jimmy,' Alec said. 'He'll be safer there than fighting on some battlefield. Well away from any bombing raids, and I understand the treatment is plenty of rest and plenty to eat. It looks as though the war's over for him.'

'And not a bad thing from our point of view,' Lennie said. 'He can't spend too much money while he's in a sanatorium and as his mother will be a long way away from him, he's less likely to tell her our secrets.'

Ben shivered. He felt sorry for Jimmy Cox; tuberculosis was a frightening disease.

A LUCKY SIXPENCE

* * *

Milly knew Lizzie was still being tortured with cravings to have another bet, and that at times she was convinced it would be possible to win back what she'd lost. Whenever Ben was out she went up to spend time with Lizzie and tried to persuade her otherwise. She'd taken charge of her post office savings book but when Lizzie was feeling really bad she pleaded for enough money to allow her to place a small bet, and when Milly refused she would get angry.

Milly was glad Jimmy Cox had gone. It meant Lizzie could no longer place bets with him. She welcomed anything that made it harder for her to gamble.

Once in a while Lizzie brought home one of the sporting papers which she picked up in the factory. She'd point out a horse she'd fancied to Milly and tell her that it had won, that she'd lost an opportunity to claw back some of what she'd lost.

Milly found it harrowing to see Lizzie in this state and begged her to talk to Ben about it, or Mum. 'No,' she said, 'and don't you tell them. You promised you wouldn't.'

'They'd understand and want to help you too,' Milly said. 'Anyway, with Jimmy gone, you can't.'

Lizzie wouldn't have that. 'There's a man at work who puts bets on for others. He'd do it for me.'

'Have nothing to do with him,' Milly advised. 'Don't go near him.'

'Just let me have three pounds of my savings account.'

'Not to gamble. You asked me not to.'

'I know Ben keeps quite a lot of money in his bedside drawer,' Lizzie told her, 'and I don't think he'd miss it if I borrowed some.'

'Don't you dare,' Milly said. 'You can't guarantee to put it back. How did you feel when you took money from Mum and couldn't put it back?'

'You'd give it to me for that.' Lizzie was defiant. 'I know you would because you helped me put the money back when I took it from Mum.'

Milly was writing regularly to Laurie now and unburdening her worries about Lizzie on him. After all, he already knew about her troubles, and he replied offering suggestions and telling her what was going on in his life. She looked forward to his letters; they were the only support she had to keep Lizzie to their original agreement. His mother still offered her the letters he wrote to her. She always read them but she no longer needed them. She felt she was much more in touch with Laurie since his leave.

In the letter that had come today, he wrote:

I've never mentioned Lizzie's name to my mother, but I expect she'll have guessed that she is the person I've been asking about. You would get more immediate advice if you spoke directly to her. She tells me you are faithfully bringing up her eggs and vegetables.

Of course Milly knew, but she didn't want to speak directly to Helen Coyne. It gave her a reason to write to Laurie and his letters were not just a help to Lizzie but a bonus to her.

Despite the war, horse racing still went on in accordance with the annual calendar, but here on Merseyside the really big race was the Grand National that took place every year in

A LUCKY SIXPENCE

March. Milly knew that in almost every factory, shop and office the staff ran their own sweepstake on the result of that race, and raffle tickets were sold for a shilling or so and were put into a hat. A list of horses was drawn up from those running, headed by the favourites, and the tickets drawn out one by one and each was allotted a horse.

It would be impossible for her to stop Lizzie taking part in that, as she had money in her purse to pay for bus fares and cups of tea, and she was afraid that would be enough to start her thinking of winning on the horses again and would strengthen her cravings. When it was announced that the Grand National could not be run, as Aintree racecourse had been commandeered by the Ministry of Defence, Milly wanted to cheer.

Milly came home from college and went straight to the kitchen. Her mother had made a casserole and asked her to put it in the oven to warm up for their dinner as soon as she got home. Mum expected to be out most of the day helping to run another bring and buy sale to raise money to buy comforts for the troops.

Milly had started to peel potatoes to go with it when her mother came home. She collapsed on a chair in the kitchen, saying she was tired out. Milly filled the kettle and was putting it on to make them a cup when the telephone rang in the hall. She wiped her hands and went to answer it.

'Hello, is that you, Milly?' She didn't recognise the voice. 'Catharine Barr here.' Milly's heart turned over; there were tears in the voice and she knew it meant disaster. 'Harry's mother. We received a letter this morning telling us that Harry's ship has been sunk in the Atlantic. By U-boat action. All the crew are missing believed drowned.'

'Oh! Oh!' Milly couldn't get her breath. 'I'm so sorry, Mrs Barr. How terrible. How awful for you to hear like that. How sudden.'

'I know he'd want me to tell you.'

'Thank you, yes. I think Harry was the bravest person I've ever known. He knew the risks he was taking. He knew this could happen to him. Oh dear, I did admire him.'

Mrs Barr was openly sobbing now and tears were stinging Milly's eyes. Her mother came to her side and took the phone from her to murmur her condolences. Milly collapsed at the kitchen table to mop her eyes.

Elsie made the tea and slid a cup in front of her.

CHAPTER THIRTY-NINE

ELSIE WAS EATING TOAST and marmalade with one eye on the clock in order to push Milly out in time to catch her bus to college, when Gladys brought the fresh pot of tea to the dining-room table.

'Mrs Travis,' she said, standing back, 'I'd like to give you a week's notice as of today.'

To Elsie it felt as though she'd dropped a bombshell. 'Why?'

Even Esmond jerked upright in his chair. 'Gladys!' he choked.

Elsie asked, 'You're leaving?'

'Yes, I am.' She was regarding them all defiantly. 'Our Clover is quite happy down at that munitions factory and Lizzie told me the other day that she was too. They earn twice as much down there as I do here. I've decided I'll join them.'

'But you only work mornings here.' Dadda was frowning. 'They'll expect you to work all day there, won't they? So of course they'll pay you more.'

'Yes, they will . . .' Gladys' face was crimson and shining with embarrassment, 'but it'll be worth it.'

'We could increase your wage . . .'

'No, Major, too late for that. They'll pay me by the hour and it'll work out more than double.'

Elsie was really shocked. 'Gladys, are you sure? I'm going to miss you. You've worked here for years. You were here before I came.'

'Yes, nineteen years I've been here, nearly twenty. Time I had a change. The price of everything is going up, you know. I can hardly make ends meet these days. I need extra money.'

Esmond took a deep breath. 'Gladys, could you please give us a fortnight's notice so we have time to find someone to replace you?'

Gladys sighed. 'You'll be lucky to find anybody now; everybody I know has given up domestic work. I'm afraid you might have to look after yourselves from now on. There is a war on, you know.'

Elsie felt desperate but remembered, 'Milly, you'll miss your bus if you don't leave now.'

'Yes, bye, Mum.' Milly jerked to her feet and was out of the door in Gladys's wake.

Esmond said, 'I'm sorry, Elsie. How are we going to cope without Gladys?'

Elsie refilled their tea cups and groaned. 'I don't know, but it looks as if we'll have to.'

Ben was late getting home because he'd spent an hour or so with Lennie in some backstreet pub negotiating with a scoundrel of a dealer who wanted to buy their ration documents at a discount.

As he let himself into Oakdene Farm he saw the major striding up the hall to meet him. Had he been waiting for him? Ben closed his eyes. Not again. Not tonight, please.

'Ben, I know you were on warden duty last night,' he said,

'but if there's a raid would you mind standing in for Charles Merrit tonight? His son has just come round with a note to say he's ill.'

It was the last thing Ben wanted; they'd had two raids last night and he'd not had much sleep. 'Major, I'm dead beat . . .'

'I know, we're all getting to the end of our tether but I would appreciate it. I'll do my best to swop your duty tomorrow night.'

Ben sighed. 'Charlie Merrit does the Sandfield Road area, doesn't he?'

'Yes, both wardens there have gone down with flu, so I'll be with you.'

As far as Ben was concerned that made it fifty times worse. 'If that's the case then I suppose I have to,' he said grudgingly. 'Let's hope for a quiet night.' He went on upstairs.

'Thank you . . .' Esmond's voice followed him, 'but it's a clear evening, not a cloud in the sky. I'm afraid we're likely to get it again. I get the feeling that the Luftwaffe are coming more often.'

'They are, and they're bringing bigger bombs,' he called back. Ben changed straight away into his ARP warden uniform because he knew the major would, and he must not be guilty of holding him up.

Lizzie looked exhausted but she gave him one piece of news: 'Harry Barr has gone down with his ship. Lost at sea, all the crew were. That brings the war close, doesn't it?'

'Poor sod,' he said, but it removed one of his worries. 'Milly will be upset.'

'She's more interested in Laurie Coyne.'

'Yes, but she likes Harry, liked Harry, I mean. It seems only yesterday I saw them having tea together in Lennie's place.'

Lizzie was upset too and slow to bring their dinner to the table. He hadn't finished eating when the siren wailed across town. It gave Ben a rush of panic and a racing heartbeat. He swore and gulped the rest of it down then put on his shoes to clatter downstairs where the major was waiting for him. He'd always known this could happen; living above him as he did, it was easier for Esmond to rope him in than anybody else, and he found it impossible to refuse.

He felt jumpy and ill at ease from the start. They got a lift in a lorry to their allotted area, which was a heavily populated older part of Wallasey. The major got the passenger seat at the front; Ben had to climb into the back. This was going to be an awful night.

They could hear the bombers above them; their engines had a noticeably different sound to that of the Spitfires. Bombs were being dropped further away. The crump crump was unmistakable, followed by flashes of light in the sky. Ben felt fully alert with adrenalin when the time came to jump down and rejoin the major.

'That'll be Cammell Laird's shipyard at Birkenhead,' Esmond said, 'or possibly the soap and margarine factories further up river.'

'Perhaps not our turn tonight,' Ben said hopefully.

'I wouldn't bank on it, plenty of time yet. Here we are.' The warden's post was a concrete pillbox erected on an earlier bomb site. They went in and the major tested the telephone to make sure it was working. Ben sat down, feeling at a loose end. He'd rather be digging out bodies than here with the major. His eyes seemed to watch every move he made.

He came and sat beside him, lifting out a Thermos from his

haversack. 'I didn't have time to have a drink after dinner, I don't suppose you did either. We'll have this now while it's quiet. Elsie always sends me off with a hot drink and a snack.' He brought out a couple of slices of sponge cake. Ben was glad to have both.

Esmond went on, 'You're doing very well, Ben, for one rejected by the army. What exactly is the problem that makes you too ill?'

Ben almost gasped aloud; instantly he was suffused with fear. Did he detect a note of sarcasm? He thought he'd settled the major's suspicions on this.

'I've been thinking about the night we were fire-watching together,' he went on. 'You did marvellously well throwing those incendiaries off the roof before they set fire to the sub-station. You leapt over that balustrade onto the stairs.'

Ben knew he was floundering. Last year he'd had the story about his supposed heart problem all worked out; now he was frantically trying to recall how it went. 'I had rheumatic fever in my youth and I was told then it could damage my heart.' He could feel himself sweating, and panic was taking over; he had to hide that.

Was Esmond trying to ferret out how he'd managed to avoid being called up? He never gave up on anything. 'I remember thinking you looked very fit, like an athlete. You were hardly breathless, even after that.'

Ben took a deep breath; he found the major's obvious suspicion agonising. 'I've done my best to stay fit since then.' His voice sounded fairly calm, but he'd have been given a medical certificate or something and he was afraid he'd be asked to produce it.

He got a grip on his nerves. 'Cycling to work and back from your place has helped, I'm sure, but I wasn't really surprised that I failed my medical. It said I had an enlarged heart on my papers.'

'Enlarged heart, eh? Does it affect you in any way?'

Ben gulped. 'Yes, I do get breathless. I have my good days and my bad. They sent me to my GP who tells me it will gradually get worse as I get older but not to worry yet. I do my best to put it out of my mind.'

'The best thing,' the major agreed, 'but Elsie and I would have appreciated being told before you married our daughter.'

'I told Lizzie,' he lied – that was the best he could do.

'Well, you do look the picture of health,' he was saying, when a much closer explosion shook the ground. Esmond got to his feet and reached for his helmet. 'We'd better get out and see what that was.' Ben did the same, his legs feeling too woolly to support him, but he was glad to escape his full attention. What the major had said terrified him; it sounded as though he was out to get him. He'd always feared and been in awe of him but now he loathed him. He wanted to kill him. He'd have to do something to shut the major up.

A series of three bombs came crashing down on them and the guns in Central Park were firing back. The noise was deafening; it seemed all hell had been let loose, but for Ben it was better than being quizzed by the major. He heard him grunt out, 'The next street,' before breaking into a run.

Ben wasn't going to prove he could run faster, not after what he'd just said. He let him lead the way. Dust and debris were flying in the air, making it difficult to see anything, but they seemed to be surrounded by big old buildings, now possibly divided into rooms or flats. Ben could see that one of the buildings had received a direct hit and others round it had been half demolished.

People were crying and screaming for help. The police were already here; the fire brigade was too, their engine clanging to a halt at the kerb. At least two more adjacent houses had been damaged and were now on fire. Ben shuddered. It was pandemonium.

A tearful elderly woman tugged at the major's coat, and screamed above the noise, 'My daughter and her family are still inside. I know they are, this is their house. They'll be burned to death. Help them please.'

'How many?' the major asked. 'You're sure they're inside?'

'Yes, yes, I tell you.' She sounded desperate. 'Six children and my daughter.'

Ben felt the major's one arm against his back. 'You go,' he ordered. Ben couldn't move a muscle; he felt rooted to the ground.

'No,' a fireman bellowed as he ran a hosepipe out. 'Stay out of that house. It's in danger of collapsing, not safe.'

The old woman was tugging at Ben's coat now. 'Please,' she implored, 'all my family. My grandchildren. Please help them, please.'

'You'll be safe enough for another few minutes,' the major urged Ben calmly. 'There's a stiff breeze tonight and it's taking the smoke away from us. Quick, go on, don't waste time. Don't be a coward.'

Ben was appalled; this was a nightmare.

With an exasperated snort the major ranted, 'You'd have

been given a white feather in the last war,' and headed for the house the woman had indicated.

'No, no,' Ben shouted, following him. 'Major, don't go in, what are you trying to prove?'

'It's our duty. Why else would we be here?' Esmond screamed at him.

A lump of flying debris hit Ben on the shoulder, making him stagger. Bitter gall was rising up his throat. He itched to kill the major. If he'd been quicker he could have bumped him hard on the head, dragged him into that house and with luck he'd be thought another wartime casualty. But too late for that now, he'd disappeared inside.

Ben followed him. Once the front door swung shut behind him it was pitch black and impossible to see anything. Glass splintered beneath his feet. 'Major,' he shouted, 'where are you?' He stopped to listen, fumbling for his torch. The racket outside was more distant. 'Major?'

He could hear something. Was it babies screaming their heads off? Or was that outside? No, now faintly he heard something else: 'Help, please help me.' He shone his torch round and saw the stairs. He knew the children must be up there. He was halfway up when there was a loud explosion that shook the whole building. He had to grab for the banisters to stop himself falling. Then came the sound of a lorry tipping its load. No, it wasn't that: dust and plaster was raining down on him, making him close his eyes. The crying ceased.

Ben's heart was in his mouth but the building seemed to settle. He carried on up the stairs; the terrified crying broke out again and was nearer now. He opened a door to a deserted room, then another door and another empty room, but he could still hear the woman screaming, 'Help me.'

'Hello, where are you? Hello.' The crying stopped abruptly at the sound of his voice. Further along the passage he opened another door and found a family of distressed toddlers clinging together. 'Come on,' he gasped, smoke in his throat, 'you've got to get out of here.'

'Thank God you've come.' A stout woman came closer with a noisy baby in her arms. She pushed it on Ben; he tucked it under one arm and felt for the nearest toddler with the other hand.

'Come on, all of you hold hands and stay together. Come on.' They were whimpering now. They'd barely taken five steps when there was another almighty crash, followed by another. Ben held his breath as he felt the building move again. All the children burst into noisy tears again. 'Shut up,' Ben bellowed, his nerves frayed.

One of them carried on; she was dancing in terror, waving her arms. 'Shush, Maisie,' the mother said, 'be quiet, for goodness sake.'

Ben took a firmer grip on the wriggling baby, who was no lightweight. 'You come last,' he said to the woman, 'and make sure they all come with us.'

He got them all moving but in order to light the way he had to hold the torch as well as the hand of the nearest toddler; she was barely two and was having difficulty with the stairs. He seemed to be edging forward through a black pall, but eventually he drew the chain of four toddlers outside. Only then did he see that the woman held another baby in her arms.

'Thank you, thank you.' Their grandmother was on the

doorstep and took the baby from him. 'All unhurt, thank God, you're a hero. My darling twins.'

'I couldn't see . . .' the mother was coughing and looked close to collapse, 'couldn't see how to get them all out.'

A fireman said, 'Are you all right? There's an ambulance round the corner, better get these children checked over.'

'Just frightened,' Grandma said, 'who wouldn't be?'

Another voice said, 'Hello, Ben, what about you, are you OK?'

Relief was flooding through him. 'Yes, not too bad.' His shoulder hurt and so did his hand where something had hit him, but he stood tall and proud. He'd done his duty; not even the major would call him a coward after that.

'That was an almighty risk you took,' the fireman said, 'ignoring all our warnings, but under the circumstances I'm glad you did.'

'He's a real hero,' the grandma said. 'What did you say his name was, Ben something?'

'McCluskey, Ben McCluskey,' the fireman said, 'but I haven't seen Major Travis come out. Did you see what happened to him?'

'Strewth!' Ben gasped. 'No, I left him to go upstairs.' He turned to go back inside.

'No, it'll go up any minute now.' The fireman grabbed his arm but he shook him off and was back into that hell hole. This was a warren of a place. The major must be somewhere on the ground floor. Ben shone his torch round what seemed to be one set of furnished rooms after another. Cupboards had burst open, clothes and private possessions were strewn amongst the fallen plaster.

He could hear the roar of a fire now and the smell of smoke was choking him; he had to get out of here fast. Some of the doors were closed and he was scared to open them, as he'd been taught he might meet a wall of flames, but one door was partly open already. He tried to push his way in but something was blocking it. He pushed with all his might and found the ceiling had come down inside and there was debris and plaster bits flying everywhere. Then he glimpsed the mound on the floor covered with dust, and redirected his torch. Oh no. 'Major?' He seemed inert and lifeless.

He tried to drag him from under debris, but could shift him only a few inches. This was a building that had once been grand, with a ceiling decorated with ornate and heavy plasterwork, part of which had come down. He paused in horror as another crash made the foundations shake again; he grabbed for a handhold on furniture to steady himself. An ornate plaster decoration of scrolls and flowers round the central light crashed down around him, shattering to pieces.

Ben felt a sharp stab on his left hand and doubled up in pain. A large piece had caught him; more bits were raining down on him, but he was moving the major inch by inch out of that room and along the passage towards the front door. He was thin but he was no lightweight; both Ben's shoulder and his hand were giving him hell and the smoke was making him cough. Another heave and another; the place stank, all bomb sites did, of ancient dust disturbed for the first time in years.

'OK . . .' the fireman had come into the hall, 'let me help.' Together they half lifted and half dragged Esmond outside.

Ben could hardly get his breath and every so often was shaken with a bout of coughing. His eyes were streaming and he could barely see, but he heard someone ask the fireman, 'Is he dead?'

'Think so.' He dropped his voice. 'Come further away.'

Ben knew they'd moved but not far enough; he could still hear. 'Look at his head. He's had a right bash on top, broken his skull. See the bits of bone? Poor bugger, he's not breathing and no sign of a pulse.'

'He's copped it all right. Major Travis was a big noise around here in his day.'

'Is that his son?'

'Son-in-law.'

Ben sighed; everybody knew them round here. He felt dazed but he'd understood enough. The major was finished; he need never worry about him again. He'd really wanted to kill the bastard but the Luftwaffe had done the job for him and spared his conscience. He ought to cheer; so why was he feeling so bereft?

'You need a dressing on that hand, come with me.' Somebody took his arm and led him away. 'You're a relative of Major Travis, aren't you? A very brave man. Sorry to tell you he lost his life.' He pushed a card into his pocket. 'Details of where and how to find him.'

'The morgue?'

'No, it's full, we've had a bad night. The church hall in Willow Road will be his temporary resting place.'

CHAPTER FORTY

B EN SAT WAITING HIS turn in the first aid post feeling dizzy, disorientated and in pain. He longed to lie down. What on earth had come over him to make him go back into that bombed building? He hadn't been thinking straight. Why had he risked his life to rescue Esmond Travis when he'd made his life a misery over recent months? He loathed the man. Worse, he had been frightening the life out of him by trying to rake up things Ben needed to keep hidden.

'Mr McCluskey, come to the treatment room.' A young nurse was hauling him to his feet. 'I'm told you've been very brave and rescued a lot of people from a bombed building. How are you feeling?'

'Tired and my hand hurts.'

'Yes, you have quite a deep cut between your thumb and your palm. Can you move your thumb? No, don't worry, that doesn't mean you won't be able to later, but you may have cut or damaged your ligaments. You also have heavy grazes on both hands, how did this happen? And like everybody else you're covered in plaster dust.' It covered his clothes and was all round him on the floor. 'Let's start by washing this dust off.' Ben knew he stank of bombed buildings, dust and plaster.

'It's stopped bleeding so I'll put a temporary dressing on

381

that cut, and clean up these grazes. You must go to Mill Road infirmary and see a doctor later on this morning. They run a clinic for minor air-raid injuries in the outpatient department from nine o'clock until midday.'

'Do I really need to?' Ben wanted to sleep.

'Yes, the clinic functions every morning but you need to go today to get a proper dressing. Now, do you hurt anywhere else?'

'My left shoulder, a piece of debris fell on me, I remember that.'

'Let's have a look.' She was helping him undress. 'Can you move your arm? Yes, let's see you move your shoulder. OK, and you have no cuts or grazes here. You were protected by your clothes. I don't think you've broken anything but you'll be bruised and stiff by tomorrow. Mention it again at the hospital so they can check you over.'

Ben realised he was being driven home in a car filled to capacity with others who had been hurt in the raid. When he was being helped out at the gate to Oakdene Farm, Elsie appeared from the shelter wearing her dressing gown. 'How are you?' she asked.

'You don't need to worry about me,' Ben said. 'But I'm afraid a ceiling collapsed on top of Esmond.'

'Oh my God,' Elsie gasped. 'Is he . . . ?'

He tried to give her a hug but she backed off. 'I'm sorry to say I think he could be. Sorry, Elsie,' he said, 'sorry.'

He could see Lizzie in her siren suit, her mouth open in shock, and a few yards behind was Milly. 'No! Not Dadda,' she wailed. 'He's dead?'

'Yes,' he said. 'So sorry, Milly.'

A LUCKY SIXPENCE

* * *

Milly was shocked to the core. It didn't seem possible. Dadda had been his usual self when he'd kissed her and said good night before going out. Such a short time ago! Now Ben's voice said, 'It fractured his skull, he would have died instantly, would not have suffered.'

What would she do without Dadda? Lizzie was crying as she took them all into the kitchen to make tea, but what could tea do to help? Dadda would not be coming back. Mum was crying too and asking questions, wanting to know exactly what had happened.

'He was very brave,' Ben was telling them, 'incredibly brave going into a bombed house that was collapsing round him to help get people out. He was a hero, you can be proud of him.'

Eventually, as the night was now quiet, Lizzie suggested they all go to bed and try to sleep. Milly knew sleep was miles away for her and once she was alone her tears began to flow again. She sobbed and pined for Dadda for hours.

Elsie's head was whirling; it had happened so suddenly. How many times had Esmond gone out in the same way, and come back tired but satisfied he'd done his duty? She hadn't expected this, none of them had.

She was sorry, of course she was. Esmond had been kind to her and she was grateful for all he'd done. She'd done her best to love him, tried very hard, but she hadn't found it easy. Esmond had been a good man and she'd done her best for him, but some would say he'd deserved better. She couldn't admit to anybody that she felt free at last, and slept soundly until eight o'clock. The sun was shining as she got dressed.

She could hear Milly moving about in her room and looked in to see her. Her eyes were red and swollen. 'I've been thinking about Dadda,' she said. 'I want to ring Mr Thornley straight away and tell him I mean to write an article about how brave Dadda and Ben were last night, and ask if he'd be interested in having it for the *Gazette*.'

Elsie found Gladys was already in the kitchen, yawning her head off. 'What a terrible night,' she said. 'I hardly slept at all, nor did our Clover. 'I've heard about the major so I'll work on for a bit longer, Mrs Travis. To see you through your troubles.'

Elsie said, 'Thank you, that would be a help. I feel shattered. I hardly know where to turn next.' She sank onto a chair by the table. 'I find it hard to believe he's dead, it was so sudden.'

'I'm very sorry.' Elsie found a cup of tea had been pushed in front of her.

Milly came in. 'The lines are down again. I'll have to leave it.'

'Sorry to hear about your father,' Gladys said. 'He's a real hero, but how terrible to be killed when you're trying to rescue others.' Tears were scalding Milly's eyes again. 'Oh, lovey, I know you've all had an awful shock, but don't take on so. Come and have a cup of tea. I've just made a fresh pot. You'll miss him, I know.'

'You've soon found out about him.' Milly dabbed at her eyes with a damp hanky.

'It'll be all over town by now,' Gladys said. 'I'm putting up a family that's been bombed out. They arrived when I was getting up to get breakfast for Clover. Well, part of a family, they are related to my husband and were kind to me when he was killed. Hilda has told me how Ben saved her and her six children, how brave both he and your father were.

'Her mother took the three older children but she only has two rooms so there was no way she could fit in any more. Hilda's come with her twins and a toddler to our house. She's very nice and very grateful, and they're beautiful boys. I've given them my bedroom and our Clover's got the toddler in her room, so I had to spend the rest of the night on the couch.'

'Gosh, Gladys, how are you going to manage?'

'There's a war on, we have to, don't we? What shall I make you for breakfast, Milly? There's bacon in the cupboard.'

Milly blew her nose; Mum liked to keep the bacon ration for Dadda. 'I'm not hungry, cornflakes will be fine. So it was Ben, not Dadda, who saved your friend and her family?'

'Yes,' Gladys said, 'that's what they told me.'

Milly wanted to get all the details straight in her mind. 'It seems they both went into a crumbling building to search, and Ben went upstairs and found the family while Dadda looked in another part downstairs?'

'Yes,' Elsie added, 'and a ceiling collapsed on him.'

'Hilda said it was on fire too. When Ben heard the major hadn't come out he went back in again to look for him, though a fireman tried to stop him. Ben is a real hero. He got him out too but he was already dead.'

'Oh my goodness.' Milly couldn't stop the tears running down her cheeks again. 'Poor Dadda.'

'Lizzie went off to work but where's Ben? I hear he hurt his hand.'

'He's sleeping it off, I expect,' Milly said. 'After all, it was half three before he got to bed at all.'

'Best thing for him,' Gladys said.

'I'm going to try to write an article for the *Gazette* about this rescue,' Milly said, 'so I need to find out all I can about it. Would it be all right if I went down to your house and talked to this mother? Would she mind?'

'I'm sure she would be glad to; she's told me about it three times already.'

The morning post brought a letter from Laurie. There was a lot about Lizzie and her problems with gambling. He was out of date with the news, and it made him seem very far away. Milly longed to be with him. At this moment she needed the comfort of having him close.

She'd write to let him know about Dadda as soon as she could, but first she went down to Gladys's house and spent an hour with Hilda Jones.

'I thought we were all going to die,' she said. 'The first blast woke us all and blew out the window. The lights no longer worked and the kids were all terrified and screaming their heads off. The only light came from the searchlights and fires outside. I knew I had to get out and lifted the children from bed and got them out on the landing, but Tilly panicked and ran back. She frightened the others and made them all scream. I couldn't carry both the twins and move them all at once. Tilly is only two, and I was so long getting them all into warm clothes that everybody else seemed to have gone. I couldn't move them all at once and I couldn't bear to leave any of them behind.'

'Of course not.'

'It was as black as hell on the landing outside. I thought the only thing was to stay together where we were. It was ages before I heard Ben calling and I saw the light from his torch . . . I've never been so glad to see anyone before.'

'Shouldn't you have been in a shelter?' Milly asked gently.

'Yes, I should, and will be in future. Getting them all up from their beds and taking them two streets away to the shelter wasn't easy, I tried it once or twice but . . .'

'Don't you have a husband?'

'Yes, but he was out doing his duty as a warden. He's now gone to see if he can find us somewhere else to live. I can't keep Gladys from her bed for more than a day or two, and my mother can't really cope with the other three.'

Elsie felt terrible. Everybody had their troubles and Gladys was doing her best for others, while she was almost overcome with guilt. A good wife would be grieving for her husband; she should at least pull herself together and do something about his funeral.

Gladys was sympathetic and wished she could help more. She brought the telephone directory from the study, and underlined the numbers of three local funeral parlours, but the phone lines were still down.

Gladys was a widow too and had told Elsie how she'd lost her husband in an accident at the docks after only three years of marriage. Elsie had heard the story more than once, but it made her feel worse than ever. Ought she to see Esmond's remains and say her final goodbye? Ought she to see the building where he'd met his end? She was undecided.

At mid-morning Milly came home and gave her a hug. 'You're shocked, Mum. We all are. Come on, we'll go out. We'll both go to see the place where Dadda died, and do what else we can.'

'Yes, call in at one of these funeral parlours.'

'I'd also like to call in to see Mr Thornley.'

'Milly's been down to my place,' Gladys said to Elsie and began telling her about Hilda and the problems she had.

'Her twins are ten months old,' Milly said.

'Full of energy,' Gladys added, 'and not a moment's peace when they're awake, fingers into everything, crawling everywhere and opening every cupboard.'

'I told her I'd go to the Food Office for her,' Milly said, 'and see what I could do about getting replacement rations books for her family. She's got four toddlers as well.'

'I'm glad to hear that,' Gladys said. 'They're as hungry as hunters. I told Hilda she was daft to have so many kids. A big family like that will keep her hard-up for ever.'

CHAPTER FORTY-ONE

B EN WOKE UP AND was surprised to see it was full daylight. Half past eleven? He should be at Mill Road hospital having his hand redressed by now. He got up to pull the slip of paper from his uniform trouser pocket. Yes, but it would be impossible now to make it before twelve o'clock. No matter, the dressing on his hand was still firmly in place; he'd go tomorrow instead.

He made himself a breakfast of cornflakes and was preparing to follow that with baked beans on toast when he heard someone coming upstairs. 'Hello, are you there, Ben?' It was Gladys. 'I heard you moving about and had to come and tell you how proud we all are. Everybody reckons you're a hero.'

He pulled a face. 'I'm afraid I didn't help the major much. Would you like a cup of tea?'

'You did marvels.' Gladys helped herself from the teapot and sat down opposite him. While he ate his breakfast she told him how grief-stricken Milly and Elsie were, and what they'd gone out to do. She went on to tell him about Hilda and all her problems.

Ben left as soon as he could; he wanted to be gone before Elsie and Milly came back. He'd heard more than enough about problems and grief. He rode down to the arcade on his bike and it made him feel fully awake again.

He didn't manage to go to the hospital the next morning either because Alec had already fixed up a meeting with another jeweller, to whom he hoped to sell the last of Jasper's haul. Ben knew he'd feel better when it was all changed to usable cash, and he'd rid his flat of stolen property.

That evening, when he went home, he found Milly and Lizzie seated side by side on his sofa. 'I'm writing an article about how brave you and Dadda were,' Milly told him, 'so I need to know exactly what happened.'

'And I've only heard about it second-hand,' Lizzie complained, pushing a cup of tea towards him.

'Oh gosh, I'm tired,' Ben said. 'I want to forget all that.'

'Mr Thornley has promised to publish my article in next week's *Gazette*.'

'What?' He didn't like the idea of his exploits being public knowledge. He needed to keep too many of them hidden.

'You were very brave,' Lizzie said.

There was no escaping Milly; she'd cornered him at home. 'I didn't manage to save your father,' he said, 'sorry.' Poor kid, her eyes were red with crying. Really, she was the only one who'd really loved the old bat.

Milly rated that the worst week of her life. She'd only just gone back to college after the Easter holidays, but Mum phoned the head tutor and explained the situation. Lizzie had to go to work as usual, but Milly found there were plenty of things that needed doing to keep her and her mother busy. At least the telephone lines had been repaired, so Mum spent half a day telephoning people who needed to be informed of Dadda's death.

* * *

The funeral was very much on Elsie's mind. 'I don't know what I can wear,' she said, wanting to be in full mourning – that seemed the least she could do for Esmond. 'I've nothing in black.'

Milly said, 'Neither have I. Nothing at all.'

'And as clothes are going to be rationed it'll be difficult to find any,' Lizzie said. 'Anyway, black doesn't suit me. It makes me feel like an old witch.'

'I don't like black either.' Milly grimaced.

Elsie paused, thinking. 'You are young for full mourning, Milly, but it's your birthday soon. I think seventeen is old enough.'

'No, Mum,' Lizzie said. 'It's just an old-fashioned tradition. It would make Milly and me feel like a couple of crows.'

The following afternoon, Elsie took Milly to Mrs Field's shop in Wallasey. She was pleased to see them and showed them what she had. 'Not much choice in style these days,' she said apologetically as she flicked across the garments on a rack. 'Everything is utility.' They were all skimpy, to cut down on the amount of cloth needed, and all had a vaguely military air.

'I have this in black in your size, Mrs Travis, but . . .' She flashed a tape measure round Milly, 'I don't have anything in black that will fit you.'

Elsie tried on the black dress and coat and decided to buy them. 'We'll try somewhere else for Milly,' she said.

Milly went home with nothing, and worked on her article again. She wanted to finish it so she could deliver it to Mr Thornley next time she went into town.

That evening, Lizzie came home before Ben, and stopped

in the kitchen for a chat. 'I'll wear what I already have,' she told her mother. 'I can't get to the shops until Saturday and the funeral is on Thursday morning.'

'All right, Lizzie, love, you can wear your grey coat and hat and no doubt you'll look very nice in it. I understand many of the ARP wardens and firefighters will be there, and quite a few men from the council. I've been told that the mayor will hold a reception afterwards in the town hall, so I won't have to provide anything here.'

'Civic recognition,' Lizzie marvelled. 'Quite a big send-off for Father then?'

'Yes, he was killed while on civic duty. How is Ben?'

'He says his hand is painful, giving him gyp, in fact, and he doesn't feel too good, but he'll be at the funeral wearing his best suit.'

'Come upstairs with me,' Lizzie said to Milly as she headed up to her flat. 'I didn't think Mum would make such a fuss about clothes. Anyway, I won't need any money from you to buy anything new. Really, there's nothing I'd want to wear in the shops. I'm jolly glad I bought nice things when I could. Come and see if there's anything that would fit you.'

She opened her wardrobe and showed Milly the coat in silver grey she had always admired. 'Or there's this,' she said, taking out a suit in black and white check. 'Could you wear this?'

Milly liked it and tried it on. The skirt hung loose round her waist and was very short for her, though the boxy jacket didn't look too bad. 'You're a bit of a beanpole,' Lizzie said. 'I could wear that and you could wear my grey coat. It's a bit longer than that skirt. And what about this grey and white striped dress that I used to wear with it?'

Milly tried them on. 'Great,' she said. 'I really like this outfit.'

'I have a grey hat I used to wear with the coat. I had it last summer, do you remember?'

'No, you weren't living here then so I didn't see so much of you.'

Lizzie put it on her head and waved her towards the mirror. 'I love this and it looks absolutely right with the rest of the outfit. You put that dress on and we'll go down and see if Mum thinks we'll do like this.'

Ten minutes later, Milly pulled her into the sitting room where Mum was sitting in her usual armchair. She tried not to let her eyes stray to the empty chair opposite. 'Do we look suitably clad for the funeral, Mum?'

Elsie leapt to her feet and put an arm round each of them. 'Yes, you both look lovely. Dadda would be proud of his daughters.'

Milly was quite surprised when Mr Thornley telephoned her that evening and after a few words of sympathy asked if she would also write an obituary for her father. 'There's no hurry for it,' he told her. 'I have no space for it this week and it would be better left to next. You can take your time over it.'

'But what exactly do you want me to put in it?'

'All the major events of his life, and the things that were important to him. What he achieved, what he did in the last war and how he lost his arm.'

'I don't know much about that, he never spoke of it.'

'No, he wouldn't have. I knew him quite well: before the war we both used to enter chess competitions and he won sometimes; you should mention his passion for chess. He was a very private person and said little about personal affairs. Ask your mother, she'll know more. We ran an obituary on Colonel Greenway in the paper last month; if you've thrown it out I can give you a copy. That'll show you what I mean.'

'Right,' Milly said, 'I'll do my best.' She put the phone down in amazement. Mr Thornley had asked her to write something for his newspaper!

She sat thinking about the life Dadda had had. All too short, and it had ended in a painfully abrupt way, but she found it a comfort that other people were interested in what he'd done in life. He had been very courageous. Strange how she'd never asked him how he'd lost his arm; she should have done.

'I don't know much about it either,' Mum said when she asked her. 'He showed me some medals once that he had from the Great War. Have a look in his study, I think you'll find those in a drawer in his desk, and he was always writing. He told me once he kept a diary. You'll find things in there that will help you. I'm exhausted. I'm going up to have a rest on my bed.'

Milly sat at his desk. Dadda had spent a lot of his time here and she could sense his presence all round her. She found it strangely comforting, as though he wasn't so far away after all. It was an austere room, rather dark with heavy furniture. The large bookcase was crammed with his books, and there were several dark oil paintings with ornate gilt frames. He'd told her one was of Oakdene Grange as it had once been.

Milly began opening the drawers of his desk to look for his medals; she'd seen him wear them sometimes when he was going out to civic ceremonies like Armistice Day. She found them and spread them out before her; he had four and a silver badge inscribed *For King and Empire. Services Rendered.* But she had no idea what they were or how he'd earned them. Undoubtedly he had: his name and rank was inscribed round the rim of some.

An hour later when Mum came to join her, Milly was deeply immersed in his diary. 'But it's for this year,' she said. 'Fascinating to find out what he was thinking about, but what I really want is to find a similar diary for the war years.'

'You'll need to keep on looking,' Elsie said. 'I know he lost his arm at Verdun in 1916, and he spent the next year in different hospitals recovering from his wounds.'

When Milly went to see Mr Thornley to pick up a copy of the obituary that he'd offered her, she took the medals to see if he knew what they were.

'Oh, my goodness, yes, this is the Distinguished Service Order. The DSO was given for an act of outstanding bravery, you don't know what that was?'

Milly shook her head in amazement. 'He never spoke about it. I don't think my mother knows either or she'd have told me.'

'And this is the Silver War Badge; he'd be awarded that because he was invalided out as a result of war wounds. These other three are campaign medals – everybody got them if they were on active service in the war.'

Milly went home asking herself why she hadn't asked him while she'd had the chance. There was more to Dadda than she'd realised. She went straight to his study to see if she could find out more. There were other diaries, although not for the war years, but she found yellowing newspaper cuttings reporting it, and curling up maps of battles along the Somme and she was able to piece together the story.

He'd led his battalion across No-Man's Land under fire and they'd captured and held a village for five days before the enemy counter-attacked. He'd received his injuries while trying to hold them off to protect his men while they retreated. His batman helped to carry him back.

He had written about waking from the anaesthetic to find his arm had been amputated, and the long painful months he'd spent in hospitals, both in France and England. She wept and wished she'd known and had been able to tell him how much she admired him.

She could write his obituary now; her only problem was Mr Thornley had spoken of the paper shortage and the need to keep it brief.

CHAPTER FORTY-TWO

WHEN MILLY WAS EATING her evening meal with the family that evening, she said, 'I've found out all I need to know about Dadda. Go to the study, Mum, and read through what I've written, I've laid out everything on his desk.'

Elsie left the girls to wash up and now sat staring at the fading photographs and newspaper cuttings. According to Milly, Esmond's war history was all here, but first, while she was alone, there was something else she had to do.

Years ago, Esmond had told her he'd written a will and left everything to her. He'd shown her where he kept it; his desk had a secret drawer. She felt for the hidden catch and in the kneehole a hidden compartment appeared. It contained several documents, her marriage lines, and among others, some of which she'd need now, yes, here was his will. She opened the envelope with nervous fingers and found it was exactly as he'd told her it would be. He'd left everything he owned to her.

She'd already telephoned his solicitor to tell him of Esmond's death and made an appointment to go in and see him. She knew nothing of his financial affairs other than that he'd told her he didn't have much income and that he'd had to sell off acre by acre the land he'd inherited.

She knew he'd always had money in hand when it was

needed and that there were still thirty-four acres left. He'd been a trustworthy man, and she'd already assumed that on being widowed for the second time, she'd have a roof over her head for herself and the girls.

Having read his will, slowly Elsie began to read what Milly had set out and soon she was captivated. Like her, she wished she'd asked him more while she'd had the chance. It brought guilt because she hadn't done enough to get to know Esmond; if she had she might have found him easier to love. She had to admire his courage.

She wept for him again and couldn't stop all evening. He'd had a difficult life and she should have tried to make it easier for him than she had. He'd been bountiful to her and the girls, made life much easier for them. She wished she'd told him how much she appreciated that.

When Milly finished her father's obituary she took it to the *Gazette* to find Mr Thornley had gone out, so she left it with his secretary. Mr Thornley telephoned later to say, 'It's more personal than I'd expected but it's all the better for that. It's full of emotion. You make us all see your father as you do, a hero in the Great War when he lost his arm in action; and a hero again now when he tried to save lives but lost his own.'

Her obituary was taken up by the national newspapers, too, and Milly was pleased that the whole country would recognise Dadda as a hero.

Elsie was awakened by Lizzie's footsteps. She still had to get up and go to work early in the morning. There was a tap on her bedroom door and Lizzie's head came round. 'Good, you're awake. I've brought you a cup of tea. I want to borrow a couple of aspirins for Ben, we've run out.'

Elsie stirred. 'Is his hand painful? Pass me my handbag, I have a packet in there.'

'Yes, very painful and he says he aches all over. He vomited several times, and he's been restless all night. Really, he's not well, running a temperature now. He says he'll stay in bed this morning.'

'I'll see if he wants any lunch later,' Elsie said and sat up to drink the tea.

At mid-morning she asked Gladys to go up and see if Ben would like some breakfast, but she said his curtains were still drawn, his cup of tea and aspirins were untouched on his bedside table, and he seemed to be sound asleep. 'Sleeping will do him more good than anything else, won't it?'

It was later than usual when Elsie and Milly began to make a salad for their lunch. Elsie said, 'Run upstairs, Milly, and see if Ben wants anything. I don't suppose he'll feel like this but there's a cupful of soup left over from last night, or I could warm him a cup of milk.'

Milly went up to the attic flat and tapped on his bedroom door. She felt a bit shy about going in and had to knock two or three times, but when there was no response she quietly opened the door. The room was exactly as Gladys had described, in semi-darkness because the curtains hadn't been opened. The cup of cold tea, the aspirins and a glass of water were still untouched.

'Ben?' She went forward to look at the sleeping figure. 'Are you all right?' She felt a sudden stab of alarm. He was breathing but it didn't sound normal; it was rasping and uneven. He seemed to be struggling for breath. He didn't look normal either. 'Ben?'

She put out her hand to touch his forehead – shocked, she snatched it back. He felt clammy. She shot back downstairs to the kitchen. 'Mum, I think Ben's ill.'

'Yes.' Elsie was washing the lettuce that Milly had grown in the garden, 'Lizzie said he was.'

'Really ill,' Milly insisted. 'Go up and see him. He's still and clammy and I can't wake him.'

Her mother looked at her in horror, then took to the stairs in a rush, Milly following to watch from the door.

Elsie swept the curtains open. 'Ben, wake up. Come on.' She tried to shake him. 'Oh my goodness!'

'What can we do?' Milly felt really frightened now. Her mother was flying back downstairs to the study.

'I don't know the doctor's number.' Milly stared at her, but she was already speaking to the operator. 'Put me through to Dr Williams, please, in Atherton Street. Yes, it's urgent.' Her voice was shaking with nerves as she tried to explain Ben's problem.

It was after two when the doctor arrived with his Gladstone bag. Milly was watching out for him and had the front door open before he reached it. Grey-haired and bent, he came slowly up the garden path. 'Hello, Milly, who is this I've come to see?'

'Lizzie's husband, he seems very ill.'

'I don't think I've met him before.'

'No.' She wanted to push him up the stairs. Mum, more agitated than she'd ever seen her, was hovering at his door.

The doctor went to his bedside. 'So tell me what has happened to this young man?'

'He was all right yesterday, he went to work.'

'Lizzie said he vomited last night,' Milly said, 'He didn't feel well when he came home.'

'What's this?' He indicated his hand; the bandage was now soiled and only half on. He ripped it off. Even Milly could see it was now a seeping septic sore that covered most of his hand. 'He's neglected this.' The questions came thick and fast after that.

The doctor turned back the bedclothes, unbuttoned Ben's pyjama jacket and put his stethoscope against his chest, but he was shaking his head. 'I'm sorry. He's unconscious.'

'Is there nothing you can do?' Elsie demanded.

'This is a virulent infection . . .' he prodded towards the hand, 'and this illness is a deadly reaction to it. He has blood poisoning. Septicaemia is the medical term.'

'But what can you do for him?' Milly wailed. The doctor opened his bag, doused a large swab with antiseptic and wiped Ben's hand. He reached for a copy of last week's *Gazette* that Ben had brought home, about to wrap the swab and bandage in it.

Milly snatched the newspaper from him and removed the page printed with her article. She put the inner pages back on the bed. The doctor carried out his intention. 'You need to put this in the fire straight away,' he said.

Elsie told him that the article explained how Ben had received his injury. 'I have seen it,' he said, 'and I now realise what a hero he is. I'll call for an ambulance to take him to hospital but I have to warn you that he might not recover from this.'

'He's going to die?' Milly was aghast. 'But he's so young and healthy.'

'I'm afraid he neglected his dirty cut; sometimes this happens, I'm sorry.'

Milly was afraid for Lizzie; she was going to be devastated. Neither she nor Mum could do anything else all afternoon but sit talking about it. 'They were so happy together,' Milly said. 'Ben was a very kind person, he was the real hero. He went back into that blitzed building twice and brought Dadda out.'

Her mother sighed. 'I'll make enough dinner for Lizzie to eat with us tonight.'

She set about preparing it. Milly peeled the potatoes to help, but felt gripped by inertia. She found it hard to believe this had happened to Ben.

They waited in the kitchen for Lizzie to come home, trying to work out the best way to tell her the dreadful news. 'There is no easy way,' Mum said; 'she's going to find this very hard to accept.'

At last the front door slammed. Milly shot out of the kitchen. 'Lizzie,' she called.

Lizzie had already reached the second stair. 'Hello, Milly, I met Alec Hooper on the way home and he said Ben hadn't been to work today. How has he been?'

Milly took her arm. 'Come to the kitchen.'

'What's happened?'

Elsie had come to the door. 'Come and sit down, love, we have a lot to tell you.'

Milly watched Lizzie with bated breath, as between them they struggled to recount what had happened to Ben. She expected Lizzie to break into hysterical tears, but she was in a state of shock and stared silently and stony-faced at the floor.

After five minutes, Elsie said, 'Don't you want to ring the hospital and find out how he is?'

'I can't,' she said, and would have rushed out but Mum caught her in her arms. 'Don't go, Lizzie, stay and have something to eat with us.'

Milly caught her mother's eye and saw her nod. She went to the telephone and rang the hospital and enquired about Ben. The ward sister said, 'He's very ill and in no pain. There's been no change, he's not really conscious. You can come in and see him at any time. Sit with him if you wish.'

When she repeated this to Lizzie, she murmured, 'He's going to die, isn't he?'

'Let's eat,' her mother said, 'and then you can go and see him.'

'What's the point?' Lizzie roused herself. 'If he's hardly conscious he won't know whether I'm there or not.'

She seemed frozen. Milly thought it might help if they could get her to talk. Mum had the same idea and said, 'I'm so sorry, Lizzie, I should have called Dr Williams sooner.'

'For God's sake, give over, can't you?' Lizzie flashed at her and leapt to her feet.

Milly caught at her arm. 'Would you like me to come to the hospital with you?'

'No, just leave me alone.'

She heard her mother sigh. 'We can do no more, Milly. Leave her.'

* * *

When Milly got up the next morning she found her mother was in the study telephoning. She looked exhausted and said, 'I got up early to ring the hospital again and unfortunately Dr Williams was right. Ben died at three o'clock this morning without ever regaining consciousness.'

'Oh, Mum! Terrible news for Lizzie.'

'I've been up to tell her. She took it quietly, just said she wanted to be left alone.'

'Poor Ben, he died without us.'

'He was unconscious, Milly, he wouldn't have known.'

'Terrifyingly quick though, I can't get over that.'

'I've taken Lizzie a cup of tea and she says she's going to stay in bed. This complicates everything. I've rung the undertaker to let him know that we now need two funerals. But somebody will have to look after Ben's business. Lizzie says she doesn't know who looked after his roundabout yesterday and I don't know how to get in touch with his colleagues at the fair.'

'It's no good waiting for Lizzie to do anything,' Milly said. 'I'll go down later. I know where to find Steve Docherty, he works for Ben.'

'Oh goodness, I must ring Ben's father in Ireland and let him know.'

'I need to ring Mr Thornley – this will alter what he prints next week.'

Milly did, and found he wanted to know every detail of what had happened to Ben. 'This is really a shock,' he said. 'Thank you for letting me know and please keep in touch with details of this funeral. I have news for you too, your article has also been picked up by the national newspapers. It's a tale of heroism, Milly. You'll see it in *The Times* when it's delivered with the *Gazette* tomorrow morning. Ben's death is a terrible tragedy and it's bound to double the interest in the story.'

'Ben was the real hero.'

'I'd like to speak to your mother now, is she there?'

Milly went down on her bike and Steve Docherty was as shocked as she had been. 'Strewth, Ben was perfectly all right the day before yesterday, taking everything in his stride.'

'He neglected some cuts on his hand and they turned septic. He got blood poisoning.'

'Oh my God, that's unbelievable,' Steve said. 'Tell Lizzie not to worry about his business, I've been keeping an eye on his roundabout. He's had Bruce running it for some time now and he manages pretty well, but I'd better take a look at his caterpillar ride and make sure that's kept going.'

Milly felt a little dazed; everything around her was changing very quickly.

She went home to find a letter from Laurie waiting for her on the hall table.

I feel very upset at your news and know how you must be feeling. I wish I could be there with you. I can't get you out of my mind. I'll try and get a few days' leave and come up and see you.

For Elsie the funerals overhung everything; time seemed to be standing still. Sunday came and she made their meat ration of stewing steak into a pie. She served it with roast potatoes, roast parsnips and cabbage. When it was nearly ready she said to Milly, 'Go upstairs and remind Lizzie that she said she'd come and have lunch with us.'

Lizzie was making a first cup of tea. Milly couldn't help but notice she'd just got out of bed and was still sleepy. Half an hour later, with them round the table, Elsie said, 'Now, Lizzie, there's just me and my two girls left, there's no point in you cooking for yourself up in that flat, you'll be better with us down here now.'

Lizzie didn't need asking twice. 'Thank you, Mum. It does feel a bit lonely up there by myself.'

'Then come and sleep in your old room. You have to work hard in that factory and it'll mean less for you to do when you come home. We'll all be better off together.'

Chapter Forty-Three

L IZZIE WAS DREADING THE funeral. At her mother's request, the undertaker had delayed Esmond's interment for three days so both members of the family could be buried at the same time. At least that meant she had to go through it only once.

It seemed an age since it had all happened. Photographs of the family were published in all the newspapers, together with one of the building, now razed to the ground, where Esmond had met his death and Ben had been mortally wounded.

This morning in the kitchen, Mum was fussing again about the clothes she meant to wear for the funeral. 'That suit might pass muster for your father's funeral, but now as a young widow after only two years of marriage, I really think you should wear black.'

'No,' Lizzie said, 'I'm not going to wear widow's weeds.' She forced a smile. 'Ben didn't like me in black. Anyway, I don't want to.'

'Most widows would,' Gladys observed tartly. 'I did.'

'That was donkey's years ago, you had to then,' Lizzie said, 'but it would depress me.'

'With your bright golden hair it would suit you,' her mother told her.

'You'd look beautiful in black,' Gladys agreed.

'If only Milly hadn't written that glowing account of Father's heroic bravery, and brought it to the attention of the whole country.' Lizzie retorted. 'They talk about it all the time at work, and everybody asks me about it. Of course, Ben's death has made it a double tragedy. That has turned both of them into heroes.'

Lizzie knew publicity was the last thing Ben would want; it would scare him rigid. He'd hate all this. He'd want to remain incognito in case his black-market activities or the burning of his call-up papers came to official attention. Ben's way was not to let his right hand know what his left was doing.

But perhaps his new status as a hero would prevent anyone believing he was a thief and a liar?

The double funeral was arranged for Saturday morning and just as Lizzie had expected, it was absolute hell. Mum was tearful and as white as a ghost, and Milly's hands were frozen.

The church was packed. All their neighbours were there in their mourning, including Gladys in her ancient black outfit. She'd even fitted Clover out in similar drab garb. It looked as though the whole population of New Brighton had turned out and they were all in deepest black. Father would have loved it.

Lizzie wore her black and white suit, just as she'd intended. Milly had borrowed her silver-grey coat, but because of her youth that had provoked no comments. Amongst the huge flock of black crows they stood out like a pair of stars.

Mum thought the funeral impressive; each hearse was

drawn by two black horses with black feathers fluttering on their heads. Lizzie had to pretend to feel grief for both of them, but the sight of the two coffins and the thought of the people she knew so well inside, did give her a few qualms. Father was buried in his family grave, and Ben had to go to the new part of the cemetery.

Then there was the slow drive to the town hall for the reception, through streets crowded with people, the men all snatching their caps off as they went past.

Lizzie hated the reception. One drink was served to each of them and the mayor and several other men gave speeches about Father and his good works. Then they spoke of Ben and his bravery and were long-winded and boring. Once they started to serve the food, which looked plentiful and appetising, Mum wanted to take them home.

They were driven back in style with Mum and Milly holding hands and mopping at their eyes. All Lizzie felt was relief that it was all over at last.

The following Thursday, when Milly got up to return to college, Mum already had the *Gazette* open on the kitchen table and was poring over it with Gladys.

'John Thornley has written an account of the funeral,' she said. 'The whole town sees Dadda and Ben as heroes.'

'Come and look, there's a photograph of you all,' Gladys said. 'It was a lovely service.'

Milly shuddered to see the photograph of the three of them arriving at the church. Mum leading the way with Lizzie on one side and her on the other. That had been a hard day but all the praise Dadda had received had gladdened her heart.

'Both Major Travis and Ben deserved that and more,' Gladys said. 'Hilda is very grateful; she wouldn't have her family now if it hadn't been for Ben. She's taken her family to live in a remote village in Wales, there's very little there but a school and a chapel. Her husband found an old cottage there he could rent for her but he has to stay here to work.'

'At least she'll be away from the air raids,' Milly said.

'Yes, they'll all be safe there,' Gladys agreed.

One day, Elsie decided, 'It would be easier and warmer for us if we ate all our meals at the kitchen table,' and thereafter they rarely used the dining room. 'Also, coal is scarce and it's a lot of trouble lighting the fire in the sitting room, so I think we could use the parlour, it's plenty large enough for us three.'

'The parlour is cosier,' Milly agreed, 'provided the power is on.' Lizzie asked Steve Docherty if he could find them a second-hand paraffin oil heater, and he did.

It took the chill off the room. 'But it smells a bit,' Lizzie said.

'Better than nothing.' Elsie was glad to have it.

One Friday, Gladys said, 'I think if you're over the worst, Mrs Travis, that it's time for me to leave. Without the major making us keep up our standards there's less for me to do.'

Elsie had been wondering whether she could afford to pay Gladys's wages now, and certainly she couldn't justify keeping her services. 'You're going to the munitions factory?'

'Yes, our Clover says it's all right and so does Lizzie. I'd like to help the war effort.'

Elsie found the house quiet with her. She missed her company and strident comments.

Milly was writing to Laurie:

Lizzie's home in Alvaston Terrace has now been repaired and the landlord has written to her asking if she wants to rent it again. She showed us the letter and said she'd prefer to stay with us, but she went to see it. 'It's habitable,' she said, 'but the new paintwork is very thin. It looks a poor unfinished job, but making it habitable is all builders are expected to do at the moment.'

Mum is pleased, of course; she wants us to stay together and she's more than pleased that Lizzie goes off to work quite happily, and is content to stay at home with us in what little spare time she has. Even Mum doesn't seem depressed about Dadda being no longer with us. The important thing now, she tells us, is to win this war.

I think I miss Dadda more than she does. As for Ben, I think of his death as a terrible waste of a young life. He was a lovely person, I really took to him. This is a cruel war.

Laurie's letters were full of sympathy and support, and he was writing almost every day.

I wish I could be there with you, Milly. Dad has written to me and enclosed your articles which he's cut from the Gazette. *He says you're standing up to things very bravely and still delivering eggs to them.*

She felt the tone of Laurie's letters was changing. They were now more personal.

I do miss you Milly, I can't stop thinking about you. I do wish this war would end so we could be together.

Milly read each one of them many times.

They were washing up after their evening meal one evening when the phone rang in the hall. Lizzie was drying and went to answer it. 'It's for you, Milly,' she said. 'It's Laurie.'

Milly felt a surge of joy, snatched the tea towel from Lizzie, half dried her hands and rushed to the phone. 'Laurie! This is a surprise.'

'How are you, Milly? I've been given four days' leave and I'll be coming home on Monday. I asked for leave so I could come to your father's funeral but last week was impossible.'

'This coming Monday? That's marvellous. Absolutely marvellous.'

'I get into Lime Street at half past eight, and it'll be past nine by the time I reach New Brighton. Quite late.'

'I'll come and meet you at Lime Street,' she said.

'Oh, Milly, it's lovely to hear your voice. You've had a very hard time recently and I've wanted to be with you.'

'On Monday you will.'

'Though I'll only have two evenings to spend with you. I was hoping for a week at least.'

'I'll not go to college while you're here. I'll tell them I couldn't possibly concentrate if I did. Though I've just gone back after having time off because of Dadda . . .'

'I know, that's why I wanted to come last week.'

'Better now than never.'

'By the way, I've been promoted. I'm now a captain.'

Milly laughed. 'That's marvellous too – I don't seem to have any other words . . . This is all such good news.'

'But I'll have to start back on Thursday, it's so short. I just had to come up and see you.'

Milly was counting the hours until he came and was ready to go to Lime Street an hour too early. 'It's not safe for you to go alone,' Elsie said. 'It'll be getting dark, the streets are dangerous, Liverpool is full of foreign sailors and soldiers are everywhere.'

She suggested Lizzie accompany her. 'Absolutely not,' they chorused.

'She won't need to go out on a street,' Lizzie scoffed. 'She can stay in the underground system, and she won't be caught in an air raid, as we haven't had any for a long time.'

Milly was taken aback as they both knew Mum hated to be reminded of that because Dadda and Ben had been killed then, but it didn't stop Milly fizzing with anticipation. She went alone after a day in college. Her tutors there had read her articles in the *Gazette* and gave her permission to take two days off. The term was almost over anyway.

Laurie arrived, looking quite an important person in his uniform with three pips on his shoulders, and swept her into one of his bear hugs. On the train under the Mersey, he sat very close with one of her arms pulled through his and Milly couldn't take her eyes off his face. He was very handsome.

'I wasted a lot of time on my last leave,' he told her. 'I'm not going to do that this time.' He came indoors with her to say hello to her mother and sister and offer his condolences.

Then Milly walked with him up to his house. 'I won't come

in now,' she said. 'Your parents will want you to themselves and they will have supper ready for you, I'm sure.'

'I'll be down with Mutt in the morning,' Laurie said. 'We'll go for our usual walk.'

Milly spent a lot of time in his arms before he went in.

Milly got up to a sunny early summer morning, and couldn't wait to get outdoors. She had Dido's harness on and went out with her, even though she wasn't expecting Laurie just yet. She was surprised to see him coming down the lane. 'I've come early . . .' he smiled, 'couldn't stay away.' He drew her into his arms but Dido was sniffing at his feet. 'Hello, Dido.' He patted her head. 'Dad took Mutt out for his walk this morning before he went to work,' he went on. 'He's been doing that while I've been away. But I'm not sorry to come without him. I want to concentrate on us.'

Milly could see the postman coming. 'Come into the field, it's more private there, and anyway I want you to see your hens. I haven't let them out yet this morning.' She let the flock Ben had bought for Dadda into their run – a well-worn strip of earth surrounded by wire netting. Laurie's hens came hurtling out into the grass; they were completely free-range.

'They look very well. They haven't given you any problems?'

'None at all, they're all laying well. You can take another half-dozen eggs home with you when you go.'

'Milly, I've hated being away from you, knowing what you must be going through. I felt I should be beside you to help if I could. It must have been a terrible shock.'

'It was. Two shocks and it would have helped to have you here.'

'Being apart has given me time to think. You've been part of my life for so long. I don't know why I've been so slow to realise it but I want to spend the rest of my life with you. I really do.'

Milly's spirits soared. She clung to him.

Gently he asked, 'How do you feel about that? Will you marry me?'

She laughed. 'Of course, there's nothing I want more. It's what I've always wanted.' She wanted to spend the rest of her life in his arms; how could he doubt that?

When Laurie could speak again, he said, 'I don't seem to be able to time anything right for us. I'd like us to be married as soon as we can, but with the war and you're still . . . well, only seventeen.'

'Don't tell me I'm too young,' she said. 'I'm tired of hearing that.'

'I'll have to ask your mother for her permission before we can go ahead.'

'Yes.' Milly pondered on the trouble Lizzie had had over that, and she had been nineteen at the time. 'Mum's gone out, she's helping to set up some bring and buy sale that'll be on this afternoon.' They sat in the sun in a corner of the field and watched the hens scratching in the grass. Dido went to sleep beside them.

'I'll ask your mother for her permission when she comes home,' he said. 'I'd like to get it settled.' At lunchtime, Milly took him home and made them each a sandwich because his parents were out at work.

They took their dogs for a walk in the afternoon. Milly said, 'Mum has made a casserole for tonight, and she told me to put it in the oven to finish cooking at four o'clock. She said I could invite you to supper if your parents are agreeable.'

They both waited nervously for Elsie to come back. She came half an hour later, saying she was absolutely tired out. She went straight to the sitting room – now the weather was warmer and they didn't need fires they were using it again. 'I'll make some tea, Mum, and bring it in,' Milly called after her.

Laurie was thinking of this as a formal occasion, but when they followed her, Milly found her mother had taken her shoes off and was exercising her stocking feet. Milly poured tea for them.

'Mrs Travis,' Laurie began – he was wearing his old red pullover and did not look such an important person today – 'I have asked Milly to marry me and she's agreed. I'd like to ask your permission and your blessing before we go any further.'

'Oh!' Mum looked from Milly to Laurie, and slowly lifted her cup to her lips. The pause seemed interminable. Milly's heart sank; she'd expected her to give it without hesitation. 'Laurie,' she said, also serious now. 'I was half expecting this. I've watched you grow up and I'd be very happy to give you my blessing, but I want to remind you that Milly is very much younger than you are. She's only seventeen, how old are you now?'

'Twenty-six,' he said. 'I'm nine years older.' There was dismay on his face.

'Mum,' Milly said, 'it's what I really want.'

'Hush for a minute, Milly.'

'The problem as I see it is that you have reached different points in your lives. Milly is still at college and hoping to be taken on by John Thornley at the Wallasey *Gazette* and trained

416

to be a reporter, but to do that she'll need to stay here for the next few years.'

'Laurie knows that, Mum.' Milly was impatient.

'I do understand,' Laurie said, 'and I agree.'

'It's a very uncertain world, and I would like to see Milly learn a skill so that if necessary she can support herself.'

'For heaven's sake,' Milly burst out. 'You know Laurie is no more likely to die than I am.'

'We none of us know what the future may hold,' Elsie said.

'I would agree,' Laurie said. 'We are living in very uncertain times, but . . .'

'If you marry now, you'll want to take Milly to live with you down in Kent.'

'We'd both love to do that . . .' Laurie turned to smile at Milly, 'but it isn't likely to be possible any time soon. Accommodation near the barracks is very scarce, everybody wants to bring their family down, and besides that, I could be posted elsewhere at a moment's notice.'

'So you can't be together?'

'It might be possible to borrow a flat from a colleague when one goes on leave, but it would only be a temporary arrangement and would depend on Milly being able to get time off to coincide with the dates.'

'So do you plan to be married as soon as you can? Or wait until Milly has finished her training? Or until the war is over?'

'I'm afraid we need to think carefully about all that,' Laurie said.

Elsie sighed. 'Well, this is your problem and I think you're both sensible enough to decide for yourselves. I will not withhold my permission if you want to go ahead, and Laurie, in every other way I really do approve.'

'Thank you.' Laurie smiled more easily.

'You've been friends for years and what better basis for marriage could there be than friendship? Go away and think over your options.'

Milly kissed her. 'I was a bit scared that you were about to say no, as you did to Lizzie.'

'I think you'll have plenty of waiting to do, whatever you decide,' Elsie said.

'I always have had . . .' Milly pulled a face, 'but at the very least we can consider ourselves engaged from this moment.'

Laurie wanted to take her home to tell his parents the news, so they walked up together.

'We are both delighted.' Helen Coyne kissed Milly. 'I've not been consulted about this, but if I had you'd have been my first choice of daughter-in-law. I know you so well already, Milly.'

Ivor Coyne opened a bottle of wine. 'I want us to drink to your health and happiness,' he said, 'but it'll have to be red wine, not champagne. When is the wedding to be?' he asked.

'We'll have to decide that tomorrow.' Laurie explained their difficulty. 'I don't even know whether I'll be able to get Milly a ring,' he said. 'No jewellery is being made now, but I'm told that a few second-hand ones sometimes come on the market. We could look round the local jewellers tomorrow.'

'I've told him I don't need a ring,' Milly protested.

'I want you to wear one to show you're spoken for.'

'Wait a moment,' his mother said, and went upstairs, returning shortly. 'Milly, I have this ring which I hope you like.' It was a two-stone diamond ring in a cross-over band of gold. 'It was my mother's engagement ring, so it's very fitting that you have it now.'

Milly gasped, 'Are you sure? It's absolutely beautiful. I'd feel honoured to wear a ring like this.'

'My grandmother's ring.' Laurie studied it. 'It's keeping it in the family.' He took her hand and slid it onto her third finger.

'It's Victorian,' his mother said. 'Not quite an antique yet.'

CHAPTER FORTY-FOUR

THAT EVENING, LAURIE HAD dinner with Milly and her family, and Lizzie went into raptures about Milly's engagement ring. 'It must be worth a lot of money,' she said. 'When do you plan to get married?'

Laurie explained their difficulty to her. 'I have to go back on Thursday,' he said, 'and I don't know when I'll get any more leave. The trouble is, there's nobody to relieve me for any length of time. For these four days a vet working nearby is on call for my pigeons. He said he'd look in each day to see that all was well.'

'But couldn't we get married on your next leave?' Milly asked hopefully.

'It might be possible, I'm due for more, but I've no idea when it will come. I'll ask for at least a fortnight next time and hope I get enough notice to get our wedding organised.'

All the following day Laurie and Milly pondered whether they should marry as soon as they could, or leave it to some future date. 'It would be easier for you to concentrate on your career if we put off getting married.'

'Wait until the war is over?' she said. 'The trouble then is we have no idea how long that is going to take. It's dragged on so long already.'

'What do you want to do, Milly?'

'It might be more sensible to wait, but my heart says let's do it as soon as we can. We'll have to wait before we can live together, but wouldn't it make the waiting easier if the knot was tied?'

A big smile lit up Laurie's face. 'That's my feeling exactly.'

'Then let us do that,' Milly said.

The war was raging on: Rommel was in North Africa and the fighting was fierce around the port of Tobruk. During that first week of May, Merseyside had endured a week of very heavy raids that caused extensive damage. Everywhere there were wrecked buildings with bare roof spars; there were gaps in whole terraces of homes and very few buildings still had glass in their windows. Shop windows were mostly boarded up now, and daubed with notices reading: *Business As Usual*.

On the roads most of the rubble was cleared as soon as possible to make them usable. Since then they'd had warnings of raids but all seemed to have been false alarms.

May had brought the warmer weather and Milly welcomed that, but it also brought the end of term exams nearer. This summer she'd be leaving college. At long last she'd be grown up and able to look for a job. Would Mr Thornley take her on? She hoped very much she had a chance of that.

Finally, it was the last day of term. She'd been looking forward to it for a long time because at long last nobody could consider her still a child. She telephoned Mr Thornley the next day and asked if she could come and see him. 'I'm looking for a job,' she said.

When she went to the *Gazette*, he said, 'Well, Milly, things are really changing here because of the paper shortage, and our ration is to be reduced again. You've walked through the office and will have seen how few staff are left. Most have been called up, and one has moved to a London paper. I will be more than glad to employ you, but my secretary has left, so I'm afraid you'll be Jill of all work.'

'I can do shorthand and typing,' she said. 'I've brought my certificates to show you.'

'I'll teach you all you need to know to work on any newspaper,' he said. 'But you've proved you're a natural when it comes to putting an article together. When do you want to start?'

'Any time, right away, if you like.'

'I suggest you have a holiday first, Milly. What about the first of September?'

Lizzie was trying to take stock of what was happening to her. She still felt dissatisfied and wanted to turn over a new leaf. She hadn't expected to miss Ben, but in a way she did. She had not had a bet for almost eight months now and Milly reckoned that should have cured her cravings, but it hadn't, not altogether. She still felt a big win would settle her down.

Over the last few months Lizzie had felt a total pauper; she'd only ever had enough money in her purse to pay her bus fares and buy three cups of tea a day at the factory. Every Friday night she'd handed over her wages to Milly as soon as she reached home. Milly put her post office savings book into her hand regularly so she could see how her savings were growing, but she took it back to hide somewhere in her own room.

As a result, Lizzie found she was thinking much more about money and longed to be really rich. In that way she was more like Ben. He'd made a will in her favour, she knew, because Father had nagged about it, and now he was dead she was in a fever to know how much that was.

She asked for an hour off work one day so she could see his solicitor, but it seemed he was no wiser than she was. She had to remind him that Ben had owned three sideshows in the arcade, and the solicitor explained about probate and that she wouldn't have anything for a while. He sent her away to make a list of everything of value that Ben had owned, and asked to see his business records and his bank accounts.

She went up to their flat to look at Ben's bedside cabinet. She'd discovered long ago that he kept the top drawer of that locked, and was afraid now she'd have to break it open, but she'd already found his key ring in his pocket. There were lots of keys on it and the only one she recognised was the one to the front door. She had to try several before she found the one that fitted the drawer to his bedside cabinet.

It slid open easily and Lizzie was surprised to find it packed tight with documents and notebooks, and there was also a collection of bank books held together with an elastic band. She spread them out across the bed she'd shared with him. There was the Post Office Savings Bank, the Liverpool Bank, the Midland Bank, the National Provincial Bank, the Westminster Bank and several accounts with building societies. There was even a bank account in the Midland in her name. She could use that straight away.

Astounded, she opened them one by one. They all showed very healthy balances. Ben had been telling her the truth when he'd said neither of them would have to work ever again. There were also several envelopes stuffed with bank notes of high denomination.

Lizzie couldn't believe it; there was money here beyond her wildest expectations. Her head buzzed and her fingers were shaking too much to count it. She was a rich widow! She took a couple of bank notes to put in her purse, locked the drawer and ran downstairs to lie on her bed to think.

Ben had said he dabbled in the black market, but he'd been working on a much larger scale than she'd imagined possible. Not only was she rich, there was no need for her to worry about waiting for probate. She had an enormous amount of cash she could spend now.

She'd railed against Ben but now she thought of this as his endowment to her. It had not been earned by honest means and she'd shown her disapproval of that too. Strictly speaking, she should hand over all those bank books to his solicitor.

Definitely she was not going to do that. Some of Ben's traits seemed to be brushing off on her; she'd always wanted money, hadn't she? Now Ben had bequeathed it to her and she wasn't going to say a word about it, not even to Milly. This was an opportunity she was not going to miss; it was her big win. It would give her what she'd always wanted: plenty of money. No longer would she crave for more and hope to win it.

Not that there was much in the shops to spend it on. She'd have to be patient and wait for the end of the war, but everybody was longing for that. Once luxuries were available in the shops she'd be able to afford anything she fancied.

* * *

A LUCKY SIXPENCE

Lizzie had to get up early in the mornings as the factory shift started at eight o'clock. This morning she was getting off the bus on the prom when she met Steve Docherty, who had promised to keep an eye on Ben's business on her behalf. 'Hello, Lizzie,' he said, 'how are you?'

'I'm OK,' she said. 'Is everything all right?'

'Yes, fine, everything is running smoothly at the moment, but I'll need more help in the summer and have to take on another lad.'

'That's all right. It's kind of you to do this for me.'

'The McCluskeys have been very kind to me over the years,' he said, 'and Ben was a friend. Lizzie, you've never had much to do with the fairground and I've been wondering whether you'd want to sell up?'

Lizzie took a deep breath. 'I haven't thought . . . Can't at the moment.'

'Yes, I know, but when probate is granted?'

Lizzie didn't have to think about that; it would be very helpful. If she did, nobody would be asking where she'd got her money from. 'Yes,' she said, 'are you interested in buying?'

'I am.' He put out his hand and she shook it.

'Good, when his solicitor tells me probate has been granted, I'll let you know.'

'Think about how much you want for it.' He smiled.

'His solicitor will work out what it's worth, won't he?'

'Yes, he will.'

Well pleased, Lizzie ran down to the factory. She didn't much care about the price the business brought. She didn't need to; what she wanted was to rid herself of the fairground. She'd remember Ben for his largesse.

Anne Baker

* * *

Steve Docherty was equally pleased; he'd earned lots of ready cash from his share of the ration books sale from the Food Office job, and he wanted to put it into a legitimate business that would support him for the rest of his days.

The fairground was doing very well in wartime, as the shortages meant there was little else for the youth of Merseyside to spend their wages on. Steve was well known on the fairground as he'd been running the rifle range for as long as most would remember. He thought it unlikely that anyone would question where he, with a criminal record, had found the money to buy Ben's business.

CHAPTER FORTY-FIVE

ELSIE HEARD FROM ESMOND'S solicitor that probate had been granted and knowing that Oakdene Farm now legally belonged to her brought a sense of security such as she'd never known before. Esmond had also left her a few shares and some cash. It may not have seemed much to him, but to her it was a fortune. She had a comfortable house for herself and her daughters, and a little income. She thought she'd manage nicely, and there were still a few acres she could sell off if she found herself in difficulty.

She'd been worried about Lizzie and how she'd manage to run Ben's business when she inherited it, but over dinner last night Lizzie had said, 'Steve Docherty has been looking after it for me, and says it's doing fine. He's asked me to sell it to him when I'm given probate.'

Milly had said, 'That would be marvellous for you, Lizzie, you could buy your dress shop with that money.'

'Yes, I've always fancied my own dress shop and I'd know how to run it. That would suit me much better than Ben's roundabouts, but it'll have to wait until after the war.'

'Yes,' Elsie said, relieved to see that Lizzie was able to think of the future. 'Yes, after the war,' she agreed.

* * *

Milly was writing to Laurie again.

Lizzie is still handing her wages over to me on payday and has not mentioned gambling recently, but she asked for money to buy new shoes and she came home with three pairs.

I didn't give her enough to buy three pairs of shoes, so I had to ask if she'd placed a bet and won. She said no, she'd come across a little cash that Ben had kept at home, and, of course, she still has his clothing coupons. I'm so pleased she's spent it on shoes.

You can tell your mother that her advice about gambling addiction seems to have worked. Lizzie says she still feels tempted sometimes but she hasn't given in.

Lizzie has surprised me and Mum by accepting the loss of her husband so stoically. We didn't even hope for such a good outcome.

Milly loved working at the *Gazette* and settled in quickly, though she was given the less interesting things to write about, needing mere paragraphs. It was also her job to make the tea for her more senior colleagues, but she found them friendly and helpful, and they all praised the articles she'd written about Dadda.

Air raids were a thing of the past, but austerity was tightening. Whale meat appeared in the shops and also tins of a South African fish called snoek, both of which were very unpopular.

In the desert the Allies were having small successes but Rommel was still fighting fiercely. On the eastern front, the Germans were besieging Moscow, but they couldn't cope with the extreme cold and heavy snow. The Russians overcame them and the German defeat was hailed as the first major victory of the war.

Laurie continued to write to her every day. He said he'd written to their vicar asking him to marry them, but he couldn't book a definite date. He had hoped it would be September, but September came and went and his leave did not. Milly was thrilled when Mum suggested she and Laurie make the attic flat their first home as Lizzie didn't need it any more.

She went upstairs to look round with fresh eyes. Ben had refurbished it recently and it was fully furnished. The only piece of furniture Lizzie had taken to her own room was the old bedside cabinet. She said Ben had taken their two upstairs and this one would fit very nicely into her old room. Milly spring-cleaned the flat and considered she was very lucky to have it ready and waiting for when she and Laurie were married. She would have the best of both worlds while she had to wait. When Laurie was with her they'd have a place of their own, and when he was not, she could easily go back to living with her family.

Her mother said, 'I'll make your wedding cake, but it will look very plain without icing sugar and marzipan.'

'Your cakes always look good,' Milly said. 'There's no point in having a cardboard cut-out to pretend it is a grand three-tier job when everybody knows that's impossible. Thank you, Mum, we must start collecting the ingredients.'

'We'll have the wedding breakfast here, of course. Though what we could provide to eat I don't know.'

Milly watched the stock of sultanas with tins of fruit and spam and sardines build up on the pantry shelves as they became available and the family had the coupons to buy them. Lizzie laughed. 'Spam and sardines for the wedding breakfast? It won't do, Mum.'

Milly deserved something better than spam on her wedding day. Lizzie called in to see Steve Docherty in the fair the next morning and told him about Milly's wedding. She had money now to spend on things like this. Some luxury foods like salmon and pheasant were produced in such small quantities they could not be rationed, but they were outrageously expensive. Steve would know how to get them and if it was bought on the black market she wouldn't mention it to Milly and Mum.

Steve said, 'I could order you a selection of luxury foods from Lennie's restaurant. I'd leave the choice to him, he'll know what would be suitable and it would come ready to set out on the table. How many are you inviting?'

Lennie promised to deliver the feast early on the wedding day.

Elsie was delighted as it meant little work for her, and told her she couldn't believe it was possible to organise all this.

'I'm Ben's widow,' Lizzie said; 'they haven't forgotten him. You can keep the spam and sardines for your Christmas spread.'

Lizzie then took Milly shopping for an outfit. 'But a bridal gown is out of the question,' Milly said. 'I can't spare the coupons for a dress I'll only wear once.'

'We'll look for a smart suit or dress you can wear on other occasions.'

But, though they searched the shops in Wallasey and Birkenhead, nothing pleased them. 'You'll have to try in Liverpool,' Lizzie told her. 'I can't take any more time off. You'll have to go with Mum.' Elsie was wearing black all the time now. 'She'll need something new too. She can't wear black to your wedding.'

Helen Coyne came up with the answer for Milly. 'My niece Doreen was married in the year before the war and she's offered to lend you her wedding gown.'

Milly tried it on one Saturday morning when she'd taken up the eggs and vegetables. She studied her reflection in the wardrobe mirror in the Coynes' bedroom. It was a classic oyster-satin full-length gown, with a high neckline, long sleeves, fitted waist and slim skirt. She was pleased with it.

Laurie's mother said, 'It fits beautifully except . . .'

'It could do with being an inch or so longer,' Milly said, 'but it could be said to be ankle length. Lizzie has some lovely silver sandals she'll probably lend me, it would show those beautifully. Yes, tell Doreen I'd love to borrow it.'

'It is a gorgeous dress,' Laurie's mother agreed. 'You'll be a really romantic bride in this. Doreen had a veil and a tiara thing to fix it on her hair, she'll lend you those too.'

'Do thank her and tell her she's solved my problem. I love her dress.'

Milly was opening every letter from Laurie, hoping he'd know when he'd have leave. She was beginning to fear Christmas would come and go. But at the beginning of December, Milly at last heard the news; Laurie would be travelling up on the eighteenth of December and could take two whole weeks' leave over Christmas and the New Year. Both families were delighted with that. It gave them three weeks' notice, and they all went into overdrive with their last-minute preparations. Milly was thrilled she could now go ahead, but the fact that his leave covered both Christmas and New Year complicated things. Their families would want them at home to celebrate Christmas with them, and to be alone with just Laurie in a hotel would be marvellous, but over Christmas that did not seem right.

She went to see the vicar, who knew both of them and their families. He was happy to fix the time and date of their wedding for eleven o'clock on the morning of Saturday the twentieth of December, but it would be a wedding without frills.

'An austerity wedding,' Lizzie called it.

Laurie wrote:

I have organised my best man. I don't know whether you'll remember John Duggan? You did meet him once, a friend of mine from vet school. I don't want to spend too much time travelling on our honeymoon. Public transport is not very comfortable these days: the trains are unheated and few and far between, but they are running more to the timetable now that the Luftwaffe have stopped blowing up the lines and the stations.

Your mother has generously said we may look upon the attic flat as our first home. Couldn't we just move in there? We could set the place up to suit ourselves and we wouldn't have to go out if we didn't want to. I realise it wouldn't be very exciting for you, so perhaps a short stay in a hotel first?

We really must decide and book it. Where would you like to go?

Milly had been thinking about that: the weather would be cold so neither the country nor the seaside seemed to fill the bill. London seemed the logical place where there would be plenty to see and do, but it was too far away.

Milly liked Laurie's ideas and fancied a country house hotel with log fires halfway up the chimney in a remote village in

North Wales, but there was no easy way to get anywhere remote. There was a frequent train service between Birkenhead and Southport that would take no more than an hour, so eventually she booked the Grand Hotel on the seafront there for four nights, and they'd come home on Christmas Eve.

To have flowers would be another difficulty as there were few florists still in business and December wasn't an easy time for flowers, but Lizzie said, 'I'll be your florist. The girls I work with tell me they collect silver paper from abandoned cigarette packets in the cloakroom and use it to make button-holes. I've got enough silver paper already. I'll ask for an hour off on the afternoon before your wedding day, and we'll collect what flowers, berries and pretty leaves we can from both gardens.'

'It's going to be a make do and mend wedding, I'm afraid,' Elsie said.

Milly dusted off the old Christmas decorations and hung them up, saving some of the best for the attic flat. There was a lot of holly with berries this year and she had plenty to make the whole house look festive. She felt she'd made every preparation she could and she was ready. She spent the last days of waiting in a fever of excitement.

On the evening of the eighteenth of December, Milly went to Lime Street to meet Laurie from the train. At last this was their time, and now she was able to see and touch him she was able to relax. After the first moments it was as always, as though he'd never been away.

'You're not wearing your uniform,' she said. Nowadays, half the population was in uniform.

'I've had it dry cleaned for the wedding,' he said, 'and I've packed it to keep it looking its best.' He seemed to have a lot of luggage. 'We've waited so long for this we must make the most of the next two weeks and enjoy it all.'

'Yes, and I want to remember every single detail to add comfort,' Milly said, 'when you go away again.'

'There'll be tremendous highlights we'll never forget,' Laurie said, 'but I have to spend the first two nights at home with my parents. I'll be back with Mutt in the morning, and we'll take the dogs for another of our walks.'

Milly didn't know where the time went on Laurie's first day back as the hours seemed to flash by. There were lots of last-minute details to attend to, and they drifted back and forth between the two houses. It was beginning to get dark when Lizzie returned home but the three of them set out to see what flowers and greenery they could collect. There were a few late roses still in bloom, though the cold damp weather meant most had brown blemishes on their petals. 'Just the thing for making buttonholes,' she said, and sat at the kitchen table to pain-stakingly pull off the outer petals that were damaged. She selected one or two leaves to put with each bloom and wrapped the stems in silver paper.

Milly knew she'd intended to make a small bouquet for her from coloured leaves and winter berries, but Kathleen, her friend from college who lived further up the road, arrived with a large bunch of dahlias. 'From our greenhouse,' she said. 'Dad wanted it turned over to grow vegetables, but Mum kept a corner for flowers.'

'Just what we need,' Lizzie said, thanking her, and incor-porated some of them into the leaves and berries they'd picked, and arranged the rest in two vases. Everyone congratulated her on making an artistic and seasonable bouquet.

On her wedding morning, Milly was lying back admiring the wedding dress hanging from a hanger over her wardrobe door, when Lizzie came in with a cup of tea for her. 'You're up early,' she said.

'Yes, Mum got me up. We've a lot to do this morning.' Milly threw back the bedclothes. 'I'll help.'

'No, stay where you are and drink this tea. We've got to make a fuss of you today, you're the bride.'

Milly did as she was told and sighed with satisfaction that at long last her wedding day had come. 'This is bliss,' she told her.

'Your breakfast is to be poached eggs on toast. Mum thinks we all need something solid inside us today. She's going to make it now.'

Lizzie brought her tray up twenty minutes later. It was decorated with a specimen vase holding a single white dahlia from Kathleen's bunch. 'This is luxury,' Milly told her.

'Enjoy it while you can,' Lizzie said tartly. 'Marriage isn't always like this.'

Mum came in to take her tray away. 'Things seem even more unreal than they did yesterday,' Milly said. 'I'm lying here being waited on instead of pleading with Lizzie to give us a hand with the chores.'

'It's bound to feel unreal,' Elsie said. 'Today is a very special day for you. In a way I feel it's a very special day for me too.'

Milly stopped to look out of her bedroom window when she came back from having a bath. It looked cold and bleak outdoors, but she felt the warmth of family and friends.

'I'm ready.' Lizzie came back wearing what she used to call her best evening dress of blue-grey satin.

'You look lovely,' Milly told her.

'As your bridesmaid I have to wear something grand to tie in with your fine wedding gown,' she said. 'Come on, it's time for you to get dressed.'

'I can manage,' Milly said.

'Not today,' Lizzie said. 'What makes you think you'll be able to fix this veil on?' It took some time before Lizzie was happy with Milly's make-up and she fiddled with her hair and the veil for ages.

Milly needed help to get downstairs in the smart silver sandals and all her finery. She found her mother had changed into a fawn two-piece she used to wear for church, and had added a fox fur that Dadda had given her a few years ago. 'I always feel smart in this,' she said.

'You look smart,' Milly told her.

Lizzie surveyed her. 'I'm not sure fox furs are still high fashion.'

Elsie smiled. 'Everybody longs for furs of any sort these days.'

The taxi she'd ordered was pulling into the gate. She draped the fur coat borrowed from Helen Coyne round Milly's shoulders for the chilly ride to church.

Once on the back seat Milly said, 'I wish Dadda was still with us.' In his absence her mother was going to give her away, and as Lizzie was her bridesmaid they must all arrive together.

As the car pulled up outside the church, Milly sat up straighter. 'Gosh, there's quite a crowd collecting.'

'It's a big wedding,' the driver said.

Milly shivered with anticipation. She could hear the organ playing softly as soon as they entered the porch.

'Oh,' Mum said, 'the vicar rang last night to say his wife insisted on playing for your wedding. He thought all New Brighton would be coming. They haven't forgotten what Dadda and Ben did.'

The organ stopped and seconds later burst forth much louder. Her mother led her down the aisle with Lizzie two steps behind, and Milly saw that the church was almost full with people she recognised. Mr Thornley had come, and some of her friends from school and college.

Laurie was waiting at the altar and as she drew near he turned and smiled at her. He looked every inch a military man in his captain's uniform. As she reached his side a ray of sunshine came through the stained glass window, adding real sparkle to the moment.

Milly tried to focus on the solemn words and every detail of the ceremony. She felt Laurie take her hand and slide the wedding ring onto her third finger. They signed the register and were walking back down the aisle as the wedding march soared triumphantly.

When they reached the steps Milly saw a real crowd had collected to catch a glimpse of her. There was no official photographer, but Laurie had managed to get a film for his camera and his father was out quickly from behind to take a few pictures.

Milly felt they were whisked home, where Gladys was waiting to receive them with a tray laden with glasses of sherry. Both she and Clover had taken time off to help with the reception. The dining table was set with a buffet of luxurious delicacies to which Mum invited the guests to help themselves. They all remarked on the spread, the like of which they hadn't seen since the war started.

Later, Laurie's father drove them to the station in order to catch the train to Southport. Milly felt swept up on a wave of luxury that continued throughout their stay at the Grand Hotel.

But one of her best moments was returning home on Christmas Eve when Laurie carried her over the threshold of the attic flat and they closed the door.

They agreed it was easily the best Christmas they'd ever had.